SPRING
COLLECTION

SPRING

JUDITH KRANTZ

COLLECTION

Crown Publishers, Inc. New York

Published by Crown Publishers, Inc., 201 East 50th Street,
New York, New York 10022. Member of the Crown Publishing Group.

Random House, Inc. New York, Toronto, London, Sydney, Auckland
http:/www.randomhouse.com/
CROWN is a trademark of Crown Publishers, Inc.

Printed in the U.S.A.

Library of Congress Cataloging-in-Publication Data
is available upon request

ISBN 0-517-59334-3

10   9   8   7   6   5   4   3   2   1

First Edition

For my very dear friend of many years, Diane S., who has been a constant source of marvelous conversation and companionship. During twenty years in California she's never failed to remind me that Brooklyn lives and to inspire me to write about a Brooklyn beauty.

For my husband, Steve, with my deep, abiding love and reasons that, after forty-two years of marriage, he must know by heart.

SPRING
COLLECTION

1

Optimistic idiot that I am, I sprinted from the subway to the office at a ridiculously early hour in the morning. Believe me, nobody can move faster than I can on the streets of New York. Call me snake-hips Frankie Severino but I've never needed to push or shove in an unladylike way. During my many years of taking the train from Brooklyn to Manhattan I've patented a way to twist, sidestep and slither through any crowd. If I'd been a man I'd have made a hell of a linebacker. Riding up in the elevator to Loring Model Management where I work, I *knew* that today was the day. Last night I'd had a dream about getting the long-awaited fax from Necker in Paris that had been so incredibly real—not dream-real but *real* real—that I woke up this morning with my heart beating like crazy. I was filled with wild anticipation, every competitive instinct I have was up and screaming, all that fight-or-flight stuff made me leap out of bed, get dressed in ten minutes and race to the subway without as much as a bagel inside my stomach.

The fax wasn't there. The little incoming tray was bare, the smug metal fax machine sat primly on its table, too high to allow me even the satisfaction of kicking it the way you do an empty vending machine. Short of taking an ax to the thing there was nothing I could do except stomp away in disgust. At least I had my cowboy boots on so the sound effects weren't wasted.

After I'd coaxed a cup of coffee from our fancy, temperamental coffeemaker, I took it into the main room of Loring Model Management where, in an hour, seven bookers would be sitting at their phones around the circular desk. There our models' schedules hang on a rotating file. All day long the bookers, each responsible for ten to fifteen girls, would be talking into their headsets, twirling the file and consulting their computers. An unglamorous setting, I thought, yet on any given day a memorable page in the history of glamour could so easily result from one of the calls our bookers field so adroitly. When I'd been a booker, right after I started work here, every phone call had been a thrill to me. Now, at twenty-seven, I'm second-in-command of the business and a damn sight less easily thrilled.

It was freezing in the booking room and I still hadn't taken off the old duffle coat and two extra sweaters I'd piled over my usual uniform of tights, a leotard, leg warmers and a cardigan knotted at my waist. I decided that the warmest place in the agency on this icy morning in January of 1994 would have to be the enormous, enveloping leather chair behind my boss's desk. Justine had definitely built herself a great little fortress, I realized as I cuddled way down into her amazingly comfy chair and sipped coffee, well within earshot of the phone ring that announces a fax. Justine Loring, my peerless leader, is just thirty-four, a former model who'd intelligently abandoned her career about five minutes after it reached its peak to become an independent agency owner. She'd hired me seven years ago. The timing was perfect for me because a bad fall —where else but in the subway?—had recently brought my dancing career to an end. I'd been a serious modern dance student at Juilliard but the injuries to both my kneecaps meant that disco was the only dancing I'd do in the future.

Sitting in Justine's chair, I thought that, although no one outside of the business realizes it, it's essential for the head of any successful model agency to have a strong personal style. Every successful agency in town is defined by a single personality, ranging from preacher to pimp. Justine's style? Good question. In many ways she qualified as the ideal Girl Scout Troop Leader with all the virtues that implies, radiating strength and trustworthiness; straightforward, infinitely capable and, above all, reassuringly calm. She's the person anyone, even I, would agree to follow up a slippery mountain trail or cling to in an avalanche, certain of being rescued.

On the other hand, Justine's probably too gorgeous to be a convincing Scout. If thirty-four is mature, which I deeply tend to doubt, maturity has made her far more seriously alluring than when she was modeling, blandly ravishing, throughout her late teens into her mid-twenties, a full-fledged member of the prom-queen-all-American league. You know that look: all-but-impossibly blue eyes, features too ideal to describe, a quick, indiscriminately adorable smile, infuriatingly good teeth and the faint beginnings of deliciously squinchy laugh lines.

Now Justine's grown so interesting to watch that you wouldn't think she'd once been only conventionally stunning. Her eyes, still the very hue of victory, are thoughtful and often pensive. Her smile is meaningful and selective, a smile that has forgotten how to turn on automatically for a camera. There's a fascinatingly slow play of changing expressions on Justine's lovely face that shows a mind always at work. She's my idea of a woman who has just barely entered into the beginning of the best part of her life and eligible men, heaven knows, agree with me. But she turns them down, one after another. Sometimes I find myself in a lather of outrage listening to her explain, with that maddening, reasonable calm, just what is wrong about each one.

It must be some inherited Anglo-Saxon character trait that allows Justine to shrug off any problem she can't do anything about and simply let it go. My preferred mode, when faced by a defect—in a man or in a situation—is to attack, charge and make it right! *Fix it!* But then my ancestors on both sides came from the south of Italy.

The difference in our ways of approaching life was probably why the two of us made such a good team, I thought, not for the first time, probably the reason why I'd advanced so rapidly from the ranks of bookers to become Justine's right hand as well as her closest friend. I'm explosive enough to allow Justine to remain her glowing blond self at all times. I'm the one who understands exactly when and how to pull a major-league freak-out, who remembers to carry necessary grudges, who won't settle for the difference between the possible and the impossible, who doesn't believe in any sensible Twelve Step maxim about having the wisdom to accept things you can't change. Accept, my ass! Not when you're from Brooklyn!

"Have you been here all night?" Justine's voice asked, interrupting my reverie.

"You scared me!" I yelped, almost spilling my cold coffee. "I got in ages ago . . . I had this dream . . . oh, never mind . . . you don't want to know."

"You're right about that, girlfriend."

"I love it when you try to sound hip." I couldn't help grinning at her, vile as my mood was. "And just what *are* you doing in at this hour?" I demanded, recovering my poise.

"Ah, I had one of those bad nights. . . ."

"*You* have bad nights?"

"Even I, my mouse, even I. But last night was the worst. Every time I managed to fall asleep I had a nightmare. Finally I got smart enough to realize that I should give up on sleep and get in here and do some work in peace and quiet. I see now that was not to be."

"Not while I'm around feeling itchy."

"That sickening contest, of course."

"What else?"

Justine had the nerve to sigh at me, just like she would at a peevish child.

"Don't give me that superior attitude," I growled. "You know it's important even if you refuse to admit it. I'm going to make more coffee. Want some?"

"Desperately. Blessings on you, my child."

While I hung over the coffeepot I allowed myself to brood over the events that had started this whole waiting-for-the-Paris-fax business. It all started about three months ago. A woman named Gabrielle d'Angelle arrived in New York on a mission to all the model agencies in town. Gabrielle was a highly placed assistant to a guy named Jacques Necker. You know, the Swiss billionaire who's head of La Groupe Necker? He owns four of the world's most important fabric mills, two major fashion houses and a fistful of highly profitable perfume and cosmetic companies. Even civilians have heard of him. GN, as everybody in the business calls it, had recently decided to back the designer Marco Lombardi in a new couture house. Lombardi's first spring collection would be shown in Paris in a little more than two weeks from now.

"I'm here to find a group of completely fresh faces," the Frenchwoman had told Justine and me in her impeccable English.

"I need girls who are as unexposed as it is possible for models to be, girls who are *entirely* virgins to the Paris collections, yet they must not be too raw, too green to work with—even if they are technically children they must not look it." I tried unsuccessfully to catch Justine's eye. Of all the glossy, brilliantly dressed, annoyingly overconfident females I'd ever come across, Gabrielle took the cake. "I'll be searching for them," she had continued, "at every agency in town and making videotapes of the best of the lot. Three among them will be picked to come to Paris to take part in Marco Lombardi's very first spring collection. One of them will ultimately be chosen as the incarnation of Lombardi's style." She had smiled loftily at us. "I suppose you Americans would call it a contest, I prefer to think of it as a modern-day version of the Judgment of Paris."

"Just exactly what plans do you have for this lucky little contest winner?" Justine asked. Amazingly I heard clear suspicion in her voice. My mental eyebrows shot up at Justine's tone. What was there to be suspicious about?

From the moment it had been announced, everyone in the fashion world had been agog to see what would come of the Lombardi launch. How come Justine wasn't delighted to hear of this chance for new girls to be showcased?

"As I'm sure you realize, the first Lombardi collection will be the most watched event of the spring collections, Miss Loring," Gabrielle d'Angelle answered her, allowing herself to look ever-so-slightly huffy and sounding ever-so-faintly surprised. "The winning girl will be signed to a long-term exclusive contract and become the focus of a worldwide advertising campaign."

"Exclusive?" Justine's question was sharp and hard, all but nasty. "If the winner's so good, give me one reason why she should tie herself down to a new designer."

What the hell was biting Justine's ass, I wondered in absolute bewilderment. Her manner was utterly unlike the way she'd ever handled any prospective client.

"The contract will guarantee the winner of the contest three million dollars a year for the next four years," d'Angelle said. Her words were crisper than fresh Melba toast and she obviously expected them to cut off further discussion.

"Aren't you taking a large risk? An unknown model working with an unproven talent? Lombardi may just be a flash in the pan," Justine insisted, sounding entirely unimpressed by twelve million dollars. I had to fight not to enter the discussion, even with body language, but of course I knew that whatever mistake Justine was making, she didn't want to be second-guessed.

"Monsieur Necker did not arrive at his present power without taking risks," the Frenchwoman said. By now she wasn't bothering to hide her affront at Justine's unexpected skepticism.

Justine just wouldn't get off it. "Of course there'll be so much publicity for GN about this talent search that it'll be worth twelve million, even if the new girl doesn't work out and you dump her for one of the usual stars." Now she sounded downright hostile.

"Miss Loring, we have every intention of building the house of Lombardi in the way Monsieur Necker has planned," Gabrielle said, deeply irritated—and who could blame her? I felt like throwing up my hands and screaming. How could Justine possibly treat Necker's emissary with rudeness and scorn?

"No new house has opened successfully in Paris since Lacroix," Justine continued with one of those curt little negative shrugs I thought only the French could do. "And that was a long time ago."

"Miss Loring, if your agency isn't interested in participating. . . ." Gabrielle d'Angelle said, pulling herself together, and, while I watched, frozen, she started to rise.

"Oh, you know perfectly well that I can't say no," Justine interrupted, cutting her off. "I'll make a list of my best prospects and deliver it to your hotel with their head sheets."

As soon as the Frenchwoman left, I turned to Justine incredulously.

"What the fuck! Are you totally insane?"

"Why didn't I lick her exquisite shoes?"

"Basically yes, damn it. I was in cardiac arrest listening to you! So what if it's a long shot, even if they don't pick a single one of our girls, you had no reason to speak to her like that. She's not looking for white slaves, for God's sake. It's the chance of a lifetime for someone and you know it."

"I find all this . . . talent search . . . corrupting . . . distasteful . . . almost degrading."

"Oh, give me a break!" I exploded with all the pent-up disbelief I'd had to hold in during Justine's dialogue with the Frenchwoman. "The whole model world is one big talent search, year in and year out, and you know it as well as I do."

"Let's say that I didn't like being condescended to by that irritating creature," Justine said, conceding my point.

"Neither did I, Justine, but what the hell does that have to do with it? Every last one of our new girls would jump ship in a minute if we don't participate in this Necker thing."

"That, my mouse, is exactly why I told her I couldn't say no. The only reason, believe me."

"Were you playing some sort of dumb game?" I'd asked, still deeply confused. "The above-it-all agency head? I've never seen you do that weird number before, thank the good Lord."

"There's a first time for everything, Frankie," Justine replied, with an unfamiliar stern and blank look veiling her eyes, a look that I didn't understand and Justine obviously wasn't going to explain. And that was the last time we'd discussed the whole thing.

Our coffee machine finally came through and I poured Justine a cup, took it to her office and left her to her work. The Lombardi model search had gotten more press in the last few months than if Madonna had married Prince Albert of Monaco while she was carrying Prince Charles's lovechild. As time passed and there was no word from GN, every agency in town was growing more and more preoccupied with getting the final word.

Only at Loring Model Management did the agency head stay visibly uninvolved. While I haunted the fax machine, Justine never even asked if there were any rumors abroad, although she knew that every Friday night I had dinner with four women in the know: Casey d'Augustino, Sally Mulhouse, Josie Stein and Kate James, who are my opposite numbers at Lunel, Ford, Elite and Wilhelmina. The five of us formed a limited palship, like a group of mistrustful Mafia dons who have to stay friendly for the sake of business.

Our sincerely shifty relationship is based on the axiom, "The enemy of my enemy is my friend," I thought, back in my own office. Restlessly I drank coffee I didn't want, thought wistfully about bagels, and put my boots up on my desk as I tried to relax. There was at least a half hour to go before the staff came in, the phones could be expected to ring and I could send one of the assistants out for something to eat.

Yes, Casey, Sally, Josie and Kate and I all had the same enemies. For "enemies," read "clients," everybody who books models: magazines, ad agencies, dress houses, even charity fashion shows. It's us, the agencies, against the clients in every negotiation, right down to the question of whether the client pays for a taxi to take a model to the job.

Of course it was also each of us against each other. Who, for example, would be the first one to brave public opinion and sign a thirteen-year-old beauty to a contract? Who among us was actively stalking another's models? Little could ever be proved but everything was suspected.

It could be an astonishingly petty world inside the gorgeous girl cosmos, but, on reflection, we still needed each other for a certain free exchange of information, I told myself philosophically. We all needed to know which horny photographers are busy putting the moves on the girls. We needed to know which cheapo clients would habitually try to pay late, figuring that the money was better off in their own banks, earning a couple of extra weeks' interest. We needed to know which hairstylist and makeup artist just happened to have a few handy grams of coke or heroin in the bags of equipment they lugged around, and particularly which model had started using drugs.

"Who's starting to look too thin?" was the first question always asked at our dinners. Besides weight loss and gain, we talked about the newest diet fads going around, we shared information on the results of personal trainers, gyms and dermatologists, and we identified the clients who were giving the girls free sample clothes for working late instead of paying time and a half. There were a ton of dirty wrinkles in the business—bound to be when a certain percentage of the people who inevitably surround the girls are as welcome as body lice or genital warts.

If any of my Friday night group or any of the agencies not

included in our gang, like Boss or Women or Company or Partners, had heard from Necker, they'd have broadcast it immediately. So there was no way anybody could know more than I did at this very minute, unless there was a fax waiting at another agency and someone there to read it. I was obsessing now, definitely over the borderline, and I didn't intend to walk this territory alone. I opened the door of Justine's office without knocking.

"Do you think Necker's people could have changed their minds about using new models?" I demanded, deciding to aggravate my pal no matter how little interest she'd shown in the whole thing. "If they don't decide in the next two weeks and three days, it'll be too late, the collections will have started."

"Oh, somehow I doubt it, Francesca," Justine said tartly. "They'd look pretty silly if they do."

So it was Francesca now, was it? Only my mother had ever been allowed to call me that and Justine knew it. Francesca was the name my parents christened me in a la-di-da moment and I'd changed it as soon as I reached third grade.

"Could I ask why you don't mind being tortured by not knowing, Miz Loring?" Justine hated "Miz" almost as much as I hated Francesca. "I realize you've refused to buy into this whole thing, you act as if it's some sort of scam. I'm fascinated, in a sick way, by watching you being so unrealistically superior to everybody else, but why, for the love of God, why?"

"I've been against this contest thing, this form of pressure, from the beginning," Justine said, looking at me seriously. "The girls GN choose are going to have to be exceptionally mature to get through that ordeal in Paris. Two of the three of them will be disappointed when it's all over. A rejection like that could permanently damage their self-confidence, and a model without self-confidence can't function. Don't you think that there's enough potential for rejection in this business already without this GN hoopla that will take place so publicly? It's not as if they're going to be allowed to fail in private."

"I suppose you've got a point," I said reluctantly. "But still. *Twelve million dollars?* . . . Sure it's a war zone out there, but a well-paid one. Most of the girls I know would kill for this chance."

One of the office phones rang and I welcomed it as an unusually early sign of the start of the day's business. Justine waved me away and picked it up.

"Loring Management," she said. "Good morning."

It must be a girl calling in, someone who was really sick, I thought, as I watched an expression of concern shadow Justine's face.

"What?" Justine asked, on a far harsher note than I'd ever heard her use. As the response came I saw my friend's face change into a grimace of defiance mixed with an emotion that looked to me, for one amazing moment, like fear . . . Justine afraid? . . . Nope, not possible. In an instant her expression changed to a combination of rage and disgust. "Repeat that last part," Justine finally asked grimly. She listened again, scribbling a few notes on a pad. "What, no additional conditions? Astonishing. I'll let you know. When I decide, that's when." She slammed down the phone.

"Who in the name of God was that?"

"I knew it was coming! I've suspected it all along! Nothing else has worked so this is the way he's getting at me . . . it's *diabolical!* They know I have to go along, they've probably told the press already—"

"*Justine!* Stop! Damn it, you're raving! *What's* 'diabolical,' *who's* trying to get at you?" I'd never ever even imagined Justine in such a state, I thought in utter astonishment. What had happened to my serene, self-assured Troop Leader?

"It was Gabrielle d'Angelle. GN has chosen April, Jordan and Tinker for the Lombardi contest," she spat out in a rush of fury.

"But . . . but . . . " I sputtered, "they're all ours! All three of them—*our* girls!"

"You don't think it's a stroke of good luck, do you?" Justine asked me with bitter scorn. "You can't possibly believe that out of dozens and dozens of girls they're the only acceptable new faces in this entire town? He's planned to pull this from the beginning . . . when nothing else worked, he saw a way to sneak into my life through the business, that vile son of a bitch!"

"Justine, have you gone out of your mind?" I demanded, stunned by Justine's incomprehensible flood of words.

"It's Necker! Jacques Necker, that contemptible, evil, *evil* man —he'll do anything to get what he wants. From the second d'Angelle waltzed in here I knew it had to be something like this, but I never dreamed he'd go so far, damn him to hell . . . it stinks to high heaven, it's unspeakable—"

"Necker . . . ? Justine, I don't get it. You're not making sense. None, not one word."

I finally penetrated Justine's tirade. She looked at me and took deep breaths, willing herself to calm down enough to explain. I could actually watch the process on her features as her passion of outrage slowly changed to the decision to part with a secret she could no longer keep.

"Frankie, he's my father," Justine said in a low voice, speaking so quickly that the words ran together in her haste to get her statement over with.

"Your *what?*" I sputtered, too confused to make any sense of her statement. "What the hell are you raving about?"

"Necker, that bastard, that bloody, *bloody* rotten man, is my father. Frankie, you heard me the first time."

"But . . . but . . . Justine . . . that's the most absurd thing—"

"Now don't, *do not,* ask me anything more about it," Justine continued. "It's not something I can discuss, not now, maybe never. But I'm not delusional. I'm his daughter, God help me. I want nothing to do with him, nothing ever, *ever*—and now he's found a way to reach me, a way I can't get out of."

"But, Justine—"

"Frankie, not one question!"

"Okay, okay! I'm not saying one word about you and . . . ." I stopped and regrouped, my brain starting to function again. "The thing I don't get is how GN using our girls puts you in . . . that person's . . . power, that's all. Hey, let's take the worst-case scenario, okay? Are you with me here on this, Justine?" I spoke with exaggerated calm. "Three of our girls will go to Paris for the Lombardi collection and one of them will win the pot of gold. Can you show me the harm in that?"

"But you didn't hear all of it, you didn't listen to d'Angelle's end of the conversation, Frankie," Justine said, ferociously. "An essential part of this whole thing is that I *personally* have to accompany the girls to Paris." She said the words so furiously that it seemed as if she thought sheer anger could make them disappear.

"And it gets worse. It's not enough that I go with them, but in addition, d'Angelle—meaning Necker, of course—wants all of us in Paris three days from now!"

"What? That's two whole weeks before the collection!"

"*Exactly*. You should have heard her, false and smarmy, fronting for him, taking a fairy godmother attitude to explain something she has to know is a lie—'The extra time will give the models a chance to learn the ropes and become familiar with the job.' What a joke! They're even paying each of them an additional hundred thousand bucks for doing that one Lombardi show! Not even Iman or Claudia has ever earned half that much. Two entire weeks at GN's expense? At the Plaza-Athénée with hot and cold running limos? *Please*. Gabrielle knows that most new girls have less than two days to get acclimatized, if that. Obviously those two weeks are for Necker to get at me and break me down, Frankie, don't kid yourself. None of it makes sense any other way."

"They seem to have thought of everything," I said finally, forcing myself to push away the impossible matter of Justine's paternity and make myself consider only the business alternatives.

There weren't any. None. There was no possibility that we could turn down this opportunity for our three girls, no matter how Justine felt. How could anyone rationalize not grabbing the GN opportunity? Justine had been cleverly painted into a very tight corner. We looked at each other for a minute, as if expecting the other to come up with some brilliant idea. Finally, as the silence lengthened and felt more hopeless by the second, I roused myself.

"Justine, we're wasting time. You'll have to deal with this long-lost-you-know-what business sooner or later, but right now we should be letting the girls know that they're going to Paris."

"You do it, Frankie," Justine told her, drooping in the after-effects of her storm of emotion. "I have to think. I know I don't have to say it, but this whole mess stays between us."

"Of course, idiot." I dropped a kiss on the top of her head, and retreated to my own office, closing the door firmly. I stood still, making no move toward the telephone. I found myself shaking, cold and dizzy. My shock was so great that the only word that came into my head was the one I reserved for the great events of life. *Caramba!*

2

It is arranged, Monsieur," Gabrielle d'Angelle informed Jacques Necker, as she stood before his desk in his office in the Paris headquarters of GN.

"No problem?"

"Certainly not, Monsieur. Miss Loring had little to say but of course she agreed."

"What about the negotiation, Gabrielle?" he asked eagerly. "What details did she ask about?"

"None. She sounded frankly overwhelmed. The surprise, as I expected, was enormous. She answered me only in monosyllables and she had no questions. I'll telephone her again, tomorrow, when the news has been absorbed, and finalize everything. Then we can send the contracts to be signed."

"Report your conversation to me before you authorize any release from our press department. And I want to see that release as soon as it's written."

"May I say anything to Monsieur Lombardi? A day doesn't go by without his asking me about your decision."

"Lombardi will have to be patient," Jacques Necker answered curtly, dismissing her with his habitual abrupt nod.

She too would have to be patient, Gabrielle d'Angelle thought as she walked quickly out of the vast office. She would have to restrain her curiosity until she discovered exactly why, out of hours of videotape and the copious notes she had taken on her impressions of literally dozens of new models from every last agency in Manhattan, Jacques Necker had rapidly chosen three girls. Particularly three girls from the same agency. They were the best of the Loring Model Management lot, exceptional girls, but not, no certainly not, unique. Nothing explained the haste of his choice, nor his impatient insistence that not one of her other suggestions could even be considered.

She would have to be clever enough to find out why she had been sent on a scouting trip to New York when she could have accomplished everything Necker wanted merely by sending a fax to Loring Management with a request for photos. And why had that unpleasant, ungrateful female, Justine Loring, been overwhelmed neither with delight nor with any other positive emotion in spite of this gigantic plum falling into her lap? The agency owner had been angrily and resentfully unresponsive. A series of grunts when handed the coup of a lifetime? An impossibly rude attitude? Hanging up on her? What kind of reaction was that? It was astonishing but not something she intended to tell Necker, since she habitually tried to give him the impression that she had every aspect of a situation under control.

No, watchful patience was required in an extremely odd situation in which the oddest question of all was why Jacques Necker, one of the busiest of men, who ran an enormously complicated group of companies and ordinarily delegated authority in a masterful manner, should have concerned himself for more than a passing minute in this relatively unimportant decision about the models for Lombardi's spring collection. Why had he himself developed the initial idea of using untested models, for all the world as if he were a bright young publicity attaché? And why was he now asking her so eagerly about routine negotiations with such tense interest?

In addition to the mystery of these questions, Gabrielle d'Angelle considered that she herself had reached far too high a level within GN to have been asked to go to New York on this matter. Any stylist from one of the couture houses could have accomplished it.

In the twenty years Gabrielle d'Angelle had worked for GN, rising steadily from the typing pool to the job she held now as chief administrative assistant to Necker himself, she'd advanced herself with intelligence, shrewdness and sheer hard work. At forty she had achieved a consummate polish, the impeccably finished and flawlessly groomed freshness of a woman without family responsibilities to occupy her, a woman who is highly paid and has access to the best craftspeople of Paris. Yet, as Gabrielle d'Angelle glanced at herself in the mirror, smoothing her casque of shining dark hair that was cut to the perfect length for the shape of her face, approving of the cut of her new grey suit, she felt no satisfaction at her faultless image. The Lombardi contest left her feeling powerless, because she didn't know what it was really about. And the one rule that dominated her still unsatisfied ambition was that knowledge was power.

As soon as he was alone, Necker jumped up and walked over to the bank of windows on the top floor of the imposing GN building on the west side of the Avenue Montaigne. He gazed at the sky on this unusually clear January day and wondered how he could possibly contain his excitement. As he looked down it seemed to him that trumpets must be blowing, that flags must be flying from every building, that the branches of the bare trees that lined the avenue must now be laden with the white torches of chestnut blossoms that mean spring to Parisians.

On the left he could see all the way to the tree-encircled Rond-Point of the Champs-Elysées, and on the right, only blocks away, the waters of the Seine below the Place de l'Alma flowed swiftly, reflecting the gaiety and brilliance of the sky. Directly across were the fantastic turn-of-the-century glass and iron domes of the Grand Palais and the Petit Palais, and beyond them the view stretched past the gardens of the Tuileries to the Louvre itself.

But Paris in all its beauty couldn't begin to satisfy his excitement. His view, startling as it was, had no relation to his mood. He had to get outside, Jacques Necker realized, and walk off some of his elation. He punched the intercom, told his secretary that he would be out for the rest of the day and took his private elevator down to the street.

He walked quickly, at random, for fifteen minutes, with only one thought in his mind. *Justine was coming!* Try as he would, he couldn't absorb it, he couldn't make himself believe it was a reality. The words had no solidity, no ring of truth. All he could imagine, in the midst of his joy, were the things that could go wrong. Justine's plane could crash, he could be killed in a car accident before she arrived . . . and why not the end of the world, he asked himself in exasperation, while you're about it? A great fireball from outer space? Judgment Day for everyone, not just himself?

Jacques Necker's basic good sense asserted itself and he told himself that perhaps if he bought his daughter a present right now, before he let another hour go by, if he found something to give her that had weight and three dimensions, something tangible, he'd be able to feel and actually experience the amazing fact that she was going to arrive in three days.

Obviously, even though she'd never answered his letters, never even read them, Justine now realized that they would see each other, speak to each other. It was inevitable. No destiny could deny him that meeting. Ever since he'd learned of her existence, only months ago, he'd known that it was absolutely essential for him to talk to her.

He had to tell Justine that he was more deeply ashamed of how he had treated her mother than he was of anything in his life. He had to tell her that for the past thirty-four years he'd blamed himself endlessly for having deserted Helena Loring. They'd both been barely nineteen, both students in New York, when she had discovered that she was pregnant. He'd fled in a blind panic, returning to Switzerland, leaving Helena alone, unprotected. Nothing could ever excuse his foul cowardice. His punishment had been bitter, yet far less than he deserved. It was not an accident, he thought in his darkest moments, that his wife, poor Nicole, had been unable to conceive, but a judgment on him, visited on a woman to whom he had been resolutely faithful until her death several years ago.

Jacques Necker was not a religious man. He thought that he relied only on what he could feel and touch and prove. Now he found himself addressing a God in whom he didn't believe. Please, he prayed, let my daughter show a little kindness to me. I can't ask for forgiveness. I don't deserve it. I only want to know her. She is the only child I will ever have in this world. Please give me a chance, if only to be with her, to look at her face, to hear her laugh.

He had photographs of Justine, scrapbook after scrapbook of them, heartbreaking photographs over which he pored each night, Jacques Necker thought helplessly, but he knew nothing about her in truth, except the bare facts of her growing up to start her successful business and lead a life that had never included marriage. He had not the slightest insight into any detail of her inner life, he possessed nothing but the pictures of a marvelously pretty little girl growing up into an alluring young beauty. How could she never have married? He didn't have any idea if Justine was happy or not, and, for some reason he couldn't understand, this was the most important question he needed to ask her.

Female heads turned as he walked oblivious to anything but his thoughts; a tall man without a scarf or topcoat, his thick blond hair cut very short, with crisp grey curling at his temples; his blue eyes thoughtful, his tie flying in the breeze. No Frenchman, each woman thought to herself. Perhaps English, the tailoring surely, and the shoes. Or perhaps Norwegian or Swedish, the hair, the eyes, the height? Perhaps a rich American? No, too assertive in these crowded Paris street corners to be American, no matter how rich, too much at home to even glance into the shop windows. But surely someone important, someone to reckon with, someone to dream of meeting, perhaps even someone famous, for there was a familiar quality to his face even though no name attached itself to the stranger who walked so quickly.

Necker looked around and found himself in the Rue de Monceau, near the Parc de Monceau. Excellent, he thought, directing his steps toward a familiar doorway, on which a simple brass plaque read Kraemer et Cie. This would do perfectly. He rang the bell of the magnificent yet anonymous mansion with many tall, curtained windows looking out on the quiet street.

"Is Monsieur Philippe at home?" he asked the manservant who opened the door.

"Of course, Monsieur Necker. Monsieur Laurent and Monsieur Olivier are here as well."

"Good."

The father and his two sons were among the most important dealers in fine French furniture in the world. Nothing they possessed and displayed, in their nine salons of furniture and objects, was less than perfect.

Their philosophy was that in matters of antiques, since they could discriminate clearly about such questions as authenticity, condition and artistic beauty, *literal* perfection was indeed attainable as it was in no other field except perhaps that of diamonds. And who, they often asked each other, would be so lacking in mellow judgment, in a feeling for beauty, as to prefer to buy a handful of crystals, no matter how flawless, when they could possess a pair of matching Boulle cabinets for twenty million dollars, cabinets that had belonged to two kings of France? Who would prefer to live with cold stones created by the unthinking passage of eons when they could spend their days amid the warmly glowing shapes of great furniture, created by men of genius?

"Jacques, it's good to see you," said Philippe Kraemer entering the reception room, a twinkly-eyed, round-faced man with a charming smile and exceptionally bushy eyebrows under a half-bald dome. His grandfather, Lucien Kraemer, had founded the business in 1875. "Come in and let me offer you something to drink."

"No, Philippe, no, thank you. Ordinarily, of course, yes. But today I have serious business with you and no time to chat."

"No time to chat? Well, well! I'll do my best to accommodate you, but Jacques, it won't be easy. Dealers only go into the business to chat, surely you know that. How serious is this business?"

"A present for a lady."

"Ah." He paused, reflectively. "I see. Of course. The most serious of all business, I agree. Shall we look around?"

"Please," Necker answered impatiently, striding into one of the salons. He knew the house intimately for he had long collected great French furniture. Both generations of Kraemers lived and did business there as well. Among them they occupied four apartments and they had installed two elevators and an indoor pool, as well as the nine showrooms where their magical wares filled every nook.

"Are you looking for something from the seventeenth century or the eighteenth century, my friend?" Philippe Kraemer asked, for they carried no other merchandise.

"It doesn't matter. I'll recognize it when I see it," Necker said distractedly, threading his way between a gloriously inlaid Louis XV secretary and a gilded armchair made for Versailles, in order to inspect a clock that was cleverly hidden in a bronze-mounted celadon vase.

"Perhaps something small?" Kraemer suggested. "For a gift an object is often the best choice. Furniture is less easy to place, unless, of course, you have the room in mind."

"Yes, you're right," Necker answered absently, busily scouting about, picking up candlesticks, inkstands, boxes, decorative urns and vases, looking at them intently and then replacing them with a negative shake of his head. He lingered for a contemplative minute over a Limoges chocolate service, and quickly ran his eye over the wealth of small pictures, plaques and sconces that hung on the paneled walls. He walked from one salon to another in which nothing was for sale that had been made after 1799, seeing dozens of rare pieces he might be tempted to buy for himself, but nothing right for Justine.

Kraemer, preserving a courtly silence, followed him in growing wonder. This was not the Jacques Necker he knew who sometimes returned four or five times to spend hours slowly walking around a single piece of furniture, examining it with a true collector's knowledge, before committing himself to its purchase. Today he was like an uncertain child let loose in a toy shop, unable to settle down to a single choice. He had already turned down a hundred objects that any woman on earth would be enchanted to receive.

"Ah!" Necker stopped abruptly. "Here it is. I knew you'd have the perfect thing." He pointed at a small writing desk, a piece of cabinet making that looked as if it could have floated into the Kraemers' mansion. It was delicate beyond delicacy, and rich beyond richness, for it was ornamented wherever ornamentation could be placed so that the richly carved wood had almost disappeared. The upper level of the desk and the front panels of its drawers were covered with inlaid medallions of Sèvres porcelain in pastel shades of pink, green and blue on which a wealth of small flowers and wreaths had been magnificently painted. "This is right for her, those are her colors."

Kraemer said nothing, gazing reflectively at the piece he had just bought at auction in Geneva. It was a *bonheur-du-jour*, a boudoir writing desk, made in the middle of the 1700s, shortly before the death of its owner, Madame de Pompadour. The desk was among the most perfect examples of furniture created in a time when every single one of the great *ébénistes* of France had devoted themselves to pleasing the exacting, exquisite taste of the marquise who had long ruled the heart of Louis XV.

"Yes," Necker said in delight, running his hands carefully over the surface of the desk. "It's a perfect size. Small enough to go anywhere. Philippe, can you please have this sent at once? Here, I'll write down the name and address. It's to go as soon as possible, by air, you understand, with a courier, to New York. Can you do that? Good. Do you have a plain card, Philippe? Excellent, thank you." He thought for a minute, wrote a short message, and put the card in the center drawer of the desk. "Now, forgive me, but I have to get back to the office." Necker shook hands hurriedly with the antiques dealer and strode back through the salons.

As Kraemer heard the front door close behind Jacques Necker he realized that, unthinkably, his old friend had not even bothered to ask the price or the provenance. This particular desk, he told himself, would have given him many a delightful hour as he recounted its history to the numbers of people among his exalted clients who would admire it but who, on reflection, would find that even they did not choose to spend quite so many millions on such a small piece, no matter how great its delicate charm. This gem had been installed in his showrooms only two days ago, no one in Paris had yet seen it, and now, poof, it was gone. And to New York! Of course, he'd always said that buying the best was a good investment at any price, but decidedly there were disadvantages in having to sell. He felt as if someone had just kidnapped a lovely woman he'd only now met.

But, on the other hand, how good it was to see a man he liked and admired so madly in love.

3

After Justine gave me the job of assembling our three new models so that we could tell them the astonishing news about Paris, I was immobilized for at least ten minutes. I just stood there, right inside my office, taking deep breaths, muttering *caramba!* like a mantra, and trying to regain my composure—Justine had given me the surprise of my young life. Finally I emerged and managed to give rapid instructions to the bookers who were, at last, busy at their computers.

Get April, get Tinker, get Jordan in here the instant they've finished whatever they're doing, send Town Cars to pick them up, I ordered, giving no one a chance to ask me what the rush was about. I could tell that my voice must be at its normal level of bossiness, for no booker glanced at me with a question in her eyes, but a veil had been drawn between me and the familiar scene. I felt as if I were watching a play, as if the entire agency, and everyone in it, were on a stage behind a transparent scrim and I was alone in the audience, distanced from it all, only an observer.

I kept trying to process the fact that Justine was Necker's daughter—I realized that it had to be true because she said so— but I couldn't seem to *feel* anything. Not surprise, not normal curiosity about how long she'd known or how it had come to happen. I was in a paralysis of astonishment too deep to allow room for any other emotions.

Somehow I was able to operate on autopilot until all three of the girls were sitting in Justine's office. They looked apprehensive, for it was unprecedented to be picked up right after finishing a job and driven back to the agency. When they saw both of us waiting for them, heaven knows what they thought they'd done wrong. But Justine didn't keep them in suspense.

"Tinker, April, Jordan, you've all been picked to go to Paris for the Lombardi show," she told them, forcing a big smile. "Congratulations. We're thrilled for all of you."

They did that sort of tribal thing that girls do when they win the Miss America Contest—or a Miss Weight Lifting Contest for that matter—hugging and kissing and crying and jumping up and down, wailing, "Oh no, I don't believe it!" over and over again. Justine sat there and watched them without expression while I restored order.

"Ladies, ladies, sit down and listen," I shouted. Technically models are always called "girls" but I address them as "ladies" whenever I get a chance, just to remind them that there's a whole other world out there. "*Ladies!* Okay, now there are a lot of details we won't bother you with right now, but Justine is going to be with you in Paris the whole time so you have nothing to worry about. You'll leave New York three days from now and you'll have two weeks to get to know the city and work with Lombardi. Let your families know right away and be sure to pack your warmest clothes. You're prohibited from going out of town or even out on a date, *not one*, from now on. Forget about men and consider yourselves grounded until the plane takes off. And I mean that very, very seriously. Grounded!"

I watched them closely, waiting for the one who was going to start in sniveling about having to say good-bye to her boyfriend or her mother. Not an eye blinked, not a smile dimmed. Necker, forget his reasons, had gotten himself three very ambitious girls, I thought, avoiding Justine's grim eyes and frozen face.

Last night Justine called me into her office.

"All packed?" I asked her. "Ready to leave tomorrow?" She'd been avoiding me for the last few days, although she should have known better than to think I'd try to drag any more information out of her. Now I was just waiting anxiously for her to go to Paris and get this whole thing over with. She couldn't hide from her father forever, and maybe Necker would prove not to be the monster she considered him. To be honest, I was rooting for a change in her attitude toward dear old Dad. How bad can a guy be who cooks up a twelve-million-dollar scheme just to get a look at you?

Obviously Justine too must be feeling better about this whole thing, I thought with relief as I entered her office and felt a lighter, more relaxed atmosphere in the air. My old buddy was coming back to normal, I decided, as I glanced at her.

She looked up at me as I brandished the screwed-up booking file I'd taken away from one of the bookers who was almost in tears. It belonged to one of our stars who'd just had the nerve to book out for three weeks merely to get married. If you ask me, the very concept of a right to a honeymoon should be specifically forbidden in every model's contract.

"Surprise!" Justine said, crinkling her eyes at me in a bigger smile than I'd seen on her face since Gabrielle'd phoned.

"Don't *do* that, Justine! I've had all the surprises I can handle for 1994 and it's still the first week of the year."

"You're going to Paris, Frankie. Tomorrow."

"You know I can't possibly come with you and hold your hand. Somebody's got to watch the store."

"Oh, don't worry, I'll carry on, right here," she said with a shit-eating grin.

"YOU CAN'T NOT GO!"

"Says who?"

I sputtered away with a list of good reasons until I realized that I didn't have a chance of changing her mind. As far as Justine was concerned, she'd been most basely and crassly deceived, and she owed Necker less than nothing. To give her credit, she presented me with two new suitcases filled with clothes she'd gone to buy for me at Donna Karan, things she told me were necessary for my trip and my new official position as duenna to our girls. Apparently my comfortable dancer's clothes that Justine had forced herself to endure for so long were no longer suited to represent the agency, not quite "grown-up" as she put it, trying to be tactful, as if I didn't know how much she disapproved of the way I dressed.

All I had to do was go home and pack my cosmetic case, she told me brightly. How was I going to explain to Necker? Simple. She planned to fire off a fax to d'Angelle that would reach Paris after we were safely en route, saying that a bad ear infection prevented her from flying and she was sending me in her place. Everybody knew you couldn't fly with an ear infection, her own doctor had assured her of that when she called him, looking for the most convincing medical cop-out she could plead short of putting herself into a full body cast.

What could I say in the end? First of all, Justine was my boss and she was giving me orders. In addition, wouldn't you have decided that, since there was nothing you could do about it, flying off to Paris simply had to be more of a kick than staying behind in New York? So help me, I had almost forgiven Justine before she finished explaining. Those suitcases . . . from the second I learned about them I'd been busy wondering if wearing Donna Karan might not be a seriously good career move after a lifetime of leotards and leg warmers. I'd guess I'd always been too cheap to spring for a whole new wardrobe. Okay. I'm easy.

We'd reached our cruising altitude, according to the pilot's announcement, when I put the copy of *Allure* I'd been brooding over in the seat pocket in front of me and snuggled back with my eyes closed, thinking how much I hate Paul Mitchell. I don't even know if there is a real human being named John Paul Mitchell, but if there is, someday I'll get him good, right between the eyes. You know those ads for his products, usually in sepia, full-bleed photographs of the head of a model tossing around hair so luscious that it *could not possibly grow* on any human being? Hair you want to eat, like candy, or pull out by the handful. And the copy—who writes that stuff? "Hair . . . hair that is free-flowing like the sea. Living in Harmony with light; dancing in its shadows, Fit, vibrant hair . . . nourished and cared for by the elements of our Earth. This . . . is Paul Mitchell hair." Level with me, does your hair rhumba and cha-cha in the shadows? How can hair be "fit," as if it had muscles and was in training for a triathlon?

Why do I get outraged by Paul Mitchell, who's only trying to make a buck selling salon treatments like something called "The Detangler"—hey, Paulie, ever hear of a comb?—when I can smile indulgently at Helmut Newton's brilliant excursions into not-so-soft porn with overexcited Dobermans slobbering over girls in Chanel?

Once a month I claim the prerogative of leafing through all the new magazines, domestic and foreign—would you believe that the new Italian *Vogue* costs thirty-three dollars by the time it gets here?—and pulling out every picture I can find of our girls who are working in Europe. Any booker could do that job of course, but it keeps me abreast of the competition and the new directions of European hairstylists and makeup artists, who are so much more daring than those in New York.

Invariably, that day I have one of my Paul Mitchell attacks. Because of a set of circumstances I'll tell you about later, no model has ever made me feel inadequate, but even a single Paul Mitchell ad will set me off. I can't stop myself from going home and checking out my own bunch of hair to find out if it's anywhere close to being free-flowing like the sea. I'll say this much for it, it's long, right to my waist. It's an acceptable medium brown with a bit of red in it if you look closely—no, I see no sparkling diamond-like evidence of "vibrant"—but it performs the task I demand of it which is to cover my head and serve as an homage to my lost art. I haven't called upon the "elements of our Earth" to care for it. Baby shampoo seems to do the trick.

I don't spend a whole lot of time in front of the mirror after I've confirmed that I still don't have Paul Mitchell hair. I don't need a mirror to know that I've got my father's nose, indisputably Italian, the most prominent feature in my face, slender, high, arched, definitely aristocratic in the European way. It's a Real Honest to God NOSE, almost a Sophia Loren nose—Paul Mitchell's copywriter would have to give it at least that. I have my mother's brown eyes, a whole hell of a lot more vibrant and dancing than my hair.

But the big Paul Mitchell question, does this face "live in Harmony with light"—Paulie, kiddo, we don't usually capitalize the word "harmony"—there you've got me. How the hell do I know? It's bathroom light I'm looking at myself in, not outdoor light, and harmony is such a neutral word. It's certainly not one I've heard used about me. "Check out Frankie, man, there's one harmonious chick." Nah, never, not even once.

Women who aren't in the beautiful girl business often ask me, ever so subtly, if I don't get "depressed" being surrounded by models so much of the time. They don't mean it as an insult but as a reflection of the way they imagine they'd feel if they had my job. The fact is that my formative years, my dancing years, from six to twenty, have given me a crossover understanding of models that almost no woman can be expected to have. As a dancer I too, like any successful model, had aced all the tests without studying. I too was born genetically *designed to perfection*. Oh, lordy, I remember all too well how it felt to possess all the right stuff without having worked for it.

When I was seventeen, during my senior year in high school, I was accepted at the Juilliard Dance Department. I was one of a class of less than a hundred students, selected from the thousands of would-be applicants from all over the country who wanted to go to Juilliard. In my evaluation I was told that my body type was the ideal for a modern dancer: extra-long arms and legs, a natural turn-out, an unusually supple back and tremendous flexibility in my joints. I also had a dancer's ideal eyes, wide-set and extra large, important for the communication of emotion. Call me immodest, but during my dancing years, particularly during my three years at Juilliard, I was high as a kite on unearned pride.

So, *no*, the answer to how I feel about models is that I realize deep in my very own, splendid Severino bones and ligaments that it is an utterly *innocent* stroke of luck when any girl is born having hit the particular genetic jackpot she needs for her work. I know that models are not *responsible* for creating a single one of the intricate and magical connections of their features.

I have a theory that when every girl child is born, a multitude of fairies gather around her crib, the fairies in charge of distributing perfect skin and great legs, the fairies who hand out symmetrical noses and full lips, the fairy of wide eyes, the fairies of chinlines, of cheekbones, of beautiful hands and long waists. Every once in a great while, one time in tens of millions, every last one of the fairies—with the frequent exception of the tooth fairy—will decide to bestow her particular gift on just one baby and of those few babies, some will grow up healthy in the Western world, and of these little females, some will become models. It's not abnormal that this happens, it's just the random way nature, and fairies, work.

I equate any model's looks as no more unfair a blessing than my truly *great* feet. I have the most remarkable, long and lovely feet, thin feet, strong feet, with a perfect arch and magnificent toes. Important toes. Even the pinkie toes stretch straight in line with the others. I'm not quite five-feet-seven and my feet are a wondrous size ten! If it hadn't been for my accident, those feet might well have been my launching pad to dance stardom.

I hadn't grown into all this, of course, when I was six and started studying dance with Marjorie Mazia, who had a studio out in Sheepshead Bay, not even a mile from where I lived with my parents in Brooklyn.

Marjorie had been a great Martha Graham star in her day—her husband was Woody Guthrie, an oddball fact that always thrilled me—and I studied with her for eight exciting, dedicated years. I was so skinny that most of my classmates made fun of me, but I knew that for a dancer skinny was good, so I held my big nose high, trod proudly on my big feet, and ignored them.

During high school I went to the Martha Graham School in Manhattan, taking the subway into the city after school and doing my homework on the way. It was Marjorie Mazia who encouraged me to continue my education at Juilliard after I graduated from Abraham Lincoln, the best arts-oriented public high in Brooklyn.

I waved off the flight attendant offering more champagne and wondered if everyone is like me about plane trips. I always find myself evaluating my life on any flight that lasts over an hour. Perhaps it's because of the slight undercurrent of risk that even good fliers can't totally forget, but as the feeling of a long plane flight took hold I started to think how lucky I've been with most things in life, starting with my beloved parents whose only fault was the name they tried to stick on me. Francesca Maria, the name with which I was baptized, always irked me because it sounded meek, dutiful and semi-saintly, all wrong for a Catholic who lapsed so young that I never made it to my first communion.

On the first day of freshman year at Lincoln I told everyone my name was Frankie. I took a lot of kidding about it, but it stuck. My parents weren't thrilled by this transformation, but, as usual, they ended up thinking everything I did was marvelous. I was their only child, conceived after their twentieth anniversary when they'd given up hope. Ma was forty and Dad was fifty when I was born, so naturally I was brought up like a future Dalai Lama. My folks both died five years ago, in a car accident on the Amalfi drive. The only thing merciful about it was that they were together.

I still live in the six-room co-op they owned in a nice apartment house on Brighton Beach, overlooking the boardwalk just before it turns into Coney Island. It's on the ninth floor, with an endless view of the ocean. There's a balcony big enough for beach chairs and at night, when I sit out there and listen to the waves crashing below, with the gulls sweeping above my head, the smell of the ocean fresh in my face and the stars above, I can easily believe I'm on my own yacht. Justine considers it a scandal that I'm still living in Brooklyn. She believes I'd be better off in a tiny, overpriced, chic little place in Manhattan, because she refuses to understand what a great neighborhood this is.

My parents were passionate beach people and they turned their back on Avenue X, the Italian neighborhood nearby, to settle here, where you can take the elevator straight down to the lobby and find yourself a hundred feet from Bay Six, the name for the part of the beach opposite our house. Jetties break the surf so the swimming is fine and the sand is white powder that never sticks to your skin. What can the East 70s offer to compare to my place?

When I was growing up this was an almost totally Jewish neighborhood, and since my father didn't think the nearest Catholic school was challenging enough for his dancing darling, he sent me to Lincoln, where I was sometimes the only kid in class on Jewish holidays. My one intensely serious crush in high school was on a Jewish guy, but when I got married, the single biggest mistake of my life, it was to a Catholic, and a moody Irishman at that.

You know how you grow up realizing, without being told, that the world is full of males you must never take seriously? Males who should only be let out in public with "not even once" tattooed on their foreheads? Why is it that you can sniff out the wrong guy any one of your friends is dating and yet fail utterly to recognize your particular doom when he comes along?

Mine was named Slim Kelly. He was, and is, a very good sportswriter for the *Daily News,* and the last time I saw him he looked like a young Pat Riley: intense, poetic, powerful. Face it, I didn't have a chance. Slim was intoxicating until about six months after we got married, when his moods began to get to me. Three years later, when we got divorced, we were both so tired out by the effort to stay together that the only thing we argued over was the custody of Big Ed, our favorite neighborhood bar. We tossed a coin and I won. Since then, almost a year ago, I've been living, by choice I assure you, in a state of chastity, abstinence or celibacy, whichever term turns you on.

I'm off men, all men.

But with custody of Big Ed, who needs them? My social life is provided for—which really drives Justine up the wall. She knows that Big Ed is my version of Cheers and she foresees a future in which I become an unmarried fixture there.

The thing that makes Big Ed indisputably the best sports bar in Brooklyn is Mrs. Ed's Happy Hour food, a full Mexican buffet, platters of barbecued baby back ribs and, best of all, Buffalo wings, those delicate deep-fried chicken wings, so spicy that you have to dip them liberally in the blue cheese and sour cream sauce to calm them down enough to eat them. Justine points out that Buffalo wings have put at least six pounds on me since my divorce but I informed her that if you're going to be celibate, you'd better have a substitute or you'll turn nasty. Sometimes she has a tendency to treat me as if I were one of our models on whom six extra pounds could be a court-martial offense.

I wish my mind hadn't drifted to Buffalo wings: as usual, even in first class, it took forever before they stopped pouring drinks and served lunch.

Now I feel better, after two portions of foie gras and two helpings of caviar, not just my own, but Maude Callender's as well.

Maude, who plunked herself down beside me at takeoff—our little Paris-bound band has the first-class cabin to itself—is generous with anything fattening because she's on a lifetime deprivation diet so that she'll never expand by a quarter inch. That's just as well when you consider she always dresses as an Edwardian dandy in custom-made costumes too special to be called clothes. She wears pants made of fine, English wool, as skintight as if she were Beau Brummell; frock coats; elaborate vests; ruffled shirts; and what I imagine would be called a four-in-hand. She's Oscar Wilde revisited, but at least she never has to wonder what to wear. Actually it's a damn clever idea for anyone with her great legs and the nerve to carry off the burden of becoming a professional personality. Maude has nerve enough to be a multiple personality and still have something left over for the weekends.

Maude became a member of our group when Maxi Amberville, the publisher of *Zing,* the fashion magazine that is doing almost as well as *Vogue* these days, got so interested in the Lombardi model contest that she decided to do a major cover story on us. The piece was assigned to Maude, who writes regularly for *Zing,* and Mike Aaron, the magazine's top photographer, who's with us too. Their brief is to create a version of *Innocents Abroad.* The piece will cover every move we make from the minute we left New York until the show is over and the winner is chosen.

Justine had agreed to a hurried setup of this wall-to-wall coverage because she and Maxi are such close friends that she couldn't refuse. However, much as I too love Maxi, it's becoming uncomfortably plain that Maude is sitting next to me, when she could have a row all to herself, in order to grill me during the flight. As I was waiting for the main course she started in with an ever-so-casual question: how do models stay so thin? Oh, the ones who don't have bulimia or anorexia all live on cocaine and speed, I was tempted to tell her. And of course they smoke at least five packs a day.

The fact is that there always are some girls on drugs and there always will be. If it's a serious problem they ruin their health and eventually their looks. On their way to this inevitable destination, they become difficult to work with; arrive late for jobs; say nasty things to the other girls; turn uncooperative with the photographers, and within months, sometimes years, depending on how much dope they're doing, their bookings taper off, no matter how beautiful they are.

As for the top girls—the so-called supermodels or megamodels, or maybe we should all fall down and worship and call them

Deities—they're deeply into serious upkeep and fitness, for their careers depend entirely on their staying on top of their game. I've never known one who didn't have a personal trainer; almost every one of them wore braces for years—because of that hard-to-please tooth fairy, perfect teeth aren't automatically included in genetic luck—and calls her mother once a day. And, for what it's worth, they each own a minimum of a half dozen leather jackets, too many jeans to count and an average of seventy of those Azzedine Alaïa "band-Aid" bandage dresses that all look more or less the same to me.

The part about calling home has always puzzled me a bit—how can there be so many good daughters?—but I assume it's because they're so young.

In the last three days, since we heard from d'Angelle, I'd often wondered who at GN had chosen April Nyquist, Jordan Dancer and Tinker Osborn out of the twenty head shots Justine sent. Was it Jacques Necker himself, or Marco Lombardi, or Gabrielle or even someone we don't know? Whoever it was had picked our three tallest girls; Tinker and Jordan are both five feet, eleven inches, and April's half an inch taller than either of them, just under six feet. What's more, they seemed to have been chosen for contrast, like a Clairol ad, April the blond Viking, Jordan the dark-haired "woman of color" and Tinker the redhead. In any case, new though they may all be, each of our girls is still gorgeous enough to hold her own physically on any runway Paris has to offer.

After all, any busy New York agency sees about seven thousand girls a year, of whom some thirty are picked to go through a training and grooming process. At the end of that time, only four or five of them are finally signed to a contract, and the vast majority of those girls will never become stars. Even among the stars, only five, right now, are internationally famous and still at their peak: Claudia, Linda, Kate, Naomi and Christy. And I'm far from sure that everybody knows Christy's last name is Turlington. Go know! It's all such a crapshoot.

Take April Nyquist, for example, sitting across the aisle. She comes from Minneapolis, the natural-blond capital of the United States. There are people who might ask, "Why April, out of all the blonds in Minneapolis?" For one thing, the Scandinavian gene pool, undiluted for tens of thousands of breeding years, that went into producing April's treasure of buttercup yellow hair, would make Paul Mitchell cry with joy. In addition April seems to breath air that is fresher than the air available to the rest of us, and her classically perfect features are relieved only by an unexpectedly endearing, ever-so-slightly crooked smile that makes her look even younger than her nineteen years.

April's been working from the first day she left the training program, although not nearly as much as Justine and I would have liked, because April's type is deeply *regal* and regal is always a hard sell to advertisers.

"What sort of living arrangements do most models have?" Maude asked me in her low, confidential voice, as if she were telling me a secret instead of trying to find out to what degree they were sluts.

"As far as I know, they live alone in New York or they live with their boyfriends, about fifty-fifty," I answered. "And a few of them live with a roommate." I didn't like being treated as the statistical expert on models' behavior, but I'd been in the business long enough to know what I was talking about, and better that Maude got it from me than from somebody else.

The flight attendant arrived with lobster, carefully removed from its shell. I looked at Maude expectantly but apparently lobster was okay on her diet. I addressed mine with concentration, after observing Jordan Dancer, who was sitting next to April, wave hers away with an imperious gesture and unwrap the container of health food she'd brought on board.

Jordan, when she's serious, calls herself "black," although one day when we were horsing around, she informed me that her skin was the subtle honey-brown color of a young alder tree when the sunlight hits it. I told her that I doubted she'd ever spent a night in a forest and I thought her skin was more the color of an herb tea I favor called Autumn Garden with milk and sugar added, but I wasn't about to bicker about technicalities.

Justine and I both cherished high hopes that Jordan would become the first true breakthrough girl, the one who finally and conclusively proves that a woman of color is as unquestioningly across-the-board commercial as a Caucasian. Jordan—think Ava Gardner with a suntan—had the potential to be seen as a beautiful woman who simply transcends color or race.

Jordan's twenty-two, the daughter of a career colonel in the Army, a Cornell graduate who majored in French and minored in art history. She's poised, mature and sophisticated far beyond the usual new face or even the usual twenty-two-year-old. There's a total dignity in her bones, yet, when I look at her, I want to start blowing kisses.

Jordan had finished her health food and composed herself for sleep before I glanced her way again. I enjoyed looking at her and calculating the amazing variations on the oval of which her face was composed: arched oval eyebrows over miraculously deep eyelids; long, uptilted oval eyes with hazel pupils; exquisite oval nostrils at the end of a small, straight nose; and a sultry oval mouth. The outlines of her eyes and lips were drawn with a simple, bold clarity almost no Caucasian models possess without makeup. Her hair was a rich dark brown, worn off her forehead in short, cherubic curls. I don't think anybody would ever ask, "Why Jordan?"

"Frankie," Maude Callender all but whispered, "don't you agree that fashion is nothing more than one giant conspiracy to make women unhappy with what's in their closets? A lot of basically male-inspired intimidation to make them spend money unnecessarily?"

"Listen, Maude, more money is spent on fashion, worldwide, than is spent on armaments. Make fashion, not war, that's my motto."

"I hadn't realized that," she said dubiously, although my statistics are exact.

"What's more, American women spend over three million dollars a year on leg waxing alone," I said, improvising in irritation.

"Oh, everybody knows that," she told me, condescendingly. I could see that Maude was bringing her own prejudgments to this "Innocents Abroad" story, but that wasn't my problem. On the other hand, Tinker Osborn was.

Our third model had a rough emotional history and Justine

and I knew that her success was problematic, although, of all our new faces, she probably had the greatest potential.

Tinker's test shots had sent us into a trance. Glamour is real, and she had it. Charm is real, and she had it. The particulars of her looks are all but irrelevant: masses of vaguely wavy, long, pale-red hair, almost a coral color, the color that Venetian women were working on five centuries ago, sitting on their rooftops in the sun with henna or some such muck on their roots; perfect skin; and vast, silver grey eyes. Moonriver eyes I called them. They express more soul, more mystery, more *edge* than April or Jordan will ever have. Her eyes make you want to really know her, ask her questions, watch her live. Yet Tinker's face, without makeup, is the perfect blank canvas, like an albino chameleon on white paper. Makeup artists will worship at her feet.

Tinker comes from Tennessee, where she became a star of the kids' beauty pageant circuit at the age of two, growing up under the inhuman pressure that those kids are subjected to.

She continued to win pageants until she turned twelve when Tinker, no Brooke Shields, hit the awkward age with a crash, entering adolescence in a hormonal shitstorm that included acne and a huge weight gain. It took almost six years until she grew out of it, and into her present looks. She'd had no school friends to suffer adolescence along with her, no school achievements, just, thank God, an interest in reading that she depended on more and more in her lonely exile from the only world she'd known.

"During my senior year in high school," Tinker told me, frowning, "I dared to look at fashion magazines again and try out makeup and hairstyles in my room. I got the idea that maybe, just maybe . . . I could get my *identity* back, maybe I could model for magazines and become a winner again. That's why I came here."

I don't remember if I groaned out loud or just internally. Of all the reasons for wanting to be a model, a search for identity was the worst. Any kind of ambition was acceptable to me, from achieving worldwide adulation to serial marriage with rock stars. Some of the most successful and strongest girls are in the business simply for the money and that strikes me as the best motive of all. But identity! No way. It's only common sense to know that a job based on something as fleeting as looks will never give any girl an identity she can count on.

Justine and I realized how emotionally fragile Tinker was. However we knew that she was determined enough to go on making the agency rounds until someone else signed her. At that point we decided that we'd take her on and protect her as much as possible.

Tinker had barely graduated from our training program when Gabrielle d'Angelle came calling. Justine and I would have preferred GN to tap any of our other models than Tinker. This was a girl who'd never set foot on a runway. She hadn't even started to build a career and now she'd have to do an haute couture fashion show in the electric atmosphere of the spring collections. The very last thing she needed was to flop in the glare of publicity surrounding the new Lombardi face. Yet there was nothing we could do. GN had made its choice.

At least she'll see Paris.

"May I have another lobster?"

Right behind me, occupying two seats, one for him, one for the cameras he deemed too important to let out of his sight, I heard Mike Aaron getting, without even saying please, the second lobster I'd been too restrained to ask for. Naturally Mike Aaron hadn't recognized me. He'd been a senior at Lincoln during my freshman year. He'd been the captain of the football team *and* the captain of the basketball team and the editor of the yearbook and president of the photo club and president of his class. He'd been light years beyond a legend.

Mike Aaron was the guy I'd had that crush on all through high school. Now, all those years later, I have to admit that it was more than a crush. I'd loved Mike Aaron for years and years after he'd graduated and disappeared, loved him with a hopeless, wild, adolescent purity of passion I don't think I ever felt for my husband, Slim Kelly, on his best day. How could any girl have been so dumb?

And what an arrogant son of a bitch he'd turned out to be, now that I'd encountered him again. I didn't like the private sense of amusement I could all but smell on him, I didn't like his power to charm that I'd watched him use on the girls, a power he probably practiced in front of a mirror until he'd hypnotized himself into making it seem natural. I didn't trust his big salty grin or his big, happy-go-lucky laugh and his extravagantly offhand gangsta style, all beat-up leather and charisma. The bastard even had Paul Mitchell hair.

4

Peaches Wilcox lay flat on her back on the carpet of her bedroom in the Plaza-Athénée hotel, holding a hand mirror directly above her face and scrutinizing her image intently. Very slowly, using only her formidable stomach muscles, she rose until she was in a sitting position, never taking her eyes from the mirror. Finally she permitted herself a satisfied smile.

Her features, viewed in the prone position and the sitting position, looked exactly the same, just as Dr. H. had promised in New York, two months ago. No section of facial skin or muscle had undergone a change as the pull of gravity worked on them. Of course, she knew better than to look at herself with the mirror on the floor as she bent over it. That was one sure way to ruin her day. How many women realized that the often-scorned missionary position took fifteen years off a gal's face? Only a really young thing could afford to be seen when she was on top with everything hanging down, no matter what improved friction the astride position provided.

It had been a good long while since she'd had that horsey luxury, Peaches reflected, as she rang for her maid to bring the herb tea, grapefruit and dry whole wheat toast that made up her breakfast. Yes, indeed, there were a few things money couldn't buy, not even with the five hundred million that darlin' Jimmy had left her free and clear, with no horrid nonsense about trusts that would have given her only the income to spend. With no children to provide for, with the Wilcox Foundation already funded, Jimmy'd wanted her to have everything money could buy. She already had more than her fair share, as Jimmy knew: good health, good skin— which was, let it never be forgotten, the largest organ in the body

—good hair, and a glorious ass; but he'd wanted to ensure her a happy future.

Poor darlin' Jimmy died without knowing that certain things existed that no amount of money could buy. Peaches searched her mind for something tangible but only an aircraft carrier, a national park and Swiss citizenship came to mind. She had more than enough real estate, thank you, she got seasick in a rowboat and she'd never want to be anything but a Texan. But, as they said, it was the intangibles that counted. Like having only happy dreams and being forty-six again. Both were equally impossible. Nightmares happened from time to time, even to her, in spite of a clear conscience, and her forty-seventh birthday had arrived, unmentioned and unwelcome, two weeks ago. Youth was as unattainable as the possession of Marco Lombardi, who should, by all rights, be nailed down with long, rusty nails on a hot stove in eternal hell for what he was doing to her.

It was downright humiliating at best for a woman who was entertained by everybody who mattered to be languishing for an Italian dress designer, unknown as yet, and twelve years younger than she. And wouldn't you know he'd be so notoriously gorgeous that it was an obviously pathetic lapse in taste to go for him? Yep, a reversal of passion, there was another thing money couldn't buy, Peaches brooded. There was no other word than passion for how she felt about Marco. If only he weren't straight this would never have happened, she thought as she put on her leotard.

Peaches McCoy Wilcox just did *not have* man trouble, she told herself firmly as she began the obligatory stretching and mat routine before starting a half hour on one of the identical Nordic-Track machines that she kept in each of her four homes as well as in any hotel in which she planned to stay for more than a night.

Starting with her daddy, who'd owned every Caddy dealership from Houston to Dallas, she'd had good luck with men. Her parents had blessed her with adoring brothers and no troublesome sisters, she'd had a string of boyfriends so persistent that it had taken her years to work through them, breaking hearts ruthlessly, as was only her due, and she'd finally decided to marry darlin' Jimmy, who'd never looked at another woman until he'd died three years ago. Jimmy had been in oil of course, there was really no other way to go making serious money unless you were in real estate, the record business, big-time, or geeky enough to invent yet another unnecessary version of computer junk.

She'd mourned Jimmy well and truly for six months and then started making the rounds that could be counted on to keep a widow in her position busy without having to pretend interest in a lot of boring committee meetings: the villa at Cap-Ferrat for two months in the summer, Venice for September, New York through the holidays, Saint-Moritz after Christmas; and, of course, a few days to rest up at the Texas ranch every now and then.

The essential constants of her life were the spring and fall couture collections in Paris, which was how she'd come across Marco Lombardi to begin with, Peaches thought wrathfully. If only she'd had the sense to stay home in Texas, never messing in the high life, never needing a constant infusion of new French clothes to keep her appropriately dressed, she wouldn't have known that such a tantalizingly manipulative peckerhead existed. By now she'd be comfortably remarried to some nice guy, predictably ordering her clothes from the trunk shows at Neiman's, and never knowing the difference between Seventh Avenue and the Avenue Montaigne.

Peaches was dedicated to maintaining her flamboyant allure. She could have gone for chic, and achieved it by toning down her natural wide-screen looks, cutting the homecoming-queen hair that reached to her shoulders in blond abundance, reducing the wattage of her smile, and taming her natural inclination to buy truly rich-lady clothes.

Hell, you could always be chic if you took the right advice, but she'd be damned if she'd give up sexy before sixty—no, make that sixty-five—and chic and sexy had little to do with each other. Would Marco love her back if she were chic? Peaches shook her head severely at her wistful folly. Marco might love her back if she were twenty-five or even thirty, but otherwise she had to try to be content with what he gave her: the most glorious fucking she'd ever had and a lot of meaningless Italian handkissing. But, oh, Lord, when he bent that dark head over her hand, that incredible head with the curly hair worn deliberately too long, with eyelashes that were equally excessive, with those slightly pouting lips that were too perfectly cut for a man, with his warmly olive skin . . . *damn him for not being gay!* If he were gay she could rumple his hair and tease him about his being too handsome for words and forget about him as soon as he left the room.

But no, Marco created an agonizing sexual tension in her that never disappeared except for a few minutes after they'd made love and when she was concentrating on her morning workout. No man had ever had the upper hand with her before, no man had ever made her beg for it. She'd spotted him running up the staircase at Dior over a year ago, and demanded that her vendeuse introduce them, something that apparently wasn't done from the woman's surprised expression. Impulsively, she'd invited him over for drinks that same night, knowing that the importance of her guests would be bound to make an impression on anyone, especially a mere assistant designer.

Marco had stayed only a half hour, displaying such quiet self-assurance that every woman in the room had called the next day, enviously trying to find out where on earth she'd found him. As he left he'd asked her if she'd like to have a hamburger with him at Joe Allen's some night soon.

And that was how it had started, Peaches thought, as she left the NordicTrack, her heart pounding as it was intended to, and started in on the free weights that were the last part of her two-hour-long exercise routine. He'd told her all about studying at the Rome Academy of Fine Arts and realizing, after a few years, that while his talents might lie in the pursuit of architectural history, he would be better served by his curiosity about the architecture of the human body. He had left the Academy and become an apprentice for the great couturier Roberto Capucci, a designer little known in the United States but considered a superb artist by museum curators in Europe and the Far East.

"Buildings have been constructed in a relatively limited number of basic ways for the single primordial purpose of housing human beings," Marco had said seriously as he passed her an unwanted dessert brownie in the noisy room full of French Yuppies having an American experience. "Yet clothes, which are just as primordial, come in thousands of varieties. Why do we have so many different envelopes with which to surround the shoulders, the breasts, the waist, the hips, the legs, none of which changes basically over the ages?"

Peaches remembered clearly that she had been unable to form a remotely intelligent answer. Looking at him had blasted a short circuit in her brain cells and turned her into a creature of pure body who only wanted his cock. Years of training in being a Texas lady, years of keeping the most desirable men at the University of Texas in a state of staggering confusion and lust, had stopped her from making an overt move. Some old habits never die. It had taken Marco a whole week to stop toying with her in that deceptively respectful manner and give her what she needed so terribly.

Peaches Wilcox put down the two ten-pound free weights, afraid that she'd throw them through the window of the hotel in rage and kill someone walking by on the Avenue Montaigne. Marco hadn't returned her calls in five days. How *dared* he?

Why was he reaching for a cigarette he hadn't had in his pocket for three years, Marco Lombardi asked himself irritably? He hadn't really wanted one for a year. Why now, when his designs for the spring collection were all decided on, when the actual samples were being finished, did he feel a nervous straining itch to start sketching another replacement collection that would be more circus-like in its unwearable humor than Jean-Paul Gaultier, go further into the vulgarity of strip tease and bondage than Versace, be more pretentiously opulent than Lacroix, more absurdly avant-garde than Vivienne Westwood? In other words, a collection that would create such a shock, even a scandal, that the press would be forced to mention it?

Marco left his studio hurriedly, before he had time to entertain any more disturbing and unworthy thoughts. He was stopped by his secretary, a middle-aged Frenchwoman, stern of manner and plain of face, who looked up at him sharply.

"You should start returning these calls now, Monsieur Marco. I have a long list of people who should be called back before tomorrow. Madame Wilcox called again as well."

"Tell me, *cara* Madame Elsa, what do you think is the worst thing that will happen to me if I don't return those calls?" Marco asked in a voice that became a caress as he spoke.

"I . . . but you know how important they are," she said, trying to sound as severe as possible. "And if you don't answer them today, they will still be here tomorrow, along with many others."

"Did you ever see *Gone With the Wind, cara* Madame Elsa?"

She looked at him warily. He was the least predictable man she'd ever been asked to work for. He'd tried to get her to call him by his first name, but she refused, finally letting him tease her into accepting a compromise that retained some proper formality. But everyone knew that the Italians were children, you had to make allowances for them. Of course she was too clever not to understand that he counted on his looks, this man who was too excessively attractive for his own good, but she congratulated herself that she had refused to become one of his gasping worshipers like so many of the women who worked for him.

"Of course I saw it," she admitted, thinking that he should be forced to get his hair cut, as she had been urging him to for months. A serious couturier shouldn't look like a wild young art student sculpted by Michelangelo, racing around Paris in a tweed jacket, flannel trousers and a scarf flung around his neck.

"Then you remember the last line of the movie, that tomorrow will be another day, that she will worry tomorrow, something like that? You see, I'm just not in the mood for the telephone." Marco gave his secretary a smile that told her that he wouldn't have admitted this to anyone but her, a smile that invited her into his world. "I need to take a walk . . . I need to escape. Perhaps I am even a little nervous, no, Madame Elsa? Wouldn't that be natural? Aren't you a little nervous for me?"

She nodded, reluctantly. She'd worked in couture too long not to be nervous before any collection, but nevertheless, those phone calls. . . .

"But we mustn't be nervous, must we, you and I?" Marco told her, leaning on her desk and looking at her intently. "Every designer in Paris gets nervous at the same time each season, why be like the others? Come, let's change the subject, Madame Elsa," he said, tapping lightly on her arm with an air of gentle command.

"How pleasing I find your name. Do you realize that even with familiarity, it sings in my ear, it reverberates? . . . Elsa . . . yes, you are fortunate indeed, and so is your husband."

"Thank you," she said, suppressing a gratified smile. "As you know, it was my grandmother's name."

"Old world and gracious. Yes, it suits you. If dresses were still given names, as they used to be, I would baptize my first dress 'Elsa' in your honor. Now, I leave you to hold back the barbarians as they pound on the gates."

"But what if Monsieur Necker calls again?" she asked in alarm. "Or Madame Wilcox?"

"Ah, Madame Elsa, how can you ask? You, a woman of imagination as well as charm? Make up something . . . I count entirely on your tact. After all, even Monsieur Necker doesn't expect me to be shut in here all day like a schoolboy when inspiration is everywhere. Tell Madame Wilcox nothing. I've disappeared, that's all you know. A domani, cara Madame Elsa."

Marco escaped his secretary, that superior, righteous and vigilant woman Necker had installed in his office to make sure that he was kept in order at all times. It had taken a few days of observation before he'd discovered her areas of weakness: her still youthful complexion, her well-shaped ears, her slender ankles and her first name. She'd never be of any use to Necker again, for now she took her orders only from him. He could bring a blush to her cheeks anytime he cared to.

Marco's workrooms and studio were installed in a building on the Rue Clément-Marot, around the corner from GN's headquarters. As he headed for the street, he suddenly remembered a dress that he had ripped apart yesterday after seeing it on his fitting model. He ran up a flight of stairs to the atelier in which the dress was being resewn by his most experienced hand, the redoubtable Madame Ginette, who had worked at Lanvin before World War II and after the war at Dior, until she'd been lured away to Saint-Laurent. Now, a decade and a half after her well-earned retirement, Necker had persuaded her to come back to work for this particular collection. Marco found her bending over a seam and he took her shoulders gently in his hands as she paused to look up at him, putting down the work.

"So, *ma toute belle*, do we make progress?"

"You know as well as I do that working these layers of chiffon on the bias is slow work," she answered, wearily, taking off her glasses with a sigh. "I'm exhausted."

"You don't want me to look at the miracle you have wrought?" He ran his finger up her chin and tugged lightly at her ear.

"All you want is to see if I can save this dress," she grumbled. "When you took it apart yesterday, you might have been more careful, you tore a seam in several places."

"You're absolutely right. If I'd given it to you from the beginning it would never have happened. But the seams are a disgrace, admit it, *chérie*. Half of these young girls don't know their craft. I'm afraid I lost my temper."

"You're a wild, crazy Italian," she reprimanded him, croon-ingly. "Monsieur Dior would never lose his temper, like a lamb he was, poor man."

"And Monsieur Saint-Laurent?" he asked, taking her worn hand and inspecting her fingertips.

"Never a cross word. A true gentleman." And even when Saint-Laurent had been young and the toast of Paris, even when she'd still been susceptible to charm, he'd never been able to sweet talk her like Monsieur Marco, she thought. Oh, these Italians, they should be barred from entering France at the borders. They were irresistible with their eyes, their smiles. Particularly this one.

"You have beautiful hands, Madame Ginette," Marco said reflectively. "They show why your work is perfect."

"They are just hands," she said, flurried. "An old woman's hands," she added, trying to draw away. He held them firmly.

"No, you don't realize—when you've worked with beauty, year after year, the hand reveals it." He released her hands slowly, touching each fingertip in turn, and brushing it with a light kiss. "Now, may I see that seam? *Bravissimo!* Exactly what I'd hoped for —you've rescued it. This dress will be the hit of the collection."

She straightened up with melting pride and smiled at him shyly.

He made her feel young again, bless him. But to rip a seam!

Ah well, he was full of passion, this Italian, but he needed a haircut.

"For certain! Those were the days. Until tomorrow, *ma toute belle*, I count on you."

As he took the staircase down, Marco thought that it would be at least a week before Ginette started threatening to leave again, speaking of her fatigue and her advanced age. Perhaps two weeks, if he was lucky, because he needed her skills. When it came time to fit the samples on the models that tiresome old hag would be invaluable.

He should have taken his coat, he realized as he walked a few blocks. It was so sunny that he had been fooled into thinking it might, just for once, be warm in this city, but no, it was a true Paris cold, mean and damp under the deceptive sunlight. He turned into a little Italian restaurant where he sat at the empty bar and ordered a double espresso.

Oh Christ, he needed a rest! A change! And a rest or a change were the last things he could hope for in these next few weeks before the day on which his dreams either became true or he was shown up to the fashion press as a failure. Shown up before every important journalist and buyer from all over the world, shown up before CNN, shown up before *Vogue* and *Zing* and *Bazaar*, before the *New York Times* and *Le Figaro* and eventually before the smallest newspaper in the tiniest provincial town sleeping deep in the countryside of *la France Profonde*.

Why hadn't he ever realized, in his flood of ambition, that no one was judged to the harsh public degree that a new couturier was? A fledgling actor could play his first part without anyone knowing about it unless it was a success. A potential tennis champion could lose an early match without fearing ridicule from all sides. But every woman considered herself a judge of clothes.

Fashion had become the world's most written about, most photographed spectator sport and each new collection was greeted with a chorus of praise or jest or indifference from the editor-in-chief of *Elle* to the shopgirls who worked at the Prix-Unique. He could just imagine them abandoning their counters to bend over the photos in the papers with the same serene yet beady-eyed, judgmental gaze adopted by those valued couture clients who were ritually seated in the first row next to the runway.

"Lombardi?—hmmm—never heard of him, somebody new I guess. What do you think? Yes, I agree, not my style, even if I could afford it. Oh, just look at Claudia in that cute little Chanel jacket . . . now I wouldn't mind having one like that, would you? You could even wear it with jeans."

Now that the moment he worked toward all of his life was almost upon him, was it possible that he couldn't handle it, Marco asked himself, enraged at the scornful, dismissive words he'd conjured up. Was this the way other designers before him had felt before their first collections?

There was no way to know, no one to ask, for designers, like rival opera singers or two prizefighters before a boxing match, didn't get together to share their inner feelings with each other. He tried to imagine the great designers having a fit of insecurity, as he was doing now, and failed. Saint-Laurent, of course, he'd made a fetish out of his ritualistic nervous attacks, the martyr to fashion, the tormented Christ-figure dying over and over for the sake of each new collection, but there was only room for one such genius.

Marco ordered another espresso, glad that he was still alone, that no one had yet arrived for a before-dinner drink. There were three dozen things he should be doing on this winter day that had turned to twilight outside the window, a hundred details he should be inspecting, and, yet, for the love of God, he didn't even know who the three new models for his show would be. What excuse did Necker have to impose on him three green girls when he absolutely needed the security of using none but experienced models who made anything look good, supreme girls the photographers would automatically focus on. But no, Necker had chosen to meddle, declaring a contest as if it were the Judgment of Paris all over again. How could Necker have dreamed up such a criminally stupid stunt?

He could kill Necker! All Marco's apprehension was suddenly channeled toward the man who had put him in this position. What right did that Swiss bourgeois have to impose his own taste on the presentation of the collection? Did his financial backing give him a free rein to call all the shots? He was the one who decided to show the spring collection in the great, cloud-frescoed space of the spa and beauty salon that had been built under the Ritz, where the vast pool could be covered over and the gigantic room could be turned into a venue for any kind of party or exhibition.

"It must be a real gala, Marco," Necker had announced. "We'll show at night, black tie, followed by a buffet. That's the only way to start with an unknown. The press and buyers have such impossible days merely covering the established designers that they'd never be able to fit you in otherwise. At collection time hype and megalomania take over. A more distinguished approach is necessary."

How the devil did Necker know? He was a businessman, a successful businessman but a *mere* businessman, an owner of fabric mills, a buyer of other people's talents, a merchandiser, a hawker of the fleeting illusion of hope wrapped in perfume bottles—not a designer, for the love of God, not an artist who had to reach into his own guts and imagination and find a way to create something new.

Ah, but Necker was smart. He gave the son of a bitch that. Smart enough to make sure that he, Marco, the engine that pulled the train, was kept short of fuel. Of course there was no way in which he would have been able to suitably launch a major collection on his own; he needed enormous funds to back him.

"You'll get your salary, Marco, a very large salary, you have to admit. But I have no intention of giving you a piece of the profits. In the first place, there may never be a profit. GN is taking a calculated risk in backing someone new. This is a speculative risk for me, an investment that may fail. I'll lose money on the couture, like everyone else. Each dress we sell will cost more to make than you can charge for it. You know the couture only exists to get publicity. The ready-to-wear will take several seasons to prove how successful it *may* become and the perfume, if there is to be one, may be years away. Marco, I admire your talent, but business is business."

All his life Marco had been a wage slave, assisting and designing for others, and this was his only chance to have his own label, so he'd taken it, of course, as Necker knew he would. He'd never forgive the Swiss for his refusal to allow as little as one crumb from the table to fall into his hands. Where would fashion be without the handful of men and the few women who had creative talent?

He caught himself trying to find a cigarette in his pocket. In another minute he'd be ordering a pack from the barman. These hours of freedom, instead of calming him, were proving counterproductive. What he needed was a woman, Marco realized suddenly. How long had it been? Two, perhaps three weeks since he'd had the time to spare for sex?

Yes, a woman, an uncomplicated woman who would not need one word of the endless seduction the harpies at work required every day. A brief, brutal relief from nervous tension, the kind of animal release only a whore could give you, and he never used whores. An appraising look came into his eyes as Marco mulled over the possibilities available to him with the kind of close attention he'd give to the menu in a new restaurant.

After a few seconds he sighed with resignation. He didn't have the time to bother finding anyone except Peaches. She had wearied him for at least six months, her attempts at possessiveness angered him, her utter availability made him disdain her. Even now, when she should be following her enviably worldly schedule, when she should be in New York for a dozen galas, she was shamelessly hanging around Paris trying to reach him. Was it possible that she was the same woman he had once, for only an evening, imagined to be, if not out of his reach, at least difficult to attain? A woman with whom he had bothered to make the kind of quasi-intellectual conversation designed to impress? Yet how could he have expected that Dior's best customer, a woman world famous for her wealth and social standing, would be so easy, so avid, so lacking in the dignity he considered proper to her age?

Nevertheless, Marco decided, physically she was exactly what he had prescribed for himself, an open pair of thighs with no questions asked. He made a quick phone call to make sure that she was in her suite and in a minute he was on his way to the Plaza, right around the corner.

Peaches felt pleased with herself as she put down the phone. She'd told Marco to come right on over, in a sweet, level voice, but she hadn't told him that she was giving a cocktail party for a good-sized group of visiting Texans, some of whom were already in the large sitting room scarfing up her caviar.

Instead of the discreet personal maid who normally ushered him into the suite, a white-coated butler opened the door as he rang, and a waiter took his scarf.

"Madame Wilcox is in the large sitting room, Monsieur," the waiter said. Marco had imagined that Peaches would be lounging expectantly in the smaller sitting room, by the flattering light of her artfully small lamps, wearing one of the hundred elaborate dressing gowns she possessed. He was taken aback when she came toward him, leaving a cluster of her compatriots by the fireplace. She was very Catherine the Great tonight, wearing a red velvet dinner suit with a closely fitted, gold embroidered jacket, its cuffs and wide skirt both trimmed with bands of sable.

He took her hand and kissed it on the inside of her wrist, knowing that not one of her guests would realize that his gesture indicated a degree of intimacy that should never be revealed in public.

"Champagne?" she asked, with her flashing, red-lipped smile, as if she'd seen him five minutes earlier.

"Why didn't you warn me you had guests?"

"But Marco," she said, opening her beautiful eyes in mock surprise, "every one of these old gals is a good potential customer. You have all evening to charm them, we're going on to dinner later."

"I'm not here to sell dresses."

"Really?" she retorted, as if surprised, leading him into the room. "Come on in and say hello to the Andersons, Selma and Ralph, from Fort Worth, and these lovely folks are Betty Lou and Hank Curtis from Houston. This is Marco Lombardi, everybody, he's a dress designer and you're going to be hearing a lot about him."

As he shook hands with the Texans and heard Peaches greet another couple who were just entering the room, Marco promised himself that he would leave in three minutes, simply slip out of the room, and walk down the hall to the elevator without even saying good-bye to Peaches. He asked for a Scotch, drank it quickly and accepted another.

Peaches, Marco noted, as he was introduced to more of her guests, was enjoying this to the same degree that her friends ignored him, too delighted to see each other to bother wasting more than a quick smile on some unplaceable foreigner. Although he spoke French with fluency, and his infrequent mistakes were always regarded as charming, he had never felt equally at home in English, a language he knew he spoke with a distinct Italian accent and a sometimes imprecise grasp of grammar. Standing slightly apart from the others, Marco observed Peaches flaunting her fake indifference as brilliantly as the great and indisputably genuine diamonds at her ears. Oh, yes, she knew perfectly well that she made her expensively gowned friends look drab and provincial in contrast to her vividly blond presence. He found himself in a state of sudden fury as he surveyed her, the center of everyone's attention. So she thought that he would stick around through dinner with these creatures, did she? He crossed the room and took her by the elbow, drawing her to one side.

"I want to speak to you."

"That's not possible right now, can't you see that?"

"I'm going into your bedroom. Follow me."

"I'll do no such thing," Peaches said, her eyes sparkling with malice.

"Do you want a scandal?"

"Don't be silly, Marco."

"I'll make one this instant and your friends will tell everyone in Texas, I promise you."

"That's blackmail!"

"Follow me, I warn you," he repeated, and wove his way across the large room, across the entry, through the smaller sitting room and into her bedroom. A few minutes later she joined him there, flushed with triumph.

"Are you happy now?" Peaches asked, as if speaking to a child. "What exactly do you think you're proving besides appallingly bad manners?"

"Close the door behind you."

"I'm going back to the party," she said, turning away.

Swiftly he pushed her aside, locked the heavy door and gripped her hand so tightly that she gasped in the astonishment of pain.

"I'm going to fuck you. Now. Here."

"The hell you are! I'll scream. Marco! My fingers!"

He held her pinned to the door and rubbed violently against her as his penis, already hard, grew quickly.

"Stop that! *Let me go!*" She was stunned by disbelief. He'd hurt her hand badly.

"I don't think so," he muttered. Quickly, using his considerable strength, Marco lifted her and dumped her on her bed. As she struggled to rise he clamped her slender wrists together with one hand and with the other he flipped her skirt up and pulled her silk and lace panties down so that her lower body was exposed, naked except for her garter belt and her stockings.

"Let me go!" she shouted.

"Nobody will hear you, not with all the noise they're making. Shut up or scream, it won't make any difference," he grunted, unzipping his pants.

"Marco, no! Stop! Don't do this!"

"You're dying for it, don't pretend you aren't." He tore off her panties and wrenched open her thighs, taking her knees and forcing them to bend so that her legs were raised. Holding her thighs apart he quickly positioned himself on the bed over her so that his weight kept her from moving her body, as her fists beat ineffectually on his back and her legs thrashed in the air. He lifted himself off her just enough to take his penis in his hand.

As he ground it into her he found himself so intoxicated by the novelty of her dryness and her resistance that he no longer heard her begging him to stop. The universe was reduced to the monstrous orgasm he felt building from the base of his spine. A man threatening him with a gun couldn't have stopped him now as he used Peaches mercilessly, quickly losing himself in a series of spasms that made him cry out as wordlessly as an animal.

When the last drop had been wrung out of him, he reared

back on the heels of his hands and looked down at her face. Her eyes were closed and her face was set in an expression he didn't recognize.

"Oh, don't worry, I'll make you come now," he promised her, breathlessly. "With my mouth, the way you adore it."

She opened her eyes and he saw the look of rage that filled them. "If you touch me, I'll have you killed," Peaches said in a cold monotone.

"Don't be melodramatic," Marco scoffed lazily. If she wanted to play at being angry she didn't impress him. No woman had ever desired him as ferociously as this one did.

In a flash Peaches had wriggled out from the cage of his arms and was on her feet, by the bed.

"Get out. Get off my bed, get out of this room, leave here right away," she ordered him.

"You're a ridiculously delicious girl, did you know that? Just look, you're impeccable, even your pretty hair isn't disarranged. Come on now, come back here, let me suck you off. I need to taste you. You'll come so soon, so deeply, right between my lips, right on my tongue . . . it will be good, so very good, even better than the last time, I promise. That's what you need, *bella*, that's why you're so angry, don't you understand?" he coaxed, rolling over and beckoning to her. Peaches turned her back on him, stepped into the pumps she'd kicked off, smoothed her skirt, checked her image in a mirror and left the room, all in one seamless flicker of movement.

Marco cursed, realizing that the door was still wide open and he was lying on the bed with his trousers open and his limp penis hanging down. He hastened to make himself presentable and hurried to the entry, where he was stopped by the butler who had taken his scarf. In the few seconds that it took the man to find it, Marco heard Peaches' laugh ring out from the room where she was again entertaining her guests.

5

Possibly she ought to feel guilty about sending Frankie off with such little notice, Justine told herself, but on the other hand, shipping her off to Paris with a new wardrobe and a whirlwind of activity ahead of her was probably the sort of shock therapy Frankie needed to get her out of the slump she'd been in ever since her divorce.

Yes, Justine thought, as she prowled restlessly from her office to the main booking room, it was high time to take action. Who knows where that girl would end up if somebody didn't take care of her? Actually she should have done something like this a year ago, but no exceptional opportunity had presented itself. She'd exhausted her powers of suggestion and canny advice, powers that had been honed by years of whipping raw girls into shape. Then she'd degenerated into mere nagging, and even that didn't work on a person who was so maddeningly stubborn, planted so squarely on those gigantic feet she was so proud of, operating from a center of gravity in her solar plexus so powerful that you could almost see it. Martha Graham had a lot to answer for, she thought darkly.

Justine kicked off her shoes and lay back on the couch in her office, putting her feet up in a position that should make her feel pleasantly relaxed. She breathed deeply, Pilates style, for a few minutes, and then, with an angry shake of her head, started picking at her nail polish, something she hadn't done in twenty years. Frankie really got her goat, she thought, her frown deepening. She hated to see somebody piss herself away! There was no other way to put it, not when she considered all the natural advantages Frankie brought to the party.

She was such a crazily terrific-looking creature, with a magnificent body that she was well on her way to treating as if she were its evil twin sister. From the day she'd first walked on a sidewalk with Frankie, Justine realized that the girl never even noticed how men turned to look after her as she swept by with her swift and sinuous step, men who were clearly intrigued and attracted by the brief glimpse they'd caught of her flashing vitality, by the haughtiness of her carriage, by the cloak of unconventionality that she seemed born to wear. Damn the girl, she escaped any category. Still and all, Justine admitted to herself, Frankie did hold herself pulled up high in a dancer's stance, her head tilted on her fine, graceful neck in a way that implied that she held a license for arrogance. Every morning that infernal creature spent twenty minutes applying eye makeup that could be seen from the second balcony of any theatre, and then she'd pile her long brown hair on top of her head and skewer it with two tortoiseshell pins in five seconds flat, without even the aid of a mirror.

If Frankie'd been a model, Justine told herself, she would have fired her ass after she put on the first two pounds. To say nothing of the dogged way she managed to conceal the incalculable asset of her magnificent head of hair! Thank God she couldn't take the veil and hide her arrestingly dramatic face. Not another beautiful face, not another pretty face, thank God, but something much more interesting, a face full of living and fun and drama, although Frankie'd never admit that there was anything special about her, the pigheaded bitch! Frankie was suffering from a case of terminal contemporary dance, that was her problem. Didn't she know that a well-paid, highly professional woman who got herself up as if she were going to a dance rehearsal hall every day of her working life should probably be in therapy? Oh, to hell with her, Frankie wasn't her problem.

Justine listened to the noises in the booking center that filtered through her open office door. Everyone seemed to be on the phone, as usual, but there was a quality of diminished attention, as if they were all working by rote, instead of keeping themselves alert to every future possibility concealed in their conversations, like Indian scouts in old movies listening to the humming of the railroad tracks.

As she'd impressed on them many times, if they could tell her why any given girl *hadn't* been booked she could learn as much about the future as she could from knowing who was suddenly in demand. She depended on them for that kind of information. Was it a post-holiday letdown? No agency could afford that. Fashion photography was a round-the-year business. But she didn't feel in the mood to go and investigate. Oh, to hell with them too, the bookers weren't her problem.

She felt . . . anxiety . . . as if something bad were waiting to happen, which made no sense at all. She should be feeling enormous relief, Justine told herself. She'd been waiting for the day when the girls would leave for France, poised in a paralyzed combination of the instincts of flight and fight, determined to escape the snare that had been set for her. But even with Frankie, the girls, and the team from *Zing* all safely aloft, she still felt that nothing had been resolved. Maybe *that* was the problem? In any case, Frankie's absence left the office feeling desolate. Knowing that she was there to talk to about business, to gossip with about anyone in complete confidence . . . yes, she'd come to rely on that feisty, upbeat presence.

What if Necker were to come to New York and walk in on her?

Damn! Justine found herself on her feet, her heart pounding, as if he'd just appeared in the doorway. This was exactly the kind of crazy thought that had awakened her, sweating, in the middle of the night for the past three nights. She closed her office door firmly and made herself sit down behind her impressive desk, the one place in the world where she felt most in a position of command. She must think this through, Justine informed herself sternly, or she'd become a victim to her growing apprehension. What, after all, had she accomplished in not going to Paris? She'd merely postponed events. She was too based in reality not to admit that eventually a confrontation with Necker was inevitable. She was reacting, damn it, instead of acting, and that ran contrary to the way she wanted to live her life.

Normally, that is. Normally she didn't hide, she spoke her mind clearly, she made decisions without waffling. She liked to think of herself as a decisive woman, a late-twentieth-century working woman who was fully in charge of her destiny.

Yet one of the pillars on which her life was based had been far from normal, no matter how you looked at it, Justine brooded.

When she was thirteen, as soon as she'd had her first period, her mother had told her that the father she'd always believed had been killed in Vietnam, was still alive.

"He was my first lover, and he left me in the lurch as soon as I found out I was pregnant with you. I've never seen or heard from him again. I'm forced to tell you this, Justine, now that you've become a woman, physically capable of getting pregnant. It's essential for you to know what every male, no matter how you think you love him or he loves you, can do to you, Justine. You must never, ever forget the lesson I had to learn."

"But who is my father?" she had asked her mother, over and over. "What was he like? How could he leave you like that? How did you meet him? How long did you know him?" Endless questions until she finally realized, with painful frustration, that her mother never intended to give her any information, no matter how many times she insisted that she had a right to know something, *anything,* about her father.

"Nothing about that person is important, darling," Helena Loring had invariably responded to her questions, "except for the fact of *what he did* to me. If you'd been a boy, I wouldn't have owed it to you to say a single word about the matter. It's a closed subject, Justine, I've earned the right to keep it private."

No question about it, Justine brooded, her mother had been a formidable woman, quite apart from her stubborn silence. Eventually, as Justine grew older, Helena Loring had been willing to tell more of her own story. Justine learned how her mother had refused to fall apart when she found herself alone and pregnant. She'd cleaned out the savings account she'd built up through years of summer jobs and birthday presents and she'd gone to have her baby in a middle-sized city outside of Chicago where no one knew her. Out of a massive streak of independence, she'd concealed Justine's birth from her own parents until a few weeks after it took place. Then, wrapped in a sense of rightness, Helena Loring had told them only that although she'd made a mistake, she was determined to bring up her child on her own.

In less than three weeks after Justine's birth she'd found a kind, capable woman to take care of her infant and secured a job as a salesgirl in the best local department store. Helena Loring had worked so single-mindedly that she rose rapidly to assistant buyer, eventually to department manager and finally to executive vice-president of the entire store.

Her mother had loved her dearly, Justine knew, loved her exclusively, for she'd never responded to the few men who dared to try to get to know her better. She had a circle of friends, couples and single women, but they were all deftly made to understand that she had been so devastated by the death of her husband that she never wanted to marry again.

"Risk." Justine said the word to herself, feeling the familiar, complicated twist of emotions it always gave her. Her mother had been risk-adverse with her emotions, as if to expose them to anyone but her daughter, and that only briefly, would be to see her life lying about her in ruins. Justine's grandparents had both died before she was ten, and there had been no other family in her life. She'd been popular in school but she'd never confided a word of the story of her parentage to a single friend, knowing that there was no one she could trust with this dangerous knowledge in a gossip-loving circle in which everyone knew everyone else. In high school it was soon understood that the class beauty, Justine Loring, never granted any boy more than a peck on the cheek, although she never lacked for constant male attention.

At seventeen Justine had been discovered by a scout for Wilhelmina and when she moved to New York she brought with her years of her mother's warnings firmly embedded in her consciousness. Yet, in her natural curiosity, she'd dared to have affairs, the first of which had only confirmed her mother's words. Several times in her life Justine had come close to falling in love, but every relationship had withered before it became serious. For one reason or another the songs of summer never carried over into autumn. There were always plenty of men in her life, but they took a distant second place to her agency.

When Justine entered her thirties, she'd briefly considered psychotherapy, but the whole process seemed unthinkably time-consuming, particularly when she considered the low rate of success it seemed to have among her friends. She'd even flirted with the frivolous notion of marrying and divorcing the next suitable man who asked her, just to get the necessary ritual over with. A divorcee wouldn't have to endure the unspoken curiosity about why she'd never married that she sensed rightly in everyone she met. However, her common sense and pride held her back; she didn't need the explanation of divorce to make her seem like a whole person to herself. Let people speculate about her—she didn't give a damn. Certainly her mother's experience had given her a one-sided view of the male gender, but it seemed to Justine, as she observed the messy love entanglements of her models, that men were *not* to be counted on, that her mother hadn't been wrong, that the expression "a good man" was an oxymoron.

Several months earlier, when her mother found out that she had only a short time to live, she'd called Justine home and told her that Jacques Necker was her father.

"Why are you telling me *now?* I'm thirty-four, for God's sake," Justine had asked, incredulous and suddenly angry. "I don't need a stranger for a father. I grew up without one, remember? And why on earth did you wait so long, Mother—over twenty years!—if you planned to tell me someday?"

"I never intended to tell you, darling. You didn't need to know and he doesn't *deserve* to know. I had no idea what had happened to him until he became so successful that there was no way to avoid reading about him. When he married, I waited for him to have children. As the years went by, I realized that he was childless. Now that I'm staring at the end of my time, things look different to me. I realize how desperately much I've missed because of that man. He took my life away from me, Justine, and I find that I don't believe there's going to be anything after this is over. So I decided to take my revenge. It's the only thing that gives me any comfort."

"What revenge, Mother, for heaven's sake?"

"The scrapbooks," her mother had replied, with a strange smile of grim contentment that Justine didn't recognize.

"The scrapbooks? The ones . . . the scrapbooks you've made of me?"

"Yes. All of them, starting with the picture they took in the delivery room the minute you were born. All the pictures, Justine, pictures of me giving you your bath when you were tiny, pictures of your first birthday party, pictures in kindergarten, in high school, in ballet class, in the school plays, tear sheets of all your most successful modeling jobs, pictures of your growth from a beautiful baby to a beautiful woman—he has all the scrapbooks now. I won't need them anymore."

"*Why!!*"

"So he'll realize exactly what he's missed in his life—there was no other way for him to know. So he'll suffer, oh, not as much as he made me suffer, but almost enough to satisfy me. Isn't that obvious?"

"But what—what will he *do?*" she asked, stunned by her mother's tone of utterly ruthless victory, a note she'd never heard before from her mother's lips.

"Darling Justine, what can he do? He can't hurt you or help you. You've made yourself independent of a man, just as I did. But I know how he'll *feel* and that's enough to let me die in peace." And her mother had fallen silent, exhausted but still smiling an uncannily happy smile of frozen triumph. From that time on Helena Loring turned inward, speaking less and less, but a smile of unmistakable fulfillment reappeared faintly on her lips many times as Justine watched over her until she died several days later.

The letters from Necker had started coming only a week after her mother died. After much thought, Justine decided to simply send them back unopened. To her this gesture was the only tribute she could make toward her mother's memory, the only way she could compensate her mother for a life whose best years had been devoted to her, a life that had been completely blighted by Jacques Necker.

She had rarely been so glad to get home, Justine realized, as she sat before the fire in her parlor at the end of the cold January day. Of course nothing unusual had happened at the agency, there had been no reason for her to have such a ridiculously paranoid attack that she'd ruined her polish completely. Only sheer force of will had kept her from starting in on her cuticles with her teeth.

She relaxed finally, gathering her house around herself like a giant quilt. Everywhere she looked, in her brownstone between Park and Lexington, she saw the results of ten years of hard work and thrift. She had bought the house three years ago, when over-priced New York real estate became less expensive than it had been during the '80s, and she'd never regretted it for a minute, even when she made out the enormous monthly check for her mortgage. There was, Justine mused, as she sipped her tea, something so wonderfully comforting about owning a house that had stood on its own plot of land for one hundred years, a house that had been lived in by generations until she bought it from the estate of the last member of the family.

On the other hand, one hundred years of living, with a minimum of modernization, had left the house in a condition that even the real estate agent admitted needed "a little loving care." If it had been in perfect condition, even in good condition, she could never have afforded a four-story town house on one of the best streets in the East 60s. Loving care, my ass, Justine thought, even as she admired the handsome carved marble mantel and chimney piece of the indubitably Edwardian fireplace. If her poor beautiful house were a person she'd send it off immediately to the Mayo Clinic and then to three restorative months at the Golden Door.

The roof was in good shape, she'd had to take care of that right away, but otherwise she'd lived in it pretty much as she'd found it, making only cosmetic changes, using wallpaper and fabric and all the amazing collection of quaint tat and charming Victorian antiques she'd collected over the years, to conceal the need for a great deal of basic renovation.

When she went to auctions and off-the-beaten-track little antiques shops Justine was attracted by unfashionably battered things, obviously broken and mended objects, almost-worn-out rugs and cushions, mirrors with their mercury dim with age, furniture with its gilt gone and its paint problematic, pieces that, as dealers said shrugging, had "suffered."

Perhaps it was in reaction to the newly minted freshness and first-class quality of the girls she saw every day, perhaps it was in reaction to the rigidly immaculate, modern interiors, without a single nostalgic touch, that her mother had favored, but show Justine a chair or lamp that needed a home to shelter it and she was a pushover.

However, there was a limit. Even Justine had been pushed to

the wall by a heating system on its last legs, plumbing that went on strike every other week, and a kitchen and bathrooms so old-fashioned that her housekeepers left after a few months even though they weren't asked to do anything except clean and leave her some dinner in the fridge. There was only so much that could be camouflaged by even the cleverest, three-dimensional collage of threadbare Victoriana, thought Justine ruefully as she waited to interview the contractor who came with such high recommendations.

Why did she *know* that he was going to rip her off? Why did *everybody* know that about contractors? Such a nationally bad reputation must surely be deserved. If there was one time in her life that Justine regretted her single state, it was now. It was a male's divinely appointed duty and obligation to deal with contractors, not a female's, at least not until other women started becoming contractors. She needed a husband for this, she thought, rebelliously, and for nothing else whatsoever.

She answered the doorbell. Well, she had to admit that he was punctual, but wasn't that exactly what he could be counted on to be, wasn't that precisely the best way to make a good impression, get the job, start the work, make gaping holes in the walls and floors of every room and then disappear, never answering her telephone calls and leaving her with a disaster that no other contractor would take on? Oh, she knew all about those tricks but she had a few of her own up her sleeve, Justine reminded herself as she opened the door.

"Miss Loring? I'm Aiden Henderson," he said with an unexpectedly pleasant smile. Very clever, Justine thought as they shook hands, he'd managed to present himself in a way that would make an unwary person think that he was probably a decent sort.

Justine had a highly developed ability to absorb people with one glance, to judge them in a flash, to capture the instant meaning of a person's stance, to intuit personality as it was conveyed through the general set of the features. In the second wave, after a first impression, she'd trained herself to make an inventory of separate details.

Aiden Henderson looked honest, he looked reassuring, he looked capable. Well of course he would, she thought with increased suspicion. What better disguise for a contractor? The honesty came from a fortuitous combination of a direct glance, friendly blue eyes, firmly set lips, an attractively broken nose, a well-shaped head of plain brown hair and plenty of it. He was nice to look at, in an outdoorsy way, but not suspiciously handsome; a noticeably big man—which, unfairly, inspired confidence, statistically the taller candidate almost always won any election—he was muscular, built on strong and generous lines, wearing horn-rim glasses— that's where the capable and reassuring part came from. The glasses were a master touch, she told herself coldly. She'd bet he didn't need them.

Worse, he was cannily dressed, in clothes that indicated that although he might be a blue-collar worker—or was a contractor actually blue-collar?—he had some background. A properly weather-beaten duffel coat, a decent tweed jacket, cords, an open-necked, button-down shirt in Oxford blue, all comfortably well worn—oh, no lumberjack was this Aiden Henderson. He had probably worked on the look for years.

"I admire your house," he said, as she hung up his coat.

"How can you possibly say something like that when you haven't even looked at it yet?" Justine asked, provoked.

"I don't need to inspect its guts to admire it," he laughed. "The exterior is absolutely intact. How many private houses are there left in this neighborhood like that?"

"Probably thousands," she snapped over her shoulder as she led him to the parlor. "Tens of thousands."

"Not really. As a rule people tear down that exterior staircase to the parlor floor and put the entrance on the street floor."

"Oh, they do, do they? Well, good for them. Would you like some tea?" she asked as uninvitingly as possible.

"That would be wonderful, thanks," Henderson said, following her into the kitchen. *"Good Lord!"*

"Yes," Justine said with a private smile, "how many people still have the original stove that came with the house?"

"To say nothing of the original teapot."

"Still admire it?" she asked.

"Yep. I think it's something of a coup. Like time travel. Very

Ray Bradbury, but in reverse. May I?" He sat down at the kitchen table.

Justine waited for the water to boil, watching the contractor out of the corner of her eye. Too obviously American for Armani, she thought, casting him automatically; too blunt for Ralph Lauren, decidedly too butch for Calvin, yet not quite the hunter-gatherer needed for Timberland. Guess Man? Not oddball enough. If she had to place him—Marlboro? Maybe. Dockers? Possibly. Or Hugo Boss? For heaven's sake, this man wasn't here for a modeling job, she had to remind herself as she poured water into the pot, he was a tricky, untrustworthy, highly dubious contractor.

"How long have you owned this house?" Aiden Henderson asked her curiously, calmly putting two teaspoonsful of sugar into his tea.

"Four years," Justine answered, sitting down at the table.

"What's the extent of the work you're planning to do?"

"Absolutely as little as possible. In fact, left to myself, I wouldn't touch it, but I've been told that a few things seem to require attention."

"Does your husband like living with so much Victoriana?"

"Fortunately I don't have to answer to a husband's taste in decor. Or anything else. Tell me, Mr. Henderson, does your wife pick out your clothes?" she heard herself asking in surprise.

"No. She's gone on to a better world."

"Oh, I'm sorry . . . I didn't know. . . ."

"She's not dead," he added hastily. "She's married to a guy who gets all his stuff custom made. At Sulka. And Dunhill too, lest we forget."

"Oh."

"That's life," he said cheerfully. "At least we didn't have any kids to mess up. You have kids?"

"Certainly not!"

"It's not insulting to be asked, is it?"

"Theoretically no, I suppose, but since I just said I didn't have a husband, yes, it is," Justine said, as haughtily as possible.

"I assumed you'd been married. There's no way you wouldn't have been. Unless you're gay, of course."

"As it happens, I'm not gay, but what kind of question is that? Is that the kind of information you could possibly need from people who might decide to hire you to work on their houses?"

"Miss Loring, you have to tell a contractor everything. How else do you expect him to be able to understand your special needs? And minister to them?"

"My special needs are for heat and hot water," Justine said, laughing in spite of herself.

"I can guarantee you that much," he told her. "That's basic. But you'll probably find that your needs go further."

"Ah ha! This is where you talk me into making all sorts of unnecessary changes I can perfectly well live without."

"No way. We can leave it at heat and hot water," Aiden Henderson replied seriously. "I get paid ten percent over labor costs to get fair bids on the job, pick out good workmen and supervise them. I've got so much work that the only reason I'm here is as a favor for those friends of yours who insisted that you needed a contractor. 'Desperate' was the word they used, to be precise. 'She's quite desperate, Aiden, you absolutely have to make time for her.' "

"Where did you go to college?" Justine asked impulsively. Anything to make her seem less in need of his services.

"University of Colorado. I'm from Denver."

"Football team?" she rapped out, accusingly. A cowboy, that explained the whole all-American look.

"Nope. Track and boxing. Ski team too, of course."

"Of course. How silly of me not to have known that you couldn't possibly *not* be on the ski team." She frowned beautifully at him.

"That's a complicated sentence. What's it supposed to mean exactly?"

"Probably envy of people with nothing better to do than go up and down mountains and get credit for it. I started working right out of high school," Justine said with a hint of a pout.

"Doing what?"

"Modeling."

"Yeah, I thought so. In fact, I had a picture of you on my bulletin board in the dorm."

"Well then, if you knew, how come you asked?"

"It's been, let's see, well, I'm thirty-six, so that makes it about sixteen years ago. You were just a gorgeous kid. You're so much more beautiful now that it was remotely possible you weren't the same person."

"Only hot water and heat."

"Still think I'm trying to hustle you? Listen," Aiden said earnestly, "let me find you another contractor and let's start all over."

"Start what?"

"I think you know what."

"Oh, really!" Justine said, trying to sound mocking.

"Yes, really." He took off his glasses and looked at her steadily. "Really and truly."

"No," Justine said flatly. She was only being sensible, she reflected, only acting on her judgment, which couldn't possibly be affected by the small scars above one eyebrow and another slightly larger, on his chin, which endowed him with a veritable Harrison Fordesque degree of trustworthiness. Sports injuries? That boxing team? Car crash? She was dying to know, Justine realized in horror.

"No? No what?" Aiden asked, slightly confused as to the precise nature of her rejection.

"I don't want another contractor. Consider yourself hired."

"Fine. Now, can I take you out to dinner?"

"That's another matter entirely."

"What's the answer?"

"I'd love it." Her first impressions were famously infallible, Justine reminded herself, with what were left of her wits, and it was wrong, even un-American, to be prejudiced against a person because he was a member of a dubious profession. It was like not exercising your right to vote because you don't trust politicians. There had to be some good apples in the barrel, didn't there?

"Tomorrow?"

"What's wrong with tonight? I'm starving. My microwave doesn't work," Justine lied piteously.

"You can't possibly operate a microwave in this kitchen. If you did the fuses would blow."

"Well, that makes me a hardship case, doesn't it?"

"Only on the Upper East Side. Northern Italian? Thai? Cajun? Tex-Mex?"

"Do you still . . . eat meat?" Justine wondered. For some reason she wanted to keep him here in the kitchen, on her home territory.

"Yep. And I still drink martinis."

"I think I need a steak. I feel sort of . . . weak." She was flirting, Justine told herself sternly, flirting helplessly, as if a team of horses had run away with her. She'd been flirting since this man walked into the house, although he certainly couldn't have any idea of it. And she didn't even feel ashamed of herself.

"So do I. The best kind of weak."

Justine stared at his hands, fighting a lost battle to make her doubts still seem legitimate. But Aiden's hands looked warm and safe. Gentle. So big and so gentle. She loved his calluses. She wanted to hold his hands. Justine picked up Aiden's glasses from the table and peered through them. Shit, she couldn't see a thing, they weren't fake. She put them down and realized how vulnerable he looked. Vulnerable, gentle, bringer of heat and hot water . . . who could blame her for deciding to hire him?

"I could make you a steak right here," she offered, unfolding the strategy that had come to her seconds before. "The broiler works and I happen to have a steak in the fridge. And there's a bottle of gin in the pantry. And vermouth . . . and even . . ." she searched for inspiration.

"Even?"

". . . cocktail onions! I could make a Gibson. It's one of my talents."

"I'd walk a mile for a Gibson."

"Well, that settles it, doesn't it?" Justine said with a look of serene hospitality. Aiden Henderson was about to share the only thing she knew how to cook. They could hammer out the business details later.

6

I got the sleaze-ball message the instant we walked into the lobby and smelled a combination of expensive cigars mixed with rich man's cologne. The Plaza-Athénée is one of the top five-star luxury hotels in the world but it attracts far more than its fair share of creeps, many of whom I saw planted in their Valhalla, the deep armchairs that were scattered all over the large lobby in cozy groups.

I'm sure that those very same Fat Cats had been there the last time I'd been in Paris over a year ago when I'd stayed at the much less expensive La Trémoille around the corner. They were international-style iffy guys, definitely not family men, at their ease, sipping drinks, sending faxes, getting phone calls and waiting for exactly the sight our little band presented. Three Magnificent Girls Three. Since the Plaza is right on the Avenue Montaigne, across from Dior and surrounded by other dress houses, it's the red hot center of town for checking out new arrivals.

"Come on, kids, follow me," I said firmly to my charges, herding them across the lobby to the reception desk and slapping down all our passports. I'd been to Paris twice before, to check out the busy French agency scene. I'd never been a chaperone before, and my new role brought out my leadership qualities. Without turning around I could tell that we had become the attraction du jour. Who could be blamed for staring at three gloriously towering girls all wearing skin-tight cross-country skiing pants, down-filled parkas and those Army boots that models were into this winter?

Finally we got to the third floor where we were billeted, accompanied by a small mob of tip-hungry hotel flunkies who didn't allow us to carry anything but our requisite backpacks. Before I found my own room I made sure that each girl had a suite, as promised. Except for Jordan, who kept her cool, they were like puppies, rushing around and opening doors, switching closet lights off and on, exclaiming over the flower arrangements and baskets of fruit and iced champagne waiting in tall coolers, even bouncing on the brocade- and satin-covered beds, while Mike Aaron, curse his voyeuristic photographer's heart, recorded it all for *Zing*.

He was good, I had to admit it. He'd been working steadily and inconspicuously since we all met at JFK and by now my models took his presence for granted. They'd forgotten that they were starring in an epic of photojournalism and behaved as freely as if he wasn't always training a camera on them, with two more loaded cameras around his neck. I was nervous enough without the added strain of finding a lens looking up my nostrils at unexpected moments.

"I'm *not* your story." I'd gone over to set him straight as we were waiting to board in the departure lounge. "The girls are. So bug out, Aaron. I can't stand having my picture taken, especially since you're forever creeping up on me."

He'd looked down at me and favored me with what he probably imagined was a sincerely wounded look. Manipulative must be his middle name, I thought, taking inventory of the changes in him since he'd graduated from Lincoln. Basically he'd turned from a tall, agile, diabolically attractive boy into an even more attractive man. Dark hair, dark eyes, great everything . . . the same face of my countless dreams, but resistible now that I'd been immunized by the passage of years. Yeah, I know he had something new; his major reputation, the vitality of real achievement, the inward substance won when a person has grown into his power. So what? I wasn't going to let him dominate our trip, the way every successful photographer figures it's his God-given right to do.

"Maxi told me," Mike protested, "that Justine was an integral part of the story. Since I haven't got Justine, you're it, pal, I've got no choice. Everyone they have contact with is part of the story. So how come you're camera shy? No, don't bother to tell me, it's your nose, isn't it?"

He grabbed me by my arms and turned me around to the light and before I could force myself out of his grip, he'd subjected me to a rapid appraisal from every angle except the back of my head. I felt as if I were something for sale that was unquestionably a fake, the only question being, a fake *what?* Every blink of his eye announced, "Get the hell out of my way, I'm in charge here and you're not."

"Nothing wrong with the schnoz," he finally said as if to reassure me. *Me!* I was so furious on behalf of the insult to my fine nose that I sputtered and couldn't get the words out before he continued. "Half the duchesses in Italy have one just like it," he said, as if he were giving me news I was too dumb to know. "American women don't understand the appeal of a real nose. Someday I'll explain it to you. If I have time, that is. You could probably stand to lose a couple of pounds, pal, but personally I'm not offended by a woman who's a bit zaftig. And you're a terrific contrast to the girls. You'll make the readers understand the huge difference between models and ordinary people, they'll be able to relate to you."

Then Mike Aaron, that insulting pond scum, had the incredible balls to actually smile at me, right into my eyes, a patented smile if ever I'd seen one, as if I, poor mere mortal, was going to be so impressed by eye contact—be still my heart!—and his cocky show of perfect teeth that I wouldn't mind his using me as an example of Everywoman. If he'd given me that smile years ago, when I was a freshman in high school, I bet I'd have fainted. I *know* I'd have fainted. Forward, into his arms . . . I was never one to lose an opportunity.

But today I was another person, tested and tempered by time, all passion spent, as someone once said.

"Justine modeled professionally for years, Big Game," I managed to say coldly, but without sounding irritated. "I'm a civilian and that changes the rules."

" 'Big Game'? Nobody's called me that since I was a kid."

" 'Big Game Aaron,' the boy wonder of Abraham Lincoln," I sneered, with a pretty terrific smile of my own. "Always came ready to play, yeah, that's what they said. I was there when you lost to Erasmus. *Personally* lost, blew it all by yourself. That last crucial free throw, remember? What an air ball! It must have been ten feet short. Bad luck, Big Game, or was it, could it have been . . . *nerves?*"

"You are one mean bitch!"

"Got it in one, kid. Congratulations. So keep out of my face!"

And he had, more or less. He certainly hadn't tried that smile on me again and if I happened to be in the shot he was getting, at least I knew it wouldn't be a close-up. I don't think Mike wanted to hear more about his sports career. Even the best players have off-days and he couldn't know that I'd only watched him play his senior year, which had been, the Erasmus Hall game aside, fucking brilliant.

I left Mike and Maude with the girls, who were clustered together, leaning, no doubt photogenically, over a balcony and getting their first breath of Paris air. The clerk from Reception, who'd never left my side, led me to the door of my room and flung it open, motioning for me to walk in.

"What on earth is this?" I asked him.

"This is what Madame d'Angelle herself arranged for you."

I looked around the gigantic corner suite. There was a vast, almost circular sitting room with three sets of floor-to-ceiling French doors that opened onto balconies of their own. There were two magnificent bedrooms, one even bigger than the other, with large dressing rooms and gorgeous bathrooms, plus a guest john in the entrance hall. The whole thing was ridiculous.

"Madame d'Angelle didn't know if you'd prefer to sleep on the Avenue Montaigne side or the courtyard, so she took both bedrooms," he explained. "The courtyard side is perhaps more quiet."

"But these flowers?" I flopped my hands at the lushly filled vases that stood everywhere I looked.

"I don't know, Madame. I haven't read the cards." He gave me that nervous shoulder twitch known as the Gallic shrug, as if the French had invented it.

"May I summon the maid to unpack for Madame?"

"Yeah, sure, why not? And please get me a Valium on ice. The big blue one, not the little yellow one."

"Madame?"

"Never mind." I'd finally realized that all this had been intended for Justine. When had she sent the fax saying that she wasn't coming? When had Necker gotten the news? Not before this morning, obviously, or I wouldn't be surrounded by so many flowers that there was every chance I'd get hay fever in the middle of winter. Frankie, I said to myself, enjoy it while you have the chance, tomorrow you'll be moved to a broom closet.

"Madame d'Angelle left me this note to deliver to you by hand," he said as he was leaving.

Dear Justine,

Bienvenu à Paris! I hope you and the girls all had a most pleasant flight and that the accommodations are comfortable. On the part of Monsieur Necker I should like to invite you and your three "debutantes" to an informal dinner at his home this evening at eight. There will be a car arriving for you at seven forty-five. If there's anything you need, please let the hotel manager know. He has instructions to provide anything you request.

I'm looking forward to tonight with great pleasure,

Most sincerely,
Gabrielle d'Angelle

I read this note over twice. This was a clear-cut command performance with no chance to refuse. How could Necker be so cold-blooded that he'd use Gabrielle to invite Justine to dinner in a group instead of arranging his meeting with her himself?

Then I started thinking about alternatives. The girls would be thrilled to be invited to a dinner party their first night in Paris and if we didn't celebrate somehow they'd be disappointed. And did I really expect Necker to make an ordinary phone call to Justine? Wasn't a party, with other people around to cushion things, the best way to handle this tense meeting?

On reflection, I thought the plan was as good a one as could be worked out. Talk about your awkward situations! There was only one problem, Justine wasn't in Paris. No, make that two problems. She wasn't and *I was*.

I left the maid to unpack the suitcase full of new clothes I hadn't seen yet and, since I still didn't know their room numbers, I went down the wide corridor to find the girls and tell them about dinner. Standing by the elevator I spied Mike bending with what looked like tender interest over the hand of an unknown blond who had her back to me. As fast a worker as ever, I thought scornfully, and walked past him without stopping.

"Frankie, wait up! Meet poor, unfortunate Peaches Wilcox," he commanded.

I turned to say hello to the world's merriest widow, who looked as if she were tap dancing happily somewhere in the neighborhood of thirty-six. Whoever had done her face had done real good.

"Hi, neighbor," she drawled. "Isn't it wonderful! We're all on the same floor! I've been reading all about this Cinderella story in *Women's Wear*—I'm so thrilled to be in on the action. Can I give a party for everybody just as soon as possible? Introduce the girls to some cute guys?"

"We'd love it," Mike Aaron answered for me. "Peaches bruised a couple of fingers skiing," he explained, still holding her injured hand solicitously, "so she left Saint-Moritz . . . can't grasp her ski pole tightly enough."

"Do you know anything more frustrating than having to sit around a hotel when everyone else is charging down the mountain?" She flashed a smile even I, critic though I am, had to admit looked as if not only the friendliness but the teeth themselves were genuine.

"Golly, no," I agreed through my very own original teeth. "I just hate it when that happens."

"Mike photographed me for a story on the most glamorous women in Texas," she said demurely. "That's how we got to know each other. Isn't it a coincidence that we'd bump into each other here?"

"I just love it when that happens."

"So do I," Mike said, giving me a dirty look. "You trying to find the girls?" he asked.

"That seems to be my lot in life."

"They're all in Maude's room, telling her, on the record, how they lost their virginity. I had to leave. It was much too graphic for me and I just hate it when that happens."

"Thanks, Aaron," I said and charged off down the hall.

"Room 311" he yelled after me.

I knocked on the door of 311, breathing fire. Not one of my girls had ever been interviewed before. They had no idea of how even a few words could be twisted and quoted out of context by any magazine writer, particularly Maude Callender. She opened the door, frowning when she saw me. Her ascot was off and her buttoned boots were lying on the floor. So were all my charges, sprawled out, eating enormous club sandwiches from a pile on a platter and drinking Cokes.

"Have you girls been read your Miranda Rights?" I asked angrily.

"Astonishing," Maude said acidly, "all three of them turn out to be virgins. Who would have bet money on that?"

"Isn't that why *Zing* is calling this story 'Innocents Abroad'?" Jordan asked, darting me a private look that might as well have been a wink.

"We thought that was the reason we were picked," April added, lifting that head of hers that lacked only a tiara to finish it properly. "At least I know I did."

"I've been kissed," Tinker offered, plaintively, her million-dollar pout working overtime. " 'Soul kissed,' I think he called it. Does that count? It was only the one time and I didn't like it much."

"Don't let anyone do that to you again," Jordan snapped. "That's the first step on the road to perdition. It's a well-known fact."

"But it was New Year's Eve," Tinker explained.

"That's not an excuse," Jordan told her. "They'll always find something—if it's not New Year's Eve it's Saint Patrick's Day or Presidents' Day—just say no."

"Well, this hasn't been an entirely wasted session," Maude announced. "At least I know that you girls are accomplished liars, a fact that doesn't do me any good because it's not as if I had proof."

"The four of us are invited to dinner tonight at Monsieur

Necker's," I told the girls. "So go decide what you're going to wear. Come on, all of you, off the floor. And that better be the last club sandwich any of you eat before the collection."

Maude looked at me in a way I didn't like one little bit. I could hear her thinking that I was not in a position of strength to enforce dietary discipline. Somehow she knew about my six extra pounds. She had a point. Nightmares of the girls ordering room service at any hour danced in my head.

"After this dinner party," I heard myself saying, "I'm going on a diet. I'm counting on the three of you to make me stick to it and inspire me by your example."

"You're starting a diet in Paris?" Maude asked incredulously, scribbling away in her notebook. "Is that on the record?"

"Maude, this story isn't about me, it's about them."

"It's about what Maxi Amberville wants, as usual," Maude said. "And she didn't put anybody off limits. Are Mike and I invited to this party?"

"Nope, this party is about what Necker wants and he doesn't know anything about *Zing*. Sorry about that."

"Frankly, I'm not. I need a good night's sleep. I'll catch up with Necker later," Maude said, wriggling out of her dandy's jacket, unbuttoning her vest and stretching widely as she took that off too.

She looked relaxed for the first time since she'd joined us on the trip over. In just her trousers and ruffled shirt I was interested to see that she looked no more oddly dressed than any of us and a thousand times more attractive than I would have imagined. Her costume, her carapace of strict tailoring from another century, certainly worked to give her a safe place from which to quiz the world. Amazing what the choice of a uniform can do. Now, with her short ash-blond hair messed up and her observant expression turned off, Maude was, and no other word will do, truly *pretty*. I looked at her closely and realized that she couldn't be more than thirty-nine or forty. She had a surprisingly voluptuous and feminine body once she lost her jacket and vest, terrific breasts under that shirt, a slim waist and decidedly feminine hips. The half-boy, half-girl look disappeared with her clothes.

"I'm whipped," she said. "Jet lag is bad enough without trying to talk to a bunch of kids. Want a sandwich?"

"No, thanks," I said regretfully. She didn't know it but my diet had just started. "Zaftig" has never been one of my favorite words and when that eagle-eyed Aaron used it about me, I hate to admit it but I winced.

"Diet Coke?" she asked, waving me to a chair.

"Love one," I answered, sitting down. It occurred to me that it would be smarter to be friendly with her than not.

"Maude, I know you have to ask a lot of questions for your story, but why don't you wait a little, until you get to know the girls naturally? They're basically good kids but they're gun-shy. People are always prying and poking at models, as if they weren't really human. Why, for instance, are you so interested in whether they're virgins or not? After all, this is the nineties, what difference does it make?"

"Because of all the talk today about chastity and abstinence —two years ago I wouldn't have dreamed of asking that question, but now it's become interesting again, even important, because they're role models to other girls. If one or two of them are virgins, that's meaningful, even newsworthy. Three would be a banner headline."

"I see your point, but I still think that it's too early to expect them to be honest with you. Remember, they're used to being treated like freaks by everyone but each other and their agencies, and that makes them gun-shy."

"But they *are* freaks," she protested. "Not one woman in ten million looks like them. They're aberrations of nature."

"Yeah, but Maude, they *can't help it*. You should get used to seeing them as superlative human animals, not freaks. And the statistically astonishing fact that not one of them smokes, thank God, is a better angle than their sexual habits, if you ask me." I think I set her off on the right path. Somewhat. Anyway, we made friends. A little. No one in the agency business believes that a journalist can be a real friend. We've all been burned too often.

By the time I got back to my private perfumed palace both beds had been turned down, the lamps were lit, and a fire glowed nicely in the sitting room. I walked into one of the dressing rooms and almost fell down in surprise at the sight of what the maid had unpacked.

Justine must really have felt guilty! There was a whole rack of stuff; dresses, pants, jackets, and two long coats, one in camel hair with a red shearling lining, the other a floor-length, black cashmere cape with a zip-in black satin quilted lining for evening. There were a half dozen pairs of shoes on the floor, yards of cashmere mufflers, handbags, gloves and piles of lingerie and pantyhose in the drawers. I ruffled through the clothes, discovering a paradise of more cashmere, silk and leather, all in the kind of good-taste colors from black to ivory with a few stops at red, pewter, moss green and subtle browns that makes it impossible to go wrong no matter what you throw on. Lots of the fabrics had that kind of reassuring stretchy feeling that promised a righteously helpful mixture of Lycra or spandex. I hope Justine got it all wholesale. On the other hand, as we taxpayers all know, there's no free lunch, and there sure as hell is no free Donna Karan. What was I going to have to do for this?

I soon found out.

"What are you doing here?" Gabrielle d'Angelle gasped. She was standing right behind the manservant who had opened the door to Necker's house on the Avenue de Suffren, bordering the garden of the Champ de Mars.

"Didn't Justine explain in her fax?" I was as surprised as she was.

"Fax! We received no fax!"

"That's *impossible*," I said flatly. "She sent you one the minute she was sure." Instinctively I vamped for time. The dog had eaten my homework and my memory had stopped working from shock.

" 'Sure' about *what?* Monsieur Necker expects Miss Loring!"

"Well, that's tough, but when the doctors all say you can't fly, you can't fly. You understand that as well as I do, Gabrielle, and thanks for all the magnificent flowers, they're incredible, even if you sent them to the wrong person. I'll tell Justine how beautiful they are when I phone her." Right! A monster ear infection. It all came back to me in a glorious flash. All, that is, except why she hadn't sent the fax.

"We'd better both pray that the antibiotics work," I added, "and that she recovers quickly enough to come over here before the collection. Those ear infections are dangerous, don't you agree, Gabrielle?" When I've got trouble I always try to make it the other guy's problem too.

"Come on in girls, for heaven's sake," I babbled on. "Gabrielle doesn't want you to stand there in the cold, do you, Gabrielle?" I shooed them inside before she could answer. "The important thing is that the girls are here, safe and sound, isn't that right, Gabrielle?"

"Of course," she answered, transforming herself back into the smoothie I remembered. "Welcome to Paris, all three of you. I'm enchanted that you're here."

As she shook their hands I observed her body language and decided that she didn't have an idea of what Necker was up to. She still looked slightly miffed at the change of chaperone to one of a lower status, but not one tenth of one percent as upset as her boss was going to be. What I was burning to know was how Justine could have screwed me like this. She'd sworn that she was going to send the fax once our plane took off. What the bloody hell could possibly have stopped her?

"Monsieur Necker is waiting to greet you upstairs," Gabrielle informed us. "We'll take the elevator." Only then did I look around and realize that we were standing in a room with a black and white marble floor and the dimensions of a ballroom that could only be the entrance hall to the largest and grandest private house I'd ever seen. Since there was a staircase curving up against one wall, the sort of majestic staircase you've seen in the White House, with a presidential couple descending to greet distinguished guests, I didn't see why we couldn't walk up. Especially since it would take longer. Even one second longer was better. *Never* would be an ideal time for me to meet Necker, but the manservant was already taking our coats.

However, taking the elevator began to make sense as it continued to rise. Evidently "upstairs" was the top of the house, which had looked, from the street, as if it were at least five stories tall. As the elevator stopped, much too soon, I managed to squeeze between the girls like one of those characters in a Western who hunkers down inside a group of horses. There was a confusion as all five of us tried to be polite and let everyone else go first, which was exactly the effect I'd been hoping for.

We finally sorted ourselves out and, since there was no way I could postpone it any longer, I pulled myself together and prepared to meet Justine's father. I looked up, rather bravely, if I say so myself, but I didn't see anyone in the vast room that stretched dimly forward toward a wall of solid glass two stories high from floor to ceiling. Beyond the wall, perhaps a thousand feet away, was a section of the base of the Eiffel Tower, brilliantly illuminated by floodlights.

The girls and I were so stunned by this unexpected iron giant out of Jules Verne, so amazed by seeing it floating so close to us, that at first we stood there and gaped. It was like part of the most enormous Tinkertoy you could imagine. The sight was irresistibly wacky in its scale and drama, and the girls all rushed, magnetized, toward the wall of glass and craned their necks up, exclaiming to each other. I stayed close to Gabrielle. Time enough to look at the view after I'd delivered the medical bulletin.

"Jules," Gabrielle said to a butler, "where is Monsieur?"

"I don't know, Madame."

"Go tell him his guests have arrived." She was clearly surprised not to find him waiting. I had a flash. Necker was as nervous about this as I was. He was hiding out the way I had in the elevator. No, better! Necker was as nervous about this as *Justine* would be if she were here. So I had nothing to be nervous about! I was just the messenger.

Well. That bit of logical thinking made me feel a little better. Then, Necker entered the room and I felt, suddenly, a whole lot worse. His expression was utterly composed but my curiosity made me glance quickly at his eyes. I saw a look so full of joyous expectation mixed with timidity and humility and hope, that it broke my heart. He stopped dead inside the doorway, instantly looking away from me toward the girls at the window and then back to me. He walked rapidly toward Gabrielle.

"Where is Miss Loring?" he asked her.

"Miss Severino will tell you," she replied.

"Miss Severino?" He shook my hand automatically. "Is Miss Loring delayed?"

"Yes, that's correct, Monsieur Necker, she's delayed. That is, she's delayed in New York, not in Paris. I don't understand why she hasn't let you know, there's obviously been a communications failure, but Justine's sick, really ill, with a middle ear infection. The doctors wouldn't let her travel under any conditions, she's on antibiotics up to the gills. She made me promise to tell you how sorry she was that this happened at the last minute. She intends to get over as soon as she can travel. In the meanwhile, she sent me instead—"

"She is *not* in Paris?" There was no question in his flat words although he'd framed the statement as if it were, as if he hadn't quite understood me.

"No."

He didn't buy it. I knew that right away, although I'd put my best into the explanation and I've always been a gifted liar. Anyone but Necker would have believed me. That complicated look in his eyes had died although his expression would never have told anyone that he'd just had a body blow.

"She sent you 'instead'?" He repeated my words in a monotone as if they were only about a minor question of delegation of authority.

"Why yes, of course, I'm Justine's second in command, so obviously it had to be me. It was such a rush, getting packed at the last minute, I hadn't expected to leave New York, you can imagine. . . ." I ran out of gas because I couldn't find anything at all to say that would give him hope. I looked helplessly at the utter desolation in his eyes.

"So. I see. That's a shame, isn't it? I sincerely hope she gets better soon. And, in any case, you're here, looking charming, and you're most welcome in my home. I trust they've made you comfortable at the hotel." He took a deep breath and gave me a brief formal smile that hurt to look at. "Now, let me get you something to drink, Miss Severino, and then you can introduce me to the young ladies."

Wow, I thought, as I followed him, I knew where Justine got

that unearthly calm, that self-control. It was pure Necker. Man, if this guy had been my long-lost Dad, I'd jump into his arms, no questions asked, all the past forgiven and forgotten, and not just because he was rich but because he had so much class. To say nothing of being one of the best-looking men I'd ever seen at any age.

By this time the girls had noticed Necker and were coming down the length of the room. I suddenly remembered that this was, for each of them, a highly competitive moment. None of us knew what part Necker would play in choosing the Lombardi girl, but we had to assume that it would be a major one.

First came April, moving with an easy, unstudied grace. She'd picked her dress cleverly; a bare, but somehow demure, black silk slip dress with a graduated string of pearls that showcased her exquisitely well-bred look more emphatically than anything elaborate. Her sudden smile flashed, but not too broadly, her amazing hair was pulled straight back from her face and flowed simply down her back like Alice in Wonderland's. I thought that if there were a young Grace Kelly today, this was how she would have been dressed for an important meeting with her future mother-in-law. Oh, proper, perfect April!

After Necker shook hands with April he greeted Tinker. I had wondered which of her incarnations she'd put on tonight; were we going to be treated to a high-fashion diva or the ravishing little orphan dreaming of a rainbow? I'd been too busy being nervous to check her out before now. Ah, the princess bride approached, clad —you couldn't say "dressed" with Tinker—clad in pure white satin, a short dress as simple as April's but with long sleeves and a demure scoop neck. She'd fiddled with her hair until she'd produced a sort of casual updo with curling tendrils framing her face, and pinned a few fresh rosebuds in it here and there, making good use of the flowers in her suite. Tinker had obviously learned a lot from the many makeup artists who'd worked on her. Tonight she was all extraordinary eyes and the palest pink mouth, with no other makeup. She looked about twelve, a grave, thoughtful and dangerous twelve you'd marry off in a hurry if you were her parents. There should be a law, I thought proudly, until I realized that for all our efforts with her she still walked badly. Her body language didn't say triumphantly, "Look at me," but told you she'd much prefer to be ignored. It wasn't so much that she was totally awkward but that she had a strong quality of inner tentativeness that made her seem not quite *here*. As she came nearer I spotted the trembling of her lips, the not-quite-hidden fear in her eyes.

And then came Jordan. The others disappeared in comparison. She was wearing a long slender turtleneck tunic and wide-legged pants, both made of dark scarlet crushed velvet, with flat silver slippers and large rock crystal hoops swinging from her sublimely set ears. The other two girls wore their highest heels, which made them inches taller than Necker. Only Jordan seemed life-sized in relation to him. But it wasn't the sensational outfit that caused her to eclipse the others, it was her attitude. She could have been the hostess and Jacques Necker the guest. She looked so much at home that it seemed impossible that she had just arrived in this room. Although he'd shaken hands with me and the other girls, Necker kissed hers, which Jordan seemed to find only natural. He might be Swiss, I thought, but he has French reactions.

I was only too happy to keep my eyes down and my nose in my drink while Necker put April and Tinker at their ease by asking them questions about their lives. Jordan, having made her point, drifted away and stood in front of a long desk with a worn red velvet top and lavish, gilded carving decorating its dark wood. Small precious objects were precisely arranged on the desktop, giving place of honor to a small painting of a rearing black and white horse in an elaborate frame. I watched her as she left her contemplation of the desk and walked quietly from one piece of furniture to another, apparently deep in thought and oblivious to the conversation of the others. Was Jordan shy, I wondered? Or just unwilling to compete for Necker's attention at this point in the evening.

I knew it couldn't be the furniture that really interested her. As far as I was concerned, the various pieces all looked more or less the same to me. They were all, I assumed, the height of magnificence, yet I found them boring, as if I'd seen them all before. The only thing that kept the room from being overpoweringly grand was the view and I was too nervous to appreciate it.

Eventually dinner was served and Necker placed me at his

right, in the place that had been meant for Justine. He casually motioned Jordan to his left and told everybody else to sit wherever they wanted. Over the muted hum of female conversation I heard Jordan speak.

"The painting on the ebony *bureau plat* upstairs, Monsieur Necker, could it be by Jean-Marc Winckler?"

"It is," he answered, clearly surprised. "The horse belonged to one of the princes of Liechtenstein. How did you guess?"

"I wrote my college thesis on Madame de Pompadour and how a king's mistress was decisive in influencing the world of decorative art."

"Yet decorative arts continued to evolve under another Louis," he said with an abstracted smile that reminded me so much of Justine that I almost gasped.

"How can one Louis not lead to another?" Jordan laughed. "After Louis XV I studied on my own and eventually I found myself almost as attracted by Louis XVI . . . I never would have imagined that any private person could own such magnificent examples of both periods."

"I started collecting when it was still out of fashion," he explained.

"I didn't know that Joseph or Leleu could ever be out of fashion. They're *beyond* fashion," Jordan said with spirit.

I drank some wine in a silent toast to a hopeless cause. I knew what she was up to, all right, but it wouldn't do her any good, not when the poor man had just had such a heartrending disappointment. But bless Jordan for making conversation. It took the heat off me. And it was a learning experience. I'd just discovered that I knew *bupkis* about furniture.

Dinner went on too long and I was grateful when Gabrielle suggested, soon afterward, that we must all be tired and want to leave early. It was just past eleven and I couldn't begin to figure out how many hours it had been since I'd left New York.

There seemed to be a lot of unnecessary giggling in the limo which kept me from falling asleep. Jordan, speaking rapid, and obviously, for me, incomprehensible, French, was making friends with Albert, the dignified middle-aged chauffeur. First Necker, now the chauffeur, I thought in weary wonder as we finally came to a stop. The girls piled out of the car. I opened my eyes. No hotel.

"Where the hell are we?" I demanded.

"Les Bains Douche, as the young ladies requested," Albert replied, coming to open the door for me.

Even I, cloistered as I am, had heard of the most notorious and, as the girls would say, "happening" club in Paris. "Everyone" went there, from drag queens to drug dealers to rock stars. It was quartered in a turn-of-the-century bathhouse but there were doubts about how reformed the atmosphere was. Certainly no one went there to get clean.

"Tell them to get back in here this minute!" I shouted.

"But, Madame, they have already been admitted."

Bitches! I'd kill them with my bare hands. An adrenaline rush got me to the pavement, fighting mad.

"Take off your cap and come with me," I ordered Albert. "I can't go in there alone."

"Madame!" he replied, shocked.

I snatched his cap off his head and threw it in the car. He made a perfectly respectable escort, if a little long in the tooth. I marched him past the three hulking doormen or bouncers or whatever a place like that has to keep out undesirables—or to admit *only* undesirables, depending on your point of view—with the unquestionable authority of an undercover cop, a version of Andy Sipowicz crossed with Serpico.

"Room for two more at your table, ladies?" I asked, glaring at Jordan. The girls were seated right on the mobbed dance floor, obviously the table of honor, and so far they were alone. I could feel the greedy, mesmerized gaze of the entire crowd on them. It was like being in the eye of a tornado.

"Oh, Frankie, we thought you'd passed out cold," Jordan answered, so help me, without turning a hair, "or we would never have left you."

"Thanks for your consideration. I'll keep it in mind when I handcuff you to the radiator."

"Please, Frankie," April laughed, "don't be mean. You were young once, way back when."

"Oh, you're looking for it too, are you? Come on, girls, we're out of here."

"Surely, just one dance," a man's voice said, and I saw a guy grab April by the hand and whirl her away. Another fellow had Tinker on her feet and there were two of them fighting over Jordan. That was all I had time to notice before somebody or other yanked me up and I was dancing myself.

We got back to the hotel safely, at dawn. Do I have to tell you that I made those girls look as if they were still learning how to do the box step?

7

"What's with Justine?" asked Carrie, one of the bookers, when the phones fell silent late in the afternoon of the day after Frankie and her charges had taken off for Paris.

"Maybe she inherited money from a cousin she didn't know she had," Dodie, another booker, replied. "She was humming something familiar this morning and when I asked her what it was, she looked surprised and said she didn't have a clue. Later it came to me, a golden oldie called 'It Might as Well Be Spring.' Weird, huh? Justine's not one of nature's hummers."

"She could be trying to exercise a positive influence on the weather," hazarded Johanna, a third booker. "Did you listen to the radio this morning?"

"Blizzard and major freeze expected," Carrie groaned. "Maybe Justine is one of those people who feels good when there's a big storm brewing. If it gets any colder than it is already, they should shut down the city out of common kindness."

"Maybe tomorrow will be a 'snow day' like we used to have in school," Dodie said wistfully. "Remember finding out that you couldn't go to school so you could watch soaps all day long? God, I miss being a kid on snow days."

"Go on home, everybody," Justine said, suddenly appearing in the booking room. "It's Friday and almost quitting time anyway. Nothing's going to happen that I can't handle."

After her grateful bookers had scurried off, Justine turned off the lights of the office, sat in one of the bookers' chairs and put her feet up on the circular desk. She loved to be alone here, in sole possession of her domain high above the nearest buildings. There was a wide view from the large windows of the booking room which included a slice of street that cut straight across the city clear to Central Park West. Behind the fanciful silhouetted towers of those fine old apartment houses Justine could glimpse, across the Hudson, the last fragment of sunset fading into the dark plum of a winter sky.

Who would want to live anywhere but on the edge of a continent, Justine asked herself. Who would want to live anywhere but here and now in the last years of the twentieth century? Who would want to live earlier in history, before Novocain, before hair spray, before telephones, before air travel and glossy fashion magazines full of nonsense? Who would want to be a woman in the days when a woman couldn't build a business on her own, unless she opened a whorehouse? Why did she so rarely take the time to realize how wonderful her life was?

Justine relaxed more deeply in the chair, slumping until she was almost reclining, bathed in a feeling of free-floating happiness. There was really nothing special to account for the quality of her mood, she reflected, unless a rare steak had powers she'd never known about. Amazing what a good cook Aiden had turned out to be—he'd even made a salad—and what a deft hand he had at Gibsons. It *had* been sort of nice to let a man make the drinks and take over in the kitchen. Definitely the sort of pleasant evening a sensible person should permit herself to enjoy every now and then —a dollop of gin, something basically satisfying to eat, a nice long, rambling chat in front of the fire, a kiss goodnight—or had it been two, one medium slow, one very quick, or the other way around?

She was glad she'd listened to Aiden when he'd looked around her basement and told her that there wasn't a minute to lose in replacing the furnace. He'd called her secretary this morning and reported that his supplier had the right model in stock, so the new furnace should be in by now. Apparently it was a simple process. She'd never planned on such a rush job, but the weather reports were so ominous that Aiden had convinced her of the need for haste.

What, she wondered, would the weather be like now in Paris? Would Frankie be bundled up in one or another of her new coats?

FRANKIE!

Jesus Christ! She'd forgotten to send the fax to Gabrielle!

Justine almost fell out of the chair as the realization hit her. She righted herself, got up in a hurry and started to pace the floor, feeling the sweat break out on her brow. She'd never done anything so completely irresponsible before! Never, ever! My God, what could have come over her? This was utterly, completely and impossibly *unforgivable*. She'd sent her best friend right into the lion's den without anything to protect her.

Frantically Justine tried to figure out what time it must be in Paris at this moment at just after five in the evening in New York. Add six hours, that made it past eleven at night. Didn't she have to add in the travel time too in order to figure it out? Her mind wouldn't work. She'd send that fax immediately, but by now it was too late. Or maybe not, maybe nobody from Necker's knew yet. Oh, shit, as if Necker himself wouldn't know she wasn't there. He'd probably met the plane.

Feeling increasingly incredulous at her own behavior, Justine tried to recapitulate the events of yesterday. She'd been in a terrible, gloomy, evil mood all day, and then, forgetting to send the fax, she'd gone home and calmly had a cup of tea and interviewed a contractor, had an unexpected evening with him and gone to sleep. Today she'd worked all day, with a fax machine no more than twenty feet away, and now, *only now*, at least a day too late, she'd remembered. And it wasn't as if she needed a fax machine to alert Gabrielle d'Angelle, she could have phoned her yesterday, right up to the time that Frankie's plane had landed. The fax was preferable because you could lie more easily on paper than in person.

Somewhere, embedded in all of this, was the reason why she hadn't sent the fax, Justine told herself, thinking hard. She was a clearheaded woman who simply did not *allow* herself to behave in an irrational way. It must have something to do with her mood of yesterday, something related to that paranoid but recurrent fear that Necker might suddenly materialize physically in the doorway, a notion that had haunted her ever since the search for the Lombardi face had been settled. In the space of a phone call she'd found herself trapped and powerless to deny this chance to her girls.

But not powerless, after all, Justine realized. Not so trapped that she could be manipulated! She'd shown him that, by God!

"Hah!" Justine shouted as she finally understood that she'd forgotten to send the fax on purpose. She'd known that Frankie could be counted on to handle the situation and she'd known that Necker would understand that his entire elaborate plan had failed. She'd rejected him again, and without having to send so much as a word on paper. What an amazingly efficient subconscious mind she had, she thought triumphantly. It had known that it wasn't enough to send Frankie in her place, it had also arranged for her to "forget" to send the fax.

"Good show, old girl," Justine said, congratulating herself out loud in the empty office. After a few minutes of victorious musing she found that as her elation faded, the big booking room was beginning to feel cold. She took herself into her own office where the windows didn't leak as much air and sat down behind her desk, where a lamp was still switched on. Her eyes fell on a framed photograph of her mother holding her as a baby, a picture so familiar that she no longer really looked at it. Suddenly Justine felt curious enough to pick it up and study it intently. Her recent actions toward Necker had made her feel closer to her mother than ever.

Justine picked up a magnifying glass and concentrated her attention on her mother's head. Helena Loring had been a true beauty, she decided with professional dispassion. She was just over twenty in that photograph, and allowing for the changes in hair and makeup in the last thirty-three years, she could have had a modeling career if she'd wanted it.

But of course that would have been too chancy, with a child to support. No, her mother had chosen a path that would, before all else, protect her daughter from the ups and downs of fortune. She had given herself entirely to her department store job. As she thought about it, Justine realized that she herself had never truly understood what sacrifices her mother must have made to give her the best possible upbringing.

Justine counted her advantages. She'd gone to the best private school in the city; she'd been encouraged to invite her friends home; she'd had ice skating lessons and ballet lessons; every summer she'd been sent to a fine camp in Upper Michigan, and for as far back as she could remember, she'd had all the appropriate pretty clothes any little girl could want. Tears came into her eyes, as she thought of the woman who had loved her so much, a mother who had never burdened her with a sense of guilt in return for her devotion. How many daughters could say that? Whatever she did to Necker would never be enough to make up for what he'd done to her mother.

At least, Justine thought, putting down the photograph, her mother had lived to see her successful, with her own flourishing business, a kind of security her mother hadn't felt working for others, no matter how much she was valued. She'd always encouraged Justine to look ahead to the years after modeling, and even in her early twenties Justine had been thrifty and on the alert for business opportunities.

Yes, she'd had an advantage that most of the other models didn't have, Justine thought, she'd had her mother's forethought and she'd had her own eye for excellence. All through her working years she'd studied the top girls, placed as she was to appreciate every crucial shading of difference between the good-enough model and the potential star.

When she discovered Lulu, who'd just started working as a photographer's stylist, she'd pounced on the raw material of greatness. In one day she'd talked the shy teenager into going to see three photographers, making an overnight leap from model to model's agent. Although Lulu had been an immediate sensation, making *Bazaar*'s cover in her first month of work, the agency business had been terrifyingly rough going. Her fanatical savings from eight steady years of work had tided her over until she was able to arrange a line of credit to cover the weekly payroll. Nothing had been easy, but during those first years Lulu had been Justine's launching pad into the agency business. Eventually she'd been lured to Hollywood and swallowed up by stardom, but by that time Loring Model Management was a healthy business.

Getting up, Justine moved to the window and looked out at the city she'd loved at first sight. At night, in midwinter, there was a harder sparkle to the lights. The city belonged to the North and it responded to cold by growing brighter and clearer, cleaned by icy winds. She'd hated to leave New York, when after four months of grooming, her agency had arranged for her to go to Paris for additional polishing. Had they any idea of what they were setting in motion, Justine wondered? Did they ever ask themselves how they changed the lives of the girls for whom they arranged those necessary European tours of duty? Now that she was routinely doing it herself, she knew that an agency head had to send her girls off in the same way that parents are forced to shut off their imaginations when they send their kids away to college.

No, not even Willy herself could have known that sending young Justine Loring to Paris for six months was delivering her to the worst man she would ever meet. Frankie didn't know, they'd never guessed, she had never told anyone on earth about Marco Lombardi.

Marco had been a junior assistant at Lanvin then, only a year older than she, but fatally well skilled in the arts of seduction. If he had involved her in nothing more than a brief physical passion followed by a typical crash and burn, she would never have forgotten him, for he had been her first lover. However, he had not been content with her heart and her body, he had succeeded in possessing her soul. Marco had bound her to him until he became her world, her God. As soon as he was absolutely certain that there was nothing she could deny him, he lost interest in her. With the coldness of a scientist undertaking an experiment, he had told her that to prove her love she must make herself sexually available to his best friend. Thank God, Justine thought, what little remained of her mother's teachings had given her the strength to immediately flee Paris for New York, but it had taken her years to recover from the deliberate cruelty of Marco Lombardi's successful attempt to destroy her innocence and betray her confidence. Perhaps she'd never truly recovered. In any case, her first experience with love had been tainted forever.

Today Justine was far enough away from those events of seventeen years ago to understand that there had been nothing intrinsically *personal* about what Marco had done to her. She had happened to cross his path when he was between women and he had acted according to his character, his bred-in-the-bone need to possess and destroy. He was not a man who could settle for less with any woman.

Should she have warned the girls about him? Justine had

debated the question with herself every minute until they left and finally had come to the conclusion that whatever she said would only have fascinated them and attracted them to Marco. To alert them might be fatal. What female could resist being singled out by Marco for his attention, the thrill of being the one chosen to enter his world? Their young arrogance might well encourage them to prove her wrong. But whichever of her three girls became the Lombardi face would have to be told the whole story, that much Justine had resolved.

Justine sighed deeply. She'd never rest until they all came back safely. What she needed now was a hot bath, a hot cup of tea, a warm evening in her newly cozy house and a good book that took place in a country parsonage in the nineteenth century. With a happy ending.

As her taxi stopped in front of her house, Justine was surprised to see signs of activity inside. Lights were on all over the first two floors and the shadows of men moving about were visible behind her draperies.

"What's going on here?" she shouted as she burst into her front door.

"We're draining the pipes," a workman answered. "Should be finished soon."

"You're what! Draining what? *Who told you to touch my pipes?*"

"Aiden," he answered and turned to be off about his business.

"Where is he?" Justine demanded violently.

"Basement," he answered, and rushed away, recognizing your typical crazy lady of whom there is one on every job. Always.

If men were from Mars and women from Venus, contractors were from a black hole in deep space, Justine thought with the still lucid top of her mind while the rest of it glowed in a lurid light and led her down the steps to the basement like a heat-seeking missile.

"What the hell are you doing to my house?" she screamed at Aiden.

He straightened up from his work, industry written all over his face, naked from the waist up. "Justine! I was wondering what had happened to you. We have to get the pipes completely drained so that they won't freeze and burst. It's going to be way below zero for three days at least, a weather front straight from the Arctic. The Mayor has closed down everything but essential services."

"Where, *where* is that new furnace you promised me, swore to me, would be installed by the end of the day?" she shrieked. "You know that was the only reason I told you to go ahead!"

"My supplier sent the wrong furnace," Aiden said, justification clear in every word. "It was too big for this basement. When I phoned that idiot, it turned out that he'd been carrying the wrong serial number on his inventory," he added indignantly.

"What happened to the old furnace?" Justine asked, gazing in disbelief at the empty space where it had stood for so long. Her anger was momentarily displaced by the enormity of what had gone wrong.

"It fell apart when we disconnected it," Aiden said matter-of-factly. "By the time we found out that they'd delivered the wrong furnace the guys had already disconnected the old one. There was absolutely no way to put it back together again, it's kaput."

He'd canceled three appointments today, Aiden thought, appointments to bid on big jobs, so that he could surprise this delicious and fascinating woman with a perfectly functioning new heating system, and instead he'd found himself with a nightmare on his hands. If he hadn't been apprenticed to a plumber years ago, the pipes would have been serious trouble. He wanted to beat himself over the head with a two by four, but he was a contractor, a leader of lesser men, the building trade's version of chairman of the Joint Chiefs of Staff and he had to behave with firm resolution.

Justine sat down on the basement steps and burst into tears.

"I trusted you with my house," she sobbed. "I trusted you and look what happened. My house is going to freeze, my poor house, oh, oh, my poor darling little house." Sobs shook her body and she bent her head to her knees inconsolably, wrapping her coat even more tightly around her although the basement was hot.

Aiden's stern contractor's code of honor faltered and then failed him utterly as he looked at her with increasing dismay.

"Oh, Justine, for God's sake, please, please don't cry like that. It kills me to see you cry. I swear the house won't freeze, it'll be cold, but there won't be any damage. Only the pipes might have frozen, but they won't, Justine, I promise you, nothing will freeze, nothing, I've quadruple-checked every last pipe in the place my-self."

Aiden stood helplessly near her huddled, shaking form and forced himself to continue. "Justine, the problem is you can't live here until I get the new furnace in. There isn't going to be any heat or any hot water. And no supplier in the city can put his hands on the right furnace over the weekend. I've checked every last one of them. Not till Monday earliest, if then."

"Oh! Oh! Oh!" Her tears flowed twice as hard. Aiden sat down on his heels so that he'd be on her level and tried to stroke her hair to comfort her. Justine jerked her head and slapped fero-ciously at his hand.

"Don't touch me, you peckerhead, you evil, evil man, you, you . . . contractor!" she managed to articulate through her sobs. "You came in here and look what happened, it's a ruin, my perfect, wonderful, cozy house, everything was fine before you talked me into this, and now it's all gone to hell, it's a shell, a freezing shell, oh, oh, how could I have been so stupid? I don't have anyplace to *live*, my *home* is gone."

"Shit! You're absolutely right. Oh, damn it, Justine, I *should* have checked the new furnace before I let them take the old one out—that was pure criminal stupidity—but I was so anxious to get this in for you before the storm that I went against all my rules, I hurried the workmen and screwed up the job."

Justine finally got herself under control enough to speak with-out tears. "Is that supposed to be a reason?" she asked, mopping her face with a Kleenex. "You were trying to do me a favor? Is that your point? You were too zealous?"

"Yes! . . . I mean, oh, what difference does it make what I mean? I fucked up and that's that, the reason isn't important. I let you down and I'll never, ever forgive myself."

"*I'll* never forgive you, so you can forget about forgiving your-self!"

"I know," he said humbly. "Why should you? Unless . . ."

" 'Unless'?" she said scornfully. "How could there be an 'un-less'?"

"Well, for instance, let's just imagine that for some crazy rea-son, without logic, you decided that you wanted to be really bigger than big about this, and you gave me one free pass at being a total fuckup with the understanding that after this I would *never* get another chance. So you'd spend the weekend in a suite at any hotel in town at my expense and maybe, one day, I'll be able to convince you to trust me again."

"Why," Justine asked in wonder, "why on earth would I want to do that?"

"I don't have a decent single reason to give you. I just hoped . . . that somehow, by a miracle, it was in the realm of possibility."

Justine looked at Aiden from under her wet eyelashes. He was still the same man whom she had trusted last night, as she had trusted no other man in years, except that without a shirt she wanted him . . . well, even . . . more, yes, considerably more. Only he'd broken her furnace and rendered her beloved house uninhabitable for three or four days. But certainly not on purpose. Accidents do happen. Nobody's perfect. If she forgave him, the very *pleasant* thing that had started last night—whatever it was—would continue. If she didn't, it wouldn't make the house warm any quicker. And she hated to seem ungenerous.

"You'd never *ever* get another chance? Under any circumstances?" she murmured questioningly, weighingly, as if to herself.

"Never! Not ever! And I'd *always* owe you!"

"Hmmm."

"Justine, please," he implored her. "Please!"

"But I hate hotels," she said gloomily. "They depress me."

"You could stay with me! I have a huge loft downtown. Tribeca. You wouldn't even know I was there, if you didn't want to."

"Hmmm." She remained clearly unconvinced.

"And I have great tickets to the Knicks game tomorrow night. They won't call that off, wouldn't dare."

"Hmmm." She sounded marginally less dubious.

"I have a ton of food, I'd cook for you and clean up and wait on you hand and foot, cups of tea, Gibsons, Tequila Sunrises, milkshakes, whatever you're in the mood for. And we could explore my neighborhood, think of it as a mini-vacation. And if there's enough snow, I have skis for both of us. . . ."

Justine put her hands on his bare shoulders, looking questioningly into his eyes, as if the mention of skis had seriously tipped the balance in his favor. Did she look like a skier to him? Precariously balanced on his heels as he was, he almost fell into her lap. Aiden scrambled up to his feet and pulled her up toward him by the elbows.

"Would you make my bed?" Justine asked imperiously, leaning back and looking up at him. "I hate to make a bed."

"I'd make it with hospital corners. I make a great bed. I'd give you clean sheets every day."

"What else?"

"I promise not to lay a single finger on you," Aiden said. "I swear it, on my mother's head."

"That's more like it," Justine whispered approvingly. "But what if . . . ?"

"If what . . . ?" he breathed hopefully.

"Oh, never mind. Just thinking out loud." She succeeded in not smiling at the puzzled look on his face. Men were so hopeless. Pathetic, really. Did she look as if she drank Tequila Sunrises? Or milkshakes, for that matter? He had a lot to learn about her. For some reason her good mood had returned.

"I'd better go throw a few things into a suitcase," Justine said and pulled out of his arms. As she reached her icy bedroom she'd started humming again. A mini-vacation, she thought, might actually be a good thing, she'd been working too hard lately and with this freeze the weekend would be tedious, even if the house were warm. Even if she had a good book.

8

What had come over her, Justine wondered, locked in an agony of second thoughts, as the cab, possibly the last one in New York, continued to creep uncertainly downtown, bouncing into every possible pothole. The West Side Highway was already closed and they were taking some mysterious overland route known only to Tribeca dwellers. It had started to snow seriously even before the last workmen left. Aiden had made one more tour of the pipes before she'd locked her front door and cast a sad good-bye look at her house.

She could be settling into a warm luxurious hotel by now, Justine thought, she could be surrounded by a secure, impersonal network of room service and phone operators and assistant managers, she would have ordered flowers up from the lobby florist, bought all the new magazines and be snugly prepared to ride out whatever the elements brought to the city, but no, she'd allowed a whim, a vagrant impulse, to overtake her judgment and now she was captive of a man she had met only twenty-four hours earlier, much too up close and personal with a virtual stranger who had already proved himself a prime fuckup.

A loft in Tribeca, Justine asked herself? How could she have said yes? She'd hated lofts on principle even though they'd been the rage when she'd first come to New York. She could picture it now: defiantly ugly high tech, all one big sneer of industrial steel and exposed plumbing. The whole loft concept was crazy, except for studio space or moviemaking. People were meant to live in welcoming, human-scaled rooms, not former factories with inadequate separations between spaces for different functions. This Aiden Henderson creature probably had installed a shower in his kitchen just to show it could be done. She'd had one dinner with him, allowed one or one and a half pecks on the cheek, and now she'd committed herself to be snowed in with the man who'd ruined her house. Was she a victim of the Stockholm syndrome?

She didn't recognize the rundown West Side neighborhood they were passing through but the taxi driver was having so much trouble with his car that it was clearly too late to change her mind. They were almost in the Hudson River as it was. Shit! She hated everything about snotty downtown lowlife, she hated its pretensions to being so much more interesting and "real" than uptown with its Chinese drag restaurants that offered bad attitude and worse food, with the panting worship of film producers and restaurant owners, who were often the same people of limited talent, with the idealization of flops full of trisexual teenaged, junkie street kids, whose spacey lives consisted of skateboarding by day and raves at night, whole tribes of the living dead who thought that anyone over nineteen was senile.

Why had she been so *easy?* At the least Aiden must have been astonished that she'd taken him up on his offer. Why hadn't she told him that with her busy social life there was no way she could be free for an entire weekend? Oh, dear God, she *had* lost her mind! The traumatic destruction of her furnace had caused her to throw all normal social conventions to the wind.

Justine sneaked a peek at Aiden's profile. He looked grim and distant, intent on trying to get the cabdriver to follow his precise directions when it was obvious that the poor man hadn't the faint-est idea of how to get to Tribeca, much less Laight Street. Where was that pleasant smile now? Ten to one this thug had never gone to the University of Colorado, ten thousand to one he hadn't shown up on her doorstep just to do a favor for her friends who had recommended him.

What kind of contractor would start a job the day after he got it? A contractor without any other work, that's who. A gypsy contractor, a contractor who'd had his license taken away, a contractor in disgrace! Why hadn't she asked to see proof of his bona fides, why hadn't she called someone at City Hall and had his name and license checked out? Why had she let herself be influenced by the honest impression made last night by this great big cowboy with the kind of broken nose that had made the young Brando into more than another pretty face? Why had she, Justine Loring, expert in all the falsity of character that could be achieved by sheer physiognomy, allowed herself to be intrigued, even, admit it, slightly . . . charmed, God help her . . . by this so-called contractor's con-artist's gift for exuding a kind of reassurance that came from being large and seeming to be capable—ha!—and acting as if he had no idea of how good-looking he was? Wasn't that the classic technique? Didn't all bunko artists work that way?

The snow wasn't just getting thicker, it was sticking, wet and heavy, a snowstorm as dense as a chenille bedspread. The wipers on the windshield were barely working. Justine shivered in her long blanket coat made of heavy white wool, lavishly wreathed with long fringes of curly white Mongolian lamb from collar to hem. She pulled her old knit cap down until it almost covered her eyes and clasped her fur-lined gloves together in rising panic. Even her feet, in shearling-lined boots and thick socks, were getting icy. But, blizzard or not, if Aiden Henderson made one wrong move, just one, even a fucking *gesture*, she'd escape from that loft and get back to civilization even if, yes, even if it meant taking the subway!

Why was Justine so silent, Aiden Henderson wondered, as he covered his discomfort by helping the cabdriver find the right route. Why was she cowering silently in the corner of the cab, covered by a bizarre pile of frizzy white hairy stuff, as if she had something to fear from him? Did a couple of quick kisses on the cheek indicate that he was going to molest her? He'd never dreamed that she would take him up on his crazy offer to spend the weekend. He'd only made it under the influence of her broken heart. Christ, he didn't know if he even had any clean sheets— God willing, Mrs. Brady had managed to get in to clean today and brought the laundry. And whatever a Tequila Sunrise was, he'd never made one. Justine Loring, for Pete's sake—she must have all sorts of other things to do, men to meet, parties to go to, a big, complicated glamorous life to go with her glamorous job about which he knew nothing at all except that some silly people thought it meaningful to civilization that women grow taller and thinner every year.

Had he been dreaming or had Justine been leading him on back there in the basement? Was he some kind of exotically low new experience for her? A weekend with a contractor or how I got to wallow in the depths of depravity with a man who works with his hands? Well, he had a surprise for her. He'd only asked her to stay because he had a businessman's responsibility to provide her with shelter and she'd insisted that hotels depressed her.

Well, tough, weekend guests depressed *him*. Why hadn't he remembered that the sight of a woman in tears deprived him of all his common sense? He'd been looking forward to a quiet couple of days to go over a bunch of complicated lighting bids for the new factory he was building in Long Island City, to say nothing of the four big football games he intended to catch. Now he was stuck with a latter-day Anna Karenina buried in a pile of dead sheep, the expression on her face suitable to someone who was about to be thrown off a sled into the Russian winter. Had he really promised to *make her bed*? No way! If she even mentioned it, if she so much as breathed a word about her bed being made, he'd escort her to the subway, give her a token and let her go and be depressed in a hotel.

The cab skidded to a shaky stop and Aiden helped Justine out and grabbed her suitcase. While he paid the driver she looked around, seeing nothing remotely safe about the dimly lit street or the dark hulk of what looked like a deserted warehouse. Silently they rose in a creaking freight elevator until they reached what Justine judged must be the top floor of the building. They emerged onto an anonymous landing and as Aiden unlocked his front door Justine sniffed the air suspiciously. Odd, she thought, anyone would say woodsmoke and . . . and linseed oil? He grasped her elbow lightly so that she wouldn't trip on the sill and flicked on several light switches. Justine took one step inside and stopped abruptly.

" Oh," she said in astonishment. "I don't believe this."

"Yeah." He grinned at her tiny bewildered voice. "It took seven barns, three big and four small, all abandoned, most of them built before 1800. I salvaged them in Indiana for almost nothing. I can't get enough wood in my life, I'm crazy about the stuff, I've got seventeen varieties in here."

"But you said a *loft*," she laughed in sheer relief.

"Technically it is a loft."

"It *was* a loft. Now it's a . . . a giant . . . what? Barn? Log cabin?

Ranch house? Stable? It's a little of everything," Justine insisted, walking around the great room in enchantment, peeking through doorways to other, smaller rooms with low ceilings.

"Since I built it with my own two hands I'll let you call it whatever you choose," Aiden said, delighted with her reaction. Everybody was startled by his place but not everybody liked it as much as she seemed to. Maybe she'd even get around to taking off her weird coat if he waited patiently. He moved across the huge room to a massive fireplace, built from flat old stones, where a sturdy pile of logs was laid, waiting for his match.

"You built it yourself?" Justine asked, coming to stand in front of the fire and removing her gloves. "How long did it take?"

"Almost seven years," Aiden told her proudly. "I was working full-time and living in the neighborhood so I did it on weekends and nights, but once I found the wood, the rough-sawn poplar and the barn siding and the big oak timbers and the black walnut, the wood pretty much told me what to do with it. You can't go too wrong with old wood, it knows what it wants. I couldn't even let anyone else do the electrical and the plumbing. I got so possessive I was afraid they'd mess up. I almost hated coming to the finish carpentry, the bookcases and the cabinets—it's the end of the job, except for the painting, so it's sort of sad in a nice way."

"But who decorated it?" she asked, taking off her cap and looking around the room where each fascinatingly battered piece of painted country furniture called out for her inspection, where the walls were hung with American primitive paintings and framed quilts and faded hooked rugs were scattered over the poplar floorboards.

"It isn't decorated. I just kept looking around until I found things that looked right. Got kind of lucky, especially with the quilts. The one over the fireplace was made by my great-grandmother but the others I found in the Amish country, some upstate and a few beauties in Nova Scotia. Now there's a place to live if you don't mind the cold. Can't beat it in the summer."

"Nova Scotia where the salmon comes from?"

"The very one. If that was a hint, I'll take a look in the kitchen and see what I can dig up for dinner."

"I'll come too," Justine said, eager to see what the kitchen looked like.

"Oh, no, that's not the deal. I said I was going to feed you and if I let you in the kitchen your natural womanly instincts might take over, and you'd start doing who knows what? Anyway, you'd be in my way. I'll show you the guest bedroom and you can make yourself comfortable."

Alone in the small, deliciously cozy guestroom with its immaculate bath, both of which seemed as if they must look out on an Alp, Justine unpacked hastily. This probably wasn't going to be as bad as she'd thought. At least he had some interesting furniture, she told herself, as she shivered in excitement. Actually, if you could judge a man more by his house than by his face, Aiden might possibly be what he had seemed yesterday. Perhaps she hadn't lost her mind after all. That, in itself, was a reassuring thought. Just as the idea of him with a hammer and nails working away patiently for seven years was reassuring. Patience was a good thing. Wood was a good thing. Patience in dealing with wood was an even better thing. Or so she believed.

In the kitchen Aiden discovered that Mrs. Brady had made a large pot of Irish stew that only needed to be reheated. He put the pot in the big warming oven so that he wouldn't have to worry about it burning and started looking around in his liquor cabinet. Justine seemed to have recovered from her fit of whatever it was in the taxi, he thought. Buyer's remorse, probably, he'd felt it himself. But now, when she'd finally taken that damn cap off, standing in the firelight, and ruffled up her hair with both hands, he'd just about fallen down at the sight of so much of what must be unselfconscious beauty, because no woman with any vanity would have worn a cap like that no matter how cold she was. Wasn't vanity one of the ruling principles in women? Maybe when you've had all your life to look at yourself, even Justine could get bored. Hard to imagine.

He found a tray and some good-sized glasses, a bucket of ice, an unopened bottle of tequila someone had given him for Christmas two years ago, and a container of fresh orange juice. He thought for a minute, added a bottle of maraschino cherries, and carried the tray into the living room where he deposited it on the coffee table in front of the fire, and sat back on the big leather sofa.

"What's that?" Justine asked as she slid down next to him wearing heavy white gym socks, bright pink tights and an oversized white turtleneck sweater bearing the legend "New York Giants" on it.

"It's nothing yet but it's going to be what I promised you, a Tequila Sunrise."

"Hmmm," she said noncommittally, reserving judgment.

"Yeah," he said, "watch this. First I put in the ice, now I open the tequila and add generously, then I stingily pour orange juice until it looks exactly like sunlight and finally I carefully position a cherry in each glass to represent the rising sun. Here, have one."

"But the sun is only red at sunset," she said, taking the glass.

"Not in Hawaii."

"I see," she said thoughtfully. So this was what a Tequila Sunrise looked like. Not that different from a screwdriver, what was all the fuss about?

"I have a funny feeling," Justine whispered suddenly. "A bad feeling."

"What do you mean?"

"There's someone in here besides us," she breathed softly in a frightened voice. "There's someone watching us. Don't move, pretend you don't know."

"Rufus, come on out," Aiden said, "she's okay."

A giant white Persian cat materialized majestically from behind a tall stack of logs and stalked slowly toward them with an offended air, his tail straight up in the air. He was an extraordinarily beautiful animal, even in a race in which there is no genuine ugliness possible. The cat took over the room.

"My God!" Justine exclaimed.

"He'd agree with that sentiment. Rufus is shy with women. He's a one-man cat. Actually he thinks he's a dog. Maybe because he's been neutered, but you can't keep a tom in the city. Come on up here, kid, and meet Justine. You're not a cat-hater, are you? Or allergic?"

"Not at all," Justine answered truthfully. She adored cats and she knew exactly how to attract them. She sat absolutely still, as if she were totally indifferent, ignoring the very existence of Rufus, refusing to even attempt eye contact. They could take anything but lack of attention, the lovely, paradoxical, unknowable beasts.

Rufus levitated into Aiden's lap and rolled over, his four feet in the air. Aiden tickled his stomach. "Ever see a cat do that?"

"Amazing," Justine agreed. "Do you have any others? Did you know that Hemingway had thirty cats? Apparently even Picasso appreciated them, he said that God invented the giraffe, the elephant and the cat . . . he didn't mention humans."

"Rufus wouldn't like me to get another cat, he's jealous by nature. That's why he's pretending not to notice you, but he's really seeing you through his closed eyelids. He thinks of you as a threat to his life with me."

"Poor deluded creature. Tell him not to worry," Justine smiled. Rufus had already peeped at her curiously. It was only a question of time. She'd keep a cat herself but an unmarried woman with a cat was a cliché whereas a man with a cat merely seemed sensitive.

"Is that sweater just decorative or does it mean you're a Giants fan?" Aiden asked carefully.

"A fan, of course. Isn't everyone? I mean, the Jets are pretty piss-poor, but naturally you have to watch both teams if you call yourself any kind of New Yorker. The problem is they're both playing this weekend, at the same time, the Jets in Buffalo and the Giants in Dallas."

Justine looked at him and they shook their heads in shared disbelief. "I've been furious all week about it," she continued. "I still can't believe they'd schedule games like that! Cretins! I'd like to knock their heads together. I particularly adore watching guys play in a blizzard. The suffering! The slipping and sliding! Buffalo! The perfect thing would be to have two television sets, side by side, and watch them both."

"That could be arranged."

"Oh, Aiden, really?"

"I happen to have it all set up," he said smugly. "You're not the only sports fan in this place."

"Maybe they'll both win! What's wrong with expecting a miracle?"

"Let's drink to that."

"Oh, yes! Hmmm . . . this is really . . . an experience. Smooth, sultry and incredibly . . . civilized."

"I believe it's quite powerful."

"Not if you eat the cherry."

"Oh, Justine. . . ." he said longingly, watching the cherry disappear into her mouth.

"Yes . . . ?" She smiled innocently. His eyes were such a deep blue, almost a secret blue, so dark that they could be another color until he looked at you. There was an exuberance in his gaze, like a breeze off the ocean.

"Here," he said hastily, "have another cherry, they're small."

"You do know how to treat a lady." He had promised not to lay a finger on her, Justine reflected. And he'd keep his promise. That was the trouble with some men. But too many scruples were better than too few. Somewhere there should be a happy medium. She relaxed on the sofa, suddenly confident that she would find a way to work out this ethical dilemma. She half-closed her eyes, looking at Aiden through her eyelashes and wondering what he'd be like to kiss, really kiss, not the brush of his lips on her cheek of last night.

It would be like opening a fresh blue tin of Malosol Beluga caviar and digging in gently with a mother-of-pearl spoon, Justine thought. Just a small exploratory taste, but the best taste you ever had in your life. Then you look around and you discover you're all alone in the room with the whole tin, fourteen Russian ounces, theoretically more than anybody can eat in one sitting, right there in front of you. You tip your spoon directly into the center of the shining surface of the caviar and you take your second taste, a slightly bigger one than the first. It's even better than you'd realized . . . now the thirst starts, the galloping guilty caviar thirst that's like none other, and your third spoonful is shamelessly heaping, filling your mouth. You keep eating, one sinfully large spoonful after another, every taste bud aflame with caviar, because there's absolutely more than enough and nobody to share it with, eating as quickly as you choose, or as slowly, depending on your mood, until you've had enough, which is almost impossible with caviar, but happens eventually. And then you stop, after one last taste, but not because you have to, but because you want to. You've been utterly satisfied, and somehow you know that the tin will still be there later tonight, waiting in the fridge, as full as ever, for that inevitable moment when you have to have caviar again and if you don't brush your teeth right away there's a bonus of the aftertaste of the supreme grey eggs that lingers lusciously in your mouth for at least a half hour, almost as good as the caviar itself.

Jesus! Justine opened her eyes quickly. This drink was like magic mushrooms or something, she'd never had a hallucination like that before. She'd never had a magic mushroom either, losing control wasn't her style. She sat silently, taking only cautious sips of this dangerous potion.

Aiden looked into the fire and acted as a cat cushion, suddenly glad that Rufus was there as a chaperone. Justine, in her fiendishly alluring gym socks and that sweater that both concealed and beckoned, was too much for any man to risk being alone with. Was she a devilishly clever vamp or an angel? He was totally confused. But a promise was a promise. Was a promise.

"Hungry?" he asked, getting up and rousing himself hastily. He had to change his center of gravity.

"Starving."

They devoured the savory stew and warm French bread with a minimum of conversation. Rufus seemed to sleep under the table after he'd had his fill of milk and tuna fish, although occasionally Justine felt a slight, tentative nudge of his haughty head against her ankle. How easy it would be to slip him a sliver of meat without being noticed, she thought, tempted, but decided that bribery was beneath her. This cat was one tough number but she'd win him over fairly or not at all.

But any feline seduction would have to wait for another time. Justine felt so exhausted, all of a sudden, from the combination of the long, emotional day at the office, the furnace fiasco and the awful trip downtown that she got up from the table before Aiden could make coffee and trailed off wearily to her room, barely able to change into the silk long johns she wore as pajamas on cold nights, before she sank into a profound slumber.

Sometime during the night Justine became aware, as she was aroused from a state of total unconsciousness, that something was *kneading* her. To her sleep-dazed mind there was a nightmare impression of a large snake winding itself sinuously and silently around her chest. She lay very still, holding her breath in terror, trying desperately to figure out where she was. Someplace hideously quiet, someplace where there was absolutely no normal background sound, no city noises, no light, no clue to what kind of supernatural force was attacking her.

"Help," she squeaked softly, afraid to frighten the snake. "Help me, someone." The snake slid horribly, with relentless stealth, up her chest until it approached her throat. She was going to let herself be strangled alive without even making an effort, she thought in frozen immobility. She forced herself to open her mouth to scream, only to be tickled by the touch of a small cold nose and wooed by a friendly cat noise.

"Bastard!" she exploded, grabbing Rufus, and holding him high over her head. "How *dare* you! *Now* you want to sleep with me? *Now* you want to be friends? When Aiden can't see what a flirt you are, huh? Well, you've chosen the wrong time, you sneaky little son of a bitch. You're going back where you came from, you imp from hell." She put the cat down on the bed and pushed him roughly off onto the floor. "Out, and don't come back!" she ordered. Rufus jumped lightly up and started walking on her, from her feet to her chest, where he stopped and sat with all his densely concentrated fifteen pounds, prepared to remain, an immovable object if ever she'd met one. And it wasn't even her fault, Justine told herself righteously, it wasn't as if she'd lured him on with food.

"Go away! Scat!" she hissed ferociously, wishing she knew which human commands he might recognize and obey. "Down! Off! Floor! Out! Bad cat!" Finally he moved, leaping lightly up to her pillow and pushing his nose into her neck with interest. She'd said the wrong word, but she didn't know which one it was, Justine thought as she pushed him away. He nipped lightly on her fingers in a friendly, familiar fashion. This could go on all night, she realized. Physically neutered though he was, Rufus still had his memories.

There was only one thing that made sense and that involved the unthinkable. As she received more of Rufus' interested attentions the unthinkable became the necessary, and Justine reached for the flashlight she remembered had been on the table by the bed. She turned it on and got out of bed, putting her feet into her fleece-lined booties. She couldn't find her bathrobe so she took the blanket from the bed and slung it over her shoulders and staggered over to the window. She pulled back the blackout shades and saw nothing, not even streetlamps, through the thick scrim of falling snow. She could be in a mountain cabin deep in the dark wild woods, Justine thought. A mini-vacation indeed. Rufus followed, twining around her legs and nudging her to the door.

"Okay, okay, I get the picture," Justine grumbled, lighting her way to the kitchen. She took the milk out of the fridge and poured it into the bowl that stood on the floor nearby. Rufus lapped quickly. "Say thank you, Justine," she said to the busy animal.

Totally occupied with his milk, he didn't hear her. Now to make her getaway. Moving with steps so tiny and smooth that nothing betrayed her, not even a vibration of the air, Justine began to back away from the loudly lapping cat. She'd just reached the door and was about to streak for her room when Rufus, without preparation, was upon her again, purring loudly, and treating her legs to a tangle of furry hugs. He had trained her, Justine realized. She had made the wrong decision and now that he had her where he wanted her, he was in the mood to play with his new blond mouse.

"You're going to your boss," she said, picking the cat up by his middle and clutching him to her bosom so that he couldn't get away. By the light of a few glowing embers Justine padded softly across the great barn. She opened the door to Aiden's bedroom without making a sound and tried to pick Rufus up and throw him inside. But this cat, she discovered, could not be thrown when he didn't care to be thrown. His clipped claws had become entangled in the fine silk mesh of her long-sleeved top and no sooner had she plucked one away than others fastened onto her as if the animal was climbing a rope ladder. Never clutch a cat, Justine thought, unless you plan to keep it.

She stood in the open doorway trying to decide what to do. She could hear Aiden breathing softly and by the light of his electric clock she could see exactly where he was lying under his quilt. He was sleeping deeply, without movement of any kind.

She'd lost her blanket somewhere in the struggle with the cat. She could either take Rufus back to her room and let him keep her up all night, or she could return him to Aiden. Perhaps, she thought, if she brought the cat farther into the room he'd smell his lord and master and abandon her for his regular sleeping partner. Some faithful one-man cat he'd turned out to be.

Justine crept a few feet into the bedroom, turning Rufus' head firmly toward Aiden with one hand while she supported him with the other, afraid that if she let him go entirely, he'd grab at her with all his ten claws. Nothing happened. She advanced with even greater care, waited a while and then subsided on the rug next to the bed. What was wrong with the animal, she wondered? Even *she* could smell Aiden from here, and he smelled wonderful, kind of like a warm, just-buttered corn muffin spread with honey. A sleeping man either smelled better than he did at any other time, or he was utterly out of the question. There was no possible medium or neutral way to smell in her experience. Unfortunately there was no way to tell ahead of time.

Minutes passed and Justine began to feel chilly in spite of the cat's warm, happily pulsating body plastered all over her, his coat keeping her fairly warm. Maybe she should carry him back to the fireplace, put some logs on the fire and sleep on the sofa? Maybe she should look in Aiden's closet for a robe or a coat and wrap herself in it? Rufus couldn't stay awake forever—didn't cats sleep fifteen hours a day? Maybe she should wake up Aiden and insist that he remove his cat? That would be the most direct course to take. But she'd already made one seriously wrong decision about a male animal tonight and she didn't want to make another.

Just how wrong could it be? Aiden had been a perfect gentleman all evening long. He wouldn't turn into a cad just because his feline had taken a fancy to her. What could you really tell about a man by his cat? Oh, oh, oh, she was so confused in this strange place! Now Rufus was trying to lick the inside of her ear. This was intolerable, Justine decided suddenly. She stood, leaned close to Aiden's ear and said loudly, "Wake up."

Rufus immediately jumped to the other side of the bed, curled up next to his owner and fell into a trance of sleep. Aiden's eyes flew open; he reached out for her and pulled her down next to him, trapping her in his arms.

"I was just dreaming about you," he murmured, and kissed her on the lips. "And now you've come to visit."

"For heaven's sake," she said, "I just had to get rid of your damn cat."

"Justine, you don't need an excuse," he laughed in joy, kissing her again. "My God, you're shivering. Where's your bathrobe? Here, slide under the covers. There, that's better? Oh, my sweet beautiful darling baby, you're so cold. Here, I'll warm you up."

"It was the cat! He came into my room, he tried to smother me, he made me give him milk, he wouldn't let me throw him, he likes me better than he does you, he forced me to wake you up."

"Of course he did," Aiden said indulgently.

"Honestly!"

"This is better than the best Christmas morning. Oh, God, you taste good."

"So do you. But it *was* the cat."

"Silent be, it is the cat."

"Well, at least you admit it," Justine said between kisses. He was more delicious than caviar and there was no need for a spoon.

"Everything, anything, you're so lovely, I adore you, are you warmer now?"

"A little bit," she said plaintively.

"That's not good enough, is it?"

"No."

"You need to be very warm, all over."

"I think so. Probably. It would be safer," she said demurely.

"Oh, I'm certain of it. The thing is, you can't really get warm with that awful slippery thing you've got on, whatever it is. It traps the cold air in, so you'd better take it off."

"You take it off."

"I can't."

"Why not?" she asked breathlessly.

"I promised I wouldn't lay a finger on you."

"You said that *yesterday.*"

"Does that . . . make a difference?"

"Of course," she whispered impatiently. He was torturing her and he knew it. Cat and mouse. Cat and man. Oh, heavens above!

"Would it be wrong if I said I loved you first?"

"It would be very nice," Justine murmured primly as she slid out of her long johns. There was a limit to what she could endure from this man and his cat and she'd reached it.

9

I was still dancing when I woke up. It felt as if I'd never stopped, even though I was lying flat in bed. Had I danced away the whole day? I felt good! I felt well! I bounced out of bed, opened the curtains and discovered that it was bright day outside, with flags flashing up and down the Avenue Montaigne, sending the world a message to come out and spend lots of money. I looked at my watch. Just half-past one in the afternoon—seven and a half hours of solid dancing-sleep, preceded by violent exercise, and my jet lag had disappeared. All I wanted for breakfast was a half grapefruit and coffee. I'd discovered the Bains Douche diet! I definitely looked a couple of pounds lighter in the mirror. No wonder that place was mobbed.

I took a shower, washed and towel dried my hair and settled back in bed to enjoy that feeling of virtuously lazy, deeply-taken-care-of relaxation you can only get in a hotel with nothing pressing to do and nowhere special to go. Paris wasn't going to disappear and I was certain the girls must still be sleeping. None of them had my dancer's resilience, to say nothing of an iota of my style. Then, just as I settled into a glowing step-by-step review of my performance of the night before, the phone rang.

"Frankie?" It was Gabrielle. I tried to sound as if she'd just awakened me. She didn't respond with appropriate apologies, but kept right on talking. "Marco Lombardi has asked that you bring the girls over to his workrooms this afternoon."

"What!" I exclaimed, going from sleepy to enraged in a nano-second. "My girls have almost two weeks to work with him, and they just got here yesterday, as you know perfectly well."

"Nonsense," she snapped, and that woman has one hell of a snap. "My arrangements were made with Justine, but in the contract there was a written commitment that she would be here with the girls the whole time. Now that contract has been breached."

"Did Necker tell you to call me? Did he say that?" I demanded, my outrage escalating. The phrase "breach of contract" will do that to me any time.

"He didn't need to. I haven't spoken to him today but you know perfectly well that you have a moral obligation to comply with this request, Frankie. Lombardi merely wants to get a feeling for their capabilities, it's not a question of work. Simply put, Marco needs to know what level of performance he can hope for from them. After all they bear a heavy responsibility for the success of the collection."

"Three girls out of thirty? Lombardi's the one who's responsible, not them."

"Nevertheless," Gabrielle persisted, "they're completely inexperienced and he's nervous about them. And, Frankie, don't forget, one of them will work with him for years, but right now they're total strangers."

"Listen, Gabrielle, either it's a breach of contract or he's asking a favor, make up your mind. Justine isn't here because she's deathly ill, so sue me!"

"Morally—"

"Gabrielle, don't give me morally. It won't work. I'll do my best for you because I'm a nice person. However, the girls are probably too wiped out to do anything but rest today. We're all still jet-lagged."

"They weren't too exhausted to go dancing last night."

I was speechless for a second. I hadn't expected Albert, our gallant escort, who'd done his share of dancing, to rat us out, but obviously he reported to a higher power.

"Everyone knows exercise is specifically recommended for jet lag, Gabrielle," I said with tardy composure. "I'll check out the girls and let you know in an hour."

Jeez, I hate blackmail. But Gabrielle had a good point. If I were Marco Lombardi I'd be dying to see the girls. Sure, in theory, he had twenty-seven other models to show on, but in reality probably the only girls he was absolutely certain of were my three.

If Lombardi were established, he'd have a good idea of who he was using by now, especially if the girls liked him personally. If he were one of the major designers the girls would be fighting to do his show. But as an unknown, he must have been kept waiting with a bunch of secondary options for any of the most desirable girls. Why should a supermodel commit to him? Once they get to the head of the line, models love to give the designers as little as they can get away with, say a low-option secondary. Oh, show me a supermodel—a word I loathe but can't find an absolutely accurate substitute for—without major attitude! Sure they're hard-working professionals, but they've been idolized into taking themselves too seriously, these Michael Jordans and Charles Barkleys of the fashion world.

When we book our top girls for shows, the trick is to get them to convert a low-option second—the first step on the road—into a high-option second and eventually, if they're having a good-attitude day, talk them into agreeing to a tentative. When they finally decide to turn a tentative into a commitment, sometimes only three days before the show, it's the model's equivalent of a shotgun marriage.

If I were a designer I'd show on plaster dummies—or wire hangers—rather than go through that hassle. I'd had enough years of being in the middle. Just thinking about the nimbus of last-minute hysteria generated by spoiled ding-bat, media-darling divas, to say nothing of coping with their horrendous boyfriends, made me disgusted enough to decide to haul every one of my girls over to Lombardi.

One day, soon enough, they'd turn out to be as difficult to pin down as your cellular phone-toting Brandis, your Shaloms, your Ambers and your Carlas, but today, by golly, I still had control over them. Justine and I often agreed that it was no wonder that poltergeists, when investigated, turned out to be generated unconsciously by teenaged girls.

I called their rooms and told them to be ready to go in an hour. I phoned the concierge and checked on Mike Aaron and Maude Callender, who had every right to witness this. They were having lunch downstairs at the Relais Plaza, the Parisian equivalent of Harry's Bar in Venice, and I alerted them to the news. I tried to reach Justine at the office to keep her abreast of developments, but mysteriously nobody answered the phone and I didn't have time to worry about it.

Actually, once I told April, Jordan and Tinker why I'd awakened them I couldn't have kept them from going. They were dying to see the clothes, but more important, although they didn't say so, they each wanted to impress Lombardi. He, the designer, might well be the one who was going to pick the girl to represent his clothes, rather than Necker.

Not for the first time I wished that Justine had been able to find out how this game was being played, but Gabrielle had resisted giving us any details. All we knew was that one of the girls would be chosen to win the jackpot, but by whom we had no idea. It occurred to me, while I was tucking myself tenderly into a sublime dark green wool suit that made me look almost sinuous and decidedly omnipotent, that even if I knew the answer there was no way the knowledge could benefit me, since I was rooting for all of them equally.

Two limos were waiting for our party of six, neither driven by that fink, Albert, who had undoubtedly been promoted a day off after his exertions of last night. The trip to Lombardi's atelier was less than a block, but it said limos in our contracts and limos we had, although it would have been quicker to walk.

Gabrielle met us in the small lobby and I followed her upstairs, followed by Mike and Maude and finally the girls, with Jordan lagging behind. Another superb performance like last night's, I wondered? Who taught her that a star will always choose to come on last? Forget "taught"—she'd probably been born knowing. As we filed upstairs I wondered how Lombardi would present himself. I'd seen a snapshot of him in a group in a fashion magazine but it had been taken years earlier. The faces of the assistants to great designers are unknown by and large, since no designer wants to promote anyone but himself, or even, in most cases, is unwilling to admit that assistants exist.

Would Marco Lombardi have adopted the severe, immaculate white smock so favored by many designers, giving them a look that made for a strange combination of Dr. Frankenstein disguised as a Rockwell Kent druggist? Would he do your Calvin Klein–Giorgio

Armani plain white T-shirt with a dark jacket number—I think they look like trustees at Devil's Island—or would he be the exquisitely tailored, suave, gracious grand seigneur like Oscar de la Renta? I hadn't expected anyone like the man who came rushing down the stairs to meet us.

First of all, the guy was gorgeous. We all—even those of us who haven't the luck to be Italian—know about Italian men, right? When they're Renaissance Florentine darkly gorgeous, like Marco Lombardi, there's nothing more so, unless you insist on Robert Redford in his Navy officer's uniform, drunk at the Stork Club, sitting on that bar stool in *The Way We Were*—and that, film fans, is a whole other breed of cat to say nothing of ethnic background. Lombardi looked younger than I'd expected, he moved with a dancer's ease and precision and his beauty was unfair, the kind that any decent, thoughtful woman like me feels is wasted on a man. He was wearing clean, faded unremarkable jeans, an old pink Brooks Brothers shirt, with the top three buttons open, bright red socks and the most beautifully polished, elegant pair of brown loafers I'd ever seen. The total effect combined the Ivy League with early Gene Kelly and vintage Fred Astaire. He was a dandy, a man who played games with his own clothes. What disarming disguise, I wondered, did he put on when he wasn't expecting a bunch of Americans? Gay, I thought, but why should I have expected anything different?

In the confusion created by Gabrielle attempting to introduce us in the proper French way and Marco Lombardi introducing himself in a highly excited and enthusiastic Italian way, enough confusion and giggles were generated so that what might have been an intimidating moment happened so quickly and easily that I could feel my girls relaxing in his warmth. Gay, I knew with sudden conviction, was the opposite of whatever this man was.

The girls were dazzled by his charm and warmth. He thought that they were all ravishing, exquisite, that much was absolutely conveyed by his eyes and his hands and his smile. He adored them. They were the most welcome sight he'd seen in years. "Such beautiful girls, three perfections," he crooned in the sort of full-bodied, old-country Italian accent I hadn't heard from anyone but an ancient storekeeper who used to sell fruit to my mother. Even though Marco had just met the girls there was a teasing, affectionately naughty, harmless little boy way in which he related to them.

"And you," he said, turning to me and taking both of my hands in his, and sounding much more serious. "You are a gift, a surprise package. I was expecting someone less young, someone less"—he sketched a voluptuous bosom and a tiny waist with his hands—"But they cannot make a woman who looks like you into a duenna! What a folly, what a delusion! You are in far more danger from me than skinny little girls."

I felt myself smiling in gratification. It was nice to be appreciated by someone who knew a real woman when he saw one. I hoped I wasn't blushing and I hoped that Mike Aaron was getting a shot of this moment. Zaftig, indeed!

"Marco," Gabrielle interrupted, "can we finish these compliments somewhere besides the staircase?"

"Of course," he answered, with a flash of irritation. He didn't like her bossy manner any more than I did.

Eventually we all moved into the relatively big room in which he worked on his fitting models. There were a few uncovered dress forms pushed into a corner but not a sign of any clothes. The girls shrugged off their parkas and I was fascinated to see that they'd each had the same idea about what to wear: those second-skin ski pants that had caused a sensation in the Plaza-Athénée lobby and equally clinging knit sweaters of the thinnest materials, through which anybody with poor eyesight could count their ribs and accurately estimate their bra sizes, although they weren't wearing bras. Just in case that wasn't enough to make you sit up and take notice, they'd all put on their highest-heeled boots, the ones that sent the message "Do me or I'll stomp you." I doubted that there was even one pair of panties among them. All in all they did me credit.

The only variations on this covered-up version of show and tell was in the color of their sweaters. April's was a soft French blue that deepened her eyes, not, I assumed, an accidental effect. Nor had Jordan picked her white sweater by chance. Whenever she wore white, the contrast with her skin ensured that she was at her most compelling. Tinker wore a rather ratty black sweater that looked as if it had been chosen at random, but it enhanced the breathless underwater flash of her eyes and the artless—not on my best day had I been so artless!—high-piled tumble of her hair seemed to beg to be let loose.

"When can we see the clothes?" Maude asked eagerly.

Marco looked half startled, half indignant. "The clothes? Not yet, Signora, not yet. The collection is still two weeks away, the clothes are not completed, and even if they were, this is not the moment."

The guy doesn't audition, Maude, I thought wryly. Of all the gauche things she could have asked! My girls made teeny oohs and aahs of disappointed sounds although I glared at them. Honest to God, it's at moments like this that I feel like a gamekeeper entrusted with a daffy herd of wild, annoying, but essentially defenseless giant animals, a cross, let's say, between an antelope and a giraffe. When they lope or drift or sway through a group of normal people, taller, in their heels, than all but the tallest men, they belong firmly to a species other than humankind. Aliens among us, they sit differently, as if they have no firm idea of what to do with their excessively long legs; extreme ectomorphs, they nourish themselves by nibbling on green leaves, and, as they were doing now, they communicate among themselves in a soft animal language.

"What do you want them to do then?" Maude persisted. "I heard that you wanted to see how they looked wearing your clothes."

"No, Signora," Marco said, "I need to see how they look wearing anything at all. What they have on their bodies isn't the question, it is how they relate to it."

"Oh?" she said challengingly.

"For example, I will give them my clothes—nothing is more interesting on a woman as a man's clothes—and, if they would be so good, ask them each to put them on and show me what happens." He picked up a tweed jacket and a long grey wool scarf he'd thrown over a chair and handed them to April. As an afterthought, he also gave her the red cardigan he must have worn under his jacket. "Over there's a room you can use to dress in," he said.

"Do you want me to put on everything?" April asked calmly.

"As you wish, *bella*," he answered, smiling at her like an old pal. "There's no way you can go wrong, this is not an examination."

April disappeared behind the door and Marco engaged Mike in a technical discussion about his cameras while I waited, thinking quickly. What Marco was up to was nothing less than a probe into my girls' runway walking ability.

No matter how beautiful a model is in person, only a small percentage of them can work a runway until it squeaks. Fashion shows have become pure spectacle, a combination of theatre and circus, and it takes a very special talent to dominate an audience just by strutting down a runway. The girls have to be as show-stopping as Ethel Merman without singing, as physically electric as Josephine Baker without dancing and as glamorous as Dietrich. And there was only one Dietrich. Great runway models have to be born exhibitionists, without a scrap of stage fright, able to do that crazily sexy shoulder-thrusting, ass-swinging, pelvis-pointed walk in shoes that would kill even me. They have to play to three hundred insane photographers blasting them with a wall of blinding flashbulbs as well as to the couple of thousand fashion professionals who judge the clothes in large part by the conviction with which they are presented.

I sat helplessly, wishing I were in the other room so that I could tell the girls what was up and fix each of them to her best advantage. I felt like three stage mothers rolled into one, and yet, hadn't the girls demonstrated at Necker's that they were astute about showing themselves to their best advantage? My job is supposed to end with the booking, not to carry over into real life, and this was the first time I'd seen models in such an intimately competitive situation, so much more overt than last night's dinner party.

April entered the room. She'd taken the cardigan, slung it around her neck and tied it so that it fell over her left shoulder, like a short cape. She'd chosen to make the advantage of her hair a nonissue, pulling it back and tucking it under the cardigan so that it was all but hidden. Her thumbs were hooked into the top of her ski pants, her pelvis thrust forward and her arms akimbo. She advanced toward us quickly, unsmiling, her chin in the air, not looking at anybody and with no movement at all in her upper body. Her knees crossed each other at every step so that her hips swayed to the maximum. All the street urchin qualities that usually were totally outweighed by her regality, now were magnified and she looked tough and arrogant. April stopped suddenly a few feet away from our group, pivoted on one heel, and paused for one long, tough, don't-mess-with-me minute.

"Hey, now!" Mike said, in what I supposed was a gender-neutral statement approved by the fashion photographers' union, although, in my opinion, his tone of voice constituted sexual harassment. Even his camera seemed to be aroused. April returned the way she'd come, her fine ass swinging like a hooker's. In a second she was back, hair hanging straight down her back, as much a princess as ever.

"I left the sweater in there," she said demurely to Marco.

"*Brava*, April! You have a very bad-girl walk."

"Not always, not unless I think it's appropriate, but something about a man's sweater . . . well, it turns me on. Isn't that strange?" she wondered sweetly.

"No, it's normal," he told her, patting her hand like an uncle. "Now, Jordan, if you would be so kind?" Marco indicated the improvised dressing room and Jordan went toward it with a hint of reluctance. You could tell by her shoulders that she was not used to being the middle child. What difference does birth order make in the success of models, I wondered, not for the first time.

Jordan kept us waiting twice as long as April had. When she reappeared she wore the tweed jacket, belted in tight and wide with the long scarf that she had somehow turned into an obi. The jacket collar was up, her chin was tucked into its shelter and she wore a pair of dark glasses. She walked in a bubble of preoccupation with herself, deliberately and reflectively, looking at the floor, her feet placed perfectly parallel, her hands thrust deeply into the pockets of the jacket, with only the thumbs showing. There was no question in my mind that she was a movie star, thinking her own thoughts and hoping to pass incognito through a crowd that was unable not to stare at her. When Jordan was three feet away from Marco she stopped and took one hand out of a pocket so that she could lower her dark glasses just enough to peer at him from over their rims. She gave him a meltdown, show-stopping smile that said "Watch out, baby, I'll be back for you later," and retired, slouching as she had come.

"*Dio,*" he murmured.

"Yeah!" Mike agreed, odiously, switching cameras.

"Now it's your turn, Tinker," Marco told her. Tinker looked at me and I could see the edge of cold apprehension flickering in her eyes. If only she'd been able to go first, I thought, it wouldn't have been so bad, but after April and Jordan, what was the poor girl going to do for an encore?

It seemed to me that Tinker was taking forever to get ready. I had to stifle an urge to ask if I could go in and see if there was anything wrong. Finally she opened the door of the other room and stepped out and I understood what had taken her so long. She'd been fussing with that damn hair of hers, until it hung down over her shoulders in the kind of careless mess that usually takes an expert to achieve. She'd stripped naked from the waist up, wearing only Marco's scarf, which she'd wrapped twice around her neck, the ends drooping almost halfway down her high-riding breasts.

All well and good, but Tinker was still standing there, her arms hanging limply at her side, her nipples partly covered. *Walk,* for the love of God, I thought, just walk! That's the whole point of this, don't you realize it, not a striptease? Hair can't walk the walk, you idiot! Finally she raised her hands and grasped the ends of the scarf, making fists over each nipple. I took a breath of relief. At least there was something going on in her mind besides playing for shock value.

Tinker approached us, posture unremarkable, projecting absolutely nothing at all except total panic. She had become a pretty enough girl who'd forgotten her sweater. I couldn't believe it. Here was this girl who had more genuine glamour than ninety-nine percent of the models we represent, here was this girl whose potential had hooked Justine and me from the minute we'd looked at her, here was the girl we'd trained for months to move in front of a camera, and she couldn't fucking walk!

Now, at this minute, in Paris no less, in front of an informal group of only six friendly people, she'd frozen, able at best to put one foot in front of another, just barely not stumbling. Tinker was like a zombie when she stopped, looked vacantly over our heads, not making any kind of eye contact or body statement at what was the all-important end of the runway. The only sound was Mike's camera mercifully going nonstop. Finally Tinker managed to turn and make her way, stumbling once, back to the changing room.

The worst of it was that we were all suffering for her. She'd dragged us into her problem and if she did that to us, she'd do it to a larger audience. Whatever she wore would be a disaster, even if it were the best dress in the show.

"I will work with her, Frankie," Marco said quietly to me. "She needs training. Don't worry, I think I can show her what to do."

"Do you have time?" I asked, stunned by his words. I'd expected him to say he simply couldn't use her.

"Nobody has time at this point, but I'll manage, at odd hours. She's a beautiful girl otherwise. She needs more self-confidence, that's all."

"Thank you, Marco," I breathed in disbelief. I couldn't remember when I'd felt so grateful to any man. He was someone special.

As quickly as possible I hustled all the girls into their parkas, said good-bye to Marco and Gabrielle, and led the way back down the stairs. It was icy and dark on the street and I was glad to see the sheltering limos waiting.

"April! *Chérie*, you haven't forgotten?" a male voice called out.

"Tinker, over here!" another shouted.

"Frankie, we're waiting. Come on, we're freezing to death!"

"Jordan, what took so long?" another guy complained at the top of his lungs.

Who were these guys howling familiarly at us from a group of cars and one motorcycle? I stopped dead and glared at them. One of the car doors burst open and three young men rushed across the pavement and laid hands on me. Friendly hands, familiar hands, Bains Douche dancing partner hands. Reflexively I struggled, keeping them from tossing me in the air.

"What are you doing here?" I demanded with as much dignity

as possible. Mike Aaron was watching, shaking his head and grinning in a superior way, like someone watching kittens squirm.

"Frankie! *Ma petite adorable* Frankie, we said we'd do it again tonight."

"You promised! I've been thinking about you all day!"

"Come on, baby, the concierge told us where you were but he didn't say you'd keep us waiting in the cold. Let's go, *mon adorée.*"

"No!" I shouted at the three of them. "Absolutely not! It's impossible."

I didn't remember making a date with these big hulking cute oafs. Well, maybe I might have said something but I didn't mean it, I was just dancing. Carried away. *You know.* Still . . . it might be fun. And it was a sure way to lose another two pounds. Even three.

"Break it up fellas," Mike said, coming over and putting his arm possessively around my shoulders. "This is my wife you're talking to. We're going home to find out just exactly what went on last night, and it better be a good explanation, or she's in *beaucoup* trouble. *Comprendez?* Say, what are your names, guys? Let me see your identification."

My admirers melted away, disappointed but not particularly surprised. It probably happened all the time.

"Come on, sweetie, tell me your side of the story. I'm keeping an open mind about this." Mike was shaking with laughter.

"Thank you, thank you, master, I'm everlastingly in your debt, I couldn't possibly have handled them myself, you great big wonderful man. How can I ever repay you?" I snarled.

"Well you don't have to be snotty. I thought I was doing you a favor."

"Oh, shit, I guess you did think so. Thanks, Aaron, you were sweet to ruin my evening."

"Just exactly who were those crude characters?" Maude asked curiously.

"Old school chums," I said. "They got a date mixed up."

"Well whoever the others are," Maude said thoughtfully. "I hope they bring the girls back safe and sound."

I ran to the limos and looked inside. Nobody. In the melee with my admirers the girls had vanished into the French night with pick-ups from Les Bains Douche, one of them, God help me, on a motorcycle. Mike and Maude were watching me closely. I smiled and shrugged. "How ya gonna keep 'em down on the farm?" I asked as philosophically as possible.

"What do you suppose they're up to?" Maude wondered.

"Dinner in some wonderfully typical, authentic little bistro, maybe a visit to a famous old café on the Left Bank where students their age hang out, lots of good conversation—a really French experience, just what girls their age should have in Paris."

"Yeah, right," Mike said. "Or maybe they can find a bookstore with a poetry reading going on, or listen to some good classical music—even the opera. Or a ballet? Paris is such a cultural feast."

"Who knows?" I answered, too worried to react to him. All I wanted to do was go back to the hotel and drown myself in one of my two bathtubs.

One thing I didn't plan to do was call Justine. I didn't want to alarm her about Tinker's inability to walk. She didn't need to know anything—not one little word—about it until Marco had a chance to coach Tinker and get her over the problem. Nor did Justine ever have to know that the girls were out on their own. *Damn Justine anyway!* I felt a totally justifiable anger.

This was her bloody responsibility, not mine, and *she* should be here, not me. Whose crazy idea had it been to send the girls so early? Hers, only hers. But here I was, put upon by everyone, working like a sheepherder, one person trying to keep track of three girls, pulled in every direction, given an impossible job, having to lie and juggle and worry all on my own, fending off Maude's journalistic instincts and Mike's troublemaking because Justine didn't have the minimum of guts to meet her own father. This whole mess was fucking unfair!

Besides, I was still in the mood to dance, damn it!

10

I had to get you away from the others," Tom Strauss said as he and Tinker sat in the Café Flore, later that night. They were almost alone. The crowds were downstairs, packed into the glassed-in terrace and jamming the first-floor rooms with so much noise and smoke that he hadn't even looked for a table, but had led Tinker immediately up the creaking flight of wooden stairs, to the refuge of a worn leather banquette and a battered table.

"Why?" Tinker asked, looking at him warily. Tom was an American, one of the gang they'd met at Les Bains Douche who'd shown up outside of Lombardi's earlier that night. She had danced with him a lot but there hadn't been more than a moment to talk.

"Because you look so damn sad."

"Do not," Tinker murmured from the depths.

"You're not the same girl as you were last night. At dinner April and Jordan were happy and excited . . . you were way down, even if no one noticed but me. Tinker, please, tell me what's wrong."

"None of your business," she quavered.

"I want it to be my business."

Tinker turned her angelic countenance on him. "Go get stuffed!" she said and burst into tears. Great sobs shook her and she turned into Tom's shoulder to hide her face. He could feel her grief although he couldn't hear it, for she wept silently and bitterly. He put his arm around her quivering back and held her tightly through the mass of her red parka, making little sounds of comfort until she threw off his arm and pulled herself together enough to speak.

"Those bitches . . . such show offs . . . I can't *do* that, I didn't want to, they made me. . . ."

"*Who* made you?" he demanded.

"Everyone!" She was wracked by another huge sob.

"Everyone made you do *what?*"

"Walk," Tinker finally managed to gasp out.

"Walk? I don't get it," Tom Strauss said, totally confused.

"Of course you don't, what could you know about it?"

"Just tell me," he implored her.

"I don't even know you," Tinker wailed.

"Do you have anybody else to talk to?" he persisted.

Tinker snuffled miserably and considered his words. Everyone else she knew in Paris had been there to see her humiliation, everyone but this prying, stubborn guy who was interested enough in her to keep passing her Kleenex, who had been watching her so closely at dinner that he'd noticed her depression, who had been sensitive to the mood she thought she'd hidden so well and who'd realized that Jordan and April were driving her mad with their elated self-satisfaction.

"Oh, all right, since you're so anxious to know," she said grudgingly, through her hiccups. "I had to do my runway walk today, at Lombardi's, in front of everybody, and I proved what a total, absolute, complete loser I was."

"What's a runway walk?"

"Oh . . . it's the special way you wear the clothes, your . . . manner, I guess, the way you project . . . having a walk is like being able to carry a tune. Either you can or you can't. And I can't. Oh, shit, I just *can not!*"

"You mean it's a special talent?"

"No, not that exactly, it's something else, not having a talent but *being a talent*, being somebody special, inside yourself, being able to have fun with it, *playing with it*, oh, you know," she said impatiently, "tweaking it, pushing it, making yourself interesting until everybody who looks at you can't take their eyes away. Some girls have it, others don't. I don't."

"I thought it was enough to be beautiful."

"That shows how much you know," Tinker said, morosely. "All the girls are beautiful, beauty's expected, beauty's the basic alphabet, but the ones who make it to the top know how to put themselves over as personalities. They play themselves, they're famous characters in the whole drama of fashion. People think they actually know something intimate about Naomi and Claudia, they think that Naomi's wonderfully naughty and mischievous and mocking and sophisticated and having a ball with life, but in a fun way, an acceptable way whatever she does, and they think that Claudia must be the purest one of all, an angel, a princess royal, sweet and so basically good, so above the others that she manages to remain utterly virginal in the tiniest bikini—they think she's doing some sort of marvelous favor in actually allowing the crude public to see her solid gold belly button."

"So what the hell would they think you were, chopped liver?" Tom Strauss was impatient. He'd never seen such a truly glorious girl, never expected to see one, and all she did was put herself down, even if she did it in a way that opened his eyes to things he'd never known about.

Tinker sighed deeply, shaking her head slowly to indicate that she was finished with this conversation. She raised her hands to her hair and hid herself in its wings, hunching her shoulders and all but disappearing in its Venetian red cloud. But she'd have to talk to him, Tom decided, he wasn't going to let her sit there and molder away speechlessly in this famous room impregnated with the aura of people who had drunk, smoked and talked to each other within its walls for hundreds of years.

Tom Strauss was not uneasy with words the way painters sometimes are. At nineteen, he'd been lured out of his graphic arts training by an ad agency headhunter, and he'd spent the next eight years working as an art director with a number of highly verbal copy writers, exchanging many more ideas than images. All that time he'd lived frugally and collected an ever-escalating salary, saving most of it, because he was determined to grant himself a couple of sabbatical years in Paris before he was thirty, to find out, once and for all, if he could or could not realize his lifelong dream to be an artist with more than a facile commercial talent.

He looked at Tinker's bent head, her eyes shadowed by her lids, and continued to probe.

"So what you're saying about the walk, is that it's a question of expressing your identity, right?"

"I guess," Tinker muttered, finishing the brandy that was left in her glass. "Just drop it, would you? Please?"

"So what's your identity?"

"What's yours?"

"I asked first," Tom said.

"But I don't want to play this stupid game," she insisted.

"Okay, okay, I'll start. I'm a man, I'm an American, from Chicago, I've been a successful art director in a New York agency, I'm trying to be a painter and I think I might, possibly, have a shot, I'm Jewish but not religious, I'm unmarried but I don't intend to stay that way forever, I have two younger sisters, both still in college, I'm the son of a mother who's a professor of art history and doctor father who . . ."

"Stop! I get the picture," Tinker interrupted. "I'm a girl and I'm pretty."

"That's it? The whole one-line story?"

"Oh, I'm from Tennessee. Maybe," Tinker ventured with her first small smile, turning slightly in his direction, "if I'd been born in Chicago it would count more. Oh, my mother's a nonpracticing Methodist, whatever that is."

"You didn't mention your profession," he said, trying not to reveal how her smile hit him in the stomach. He felt as if he'd been shot out of a cannon into a wildly blue sky with land nowhere in sight. "Doesn't being a model qualify as a piece of your identity?"

"Only if you're more than that, if you've got that thing that makes you special, the thing I explained. And I don't."

Tom Strauss ordered more brandy from a waiter. "I suggest a drink," he said, "while we recover from your temporary identity crisis. It sounds like a basic country music title, 'I Found a Pretty Girl in Tennessee Who Didn't Have No Identity.' There's got to be a verse, in fact, a whole song to go with the title."

Tinker giggled and inspected him closely for the first time. Dancing with him last night, she had noticed that he was taller than she was, which didn't happen every day, but she hadn't really paid him much attention in the crowd. He was not unattractive at close range, she decided. Not bad at all. How come she hadn't noticed before? He seemed so very much at home inside his skin.

With his messed-up dark brown hair that made you want to fix it and his sort of quirky, easy mouth and that lazy grin and good teeth, and the laugh lines that sprouted from the sides of his narrow, long, dark brown eyes, and the absolutely grand way his eyebrows just swung upward and upward, this Tom Strauss person looked . . . smart. As if he thought interesting, funny thoughts when he was alone, things he didn't tell anyone. Something about that suddenly annoyed her. If he had anything interesting to say, she'd like to hear it.

"Let's work on your childhood," he suggested.

"I don't like to think about my childhood," she said, dismissively.

"But there's *identity*," Tom pounced. "An unhappy childhood automatically gives you an identity, it's practically a prerequisite. Why were you unhappy?"

"I didn't say I was unhappy, I said I didn't want to think about it. Oh, I give up, you're looking at a retired beauty pageant queen," Tinker said wryly. "I used to be a star. I reached my peak before I had my first period. Isn't that ridiculous and pathetic? When I was crowned Little Miss Tennessee in the under-three-year-old category it was my seventh pageant and I'd won all of them. Ten years later I had a hundred and sixty trophies and crowns, all won before I was twelve. That and fifty cents will get you a phone call so long as it isn't long distance."

"But that's terrible! You must have been pushed into a kind of pressure and competitiveness before you were ready to handle it, just a little kid—it's obscene."

"I don't necessarily believe that," Tinker said, frowning. "It was the only life I knew. Oh, you can't imagine how *important* it was, how important I felt! I had nothing to compare it to except school, and of course the regular kids didn't like me, how could they have? I thought I didn't care about them because on the circuit I was . . . oh, I was *such* a big winner, so envied, so admired, so petted . . . you can't begin to imagine what it was like."

"Still," Tom said carefully, "it sounds like it's something you were too young to make a judgment about."

"My mother thought the contests were good for me," Tinker said in a soft dreamy voice. "She said they would build my self-confidence. Almost every weekend we were out driving the circuit together, just the two of us. She was divorced and didn't have much of a social life so she had plenty of time to devote to me."

"Hmmm." Tom's tone was neutral and encouraging.

"Even before you get into an actual contest there are dozens and dozens of regional preliminaries," Tinker went on, remembering, "and all sorts of categories to enter . . . Most Beautiful, Most Adorable, Miss Memphis in May, Best-Dressed, Most Photogenic, Universal Charm Queen . . . it never stops. Of course they're all about how you look, not who you are, but you have to behave beautifully. All the contestants wear special, custom-made dresses that cost hundreds of dollars each and the only difference in them is how fancy they get. My mother used to curl my hair and put on my lipstick and rouge and eye makeup, grooming and polishing me . . . I grew up wearing lacy, frilly, fussy pastel dresses with puffed sleeves and so many petticoats under the skirts that sometimes they were wider than I was tall, and hair bows to match each dress. Every week I had a new pair of spotless white shoes with white satin bows on the toes and white ankle socks with ruffles around the tops . . . and I won and won . . . I *reigned* for a decade . . . I was unbeatable . . . a star, a true star."

"And then what happened?" Tom spoke as softly as if he were talking to a sleepwalker.

"Adolescence. I lost it all in less than six months. I'll spare you the details but I turned into an ungodly slob. I couldn't believe it. I . . . I basically ran away. I couldn't face my mother's disappointment with me. I didn't run far, naturally, just to my Aunt Annie and Uncle Charles's. She's my mother's sister and they don't have any kids, so they were happy to have me, repulsive though I was. By that time my mother had started dating again so she didn't mind. On the contrary, she was relieved. Aunt Annie probably saved my life. She taught English and she got me started reading . . . that's almost all I did for the next six years. I read every novel in the library stacks. That and school."

"And then you got your looks back—?"

"My looks, yes, but I still can't walk."

"But you must have had to walk in the pageants," he protested.

"And that's exactly the problem," Tinker said, shaking her head in a rush of animation. "The child's pageant walk is the absolute opposite of a runway walk. I walked like an automaton, a windup toy, a good, good, *good* little girl with the best possible posture, a little princess reviewing the troops. I stood up absolutely stiff and straight, head held high, chin up, eyes straight ahead, and I learned not to swing anything, not even my hair—the judges hate the slightest hint of overt sexuality—Lolita would never make it to the Little Miss Most Adorable Nashville contest. I was a living doll with my arms held out to the side, just so, with my hands barely grazing the frills of my dress so I didn't flutter them, my feet perfectly placed, totally stiff, a smile pasted on my face. A doll, Tom, a doll, not a child, and certainly not a personality. There's no contest for best personality . . . not even a Miss Congeniality. It's *all* about how you look. My training is as deeply ingrained as if I'd been popped into a Russian school for potential Olympic gymnasts all those years, or brought up to be the next Queen of England. Did you ever see a photo of the Queen slumping, no matter what happens to her? I knew Princess Diana was in trouble as soon as she started showing her playful side in public. I'm trying to change, but my body doesn't want to. I think they call it muscle memory."

"You were trained like a show dog!" He quivered with outrage.

"Do you think I don't know that? In my head I understand exactly what the problem is, but you can know something about yourself and still not be able to change it."

"Then why the hell are you beating your head against the wall if you don't think you can do something about it?" Tom pounded his fist on the table in exasperation.

"It's the only thing I know how to do. I have to try now that I have the chance. I want to win again," Tinker said simply.

"Jesus! That's got to be the craziest thing I ever heard!"

"To you, maybe, but I don't feel that way," she said in a voice in which finality rang clearly.

Tom studied her determined expression and fell silent. Tinker didn't think she had an identity but she had a powerful one and she didn't even know it, she wouldn't believe him if he told her, this girl who flat out told him a Gothic horror story about herself without varnish, without self-pity, in an analytical way, not hiding her fears and wounds but not giving in to them, certainly not asking for advice or help. She was strong even if she was absolutely wrong. Even if she didn't have a flirtatious bone in her body. Why should she? A girl who looked like she did never had to flirt with anyone.

"I haven't said a word about this since I came to New York," Tinker said with astonishment in her voice, "except a little bit to Frankie. In fact, I've never talked this much about myself in my whole life, to anybody at all. You know everything there is to know about me now . . . . you must think I'm completely self-centered, with nothing on my mind but a silly runway walk, as if that could possibly be important to you or anyone with any brains—"

"I was drawing you out, didn't you notice? Can't you tell how interested I am?"

"I thought you were just being a good listener, so that you could lull my suspicions," Tinker said, turning to him and unleashing her luminous glance, with the merest hint of the possibility of the chance of a smile at the corner of her lips.

"What kind of suspicions?" he asked, stumbling over the words. Oh, God, he was wrong, she did know how to flirt, Tom thought, feeling sick with swift, undiluted jealousy for every poor sucker she'd ever flirted with—there must be hundreds of them, the miserable, unworthy dickheads whatever she'd said about spending her time reading in a library. She probably didn't even know the Dewey Decimal System. Maybe she'd made up the whole story of her life, maybe she was a psychopathic liar, oh, God, he was going insane, why would she bother to lie to him when whatever she said was fascinating, even the ankle socks?

"The suspicions," Tinker explained, "that would be aroused when you ask me to go to your studio with you and look at your work. Isn't that what artists do? I've read all about it."

"Read about it?" he mumbled, feeling stupid.

"I've never met a real artist before." Now the smile was a reality. Tinker bent her head, took his hand in hers and looked at it carefully. "No paint under the fingernails," she said finally, as if in regret.

"Try my pulse," he suggested, putting two of her fingers on the inside of his wrist.

"What's normal?" Tinker inquired earnestly. "I missed First Aid, I never had time to join the Girl Scouts, not even the Brownies."

"You're utterly useless, aren't you?" He tried to sound indifferent although he could feel his pulse jumping madly under her fingertips and he was short of breath.

"Utterly," Tinker agreed readily. "That's exactly what I've been explaining to you. In a world going rapidly to hell, I have no place, not even on the runway."

"What if I could find a use for you? Would that help?" He listened to his own words in a cloud of shocked disbelief. *He* was flirting and he didn't do that, it wasn't his style, he got flirted *at*, that was the way things had always been in his life.

"Now that's the sort of question that might arouse my suspicions, if I were a suspicious type, but I'm not. I'm gullible, a sitting duck, an innocent, helpless, basically worthless little country girl from Tennessee," Tinker said with rising delight, feeling something she didn't quite understand shift in her inner landscape, lightening the shadows, making the phantoms disappear.

"Ah, shit, you win, just don't stop taking my pulse."

"Win what?" she asked.

"Me. If you want me."

"Well, I don't know about that yet, do I?" she asked reasonably.

"Will you come and look at my pictures?"

"When?"

"Now?"

"That seems to be as good a time as any," Tinker said, trying to keep the surge of eagerness out of her voice.

"Promise me one thing," Tom said, as he paused before turning his key in the lock of his Left Bank studio, on the top floor of an ancient building on an unfashionable street in an unpicturesque neighborhood of the sixth *arrondissement*. "Don't say anything about the pictures. Not a word. I know you're not experienced in making the kind of polite remarks people make when they visit a studio."

"What about impolite remarks?"

"Oh. I hadn't thought of that. Not," he added hastily, "that the pictures are good, just that people have this idea they have to be complimentary, no matter what they really think."

"Come on and open the door. I don't know anything about art, I don't even know what I like, so you have nothing to worry about from me." How come Tom had suddenly become so self-conscious, Tinker wondered. First he wanted her to see his paintings, now he didn't want to know her reaction to them. Were all artists shrinking violets when it came right down to showing their stuff? Were all *people*, even the ones who seemed the most confident, shrinking violets about going public with their personal efforts, even to one other person?

She was busy turning this thought over in her mind when Tom snapped on the lights of a room with flaking plaster walls painted chalk white, a paint-splotched floor, and a pyramid grid of white metal overhead that supported a skylight ceiling. It was a big room, divided into various areas by old, vaguely Art-Deco screens. The largest object in the room was an enormous, sagging old couch draped in a piece of white fabric adorned with a few ancient pillows, around which three space heaters were placed. The couch stood on a ratty-looking Persian rug, and some candles on the floor evidently served as a fireplace equivalent.

"Not exactly cozy," Tinker said with a shiver as all the whiteness popped into view. There must be an easel hidden somewhere behind one of those screens, she thought, and a kitchen and a bathroom of some sort, and even a closet, or didn't artists bother with closets?

"It's perfect," he objected, "perfect. I dreamed of a place like this all of my adult life. I never thought I'd be lucky enough to find it. It gets every bit of available light in a dark city . . . finding it was an incredible stroke of luck. I suppose you're wondering why Paris? Why did I go for that old, outdated, unhip, not-happening cliché of coming to Paris to paint when I could have done it better in New York where the art scene is? But New York is where I had my advertising life and my advertising friends and my advertising success. I had to get out of town, make a clean break, throw myself into another world. For some deep-down reason—probably something I read, maybe *everything* I'd read, it was important to me to live the familiar dream, go the whole way with the experience, not duck it, but buy into the whole banal old-fashioned, outdated romantic fantasy of being a painter in Paris—that way, when I go back, if it doesn't work out for me, at least I'll know that I didn't do it the safe way or halfway—"

"If you want to keep standing here talking, and putting off the inevitable, we might just as well go back to the Flore where it's warmer," Tinker said, laughing at the sight of his feet firmly planted at the entrance to the studio, as if to go in would be dangerous.

"Damn, you're probably freezing. Here I'll go turn on the space heaters," Tom said, finally moving to the couch.

"I just want to look at the pictures and you're stopping me," Tinker said, unzipping her parka. The room wasn't actually ice cold, she decided, it was the effect of that glacial white paint. She crossed the floor and began to inspect paintings that stood propped up against the walls.

"See, what it is," Tom said nervously, "is that I don't believe that there isn't plenty of room to work in the area between pure representation and pure abstraction. Most artists are deconstructing, disassembling, and certainly attempting to find some other way to work than straightforward easel painting, but I don't give a damn what the hell is fashionable at the moment. What I'm trying to do is recapture, well, try anyway, to recapture *memory*, you know, like poetry is supposed to be emotion recollected in tranquility, I try to recapture specific important memories, certain significant moments in my life, recollected in color, in fact—"

"Shut up," Tinker said, "you're confusing me." As she walked slowly, pausing before each painting, she made no judgments or comparisons, for she lacked the background to do so. She simply allowed the paintings to happen to her, she plunged her eyes into each one, reveling in the lushness, the downright unabashed gorgeousness of the colors that spilled down every inch of the canvas as well as over their wide wooden frames that were treated as an essential part of the pictures. The shapes Tom had created were mysteriously both familiar and unfamiliar. There was a singing vibrancy, an almost irresistible allure, an intense sensuous pull to each painting that made Tinker ache to touch them, to dip into them, to run her hands over their seductive, thickly painted surfaces, to find out if these marvelous, happy, dancing colors would come off on her.

"I could eat them," she murmured to herself.

"What?" Tom asked from the doorway, where he seemed to be fastened to the floor.

"An inappropriate remark," Tinker replied.

"What did you say, damn it!"

"I said I could eat them, damn it! Whatever happened to freedom of speech?"

Tom blushed with deep pleasure.

"I know that's not the right thing—" Tinker began.

"It's the perfect thing!" He crossed the room behind her and lifted her mass of hair off the collar of her parka and kissed her lightly just where the short curls of her hairline lay on the tender skin of the nape of her neck. "The *one* perfect thing—there's only one problem," he laughed, pulling briefly on one of the short curls. "How will I paint the memory of this moment without actually painting you?"

"What's stopping you from painting me?" Tinker asked, turning to face him. "Did I say I wouldn't pose?"

"I don't do portraits. I've never painted someone real, some one sitting right in front of me."

"Why not?" she demanded, her hands on her hips.

"Painting a real person involves or at least implies, getting some sort of 'likeness,' and that's a word that's always bothered me," Tom said, standing his ground. "It imposes a limit, with conventional boundaries, it's something with thousands of years of history behind it, it's one of the most ancient forms of art, it goes all the way back to drawing animals and hunters on the walls of caves and making fertility goddesses out of stone."

"If getting a likeness isn't fashionable because it's been done forever, then isn't that a good reason to do another, in your own style? I want you to put me on the wall of your cave," Tinker informed him, with the beat of teasing but real confrontation clear in her voice. "But I don't want you to wait to recollect me, either in tranquility or in hitting yourself on the head, like a total jerk, asking yourself why you let me get away when I was right here inviting you to paint me. I don't want to be a 'significant moment' in your life, dredged up years from now, turned into a bunch of colors."

"Oh."

" 'Oh'? Is that all you have to say?" she challenged him. "You're plenty talkative when you're telling me what you will or won't do in your work, how about a few words like 'yes, thank you' or 'no, thank you' when I make you an offer I wouldn't turn down if I were you."

"What a provoking bitch you've turned out to be!" he said, unable to suppress a laugh. "You come in here announcing that you don't know anything about art, you make a quick judgment about my pictures, and now you want me to change my style at your command."

"So what? It's a free country. Just what are you going to do about it?"

"What do you think?" he asked, taking her by the shoulders of her parka and shaking her slowly, a few inches in each direction. "Do I have a choice? Do I want a choice? I'm going to do exactly what you want me to do." He pulled Tinker into his arms, bent his head and kissed her full on the mouth. "That was the first thing you wanted me to do, wasn't it?"

"Right on," she quavered.

"And the second and the third—" He kissed her over and over again, kiss following kiss until they were trembling against each other, all but holding each other up in the center of the room. "What else," Tom muttered between kisses, "what else do you want me to do?"

Mutely Tinker shook her head, trying to send him a message with her eyes.

"It's up to me now?" he guessed.

She nodded, closing her eyes and holding up her lips again. "I'm shy," she whispered.

"We'll fall down if I kiss you again," Tom said, picking Tinker up and carrying her over to the huge couch, where the space heaters had created a humming oasis of warm air. He put her gently on the couch, with her feet on the floor, and sat down beside her. Tinker's eyes remained closed. "That parka . . ." he said out loud, "gotta lose the parka. . . ." With a certain amount of pulling and tugging and lifting her arms, he managed to divest her of the bulky garment, deadweight though she made herself. She lay back encased in a sweater, ski pants and boots, every inch of her long, graceful shape covered in a tight prison of black wool, stretch fabric and leather. She looked as utterly relaxed as if she were unconscious.

Tom took one of her calves in his hand, and released her heel from the boot with another, gradually easing it off her leg. He did the same to the second boot and slipped off the stirrups that held her ski pants down, so that Tinker's feet were free.

"I don't think I can manage anything more," Tom told her unmoving form, and bent over her and rearranged her on the couch so that she was lying full length. Tom kicked off his shoes, lay down next to her and put Tinker on the curve of his arm, holding her comfortably and securely, lulling her into deeper relaxation with the warmth and stillness of his big body. Motionless, he listened to Tinker breathing, while he inhaled the delicate spicy smell of her hair. A change in the rhythm of her breathing made him aware that from feigning sleep Tinker had actually fallen asleep.

After a few minutes Tom snaked his arm slowly out from under her. He'd never felt more wide awake in his life and her weight, slight though it was, was numbing his arm. Moving silently, he switched off the bright, overhead lights, covered her with the parka, and carefully arranged one of his old sweaters over her feet like a lap rug. Then Tom pulled up a chair, lit all of a group of candles that sat on the floor in saucers, and observed the sleeping girl.

Minutes passed as he looked at her in a way that hadn't been possible while she was awake, and distracting him by the play of her eyes and the range of expressions that passed over her features as she told him what her life had been like. The painter in Tom had a chance now to be as interested in Tinker as was the man.

He observed how rare the color of her hair now looked as it

rose, almost cracking with life, from the fair curve of her forehead, rare and valuable, now a pale coral red he'd only seen before inside certain seashells, a hidden red, delicate and changeable, a red born of the candlelight. Her eyebrows and eyelashes had been drawn by a calligrapher of genius and the curves of her fresh, full mouth were presumptuous and triumphant, even in sleep. There was a fascinating economy to her profile. Each feature, from her rounded chin to her straight nose to the curve of her cheek, seemed to have been sculpted with precisely the necessary amount of bone and flesh, not a tenth of a millimeter too much or too little.

Tom fell into a reverie as the time passed. This time, this hour he was spending next to Tinker as she slept, was a moment he would paint one day, he knew that already. Paint over and over. Hidden in the furniture was how he would re-create it, how he would find the way to capture the surprising, unnameable surge of emotion he felt sitting by candlelight in this white studio, guarding this precious, majestic, sleeping girl, only half-revealed in the candlelight. Now all he knew was that every moment, every detail, was important, from the hum of the heaters to the shadows her lashes made on Tinker's cheeks. A likeness . . . no, his paintings wouldn't be a likeness, they would be far more, at least to him.

What Tinker looked like was only part of the spirit of magic that had fallen over him. He wanted to give her something, wanted to more and more with each passing minute. He felt deeply connected to her in a way he couldn't logically understand or put exactly into words. She had such suddenness to her, like a bottle of just-opened champagne, she imposed an answering suddenness in him. Perhaps it had been because he'd been able to imagine her so clearly as an exquisite little girl, leading a life of an awfulness she hadn't understood and might never understand. Perhaps it had been the straightforward way she told him about herself, perhaps her impudent, artless personality and her ignorance of its charm, perhaps the almost childlike wonder of her kisses, the scent of her hair, even the strong shape of her shoulders under his hands.

Suddenly he stood up and soundlessly made his way to the cupboard where he kept his supplies of paint. He found a pad of white paper and a thick, soft pencil and brought them back to the chair. It was only a party trick, he thought, something he'd been able to do from an early age, a facile talent he'd never honored, but she'd wanted a likeness and that, at least, he would give her. He worked swiftly and surely, sketching Tinker's head and as much of her shoulders as he could see before the bulk of the parka covered her. When he'd finished the sketch he looked at it and shook his head. Yes, it was exactly like Tinker, the essence of Tinker, it could not be a sketch of any other human on earth, yet how many other artists could do the same? Or better, perhaps, with a camera? But there was something he could add that a camera couldn't, Tom realized, and he drew a large heart around the entire sketch. It was five or six weeks early, but why the hell not? "For my Valentine," he inscribed under the heart, and he was about to sign his name when he found that he wanted, desperately wanted, to add more words. "I love you," he wrote.

"I'll be damned," he said out loud in sheer surprise. "Where did *that* come from?" Tom Strauss stood up and began to pace around his studio. In this familiar, beloved, safe space he felt as unanchored as a ship tossing on a heavy sea, a ship suddenly set adrift. *"Where* did that come from?" he repeated to himself as he walked. Finally he stopped and stood clutching a window frame, gazing out of the window at the chimney pots of Paris, half-visible in the light of the moon. His heart steadied. *He meant it, wherever it came from*, he realized. Wherever it led him, he'd follow. Too overcome by emotion to even think of sleep, yet so surprised that he didn't know what else to do, he went over to the couch where Tinker slept and lay down on the rug as close to the couch as possible, looking up through the grid of the skylight at the new horizon that had opened to him.

"Why are you smiling to yourself?" Tinker asked.

"I—I didn't hear you wake up."

"How long have I been asleep?"

"I'm not sure, maybe an hour, maybe more," he said, sitting up on the floor.

"Thank you for covering me up," Tinker said, emerging from the parka and stretching lazily. "It must have been jet lag."

"How do you feel?" he asked anxiously.

"As if I've been asleep for days. Born this instant, like a chick right out of the egg."

"You mean you don't remember anything?"

"Hmmm . . . no," she said in judicious wonder. "Dear me . . . goodness, gracious . . . . I just remember looking at your pictures, and then, after that . . . it's all a blank. Say, who took my boots off?"

"The Tooth Fairy," Tom said. He sat down on the couch, scooped her into his arms and kissed her. "Does that bring back anything?"

"I'm not sure . . . barely . . . just a little." She seemed doubtful.

"Do you like it?" he asked and kissed her again, beginning to quiver. He should never have let her go to sleep, he thought, never have let her out of his arms, her emotions weren't involved like his. And yet, if she hadn't slept, would he have understood so quickly how he felt about her?

"Like it? Oh, yes," Tinker answered. "I like it fine."

"Are you still shy?"

"Ummm," Tinker growled in disbelief, "did I actually say that?"

"Don't you remember *anything?*"

"Well . . . maybe . . . I can't really say for sure." She gave him a small, infinitely provocative smile, signaling that she was prepared to toy with him until she wearied of the game. She was falling back on flirtation, reaching automatically for a technique that had worked in the past, Tom thought, but he wouldn't let her. He believed in her shyness and he knew that only shock therapy could drive it away.

"I made something for you," Tom told Tinker, pulling away purposefully and reaching down for the sketch pad he'd left on the rug. "It's a likeness," he said, giving it to her and holding up a candle so that she could see it clearly.

"Oh," said Tinker, in surprise. Then, she bent her head so that she could read his words in the candlelight. "Oh," she said again, in a changed voice, a tiny flame of a voice, an incandescent voice. "Do you mean it, Tom?"

"Yes, God help me."

Tinker sat silently a moment, her head still bent, while he held his breath. Finally he put the candle and the sketch pad back on the rug and with his finger, lifted her chin and tilted her head toward him. His heart lurched when he saw the tears welling in her eyes.

"I know you're shy, but help me out here," Tom said. "Is this good news?"

Tinker nodded slightly and the trembling tears escaped her eyes and started down her cheeks.

"Do you like me?" he asked her. First she shook her head and then nodded vigorously. "You don't *just* like me, you like me a lot?" he interpreted. She nodded even more fiercely. "You might . . . possibly . . . love me?" he asked so softly that if she didn't want to answer she could pretend she hadn't heard. Tinker forced herself to look him in the eyes and inclined her head in a tiny, single inclination of her head, a mute but unmistakable avowal. Then, galvanized, she threw her arms around his neck with all her strength and pulled him down so that they lay sprawled in a tumble. She scrambled on top of him and kissed Tom vehemently all over his face and his neck. "Here and here and here," she said voraciously, made suddenly savage by the need to imprint every available inch of him with her lips, until he started to laugh because she was tickling his ears and her elbows were sticking into his chest.

"Hold off," he gasped, catching her hands in his. "Where do we go from here? Please, Tinker, darling Tinker, *talk* to me. I know you can, when you're in the mood, you've talked before."

"Where would you normally go?" she asked.

"There's nothing normal about this. I've just fallen in love for the first time in my life."

"Me too."

"You finally said it," he cried in jubilation.

"No, I didn't."

"You just this second said you were in love with me," Tom insisted.

"No I didn't. You jumped to a conclusion. I, Tinker Grant, am in love with you, Tom Strauss. *Now* I've said it. Ouff . . . I feel better now."

"Say it again!"

"Make me," she challenged him.

"Oh, you're asking for it, you know that, don't you?"

"Is that a threat? Or a promise?" she crooned.

"Oh, Tinker, you're going to drive me mad, aren't you?"

"Time will tell," she answered, pulling off her sweater. "Time will soon tell," she repeated, as she slithered out of her ski pants and lay smiling in all her supremely young and tender beauty on the white couch.

Holding his breath, Tom touched his fingertip to the faint rose of one nipple and felt it rise immediately. Mad, utterly mad, he thought to himself as he threw off his clothes. She would make him mad and she would make him whole and she would be everything in the world to him.

11

"Frankie is in a rage," April confided to Maude Callender when they encountered each other at the lobby newsstand. "Just because Tinker didn't sleep here last night she's acting like it's my fault—since when I am supposed to be in charge of bed check?"

"When did you see Tinker last?" Maude asked with interest.

"Last night at dinner. Then she took off alone with one of the guys and Jordan and I went to another club and danced for a few hours. Now Jordan's gone off too and I've been left on my lonesome. Frankie's dragging me to the Louvre after lunch, she says we haven't been exposed to any French culture yet. Exposed! She sounds like my grandmother with Beethoven when I was twelve. She didn't want to listen when I told her there must be more fun things to do in Paris than look at a lot of pictures. Frankie's turned into a tyrant, and I'm her only target."

"Come have lunch with me instead," Maude suggested. "I'll show you the real Paris, or a small slice of it, anyway. I've lived here on and off for years and it's taken that long to scratch the surface of this city. You'd be surprised how little time I've spent in the Louvre."

"Thanks, Maude, you're the answer to a prayer. I'll leave Frankie a message. Meet you down here in five minutes, okay?"

"Perfect." And it was perfect, Maude thought. She'd almost despaired of getting one of the girls alone without their omnipresent minder, Miss Severino. The first rule of any interviewer's working life is "get rid of the minder." It doesn't matter if the minder is an official PR rep, a designated chaperone or an amateur friend, sister or mother, even a child. The presence of any third person changes the dynamics of an interview. The interviewer can't ask questions as freely and the person being interviewed never responds as openly. The official interview atmosphere never progresses into a free-wheeling conversation. Both parties consciously or unconsciously censor themselves even if all the minder does is sit in a corner, eyes downcast, pretending to read a magazine.

And it was ideal that April was the first model to escape Frankie's supervision, Maude thought. She had picked April for the winner of the Lombardi contract from the start, she'd been rooting for her from the moment they'd all met at the airport. April simply outclassed either of the others. April had deep, *deep* class, she personified the kind of beauty that was internationally recognized as the outer sign of breeding, quality and social standing.

Maude Callender came from an old Rhode Island family, rich in civic background and philanthropic tradition as well as in worldly possessions. Her private income was more than enough for her to live on handsomely; her work gave her that necessary position on the ladder of fame that is essential for any single woman who intends to be part of the New York City social world. Maude had always quietly maintained her belief in the importance of class, that politically incorrect concept she subversively upheld in today's world. It would be an interesting challenge, she thought, to find out more about April. The girl's bone structure was responsible for the regal look that was her second nature, but it told her no more about April's inner life than what you could guess about Garbo from seeing her in the movies.

She would give the girl a glimpse of the Left Bank, Maude decided. All any of the girls had seen so far had been a few places devoted to retail luxury, this overblown hotel and those clubs they went to. No, Frankie would have nothing to bitch about, try though she would.

In less than a half hour Maude and April were settled snugly in a tiny, cozy Russian restaurant, La Chaika, hidden on the Rue de l'Abbé de l'Epée, a tiny winding street deep in the Left Bank. Maude threw her dark green double-breasted coachman's coat, with its rows of polished buttons, high collar and wide swinging skirt, over an empty chair. She wore a suit of black broadcloth, its tightly fitted jacket worn over a green brocade waistcoat which provided a rich background for the starched ruffles of her white cotton shirt with its high-tied ascot. Her short blond hair was brushed forward in shaggy bangs that reached all the way to her eyebrows, and she looked like a wise, witty and wealthy don at Oxford sometime in the early nineteenth century. Only the way her gold watch chain stretched over her swelling breasts, and the eye makeup she used so cleverly, indicated that she was a woman and a most appealing woman at that. April sat tall and grave in her pale pink cashmere sweater, her single string of pearls her only ornament, her hair slipping straight forward over her breasts like twin scarves of gold silk. Exquisitely proper and perfectly groomed, she looked as if she were bursting with a grievance.

"What's going on?" Maude asked mildly.

"It's so unfair!" April exploded. "I didn't say before where Jordan was but she's with Necker, can you believe it? He called her this morning and invited her to visit Versailles. Only her! Just because she knows something about French furniture she gets a beautiful opportunity to work her way into Necker's good graces . . . that's favoritism if I ever saw it." Her powerful anger was only slightly mingled with relief at being able to speak her mind.

"That shouldn't affect your chances unless this whole contract contest is a charade, and I don't see how it could be considering the trouble they've gone to and money they're spending," Maude assured her.

"How can you possibly say that? Necker owns the House of Lombardi. All he has to do is give Jordan thumbs up."

"That won't happen because you're the best for the job, April," Maude said calmly and with utter sincerity. "You're absolutely and clearly outstanding. I've told Mike that I'm concentrating heavily on you in my article—you're going to be the star of my piece—and I warned him that he'd better have great single shots of you to go with the article. That's one of the points of having my job. I get to shape the material from my personal point of view—it's not true that a picture is worth a thousand words, you know, not when the writer is calling the tune."

"The best! Oh, Maude, thank you! I only wish I thought you were right."

How naively American April's voice was, Maude thought, so uninflected, so little-girl, high and sweet, almost like the voice of a choir boy.

"I know I'm right," she told April. "I was there yesterday and I watched the way you showed that sweater, remember? Jordan didn't have half your zip, her walk wasn't sexy at all, and poor Tinker was a hopeless nonstarter. It's lucky I bumped into you today—you can fill me in on your background while we're here. Is this food all right for you?"

"Oh, it's great, it's so . . . bohemian? I didn't know they had Russian places in Paris. I've never had two kinds of herring in dill before. I'm trying to save room for the chicken pie I ordered."

"I'll be sure to make a point of your hearty appetite," Maude said, laughing at the wholehearted way April ate. She'd been right about the Chaika, it was like a little nest, with its feminine, comforting atmosphere. She'd always found it a good place to talk, without hovering waiters.

"I'm lucky about calories, I can eat just about anything, but the food I grew up on was so basically boring that this is an adventure."

"Tell me a little bit about the Nyquist family, April. What does your father do?"

"My dad? He's a sweetie, a banker, but his work is basically boring too. My mother is the perennial golf champion of the local country club and she's involved with Planned Parenthood and some local charities. Of course we all ski and sail and play tennis . . . the usual, you know. They're great parents," April said, dismissing them.

"Brothers and sisters?"

"One of each, both terrific. Yawn, right? I wish I could be more exotic but we're a typical upper-middle-class family according to my sociology textbook. It may be an endangered species but that doesn't mean it's thrilling. It certainly won't give you anything to write about."

"Yet your parents let you go to New York to model. Isn't that unusual?"

"Ha! They couldn't even *try* to stop me. Naturally they would have preferred that I go to college but I've been modeling locally for years, earning pretty good money. They *had* to accept the fact that once I was eighteen I'd try for the big time."

Maude was fascinated at the way April's face changed when she imagined her parents' opposition. There was passion there, and contained power and a ferocity that turned the rather aloof impassivity she normally projected into the raw material of high drama.

"Were you always the most beautiful girl in school?" Maude asked, suddenly blunt.

"Well. . . ."

"April, this isn't a test of your modesty. I'm interested in the forces that formed you."

"I guess I always knew I was . . . oh, Lord, I hate to say 'beautiful' but I want to make something of myself and I can't *not* know about my looks. I'm terribly ambitious, Maude, even if I try hard not to give that impression. I want to get *somewhere!* I want to be *somebody!*''

"Don't we all? I know exactly how you feel."

"What kills me is that I don't get as much work as lots of other girls who aren't as good-looking as I am," April brooded. "Not by objective standards anyway. It's a problem of range. I'm no chameleon like Tinker who can look any way she wants by lifting an eyebrow. At least that's what Justine and Frankie have analyzed as my problem. What can you do if you don't fit into any look but your own?"

"Maybe you shouldn't look at it in a negative way, but as a challenge. Frankly I wonder why you haven't tried to experiment with your look, bend it in other directions—makeup and clothes can do just about anything you want them to, after all. You can't change your body type or bone structure, April, but that's just about all you can't change . . . I'm beginning to wonder if Loring Model Management is really the right agency for you, not that I know that much about the business. But maybe, just maybe they haven't tried hard enough, maybe they've settled for your strong primary look without developing all your other possibilities. Did you ever think of that?"

"But they've been so wonderful to me!" April protested, shocked. "I was thrilled when Justine signed me."

"Wonderful isn't always the best thing for a career. Still, I could be wrong," Maude said, shrugging. "Tell me, why do you think that Gabrielle d'Angelle picked you for the contest if you have such a small range?"

"On, no question about it, my runway walk, my secret weapon. There's a nice little contrast going with the boringly pure way I look and the way I swing my hips . . . I'm lucky I can pull that off."

"April, yesterday, when you hid your hair, what made you decide to do that?"

"I felt I had to try something a little different. Sometimes I just *can't stand* being so conventional-looking. Usually I use my Nordic blond thing to the max since it's my strong point, but every once in a while the devil gets into me. You know a model called Kristen McMenamy? No? Well she's this powerful, weird-looking girl with strong features, almost like a great-looking guy. She wasn't getting anywhere until she shaved her eyebrows off completely and started wearing bizarre white makeup and changed her attitude to a tough 'fuck-you and the horse you rode in on' look—she became an overnight sensation. Nobody's ever seen her smile. Now she's a supermodel—she's invented a whole new kind of beauty—and everybody fights over her for runway. Big deal, she's androgynous! Not only that, she's married and has a kid. How am I going to compete with that?"

"Why would you want to look so strange?" Maude asked, fascinated with April's knowing self-analysis that must be based on years and years of looking at magazines and comparing herself to the girls in the fashion photos.

"Because I'm cursed with an *expected* look, the all-American-girl sort of Ralph Lauren look, which is fine if Polo is all you want out of life. It's hideously boring! I look cold, I look like an ice maiden, and, what's worse than cold, Maude, I'm *uncool*. Do you know what that means? Today it's like the kiss of death. I haven't got a speck of funk! Kate Moss in those Obsession ads? Now that's funk. She gets out of bed naked, undoubtedly with a vile hangover and bad breath, she yawns, ugh!, her boyfriend shoots a candid and she becomes an immediate funk princess. Worse, she cleans up beautifully so she can do great runway stuff, glamour cover shots and the Calvin Klein all-American girl thing too. She damn near convinces you that she's an American blue blood instead of a too-short English girl with dishwater-brown hair." The bitter envy in April's voice rang out clearly.

"April, it's not just about funk or unconventionality," Maude protested. "That's *your* obsession, kiddo. You analyze your looks like an outsider and yet you end up underrating their value, in the insecure way only a professional beauty can. I've never known one who wasn't down on herself, who wouldn't pick out her only flaw and magnify it. You've gotten into the habit of seeing yourself in terms of the competition, instead of giving yourself the credit for being *unique*. You're a rare and special type, and you will be for the entire rest of your life. You've got true *classic* beauty to fall back on, you'll have it when Kristen McMenamy is forgotten, when Kate Moss isn't hot any longer, you're an American Catherine Deneuve, for heaven's sake."

"I'm not even sure who she is," April said, brightening at Maude's assessment. It wasn't as if Maude hadn't been around.

"She's the greatest film star in France and has been practically forever, the whole country worships her, she's Yves Saint-Laurent's friend and years ago she used to be what they call his 'muse,' his inspiration—you must know what she looks like."

"Oh, of course I know," April said. "I missed *Indochine*, but I saw the ads . . . please, let's not talk about my looks anymore, Maude. I've gone on too much about them."

"Done." Maude looked around the restaurant. April was obviously completely unaware of the other customers who had been darting fascinated looks at her since she sat down. The girl was so used to homage, Maude thought, that it had long ago become invisible, as normal a climate as air.

"Tell me about boyfriends," she said, as the fastest possible change of subject.

"That's my second least favorite thing to talk about." April made an apologetic grimace. "But I knew you'd have to ask."

"How so? Men must be falling all over you."

April smiled her wide, unexpectedly off-center smile. Maude

was so much more fun than she'd ever expected her to be. There was nothing intimidating about her when she was one-on-one, and the knowledge that she was going to be the focus of the *Zing* article was such a totally unexpected and thrilling piece of news that April had to prevent herself from thinking about it until she was alone.

Right now she was having too much fun talking grown-up girlfriend talk the way she couldn't with Jordan or Tinker because she didn't want them to know much about her. The three of them had been thrown together in an artificial way, and they had all realized it was good to keep up the impression of buddy-buddy giggling girlfriends, but down deep she couldn't trust them and they couldn't trust her because they each wanted the Lombardi contract and only one of them would win it.

"If I say something's 'off the record' will you keep it that way," April asked warily, "or is that just an expression you hear in movies that isn't true in real life?"

"Anything off the record remains absolutely secret, strictly between us," Maude told April honestly. She hadn't reached her position in magazine journalism by trashing or betraying her subjects. People would talk to her who refused to be interviewed by those writers who trafficked in the rape-and-pillage articles so many publications had demanded for years.

"Remember the other day when you were asking if we were virgins and Frankie butted in and stopped us? Well . . . I would never have admitted this in front of the others anyway, because they'd have laughed. I look uncool enough as it is, so at least I want them to think I have a sex life. But—oh, you might as well know since I've told you this much, and it's off the record. I don't."

"You mean you don't have a sex life at the moment?" Maude asked carefully.

"No, that would be like lots of girls in the business. I'd just be looking for the right guy. I mean . . . I've never had one," April said slowly.

"Well, you're so young. . . ." Maude ventured, seeing the pain and confusion on April's face.

"That has nothing to do with it. I'm almost twenty, more than plenty old enough. It's something else and it's something I don't understand. I like men well enough as people but I don't feel attracted to them, you know, physically. Maybe I've dated the wrong guys, but if I give one of them as much as a single good-night kiss, and there's no way to get out of *that*, they're all over me! It's disgusting. I listen to my friends talk and you'd think that boys . . . men, whatever you want to call them, are the most thrilling, desirable creatures in the world. I don't *get* it! I've never gotten it!"

"Have you ever given one of them a real chance?"

"A couple," April admitted, shaking her head at the memories. "I forced myself. I let them—oh, you might as well know, I *almost* let them make love to me but I couldn't go through with it. They promised to use condoms as if the only possible reason I wouldn't want to was fear of getting pregnant or HIV—I couldn't tell them that the reason I made them stop midway was I couldn't stand the thought of the whole . . . messy . . . thing. Oh, if only I hadn't even tried! They were so horrible about it afterward. I guess I can't blame them. Cock tease was the least they called me but, damn it, I hadn't *planned* to be a cock tease, I just thought I had to give it a chance and maybe I'd get turned on, like everybody else, but I didn't and I couldn't."

"So you've never . . . ."

"No. And I don't want to! I don't care if that's not normal, that's the way I am. Of course people expect that one day I'll get married just like everybody else. My mother's probably got the wedding planned already, but I can't see it ever happening. Thank God I'm still young and they haven't put any pressure on. But you've never married, have you, Maude? How did you manage that?"

"I let nature take its course. If you wait them out, people eventually accept you as an unmarried woman and deal with it. Of course it's easier if you're not a raving beauty."

"Now you're the one who's being fake modest," April teased, suddenly very much at ease, now that she'd told her secret and Maude hadn't seemed surprised or shocked. "You have such a great look! It's different, it's stunning, it's terrifically becoming and it's all your own. I wish I had the guts to dress like you."

"You never know. You might surprise yourself."

Yes, thought Maude, you might surprise both of us. She'd set out to learn more about April and she'd succeeded brilliantly, she congratulated herself, while she tried, and failed, to beat to the back of her brain the intoxicating knowledge that every one of the women she'd loved deeply had been a minor approximation of April's type. Not one of them had been the true, pure thing. Not one of them had been April.

12

Jacques Necker and Jordan Dancer strolled through the gardens of the Petit Trianon, from which the Château de Versailles was invisible. The winter sun was high in a cloudless pale sky, and it was warm enough for Jordan to throw back the hood of her long red coat.

"This is my favorite place of all," Necker said, "because it's so lacking in pomp. That lovely little pavilion over there, the Belvedere, is where Marie Antoinette was sitting when a pageboy came running to warn her that the Parisians were marching on the palace. It was the last happy moment of her life. She never saw these gardens again. Today it seems impossible that it happened over two hundred years ago."

Jordan stopped on the path and listened to the sounds of birds in the bare trees. In the distance gardeners worked quietly, preparing the ground for spring planting. "It's so quiet," she answered, "it's almost unearthly, especially after Paris . . . I feel as if I've stepped into Marie Antoinette's world. It makes me shiver—I guess it's because we know how it ended. But tell me," she asked, puzzled, "why didn't we visit the Château de Versailles itself? I thought that's where we were headed when you phoned this morning."

Jordan's puzzlement went much further than that particular question, she thought as she asked it. She could hardly tell this all-powerful businessman that after she'd received his invitation to Versailles she'd spent an anxious hour wondering about it, or indeed that she was still of two minds about the wisdom of having accepted. She'd been trying to make a major impression on Jacques Necker from the beginning but all she'd wanted was to stand out and win the contract. He was enormously attractive, no question about that, but the last thing she wanted to do was get involved with him. Nothing would be more unbusinesslike. If, God forbid, this outing was going to lead up to his making a pass at her, it would be deeply embarrassing to them both. Yet how could she have refused his invitation?

"To me the gardens are the essence of Versailles," Necker said. "The château itself is monumentally sad and empty. There's no life there, in spite of the grandeur. After the Revolution the furnishings were confiscated and sent far and wide, the tapestries and pictures ended up in a museum, and whatever little is there now is an attempt at restoration. If there are ghosts, and I firmly believe there are," Necker said slowly, "they're here, in the gardens, not in those vast, echoing staircases and corridors."

"Are we ghost hunting," Jordan asked, "or are you a nostalgic royalist? Would you like to see the monarchy restored? Are you one of the people who support the Pretender to the throne of France, with all those happily married children that make every other reigning royal family look pathetic?"

"Where on earth do you get this arcane information?" Necker smiled at Jordan with amusement. Her short curls were tumbled by a slight breeze and all the pale sunlight in the sky of the Ile-de-France seemed to be trapped in a frame around her warmly glowing face. Against the intricate background of bare branches Jordan looked as if she could start a fire by just standing in one place and twirling.

"Mostly from *Hello!*," she answered, "an English magazine where they cover the European royalty beat very seriously. It's fun to look at the pictures and decide that the Queen of England should have her hairdresser shot at dawn or that the new queen of Belgium should burn her entire wardrobe. But I don't just criticize, I'm also a groupie—my pet is Lady Sarah Armstrong-Jones, Princess Margaret's daughter, who wore floppy pants to a royal wedding and stole the show. Ah, me, it's all fairy-tale time."

"Do you have a taste for fairy tales?" Necker asked as he thought that this expedition was almost as painful as it was pleasurable. He should have been here with Justine, watching her walking in this well-loved place, he should be asking Justine these questions, he should be getting to know his daughter instead of this nice young creature whose background was as strange to him as his must be to her. Still, a daughter substitute was better than nothing at all in his present state of misery, and she was the only one of the girls who had any interest in French history.

"Beats reality, nine times out of ten."

"Let's sit down on that bench for a minute," Necker suggested. "Are you going to be warm enough? It's fairly sheltered here."

"Even if I weren't, I'm ready to sit," Jordan answered, glad to stop walking. Necker didn't realize what a brisk pace he set. "I bet the ladies of the court got all the exercise they needed just jogging from one place to another . . . how did they ever have the strength to change their clothes five or six times a day, to say nothing of dancing and flirting and playing cards and social climbing?"

"Probably because they were so competitive with each other they didn't dare slow down."

"Sounds a little like my work," Jordan laughed. "Except for the flirting and the cards and the social climbing."

"Tell me something about Justine Loring," Necker asked, abruptly, unable to hold back another instant. "Is she a good person to work for?"

"I think she's the absolute best," Jordan replied. "It's really a shame she got sick and didn't come, I know you'd have liked her. Still, we're in good hands with Frankie."

"Why do you say she's the best?" he persisted. "What makes her that?"

"I trust her totally, she never gets flustered, clients can't intimidate her and she doesn't play favorites. She's a strong, committed advocate for her girls."

"Do you think she's a happy woman, Jordan? Do you get the feeling that she's fulfilled in her life, or that there's something missing for her? I mean as a human being?"

"I can't possibly answer that," Jordan said, surprised at the tenor of his questions. "Justine doesn't let us in on her emotions, Monsieur Necker, she's not into her personal drama, she's essentially a reserved woman. She's deeply interested in each one of us but she doesn't give us any reason to gossip about her."

"Why did you say you trust her?" he asked sharply. "What's she ever done in particular to make you feel that way?"

"Trust's a funny thing, some people inspire it and some don't. I'm not saying I'm an infallible judge of character. Justine has one of the best reputations in the business, but that's really all I can tell you about her for sure. Frankie's her best friend, so if you want to know more about Justine's private life, she's the one you should be asking."

"I like to know as much as I can about the people I do business with," Necker told her, responding to the faint question in her voice. "It can be helpful in many ways."

"Well there is one other thing that means a hell of a lot to me —Justine will suggest that clients see me even when they haven't specifically requested 'a woman of color'—that's the preferred expression they use these days. Most other agencies will tell you that the clients have to ask for you in so many words before they'll send you anywhere, but Justine is trying to get me every break she can."

"A 'woman of color'?—I hadn't heard anything after 'African-American.' I thought that was the final official word on the subject."

"I'll bet there's never going to be a final agreement on that. People are going to be struggling forever how to say *it* without giving offense to one person or another."

"Forgive me," Necker said hastily, "I didn't mean to pry. It's just that for a Swiss, well, of course we have the Italian and the German and the French Swiss, but—"

"But you're all white. Lucky little Switzerland."

"I'm sorry, I've offended you."

"No way!" Jordan protested, smiling at his typical reaction. "It happens to be one subject I have plenty to say about and I've almost never found a white person who feels comfortable talking about it with me."

"I'm comfortable, and I'm interested."

Jordan scrutinized Necker and found a frank and direct curiosity in his eyes, the kind of curiosity most people who felt it would politely hide. She realized that she now felt secure with him. Nothing he'd said indicated a sexual interest in her. His air of command didn't disconcert her, nor his habit of asking questions and expecting answers. She respected this man and trusted him enough now to be open and take him at his word.

"Now take 'Black' for instance," Jordan said, "—sometimes used without a capital B—lots of people, like me, continue to insist that they're black Americans, not African-Americans, because they're so culturally distant from Africa, their ancestors have lived so many generations in the United States, *way* longer than most other Americans, that they can't feel emotionally African. On the other hand, I'm not black *enough* for a lot of my fellow black Americans."

"Now I'm totally confused."

"No more than I am. The other day I was reading an English magazine targeted at black women and it said that and I quote, there were about 'thirty-three different shades of black skin, from the palest ivory to the blue-black.' The mind reels! Who was appointed to count those thirty-three different shades and how *on earth* did they do it? Then, in the same magazine, they have a story about Roshumba, who's a top black model and they call her a 'Real Sister' because she sports a very short Afro and because she has a fairly negative attitude about some of the black models who've told her that they'd agree to have long straight hair or a nose job to get on the cover of *Vogue*. As if a white model wouldn't be willing to do the same thing without feeling disloyal to the Scotch or the Italian in her. Probably without meaning to, I think Roshumba— which means 'beautiful' in Swahili, no less—has set herself up as a high priestess of being *righteously* black. She hasn't had to compromise personally, she's gorgeous just as she is with three *Sports Illustrated* swimsuit issues to prove it. So now, as if it isn't tough enough I have to contend with being considered less-than-righteously black—not a 'real' sister!"

"Can't you be—oh, maple syrup or apple cider or very foamy cappuccino or tea with milk or a dry sherry or—"

"I take it that's Swiss humor, Monsieur Necker? At least you didn't say milk chocolate." Jordan shook her head at him with a dance of mischief in her eyes. "Now you've got me doing it—a fine single-malt Scotch with lots of cream in it comes pretty close, wouldn't you say, although a single-malt-Scotch drinker would never put even an ice cube in the stuff."

"I meant that question," Necker protested. "Don't evade it."

"The answer is that it's a waste of time to worry about your particular slot on the color chart, because you can't do anything about it. However, even if I try not to worry, I'm totally *conscious* of it. You'd think that just being black was enough to have on your plate, but no, the shade of your skin does matter enormously." Jordan was trying to be as precise as she would be with her father, since she knew that nothing less would satisfy Necker.

"Why is that? Is lighter always considered better?"

"It's not just that simple," Jordan continued, picking her words carefully, "although of course it's *never* forgotten and generally speaking, lighter is considered more desirable, particularly in a woman. But, Monsieur Necker, it's not just the reaction of white people, but the way other black people feel that matters. Blacks as well as whites are in the business of making these distinctions. I know damn well that when a black woman looks at me she wonders who my parents' mothers and their grandmothers and their great-grandmothers slept with, to end up with a descendant with my particular assortment of what are considered nonblack features. The base line is that how I look indicates how much white blood I have. It's always about race, Monsieur Necker. When another black person really scrutinizes me I know all my ancestors are being judged. And it's not as if I didn't ask myself the same questions. Who *were* those white ancestors? Did they love my black ancestors or only use them? I must have an immensely complicated family tree I'll never know anything about . . . it's sad and frustrating and infuriating."

"I had no idea. . . ."

"Most people don't," Jordan said. "I didn't know I was going to make such a speech."

"Now tell me something about your parents," Necker asked, "tell me about how you grew up."

"My father's a career military man, Colonel Henry Dancer. He was a brilliant West Point graduate who realized that he'd found a home in the Army, so long as he followed all the rules. He's tough, authoritarian and totally career-minded. He insisted that I graduate from college before he'd allow me to work—that's why I'm twenty-two—and then he checked Loring Model Management out thoroughly and grilled Justine for two hours before he'd let me sign with them. He doesn't like my being a model. I was brought up to be decorative and educated and a credit to the family. My mother's main passion is her own ambition for him; she sees him as a future general and she's probably right. Today she's the colonel's lady and one day she'll be the general's lady—she'd like me to have the same structured, safe life of a military wife—I get the creeps at the thought."

"What would be so terrible about it?"

"Ah, you Swiss! I want options, not an insurance policy. I've lived on eight different Army posts and I know the drill, I know how to charm the wife of the commandant of any post and I don't want to ever have to do that again!"

"You find it demeaning?"

"More boring than demeaning. It's all about authority and pleasing people who have it. If I were to marry the kind of promising black officer my parents would approve of, all my friends would be the wives of other officers of his rank. We'd move up the ladder together for the rest of our lives, trading dinner parties and recipes, unless one of the husbands was promoted above the others, or left behind, and then that wife would have to make all new friends. Can you imagine that?"

"It sounds incredibly constricting. Even for a Swiss." Necker laughed at her seriousness.

"Being black is more than constricting enough. My roommate at college was a terrific girl named Sharon Cohen. We used to talk for hours about being Jewish and being black. She said that just once she'd like to see what it was like to be introduced as Jordan Dancer, to see how people would relate to her if they didn't know, the minute they heard her name, that she was Jewish. I told Sharon I'd like to live inside her skin for a week and find out what it was like not to be put into a definite category the split second I walked into a room, long *before* I was introduced! That was one argument Sharon didn't win!"

"What kind of social life do you have?" Necker probed soberly.

"In college I only dated black guys, frankly it made life easier. I didn't have to be on guard all the time in a dorm atmosphere where everyone knew everyone's business. Now that I'm out of school I can date pretty much whoever I want to. That's not the problem. The real question is what will I do when I get older, when my modeling career, whatever it turns out to be, is over? I have to plan for that *now*," Jordan said fiercely, "not in six or seven years from now."

"Isn't that true for every model, black or white?"

"Sure it is, but most of them assume that something good will turn up. White girls have the luxury of easy expectations, they've had that all of their lives. But I don't dare to think that way. To get anywhere in this business I have to be so much *better* than a white girl because there are hundreds of places for them and only a few for me. I have to be special beyond special to *begin* to qualify, and I have to accept that fact and absolutely *not* let it eat at me because no one wants a black model who makes them feel self-conscious about the whole race thing. I have to seem to *not know* I'm black, so they can relax about it and feel comfortable with me."

"That must be incredibly complicated."

"It is," Jordan said ruefully, "trust me on that."

"Have you made plans for your future?"

"Not seriously, although I know I should. Do I try to lay the foundations for a business of my own? As an example, take Iman, Monsieur Necker. She worked for twenty years and now she's starting a cosmetic business. She's a legend, she's married to David Bowie, at thirty-nine she still gets forty thousand dollars to do a single runway show and if Iman's on the runway you might as well forget about the other girls. Now there's a black woman who has it all, but she's unique, one in a billion, a goddess from Nairobi. Do I dare to hope to start my own business too or do I take the easier road and look for a husband? Do I turn seriously stupid and marry a rock star or an actor or a sports hero and discover that the marriage doesn't last because those marriages usually don't? Or do I marry a black millionaire, marry for money and position in the black upper class?"

"Have you ruled out the idea that you might simply meet someone average, some nice guy who isn't a celebrity or a millionaire and marry him and lead an ordinary life?" Necker asked, his eyes twinkling at the serious way Jordan had assessed her marital possibilities.

"Sure, that could happen," Jordan said gravely, "but I don't think I'd be satisfied with it for long. You don't really get it, do you? You still don't realize how *incredibly* lucky I've been, how rare a bird I am to have been given a huge package of advantages—family, education, looks—every last one of the things most black girls can't even dream of! I've been specially blessed and I admit it's spoiled me, it's opened my eyes to possibilities beyond an average life. Everyone I know has expectations that I'll make something of myself, become more than a housewife and mother. *And so do I!* Do you think I can drift along heedlessly, hooking up with the first vaguely suitable man who comes along, or even worse, maybe falling in love with a white guy and creating nothing but problems, for him and for me?"

"Why are you so sure of that?"

"Because everyone's a racist somewhere inside," she answered in a matter-of-fact voice.

"Jordan, do you truly believe what you've just said?"

"Damn right I do. I'm a racist too, damn it! I have hateful feelings about rednecks and Puerto Rican gangs and black gangs and the kind of white groupies who get hysterically excited around black jocks, so if I have these feelings, how many times worse would it be if I married into some white family and became my mother-in-law's worst nightmare?"

"Could you be exaggerating? Wouldn't people simply have to see past the color of your skin after they got to know you?"

" 'After' . . . maybe. I'd like to think so—I know Sharon did, and lots of my other friends at college, and some of the girls I work with, but we aren't marrying each other's brothers."

"Wouldn't your looks, Jordan, help to get you over the hump of the racial thing?"

"Ha! You've *got* to be kidding! I didn't think even a Swiss could ask a question like that. I'd never expect looks to count for a second. You don't understand how sensitive the whole thing is without adding interracial marriage to the pot. Just in daily life in New York there are plenty of other beautiful black girls around. I'm not instantly recognizable, not yet. I'm no Naomi Campbell or Tyra Banks or Veronica Webb—no, make that *only* Naomi, she's the only black model everybody, more or less, knows by sight—so

I'm very careful about things you'd never think about. I don't like surprises."

"What exactly do you mean?" Necker frowned in incomprehension.

"At college, for instance, I didn't join a sorority . . . I didn't want to be one of the few token blacks in a white sorority or limit myself to a black sorority, so I concentrated on the things I could do well without joining one group or another."

"Do you think you might be oversensitive?"

"Probably," Jordan shrugged, "but it simplifies things. For instance, in New York I only go to places where they know me or where I have the right introduction. For example I'd never go to a strange hairdresser without someone who knows the owner or operators there. I'd never go shopping in a good store without a white girlfriend. If I'm taken to a fine restaurant by a white friend it's okay, but I wouldn't let a black guy make a reservation and show up with me unless he knew the headwaiter and had been there before. You look stunned, Monsieur Necker."

"I am."

"It isn't your problem. But it does me good to talk about it, especially to someone who listens as hard as you do. I've answered a lot of questions this morning, I've told you a lot of things I never dreamed I could discuss with you, because you were so interested. What I still don't understand is *why*? Why do you care? I'm one of the three models in competition for a contract with your company, is that the reason?"

"No it isn't."

"I didn't think so somehow . . . well . . . what is the reason?"

"I was just thinking . . . if I had a daughter . . . if she had an entire life I didn't know anything about . . . I'd want to know everything about her, what her problems were, what she hoped for, what her deepest thoughts were about . . . it's genuine curiosity, not idle curiosity."

"But you don't have a daughter?"

"My wife and I never had children. . . ."

"I'm sorry," Jordan said.

"So am I. Deeply. I'm not like your father who's more interested in boys than in girls. If I'd had my choice of just one child I know I'd have wanted a daughter above all, a daughter I could have made sure was . . . happy and safe."

"Well, if you did have one, she'd tell you she was hungry," Jordan laughed, puzzled by the look of loss in his eyes.

"So am I," he said, getting up suddenly. "Let's go back to the car. There's an excellent place to eat in the town of Versailles. And I know the owner."

"Hey, in France I feel right at home. Maybe I'm a reincarnation of Josephine Baker."

"I rather doubt it. You're not nearly black enough," Jacques Necker said with a grin.

"Details, details."

13

I'd already had breakfast when this fax was delivered to my room.

Assume you know that all New York is paralyzed by storm.
Tried to phone several times but you were always out having
fun. Lucky lucky you enjoying yourself like mad in gay Paree
while I freeze. Don't try to call me, I'm staying with friends
because of unspeakable furnace problems at home. Office
closed for duration, photo shoots canceled, flights canceled,
people staying home until emergency over. Envy you in nice
warm hotel. Hope girls are learning fast and giving no
trouble. As for you, try to behave yourself no matter what the
provocation.

Love and kisses, Justine.

Behave *myself!* Tinker had disappeared with some unknown
guy, April had been spirited away by Maude, Necker had designs
on Jordan, and that untrustworthy bitch, Justine, tells *me* to behave
myself?

Even worse, Justine had put herself beyond my wrath. How
come she hadn't told me which of her friends she was staying with?
I knew them all and I could reach any of them, as she damn well
realized. And so what if the city was paralyzed, you don't just close
down an office! I'd decided not to phone her anyway, but there
should be a way to communicate with her in case of an emergency.

What had happened to Justine's common sense? She'd cut me
adrift just when my worries about Tinker had more than doubled.
Two days off the plane and she'd already spent last night with a

stranger. This, friends, was not happy news, especially in view of how vulnerable she'd been after the fiasco at Lombardi's yesterday. What kind of thug had taken advantage of her? The stage-door Johnnies who lie in wait for models are beyond slime. And there wasn't even anybody to ask since the other girls had slipped the leash too.

I was crumpling the fax in my hand and cursing to myself when I bumped into Mike Aaron in the lobby.

"Ah ha! There you are, Frankie. Listen, things can't go on like this!" He grabbed me by the arm so that I had to stop and listen to his beef.

"Good morning, Mike, is something bothering you?" I asked blandly. As I see it, I'm the anointed grown-up in our little group, I supervise the homeroom, I'm the one who cleans the erasers, I can't act like a kid too. "Rise above it" is my motto when I'm in public.

"Have you looked outside today?" he asked furiously.

"Yeah, why?"

"The light is extraordinary! This may never happen again while we're here, given the kind of weather Paris usually has. There's going to be ideal light all afternoon for me to shoot the girls on the streets discovering the city—and I can't dig up one of them, much less three and *three* is the story. I can't even find Maude. What the hell is going on?"

"They've run amuck, whatever that means. You saw what happened last night."

"I thought you were in charge," he said accusingly.

"So did I. Apparently fate had other plans."

One thing I wasn't going to do was cover up for Mike Aaron and pretend I knew where the girls were. I was keeping enough secrets as it was. If he couldn't get pictures of them in the sun he could get them in the driving sleet or down in a coal mine, as far as I cared. *Zing's* problems weren't my problems.

"What kind of chaperone are you?" he said, looking at me accusingly.

"A total failure." I threw up my hands in a gesture refusing to be conscience-stricken. "Chaperoning was never a primary career move for me in the first place. I don't have the basic training for keeping tabs on three healthy but not necessarily obedient young animals."

"This whole thing is like working with a film company on location," Mike said in high irritation. "Take actors off a set, transport them away from home, put them in a hotel and they behave as if their normal lives don't exist, as if nothing they do has any consequences. Once they don't have to sleep in their own beds, no holds are barred—the bastards turn into wild animals roving the range. It's an attack of mass hysteria, focused on the genitals."

"But even wild animals, unlike models, behave in predictable ways," I added helpfully. "And a nice peaceful range isn't Paris. Well, I guess they'll show up before the Lombardi show even if worst comes to worst." I took a perverse pleasure in painting things in their darkest colors, in seeming not to care what had happened to my charges. Insouciant was the operative word here. "Chaperone" is a title I particularly dislike.

"Oh, fuck it!" he said in disgust, giving up on the subject. "Want to grab some lunch?"

"I wouldn't mind. Here or somewhere else?"

"I've got to get out of this hotel or I'll suffocate. Let's go for a walk and get a sandwich or something. Maybe we can get into the Louvre for an hour. Might as well do *something* useful." He looked utterly disgruntled.

"Swell. I was actually planning to take April to the Louvre today."

"This is probably my twentieth trip to Paris and I've never been there yet . . . something else always come up."

"I'll go get my coat and meet you back here."

"Wear comfortable shoes," he said gloomily.

On the way back to my suite I considered the enormous gallantry of his grudging invitation. Lunch with me was obviously the booby prize of Mike Aaron's wasted day. I didn't even know why I'd accepted except that I had nothing better to do. I went to the closet to find my coat and unexpectedly met my eyes in the mirror. *Oh, balls!* Who was I kidding? I was as excited as if I were back in high school, I looked as brimful of expectancy as if I were waiting for my first prom date.

I looked at myself in horror. Horror mixed with a kind of thrill. A thrill mixed with a kind of defiance. I was sick and tired of being cast in the character of reliable Frankie-the-twenty-seven-year-old-duenna, something Justine had lumbered me with only a few days ago, thank you very much. Give a dog a name . . . it wasn't fair!

It certainly wasn't the bad-tempered, bad-mannered Mike Aaron of today who got to me, it was the memory of the kid I'd been who would have given anything to take a walk in Paris with the Mike Aaron of her fourteenth year, that much I was certain of. Ah, give yourself a break, I thought. How often does one get to realize an old fantasy, even when it's been long burnt out? Go *for* *it!*

Quickly I stripped off my clothes and homed in on the Donna Karan black cashmere sweater worn with her black stretch pants, a combination that guaranteed lithesomeness, if there is such a word. It looked a little severe, I thought, studying the result. Almost too thin, if there is such a concept. I needed to balance all that seamless stretch of enticing, classic black with hair. And, thank you Lord! Only yesterday I'd washed my hair and braided it damp so I could pin it up out of the way.

I pulled out the tortoiseshell pins that held up my topknot and brushed my hair out as quickly as I could considering how thick it was, all in ripples from being braided.

Oh, most definitely, yes! Maybe Justine was right about my hair, maybe I had been neglecting a natural asset. What's more, this was a look Martha Graham herself wouldn't have disapproved of. She'd been known to use her hair in her dances as if it were a fifth limb. My long camel's hair coat with the red shearling lining, worn swinging open, its belt dangling, a red cashmere muffler flung around my neck, the ends trailing down my back, and my favorite, well-polished, low-heeled black boots that reached to my knees, completed the outfit. The beauty part was that although the finished effect was intensely dramatic, there was nothing flashy or dressy or come-hither about the whole getup, even though I'd spent another ten minutes on my eye makeup. I looked like a dangerous highwaywoman on a supreme hair day, yet all I'd done was dress sensibly for a walk and a sandwich.

I stepped out of the elevator and walked right up to Mike. I vamped a wicked little rumba hip movement ever so slightly as I walked, a maneuvre no one but a brilliantly suspicious dance teacher could have noticed. He didn't recognize me. "Ready to go?" I asked.

"Frankie?"

"Sorry it took so long. Gabrielle was on the phone and I had to lie a lot."

"Frankie!"

I looked at him with a hint of lofty amusement, as if he were a younger brother. "Forget something?"

"Huh?" His expression was startled to the core.

Really, men are inarticulate, poor things.

"I asked if you'd forgotten anything," I said patiently, pulling on my gloves and smoothing the fingers as meticulously as Marlene Dietrich ever had in any of her movies.

"No. I—never mind." As we walked out of the hotel I had the strong impression that unless I was totally mistaken—and I'm not in the habit of making certain basic errors—I had rid myself of that chaperone tag for once and for all. Even if you give a dog a bad name, every dog has her day, and today was mine.

"Which way?" Mike asked, gesturing up and down the avenue.

"Let's nip down the Rue Byard and go straight to the river," I suggested. "It's a good shortcut, I'm in a mood to walk by the Seine."

"You seem to know Paris pretty well."

"I used to come here a lot with my first husband," I lied exquisitely, walking briskly, which is almost impossible when you're hearing a waltz in your head. Ever see anybody march in three-quarter time? It can't be done, but Paris brought out my inner waltz. Could it be a Zen thing?

"First husband?" he asked curiously. "Anybody I know?"

"Slim Kelly."

"The sportswriter?" he asked, incredulous and impressed.

Now why is it that men react that way? Status by insemination? Do men have any idea how gross their thought processes are? I could have been married to Ted Koppel and they wouldn't have as much respect as they did for that riffraff, that cur, Slim, a living legend, as he had rarely failed to remind me.

"Yep."

"If Slim Kelly was your first husband, who was your second?"

"I haven't met him yet. But I've only been divorced a little over a year, it stands to reason that there'll be a second."

"And a third?"

"Time will tell," I flung over my shoulder as I zoomed up the Cours Albert Premier, headed for the Place de la Concorde.

"Jesus, Frankie, do you have to walk so fast?" Mike complained.

"You said you were suffocating in the hotel. I thought you needed a brisk head-clearing walk."

"I didn't say I wanted to *run* past the most exciting view in the world."

"Whatever you say," I slowed down. "You may be a little out of shape."

He glared at me, or at least he started to glare at me, but the combination of my hair and my superior grin—did I forget to say that my teeth are as great for teeth as my feet are for feet?—stopped him in mid-glare.

"Don't start with me," was all he said. We continued to walk upriver, while on the other side of the stone quay the Seine, powerful and determined, made its way toward the channel. Across the river lay one of the great Parisian perspectives, punctuated by the Eiffel Tower. The parade of classic buildings, one more beautiful than the next, all of them low and many shades of ancient grey, was dominated as in no other city I've ever known, by a great, blowing freedom of sky. I had the same carefree feeling here as I had walking on the boardwalk in Coney Island, although here I traded the sweep of white sand and the ocean beyond for architecture. Fair enough, so long as I didn't have to choose between them, I thought, as I hit my stride and walked on getting into a zone of pure pleasure.

"Aren't you hungry yet?" Mike asked.

I stopped and looked around. On the other side of the street was the bird market, just ahead of us was the Ile de la Cité and the towers of Notre-Dame. That meant that somehow we'd managed to walk right *past* the Louvre, which is like overlooking the Pentagon.

"I could become hungry, now that you mention it. Funny, the last thing I think of in Paris is food."

"So I've noticed. If you don't watch out, you'll get as skinny as the girls."

"What's wrong with that?"

"I'll tell you, if you'll just stop this marathon. There's a place to eat across the street and that's where we're going."

"Whatever you say . . . big . . . guy."

"Watch it!"

"Touchy, aren't you?"

"Just hungry."

We settled down in a glassed-in terrace of a tiny sidewalk restaurant called Le Bistroquet. I looked at the eloquent menu of hearty country fare.

"They don't seem to have heard of sandwiches here," I said.

"That was just a figure of speech."

"Like 'zaftig'?" I asked, studying the menu.

"I knew it! That's why you're so snippy, isn't it? Come on, admit it, you've never forgiven me for calling you 'zaftig.' Frankie, that was a compliment!"

"Not where I come from, airball."

"Zaftig—voluptuous, yummy, good in the hands, something to grab onto on a cold and stormy night, sexy, fuckable, for Christ's sake. *Fuckable!*"

"Stop screaming."

"Didn't I just say you'd better not get too skinny?" He pounded on the table. "I meant it, damn it! I married a model once, nobody wore clothes better than she did, but Jesus, there was no comfort factor there, no room for cuddling, not with those elbows. Her hip bones were like swords, her pelvis could give you a serious bruise in a delicate place, and there was no joy at her bosom—it was before implants."

"So why did you marry her?"

"Damned if I know. In bed she was like a praying mantis made out of iron, a very temporary turn-on. I was just a kid and it seemed like a good idea at the time."

"Yeah, yeah, yeah. I'll bet anything your second wife was another skinny model. Photographers never learn."

"I never married again."

"Smart move." Break my heart, he didn't.

"So do you agree to forget about my calling you . . . zaftig?"

"You remind me of Slim Kelly. He used to call a pizza a 'Guinea Pie' and he insisted that I shouldn't get upset because when he was a kid, Guinea Pie was shorthand for the best food in the world. He just wouldn't understand that I objected to the expression on principle."

"I promise never to say 'zaftig' again. If."

"If?"

"You never say 'airball' again."

"Oh, Mike, I'm so sorry! I didn't realize that *bothered* you. It's ancient history, after all. Dearie me, I didn't mean to be tactless."

"Look, Frankie," he said, gritting his teeth, "there's an airball in every shooter's life. Bill Bradley says that the hardest thing he's ever had to do in his life was to forget missing the last shot in the 1971 Eastern Conference finals because for the next *twenty* years cabdrivers reminded him of it. That's United States *Senator* Bill Bradley!"

"Are you trying to tell me that nobody's perfect?" I asked incredulously.

"You *are* an interesting bitch, aren't you?"

"I was wondering if you'd ever notice. Schnoz and all."

"Ah, shit!"

"I forgive you, I forgive you," I said hastily, laughing helplessly at the expression on his face. My laugh told him how okay it was. "I can't listen to another apology and another explanation of how aristocratic my nose is. For the record, I have always adored my nose and fully understood its natural distinction. Got that, Mike?"

"Sometimes I sound like a gold-plated asshole," he muttered.

"Elegantly put. Shall we order?"

There's a funny kind of moment that happens when two people who've had a background of mutual put-downs decide to declare a truce. It's an awkward and silent moment while both of them wonder what they're going to talk about from now on, since they've abandoned the mutual hostility that fueled their relationship.

Mike and I buried ourselves in the menus, frowning dramatically, miming the difficulty of choosing among so many possibilities, pondering the potential of the Bistroquet's kitchen as if we were two restaurant critics.

"Have you any ideas?" he asked finally.

"I thought, maybe, the stew?"

"Which stew?"

"That's the problem, there seem to be three of them. Do you have a clue?" I asked.

"A steak and French fries, can't go wrong."

"Same for me, but no fries."

"Just a steak on a plate?"

"With some . . . green beans?"

"You've got it." He ordered in the kind of French we'd both learned at Lincoln.

"Wine?" he asked.

"Yes, please, a glass of red," I answered. I never drink at lunch, but what the hell.

After the waiter filled our glasses, he held his up. "Here's to playing hooky," he said, gesturing out at the busy street just beyond the glass of the terrace. "If you're going to do it, this is the place."

"Is it ever," I agreed fervently.

"Did you ever actually play hooky?" he asked after we'd clinked our glasses.

"Once, but I told my mother in advance so she wouldn't worry if the school called to find out what had happened to me."

"You must have been one reckless, rebellious kid."

"Yeah." I giggled at the idea. "In my next life I'm coming back as Madonna. But in this one I was a pussy cat, a good little modern dancer pussy cat."

"So what happened? How come you're not still dancing?"

"In my third year at Juilliard I had a really bad fall and

wrecked my knees beyond repair. You can dance with bleeding feet but not with bad knees."

"Basketball either. When they go, it's over."

"Is that why you're not a professional player?"

"God, that is so sweet!"

"No, I'm serious, I'm not trying to make a crack."

"I know you're not, that's what's sweet about it. Listen, Frankie, I hate to disillusion you, but I was a high school hero, that's all. There are maybe a quarter of a million high school players as good as I was in the country at any given time. About fifty thousand of them go on to play college ball. Then, out of those fifty thousand, only fifty get into the NBA lottery each year. Fifty rookies, that's all, get picked by any professional team out of a quarter of a million high school hot shots. And out of that fifty, you may find a couple of dozen guys who are never heard of again and a half dozen who become starters one day. That's how hard it is."

"It's almost as bad as the odds of becoming a top model."

"I never thought of it that way."

"Does that give you more respect for them?"

"I guess it should," he said thoughtfully. "But great athletic skill still seems more . . . meaningful . . . than looking good in front of a camera."

"Forget meaningful, think of the sheer determination required to get to the top."

"I guess you're right. It's just that models never seem to be doing necessary work."

"Mike, that's not fair. Top models lead fiercely competitive professional lives for which, I admit, they're overpraised, overindulged and overpaid. But, while that's happening, they make an essential contribution to a huge industry and they turn it into one compelling, exciting show—like fireworks—for the world, and when it's over for them, it's over awfully fast and unless they've invested their money wisely, all they have are their scrapbooks. Like basketball players. Think of Claudia Schiffer as the female equivalent of Shaquille O'Neal."

"Whew! I'm glad Bill Bradley made it in politics."

"Me too."

"Do you want cheese or dessert?"

"No thanks, I'd like to wander around a few more hours before the sun starts to set."

And wander we did, along the river which, with its fourteen major bridges, will always be the most beautiful street of the two-thousand-year-old city. Whenever we were half-tempted to venture into one of the side streets the Seine lured us back, exercising that hypnotic fascination that is irresistible not only to tourists but to people who have lived in Paris all their lives.

We didn't buy anything except a couple of cups of coffee, we didn't go into a single historical building, we didn't enter a gallery or browse in the open-air bookstalls or look at anything more significant than the window of a birdseed store, we talked a lot of nonsense and sometimes a little sense and at the end of the afternoon, when the sun set, I had the notion that we had become something close to friends.

"It's getting cold," Mike said. "Let's get a cab and go back to the hotel for a drink. Maybe there'll be a message for you there from the missing person bureau."

"Hooky's over," I sighed. "But it's been a wonderful day."

"One of the very best," he agreed. It seemed to me that he sighed too, but I could be wrong. Which would amaze me.

When we walked through the revolving door into the brightness of the Relais Plaza, filled with its usual elegant crowd, sitting at a table near the bar were Tinker, April, Jordan and Maude.

"Well, there you are!" April called accusingly.

"About time you showed up," Maude frowned at Mike.

"And just where have you two been?" Jordan asked, indignantly.

Tinker had the native wit to squeal, "Frankie, fabulous hair!"

I looked at Mike and he looked at me.

"We went to the Louvre, of course," he said.

"And I didn't notice any of you there," I added severely.

Yes, I think I could say that we had made friends.

14

Justine took a deep, listening breath as she paused in the hall corridor in front of the closed door that led to Loring Model Management. Inside she heard the unmistakable sound of a large group of models, a high-pitched babble, punctuated by outbursts of semi-scandalized shrieks and thoroughly wicked laughter. They couldn't be allowed to see her like this, she realized in a sudden panic, and dug in the pocket of her coat for her old knit cap. Although it was warmish in the hall she tugged the cap down as far as it would go and still give her a minimum of visibility. She pulled her hair around her cheeks, raised the collar of her white coat and wound a white muffler around her face so that only the tip of her nose was visible. Thus disguised, almost indistinguishable against the white walls of the agency, she slipped into the reception room and skirted the furniture until, unnoticed by anyone, she slid quickly into the refuge of her own office. She breathed a sigh of relief as she reached safety and locked the door behind her.

She knew what she looked like. Lips puffed and swollen, cheeks and chin covered with whisker burn, eyes languid and almost unfocused, with circles under them from lack of sleep, tangled hair that had only been towel dried, since Aiden didn't have a blow-dryer. She looked utterly fucked-out, completely, thoroughly fucked, up, down and sideways. It felt one hell of a lot better than it looked. They'd never tried to make the Knicks game, they'd never changed the sheets, much less made the bed, they'd barely stopped to eat and she'd resented the showers they eventually staggered into together because soap dissipated the way Aiden smelled.

Stop it this minute, Justine told herself firmly, as she tried to make repairs with the cosmetics in her desk drawer. Nothing worked. She took one of the iced bottles of champagne from the bar, where it was always kept ready for celebrations, and rolled it around on her flaming cheeks, knowing that only a good night's sleep alone in her own bed would begin to help. And she didn't want to sleep alone in her bed. *Stop it!* Justine buzzed her secretary.

"Phyllis, good morning."

"Oh! I didn't see you, Justine. I'll be right in."

"No, stay out there and hold the fort. Just slide the faxes from Frankie under the door."

"There aren't any, Justine. I just checked the machine."

"But that's impossible!"

"I couldn't understand it either. They've been gone four days. I called the phone company to see if there was anything wrong on the lines from Paris to here, but everything's normal. Do you want me to phone her at the hotel?"

"No, not yet. I'll tell you when. Anything else I should know about?"

"Another call from Dart Benedict wanting to make a lunch date."

"Ignore him. Listen, Phyllis, unless it's an emergency, just take messages for me. I have a lot of stuff to catch up on in here, and since nobody's up to speed yet, this gives me some necessary time." Even without the evidence of her face, Justine thought, she'd never be able to explain her outfit to Phyllis. Pink tights and a Giants sweater weren't her normal agency-head garb. She'd have to rush home at lunchtime and change.

"Will do, Justine."

The city was slowly digging itself out of the blizzard but most of the side streets were still impassable. However, the noisy chatter outside her door was loud enough to indicate that every model who hadn't been paid last Friday had managed to show up for her check, mobbing the bookkeepers' office, clutching the book of vouchers that would indicate exactly how long she had worked, for whom and at what rate. This weekly rite was usually spread over a period of hours late on Friday, but last week most of the girls had gone directly home to escape the storm and today was a holiday for them since the photographers' studios were only now beginning to attempt to function.

Damn! It was, as Frankie would put it, a snatch convention out there. One of the chief Catch-22's of the agency business was that the more successful she was—the more bookings her girls had, and the higher their rates—the more she stretched her already frighteningly large line of credit. She could never, never, *never* relax about her credit, Justine brooded. She tended it as carefully as a prematurely born baby who was the only heir to a throne; kept it constantly warm, free from the slightest contagion and religiously fed on time. Loring Model Management, like all other agencies, paid their girls weekly, but collected far more slowly from their clients. However, every ninety days there was that huge note due to be paid, and recently everyone's clients had been holding on to their money longer than they ever had since she'd started in the business. It was something to be concerned about. But not until tomorrow.

On the other hand, Justine thought, wandering over to the window, the fact that the girls had made it through the snowdrifts, like huskies bounding for the Pole, was a good sign of their mental and physical health. The moment that it was time to become seriously worried about a model was if she *didn't* come in to get paid.

For certain girls who were halfway—or more—to becoming problems, payday was the only fixed point in a week that was a dizzy, high-thrill, addictive confusion of work, attention, flattery, free clothes, parties, gossip, sex and drugs. Or maybe, if she were halfway smart, just too much to drink instead of drugs. But when a girl forgot payday, it was the equivalent of a fire alarm, a hundred times more dangerous than a dozen hangovers, any amount of weight gain, an inexplicable refusal to go on location, bookings canceled at the last minute, weeping on the set or even a black eye or a missing tooth. Forgetting payday usually meant cocaine. Or, in the last year, heroin.

There was so little she could do about it, Justine admitted with a feeling of rage and frustration that never grew less. All the lectures and horrible examples in the world could no more protect a girl from choosing a sadistic, tormenting boyfriend than they could stop her from taking drugs, if that was the direction she was destined to take. Even if they were in high school or college, in 1994 all teenagers were, to some degree, in harm's way.

What was making her think such gloomy thoughts on a morning after the most wonderful weekend of her life, Justine wondered. Maybe it was a natural letdown from too much happiness, maybe it was some sort of hormonal revenge, but now, back in her sanctum, instead of basking in memories of the weekend, a free-floating bad mood had abruptly descended on her. Justine probed her feelings and decided that she felt an impression that something was infuriatingly *missing*, something she couldn't exactly put her finger on, but connected with Frankie. The feeling was mostly anger rather than worry. Was it Frankie's inexplicable lack of communication or merely her physical absence? The office simply didn't feel right without her gay profusion of emotions. Frankie had a basically upbeat take on the modeling profession. In spite of any evidence to the contrary, she still saw every new girl as an exciting challenge, rich in potential, a Cinderella story asking to happen, a marvelous opportunity for a girl who hadn't known it was there for her. But then Frankie had only been in the business a mere seven years, compared to her own seventeen, eight of them as a working model, nine running Loring Model Management. Frankie hadn't seen as many girls self-destruct.

Could she possibly be suffering from burnout, Justine wondered? Was that the reason that whenever she signed a promising teenager her heart constricted as she asked herself where that girl would be in ten years? Was burnout the reason she could barely bring herself to read the beauty pages of fashion magazines with their maddening reversals of position: one season touting the pale-lipped, big-eyed vamp, the next the strapping German blond, quickly followed by the glamorous brunette bombshell, soon overshadowed by the all-American freckle-face until the frantic editors, desperately trying to keep the readers' attention, came around to insisting that *the* new look and *only* look was that of yet another version of the vamp, this one red lipped, with damaged hair and eyes that had seen too much?

What normal woman, in the name of God, would pay good

money every month to have it rubbed in her face how far short she fell of a ridiculous, impossible, manufactured ideal that was constantly *changing*? What kind of collective insanity allowed the magazine editors to get away with the manipulative crap they wrote to sell cosmetics and clothes? And it wasn't just an American phenomenon, there were some *thirty* fashion magazines published by the supposedly sensible French.

Wouldn't it feel wonderful to turn her back on it all and let it slip away, Justine asked herself? Wouldn't it be bliss to refuse to spend another hour judging the chances of a young hopeful, to throw every bloody awful fashion magazine into the wastepaper basket—not even glancing at the cover, lest she be entrapped in spite of herself—to pack up and move to New Zealand, apparently a place in which you could immerse yourself in a more sensible and placid past, something that resembled a better version of the 1950s? She'd never buy new clothes again. She had enough for an Auckland lifetime. Her only makeup would be sunblock and sheer lip gloss. She wouldn't even watch Elsa Klensch on CNN, Justine promised herself. She'd sell the agency and put the money into a good old-fashioned New Zealand bank and retire to the wonderfully green countryside where she'd . . . she'd . . . raise sheep. . . .

Justine flung herself on the couch, shaking her head at her ridiculous fantasy. She'd seen sheep shearing in a movie once and it didn't look like her idea of fun any more than it had looked like the sheep's. She was in a weird mood, for sure, but New Zealand wasn't in her future.

Was it Aiden? Was it because all the world, for almost three days, had been framed by one man and one cat in a secluded forest of peace and passionate discovery? She'd been all but physically unable to leave the apartment this morning. Aiden had literally been obliged to drag her out of bed . . . just because he had to go fix her furnace. Couldn't it have waited? Aiden—Justine was conscious of her mind scurrying over the weekend, trying to find how it fit into a list of possibilities, when it was light years beyond whatever was nagging at her. Whatever Aiden was going to mean to her, whatever he meant already—and she wasn't about to try and deal with *that*—he wasn't the kind of problem that would drive her to buy a ticket for Auckland.

Did her mood have to do with the basic nature of the agency business? Had the weekend, which had removed her totally from her daily preoccupations, shone a new spotlight on the aspects of sleaze and pimping that some people thought modeling was all about? Sometimes she felt that she'd never be thought of as representing and protecting talent, or as providing girls vital direction in managing their career—there was always an undertone of, "yes, but what else do they have to do to make good?"

Justine tightened her lips in a familiar irritation. She knew that she ran as straight and shipshape an agency as there could be in a business based on renting women. At least she was a woman too and sexuality never determined a girl's chances with her. Almost every one of the traditional abuses in the modeling industry stemmed from men owning agencies. Obviously no heterosexual male should be allowed to have such power over females.

Yes, she mused, there ought to be a law about men in the agency business . . . yet, how could there be a law that said that beautiful girls were prohibited from selling their images? A law that said that businesses were forbidden to use those images to attract customers to buy their products? Imagine pages and pages of ads with no photographs . . . not even illustrations by a modern version of Charles Dana Gibson? The American way of life would grind to a halt. At the very least the industries of advertising, publishing, fashion and cosmetics would have to shut down for lack of consumer demand.

No, Justine told herself, once she'd made the decision to go into the agency business what else could she do but stick with it and run it as well and as honestly as she could? No one now had the luxury of delicate shades of discrimination such as those, years ago, that had prevented top models from doing lingerie ads. She could only establish rules that the girls would break and police the obvious abuses of a system in which reigning models proudly posed stark naked so long as the money was right and the photographer was professional. Or her boyfriend.

Abruptly Justine buzzed her secretary.

"Phyllis, are you positive there isn't a fax from Frankie?"

"I just checked the machine. Nothing yet."

"Thanks, keep checking."

"You taking calls yet? Dart Benedict called again."

"No, I'll let you know."

Is this the way you've picked to get back at me, Miss Severino? Is this your idea of revenge? Is this my punishment for not forcing myself to go to Paris? No fax since you arrived? Just because I chose to stay home is no excuse for your silence. And after all those thousands of dollars worth of Donna Karan, you utterly ungrateful, horrifyingly dressed, overweight, arrogant wench?

Anger took over entirely from depression, as Justine paced around her desk. Didn't Frankie realize that she wanted to know how things were going? Was such disregard of her feelings humanly possible? She had three girls at risk in Paris, for heaven's sake. How were they doing? Had they met any of the hideously wrong guys who hung out wherever models could be found? How had Lombardi welcomed them? Were their accommodations okay? She should have heard something by now. *Anything.* Had their plane disappeared into the Bermuda Triangle?

Furiously Justine scribbled on a yellow pad.

> *What's going on? How's everybody? Where are you and what are you doing? Send information the instant you get this. Justine.*

"Phyllis, come in and take this fax for Frankie, please."

Justine's secretary picked up the yellow sheet. "I'll type it up."

"Don't bother, send it that way." Oh, she knew perfectly well what that vicious slut was up to, Justine thought, raging back and forth. Just because she'd refused to tell Frankie the details of how she came to be Necker's daughter, Frankie was trying to smoke her out by starving her of information, playing the cards close to her chest, trying to get her to reveal that, after all, she had a little natural curiosity about . . . what time was it in Paris now? More or less dark, she calculated, but before dinner . . . they'd all be at the hotel . . . for two cents she'd pick up a phone . . . Justine lost herself in a heated recital of what she'd say to Frankie if she wanted to communicate by voice instead of using the protection of a fax, which gave you speed but could effectively screen your mood.

Phyllis returned.

"She must have sent this as soon as she received yours. It's only been minutes."

> *Your eloquent message delivered this instant. Thought you'd forgotten us while having a swell time with your "friends." Since you ask, everyone is in good health, accommodations perfect, girls happy and busy, no really major problems seem to have fully developed yet. In reply to your question about my activities, I'm in suite giving my hair a henna treatment. Will be busy at this for next hour or two. Call if you want more details. Frankie.*

Intolerable! Frankie knew exactly what she was doing. "No really major problems seem to have *fully* developed yet!" That meant "major problems looming" in any language! Justine crumpled the fax and threw it at the door. Naturally there'd be problems. Send three inexperienced girls to Paris and you could only have problems. It went with the *arrondissement*. Any *arrondissement*, but especially the eighth.

But why hadn't Frankie said anything about Necker? She knew damn well—she wasn't that stupid—that of all the things Justine wanted to be informed about, Necker was the unmentioned, unmentionable, far and away most important item. Just because she'd quite properly refused to let him put pressure on her, just because she'd been smart enough to figure out a way to keep him at a distance, didn't mean that she didn't want to know—well, for instance, how he'd reacted when she hadn't shown up, what impression he'd made on Frankie, what they'd talked about . . . all sorts of little things like that, things that would be . . . well, obviously fairly interesting to learn, details that Frankie, relishing her power, wallowing in righteousness, was leaving out on purpose.

She would *not* call Paris. There was such a thing as maintaining her dignity. But weren't friends supposed to know when to bypass your dignity, Justine wondered, miserably? Now that she knew why she'd felt so horribly out of sorts all morning, she felt even worse. She'd thought she wasn't curious enough about Necker to even care what Frankie thought of him. So much for the healing power of inner knowledge.

Two hours later, choosing a moment when almost everyone had left for lunch, Justine left Loring Management as unnoticed as when she'd entered. A cab dropped her at the end of her street and she wallowed almost waist-high through snowdrifts until she reached her house. It was as cold as ever inside, she thought, as soon at she arrived, but there were encouraging sounds of men working steadily in the basement.

"Mademoiselle Loring?"

"Yes?" Justine looked with surprise at a man waiting in her hallway, dressed in a dark uniform that had a vaguely official look. He thrust a pegboard at her, with several sheets of paper attached to it.

"If you please, Mademoiselle, sign each sheet to indicate safe arrival of the case," he said politely.

"What's this about?" Justine asked, confused, looking around for Aiden.

"A delivery from Kraemer," he said with a smile, indicating a tall packing crate that had been left on the floor next to the front door.

"I haven't ordered anything from Kraemer, whoever that is," Justine said impatiently. "Take it away . . . come on, just take it away."

"Impossible, Mademoiselle. My orders are specific, to deliver it to Mademoiselle Loring in person."

"Oh, for heaven's sake, I don't have time to stand here arguing . . . all right, leave it wherever. . . ." Justine said distractedly as she tried to distinguish Aiden's voice in the basement. She scanned the papers briefly, signed them with a scribble and waved the man out of the door. She didn't bother to inspect the crate—probably some trick of Frankie's—with luck it would contain all her unspeakable old wardrobe and the entire lot could be picked up by Goodwill, if they weren't too picky. Justine walked quickly to the top of the steps that led to the basement.

"Is Aiden down there?" she shouted.

"He's on the second floor," someone called back.

She rushed up the stairs and then suddenly stopped as she heard Aiden humming as he tapped on a pipe in her bathroom. She didn't know what to say to him, Justine thought in a rush of shyness. Her morning at Loring Management seemed to have put a year between waking up in his bed and this moment. She turned away abruptly, went into her bedroom, sat down at her dressing table and took off her cap. She picked up a hairbrush and automatically began to do something about the tangles, her heart beating heavily, not daring to look at herself in the mirror. The sound of humming stopped and she heard footsteps approaching behind her, but she continued to apply herself, single-mindedly, to the disorder of her hair.

"What a mess," Aiden said, gently taking the brush from her hands and uncovering her face. "Probably best if we cut it off. Very short, like a little boy. It's all my fault, not having a blow-dryer, so I'll cut it for you, I'm quite handy. And no extra charge."

"You fool." She leaned back in his arms, laughing for joy.

"Will it hurt if I kiss you? Your lips do look a little . . . bruised. But I've missed you so much, I've been thinking about you all morning, just let me show you how gently I can kiss. . . ."

"I don't know," Justine murmured pitifully. "It even hurts to walk. . . ."

"Oh, there's only one remedy for that," he said. "Hair of the dog." He picked her up and carried her over to her bed as he licked her lips with a soft and careful tongue, over and over.

"Aiden!" Justine said, struggling, "Aiden, for God's sake. . . ."

"Yes, my darling?"

"Lock the door!"

"Done. Can I take that to mean you're feeling a little bit better?" he asked smiling, busily taking off her coat and tucking her under the blankets in the glacial room.

"If you're teasing me I'll—" she threatened him, opening her arms.

"I'm not that kind of guy, I'm not a tease my little sweetheart, I just wanted to make sure I was welcome. Now, let's see—do you want it slow and easy—very very slow and very very easy—or could you possibly be in the mood for a quickie?" he asked, considerately, pulling her sweater up just far enough to reveal her nipples. "Or would you rather toss a coin?" he continued as he stripped her of her fur-lined boots and her pink leggings, and started to take off his own clothes, apparently not feeling the cold.

"Oh . . . oh. . . ." It was impossible, given the weekend she'd just spent, Justine thought, but she wanted a quickie and she wanted it immediately and desperately, with no more talk, or he'd make her come just discussing the possibility, while she looked at his body.

Aiden got under the blankets, next to her, his big body radiating warmth, and tried to peer into her eyes. "I have a better idea," he said, "I'll just touch you very lightly between your legs and that should give me a general idea of exactly what you want, hmmm?"

Dry mouthed, Justine nodded. She felt his possessive hand cover her pubic hair and his middle finger move with the utmost caution over her clitoris until he'd worked it with almost reluctant gentleness into her vagina. Suddenly she squeezed her thighs together so that he couldn't move, and in a violence of total gratification, rubbed herself quickly, greedily and hard against the large, callused finger. Within a few exquisite seconds she screamed out her orgasm.

"That was fairly informative," he said after she'd returned to her senses and lay limp in his arms, still panting.

"I've never done that!" Justine cried, wide-eyed and embarrassed.

"Now you have."

Justine thought it over. "It was all your fault," she muttered, still abashed.

"I hope so, my sweetheart," he said, grinning at her flushed face. "At least you're warm now," he added, guiding her hand down to his penis.

"Good heavens," she gasped, "I forgot all about you. You can't go around in that condition."

"Not and get any work done," he agreed.

"This 'slow and easy' you mentioned? Would it really be . . . comfortable?"

"You'll hardly notice," Aiden assured her. "And I'll stop if it hurts, I promise I will."

"How can I refuse an offer like that?" Justine whispered, opening her legs. She wanted him again, she realized. Badly. Very badly. The weight of his penis on her palm, burning and heavy, had been enough.

"Was I asleep?" Justine asked, startled as Aiden kissed her on the ear. She lifted her head from his shoulder, opened her eyes and realized that she had no idea what time it was. Or even what day.

"Just for a few minutes. You were sleeping so deeply that I hated to wake you, but I have to get back to work and I'm on the wrong side of the bed."

"My God, so do I! I only came home to change. Oh, Aiden," Justine cried, jumping out of bed, wearing only her Giants sweater. "Oh Aiden, what have you done to me?" she wailed, looking into her dressing table mirror.

"It's sad for a man's best efforts to be so quickly forgotten."

"Fool! I mean what have you done to my face? I don't know how to begin to fix it," Justine said, facing an unfamiliar, radiantly flaming visage.

"Leave it, darling. If anyone raises an eyebrow, say you went for a facial at lunch and the operator was too vigorous."

"How knowledgeable you are," Justine said, seized by a piercing pang of a jealousy she'd never felt with another man. "I suppose you've given a lot of similar advice?"

"Never." He pulled her up and held her close. "I don't make love to my clients—that's a rule. And I don't personally put the final touch on their plumbing either, that's what I hire plumbers for, but today was an exception. Understand?"

"Yes," she said in a small, unconvinced, unwilling voice.

"You sound suspicious. You don't have to be."

"How do I know that?"

"You can't, yet. But you'll realize it as time goes by and by and by."

Embarrassed, Justine pulled out of his arms, sat down and reached for her moisturizer and lip gloss. Jealousy was an emotion she despised and she'd been caught out in it.

"Did that courier get you to sign those papers?" he asked as he put on his clothes.

"Courier?" she asked.

"The guy I let in. He was obviously okay. He was prepared to wait for you outside, all day if necessary, but I took pity on him. He told me he'd been trying to deliver that crate to you for days but the blizzard prevented him from even taking off for New York."

"Taking off? Where did he come from?"

"Paris. I assumed it was something you expected."

"This whole thing is a mystery," Justine shrugged, as she expertly darkened her eyebrows.

"Don't you want to know what it is? A special hand-delivered mystery in a big packing crate?"

"I guess," she muttered, distracted as she hunted for her mascara.

"Come on, you won't be able to get that thing open by yourself. I'll do it for you and then you can go back to your office if you really have to. Haven't you noticed that it's getting warm in here?"

Abruptly Justine put down the unused mascara wand. "Oh, Aiden, *it is!* How wonderful!"

"The new furnace is working," he said with relief. "Shouldn't we celebrate that with a half-day holiday?"

"We've just had a holiday," Justine protested.

"No, it was an act of God, that's not the same thing at all."

"Will I ever win a discussion with you?"

"Once every year. Now, do you want to fiddle with your lashes or do you want to know what's in that crate?"

"Why don't you open the crate while I put on my mascara. I'll be down in a minute."

"Right."

"Once every year," Justine thought, he'd said it so naturally, with such casual conviction. A week ago she hadn't known him. A week ago she hadn't known herself.

A few minutes later, wearing charcoal-grey wool trousers and matching sweaters, Justine watched as Aiden finished opening the crate.

"They weren't taking any chances, whatever it is," he said. "I've never seen anything packed like this. Give me a hand, darling."

Aiden and Justine carefully removed the packing material that was wedged tightly around the *bonheur-du-jour* until he was able to pick it up and set it down lightly on the hall rug. They were both struck momentarily dumb with astonishment at the sight of the small writing table whose richness of ornamentation and utter elegance of line spoke more eloquently of its provenance than could any museum curator.

"My God, it's fucking incredible!" Aiden said finally.

"I'm afraid to touch it," Justine murmured. "There's got to be a mistake. That can't possibly be for me."

"I saw the delivery instructions, they were explicit. I wanted to sign for it but the guy said only Mademoiselle Loring could do that. Look at those legs—sycamore from paradise, and the carving is nothing short of genius." Aiden bent over the writing desk with its marquetry veneers and inlaid plaques of porcelain in wonder. "What workmanship! Justine, this is a museum piece."

"How shabby it makes everything else look," Justine said in a detached tone of voice. The jewel of a writing table, on its slender, high, ormolu-decorated legs, stood on her faded, tattered, garage sale rag rug with what struck her as haughty disdain, that of a purebred horse that had found itself in a livery stable.

"You'd certainly think twice before you used it," Aiden said slowly. "It's in perfect condition—not exactly your kind of thing. Is this your birthday, or something?"

"No."

"Well aren't you going to open the drawers—there must be a card in one of them."

Justine stood motionless. Nobody but Necker could have sent her this rich and useless toy.

"Or, do you know who sent it?" Aiden asked in a voice he tried to keep neutral.

"Now you're the one who sounds suspicious," Justine snapped.

"This is the kind of fine French furniture that's called 'priceless,' Justine. Credit my course in Decorative Arts 101—but even priceless furniture has a price. Depending on who this belonged to, it could be in the millions."

"Oh, don't be ridiculous!"

Alarmed and flustered, Justine opened each of the three square drawers, equal in size, that formed the top of the *bonheur-du-jour* and found nothing but elaborate compartments that divided the deep drawers for storage. Beneath the writing surface of the desk were three more drawers, and it was in the middle one, raised to give knee room, that she found a white envelope. She ripped it open and gave the card inside a quick glance.

"I'm counting the hours. J. N."

Justine stuffed the card back into the envelope and quickly shut the drawer on it.

"Look, darling, you don't owe me any explanations," Aiden said, looking at her closed face. "We're both grown up and what's past is past. But if there's someone in your life who's important to you—because obviously you're important to him—I want to know if you're serious about him. It's for my own self-protection—although it's already much too late for that."

"There's nobody in my life," Justine said angrily.

"Okay, if you say so."

"You don't sound convinced," she accused him.

"I've just realized how little I know about you."

"I don't know one damn thing more about you than you do about me."

"Nobody's sending me wildly expensive presents, you can count on that."

"Aiden, that's rotten."

"Just realistic."

She was not going to tell him. Justine thought clearly in the midst of her anger. Basically she knew very little about him. Sex, especially the kind of sex that made you wild enough to do things you'd never dreamed of, was the least trustworthy thing about any man, so why should she confide the deepest secret she'd ever had to him? If he wanted to think she had a rich lover, let him. Why shouldn't she have one? Or ten?

"I have to get back to the office," she said coldly. "I'd be grateful if you'd put that thing somewhere where your guys won't bump into it."

"Am I going to see you tonight?"

"No, I don't think so. I need some time to myself."

"Fine. Have it your own way," he said, his voice stiff and formal with hurt. "But don't forget to write whoever sent you this gem a very grateful thank-you note."

15

Marco Lombardi walked restlessly and without any fixed purpose around his big workroom; panic and the attempt to flee panic the elements that kept him moving. The level of his anxiety twisted higher and higher as each day whirled past, bringing the test of his first collection. During his years as an assistant designer he had been impatiently convinced that he possessed a major talent and only the lack of proper backing was keeping him from proving it. Now, with little more than a week remaining before the possibility of overnight success, to his furious disbelief all his plans seemed to be crumbling. He had a sick feeling in his bones, an intimation of potential failure.

That very morning he'd ordered the entire collection brought into the workroom, not caring that, as was normal in the couture, much of it still lacked finishing touches: crucial embroidery hadn't been delivered from the specialists; buttons and zippers hadn't been placed; even some seams were still only basted. He'd slashed through the racks of suits, dresses and evening gowns, brutally throwing to the floor more than half the collection. Better to show nothing, he'd informed his stunned staff, in a high, cold fury, than to show anything that wasn't perfect. Take everything away, he'd ordered, and never let him see those misbegotten rags again. The women scurried about, scooping up the offending garments with little chucks of commiseration, intending to hide them on their hangers in the ateliers until his mood changed.

Marco called for his house fitting model, the great Janine whom Necker had gone to great lengths to hire. He ordered her to try on each of the outfits that had survived his purge. Janine, a plain, supremely professional woman of thirty-five, with a famously faultless body on which even the least of designs would hang with chic, stood in perfect composure as he went on a rampage, pulling off sleeves, snipping off collars, cursing as he repinned skirts. Janine was weighing the merits of a new recipe, her usual train of thought during hours such as these, which came about with regularity at any house in the couture, when she realized that Lombardi had stopped in front of her.

"It would make it easier for me, Janine, if you weren't so utterly and totally uninvolved, if you weren't such a bore to look at, if you weren't merely a stupid, untalented, bourgeois housewife at heart, if you could bring yourself to pay any attention at all to the creative process."

Janine looked him in the face with no change of expression except a tiny contemptuous lift of her eyebrows. She unzipped the slim, pale grey peau de soie sheath she was wearing, folded it and handed it neatly to Marco. All activity in the fitting room came to a halt. "Adieu, Monsieur," Janine said in a carrying, utterly final voice, stepping out of her shoes. Disdaining the peignoir that was provided for her, she removed herself and her valuable bones from the room, clad only in her own tiny lace panties.

There were a half-dozen jobs she could have for the asking, jobs where her measurements brought her nothing but admiration, Janine thought as she walked away. No designer, not even in his worst frenzy of self-doubt, and they all had them, had ever had the poor judgment to blame *her* before, Janine reflected, as she paraded magnificently up the stairs to the locker where she kept her street clothes. She did not predict success for this new Italian boy, whose indisputable prettiness could never make up for his temper. And, of course, his display of vile, foreign manners would be held against him for years. She herself could hardly wait to tell her best friend, the chief fitting model at Chanel.

In the fitting room no one dared speak. Marco threw the dress to one of the women in the room. "Have you people nothing to do but gape like morons?" he demanded furiously. "Take these clothes away and get back to work. Out, everybody, this is not the circus! You, Madame Elsa, find me a new fitting model, not another used-up cow."

Now, several hours later, Madame Elsa was still unable to locate a single suitable fitting model available at the last minute during this frantic period in the rhythm of the couture. Too angry even to try to sketch, yet far more hideously humiliated by his loss of control in front of his employees than by the defection of Janine, Marco found himself reduced to waiting for Tinker Osborn.

The girl had the unspeakable effrontery to be three minutes late, he thought ferociously. He had promised, in a moment of weakness, to teach her how to walk, and instead of sitting here waiting when he returned from his hasty lunch, she was not even on time. His fury rose as he looked out of the window, and scanned the Rue Clément-Marot. Suddenly he spotted the unmistakable coral cloud of Tinker's hair. The girl stood on the sidewalk, just below the window, all but buried in the embrace of a young man. Whoever he was, he was so burly in his winter coat that he'd hidden her from sight as they'd run along the street.

Tinker quickly forced herself to leave the shelter of Tom's arms and timorously mounted the staircase to the room in which she'd been told she'd find Marco Lombardi. It was, she noted with apprehension, the same room in which she'd been disgraced. She knocked on the door and entered on his bark.

"You're late," he said, not looking up from the long table at which he was inspecting bolts of fabric.

"I'm terribly sorry—I ran—but we—I just couldn't find a taxi."

"The reason you're staying at the Plaza is that it's just around the corner," he said, his voice icy. "You're here to be at my disposal, or have you forgotten so quickly?"

"No, no, I haven't . . . it's just that I had lunch with a friend and the waiter didn't bring the check quickly . . . enough . . ." she faltered.

"The friend I noticed from the window? Don't expect me to swallow that one. Girls like you are the joke of every collection . . . not five minutes off the plane, one gulp of the air of Paris, and off you trot like a bitch in heat, panting to spread your legs for the first lout you meet. I hope you took a good bath before you came here."

"It's not . . . that's wrong—"

"The hell it is! Save your breath. I know the story, he's your long lost brother, your cousin, your uncle . . . you girls have as little shame as imagination, you'll say anything but the truth, he's a cock with a man attached to it, nothing more. Take off your clothes."

"What!"

"Your clothes. I need a fitting model."

"But . . . you said . . . my walk. . . ."

"A folly. I should never have agreed. However, right now I need a fitting model. Don't remove your bra this time, try to behave as if you're not in a striptease show. Take off your clothes or take the next plane back to New York, it's all the same to me, but you're absolutely useless as you are."

It was Necker's fault that he found himself stuck with her. Necker had saddled him with dreary Janine, Necker had never ceased to impose conditions on him that crushed his creativity, Necker who was responsible for this idiot without fire or wit, bleating her ridiculous excuses in one of those foolish American voices. God, was there no one who did anything but stand in his way?

"Go on, move! Just drop them anywhere." Marco shouted at Tinker.

As Tinker hastened to shuck her mini-kilt and sweater she trembled with helplessness. How could he be the same man who'd charmed them all? Nobody would believe her if she told them. The only thing she was certain of was that her one chance to salvage this situation was to obey him, to do everything he asked, for he had all the power. Otherwise she'd be out of the competition, and her chance, her unique and precious opportunity to become somebody, would be gone forever.

"Stand in the light, with your back to the big mirror, several feet away from it," Lombardi ordered, still bent over the dozens of bolts of cloth that were piled on the table. He looked up. "For God's sake, take those boots off. Take one step forward and stay there," he added, staring at her with an entirely abstracted gaze that made her feel that she had turned into a dressmaker's dummy. Tinker's trembling stopped, replaced by the never-forgotten iron endurance that had been trained into her throughout her childhood.

Thank God he'd gotten rid of Janine, that middle-aged work-horse, Marco thought, as his keen graphic senses worked rapidly on the image Tinker presented. Just looking at a new girl made him realize that Janine had become so much of a habit that he had stopped seeing her, Janine with her dun-colored, elegant chignon, her sallow complexion that not even her expert makeup could conceal and her predictably impeccable stance.

Every designer's ideas must come from hundreds of sources, no one designs in a vacuum—who could possibly say, Marco asked himself, how much of his recent difficulties stemmed from sheer boredom with Janine, a boredom that had been confused in his mind with a lack of faith in his ideas?

Now this one, with the freshness of contrast created by her hair and her skin, her youth that needed little makeup, and her utter lack of sophistication, her body that, in every one of its lines, was unfamiliar to him, from her ridiculous way of holding her shoulders back like a soldier, so strictly that she was standing un-naturally straight, to the tautness of her rib cage—now this one . . . yes, this one gave him new ideas.

The very ignorance that maddened him nevertheless made her utterly different from Janine. He'd often asked himself how much a model invested a design with her own individuality or whether the design could totally transform a model. Sometimes one dynamic took over, sometimes the other, but a couturier never truly knew what to expect until he saw his sketched ideas worked out on a human body.

As he continued to study Tinker, it occurred suddenly to Marco that there was no lace in his collection. Lace had seemed a matronly medium to him this spring—at least lace combined with Janine—but something about this girl called for lace, something told him that she could make lace young again, he thought, quickly unwrapping bolts of black Chantilly lace folded around oblongs of cardboard. The elaborate yet dainty floral design was widely spaced on the fine webbing and each silken bolt was so light that precious meters of it weighed very little.

Marco draped two lengths of lace over his arms. He placed the center of one full length over each of Tinker's shoulders, totally veiling her in a soft, light cloud that drifted into pools on the floor. He stepped back and looked at her in detached appraisal. It was a shame, he thought, that he couldn't send her out on the runway like that, emphasizing nothing but the beauty of the fabric; no construction, no lining, no seams, no decoration, her height and her leanness making a gesture, a suggestion of grace through the design—yes, the black and white contrast of an almost colorless face, the plume of red hair and superb black lace trailing, scrolling, fanning out behind her—but what rich woman would pay for something she could buy in a fabric store and play with for her own amusement?

Rapidly Marco attacked the fabric. He pinched and bunched the material here and there, using pins expertly to create shoulders, indicate the line of the sleeves, and suggest a high neckline. He pinned the lace wide open at the back, from shoulders to waist, and adroitly tied the two lengths together into an enormous bow at Tinker's waist, its ends long enough to make a short train. He studied the effect in the mirror, approving of the way in which the fabric now stretched backward in an illusion of flight, away from the body. But the hair would never do, he decided. There was too much of it, it fought the sweeping line of the lace.

"Your hair must be up," Marco said. "Did you bring hairpins with you?"

"No."

"You should be better prepared," he said curtly. "Don't move." In a minute Marco discovered the box of hairpins that Janine had forgotten, in its usual place on the accessory table. Taking several of them in his hand he faced Tinker and began to lift the hair that fell on one side of her face. Only then did he glance at the face and notice that it reflected no emotion at all. She had made herself as neutral as the blankest canvas, and he found neutrality in a model even more deadening than a show of temperament. Damn the creature! If he wanted the negative vibrations of an inexpressive face and a pair of lifeless eyes he might as well have kept Janine. But now he *needed* this particular little cunt. He had to have unlimited use of her, he'd realized that from the instant she'd made him feel like working in lace.

"Has no one ever created a dress on you before?" he asked her.

Tinker made a short negative sound.

This fool still had the presumption to be angry at him, Marco realized. She should be thanking the lucky stars that had put her in this position at this moment, but no, she was giving herself airs and graces, as if she had a right to be hurt because he hadn't greeted her with delight. She showed a total lack of professionalism but there was nothing to be done but charm her.

"I find that surprising," Marco said, his voice deepening into warmth. "Admittedly you can't strut, but when you stand still you're an inspiration. It's not an ordinary role. After all, anyone can learn to walk, and I haven't forgotten that I promised to teach you, but how many models can say they've inspired an artist?"

Tinker stared silently ahead, past his left ear.

"You look tired," Marco said sympathetically, lifting a few tendrils of her hair. She made not the slightest response, not a twitch of an eyelash.

Attention, he thought, she has the nerve to insist on attention before she will consent to come alive again. Marco plunged both his hands deeply into the roots of Tinker's hair and softly massaged her scalp with his fingertips. "You need to relax," he murmured, as his fingers continued their light, intimate, unmistakable caress, "even if I can't let you sit down yet." He worked his fingers slowly all the way from her hairline to the nape of her neck in a way that he knew had to feel irresistibly delicious. "Any better?" he asked as he quickly pinned up her hair.

"I said I was okay," Tinker said with no change of tone, holding her head motionless, as if he hadn't touched her. A river of anger rising from her gut made her clench her fists until her nails bit half-moons into her palms.

She was stubborn, Marco thought, turning away to unwrap more lace to fill in the wide gap in the front of the dress, where the fabric had been pulled apart to form the bow in the back. She was hostile, sullen, unforgiving. Normally, if she were this unpleasant he would have thrown her out by now. However something entirely unexpected, something deeply important had just happened to him.

As Marco touched Tinker's scalp and felt its warmth he had released a fragrance that was natural to her, a fragrance that acted on his imagination as a powerful stimulus. Suddenly ideas, unbidden, were leaping in his mind, fresh, thrilling ideas, so vivid and complete that he knew absolutely that there was no need to stop and note them in his sketchbook because he would never forget them. And Tinker was the source of these ideas.

This girl had a quality! He could have never guessed it until this minute, but now he knew that he would design *from* her. A full day's work with her would yield an entire group of sketches that would complement and elevate the best designs in his entire spring collection. Far more important, they would give the entire collection that extra leap into true originality that he'd known, and fought admitting, had been missing all along.

Marco Lombardi's anxiety left him entirely, he felt possessed of the full mastery for which he had worked so many years, the strong foundation of craftsmanship that had been obscured, for terrible months, by the need to perform. Now he was standing firmly astride the welling center of his talent, through some magic that mysteriously had been unleashed by a particular girl.

He turned back to her as she stood motionless, her naked body exposed yet framed by lace, her shoulders, neck and arms covered, her torso bare and white except for her bra. He must construct the top of the dress over bare skin. Nothing could do the ball gown justice on the runway unless it had the drama of the girl's body naked from the waist up.

Deftly Marco unhooked Tinker's bra and slipped it out from the half-finished construction. "I was wrong, no bra under lace." She made no sign that she noticed her breasts springing free as Marco pinned a long piece of lace at her neckline, again covering her to the floor. "Flat to the body in front, the drama of the bow at the back . . . yes, but it still lacks shape."

Quickly Marco used pins to outline the shape of her body from her underarms to her knees where he let the fabric spring out into ripples. Impersonally he ran his hands along the sides of her body and used more pins to mold the lace so that it lost its last wrinkle.

He stepped back again, judging the result of his work as pure line, pure drama. Suddenly, startlingly, his focus changed and Marco saw Tinker as a man sees a woman. He stepped forward and deliberately put his hands on her breasts, lingering on their delicate upward curves, weighing their light and luscious mass, without any pretense of fitting.

Tinker fought successfully to stand as stolidly as before, too molten with fury to trust herself to move. She thought clearly through her emotion. She could let him paw her and get what she wanted or she could tell him to go to hell, rip off the dress and get out of here, out of Paris, out of the competition. There were no other options. *Win*, Tinker told herself, I choose to win. At that moment Marco brushed his thumbs over each of her nipples with a deliberate contact that was so delicate that it was almost imperceptible.

Without thinking, Tinker stepped slightly backward with a single controlled and dignified motion.

"Don't worry," he assured her, pretending to misunderstand. "No one else will see them clearly, you can be sure of that . . . so very pale a pink . . . only I know exactly where they are . . . they are bigger . . . and more sensitive . . . than I saw the other day, but they will be almost invisible . . . that quality of mystery will add an immense allure! Those pigs of photographers will go crazy for you in this gown . . . and just as crazy about the other splendid designs I'm going to create just for you. You'll set off a stampede with those gentlemen of the press, Tinker, you're going to be the star of the show, I intend to make sure of that."

"How much is your intention worth?" Tinker asked, each word iced with hard suspicion. She had suddenly realized that she had gained the upper hand with Marco Lombardi. The impatient quiver of his voice, the raw sincerity that emanated from him when he spoke of designing for her—it all added up to truth, at least the kind of truth he was capable of.

"How can you wonder? It's totally within my power. I make those decisions, no one else."

"You promised to teach me how to walk. You haven't done even that, and now you say I'll be the star of the show. You insulted me when I arrived and now you promise me the moon. You change from minute to minute. Why should I count on you?"

"I was in the foulest of moods before you came. I admit that I took it out on you," he said, annoyed at the need to apologize to a model. "You might try to understand what I've been going through."

Tinker continued to glare at him with unblinking challenge, her eyes as deeply silver as if they were reflecting stars.

Reluctantly looking for a way to prove his sincerity, Marco realized that in his excitement of finding his abilities fresh and alive and intact, he still hadn't shown her the dress he'd just pinned. *That* would bring her around! He rummaged quickly in the trays of costume jewelry on the accessory table until he found a pair of long glittering pendants. "Let me show you." Marco approached Tinker and clasped an earring on each of her ears. "Now, turn carefully, very carefully, and look at yourself in the mirror, and tell me what you see."

Tinker gazed with growing amazement at her reflection, a self she had never imagined, a creature who had slipped through time from another century, a gracious era of infinite possibility and grandeur, a creature who was not a girl but a polished woman who had been born to carry precious lace and wear magnificent jewels, a woman whose skin gleamed through the elaborate material with an authority of whiteness she had never known it possessed, a polished, glowing, reigning woman whose flowering skirts showed only a tantalizing hint of legs through their shadows, a woman whose eyes outshone her earrings, whose hair was more becomingly arranged than she had ever managed to make it herself.

As Tinker stood, falling in love with her image, Marco stood behind her and found the soft skin behind her earlobes and stroked it as he whispered, "See how beautiful you are, *cara*, is that not the proof? Could I possibly not use you when you *are* a star already, a natural star? How often do you think I've had this possibility?"

Tinker shook off his fingers impatiently. She met his eyes sharply in the mirror and saw that they were unfocused with pleasure, as if he were unaware that he had been touching her.

Yes, he mused, yes, in spite of the great glamour he would bestow on her, she was still basically unspoiled, she still possessed all the vulnerability and ineptness that had caused him to volunteer to work with her in the first place. The day the three girls had first come to be inspected, he had promised himself a delicious interlude with Tinker. As much as he appreciated accomplished models, it was always an ungainly girl who had the power to arouse him. Jordan and April, charming though they were, already knew far too much for his particular tastes.

But when Tinker had walked toward him, mortified, unable to hide her embarrassment, his cock had twitched and filled and risen quickly under his trousers. As clearly as if it were taking place, he imagined her falling to her knees on the floor in front of him. She would perhaps be unwilling—oh, yes, most certainly unwilling —but too flustered, too intimidated to protest. He would inform her of his needs and watch her as she opened his belt and his zipper with tremulous fingers. As slowly as she dared she would force herself to bend her head toward his cock, still not fully hard, and take him awkwardly into her dry, quivering mouth. She would work on him with an intoxicating, uncertain clumsiness, gauche and disconcerted, not knowing whether to lick or suck or even how to touch him properly with her fingers, fumbling, painfully reluctant in her lack of experience, as he grew thicker and longer, spurred by the rare delight of innocence, that spice to which he was addicted. He could prolong her innocence, give her no help at all, mock her for her attempts, hold back his orgasm almost indefinitely until he finally chose to give her a few words of such explicit instruction that he could lose himself and come in her mouth. Of all the methods he had devised to break a girl in, making her suck him dry was by far the most direct and effective. Then, taking his time, lingering over details, he would spend weeks until he trained her to please him perfectly, to learn each one of his exacting ways. When she was expert, when she was no longer new or innocent, he would pass her along to a friend. To Dart Benedict perhaps, in return for a special favor. . . .

"Marco?"

Tinker's sharp, angry voice entered his fantasy. "Marco, the walk! That's what I'm here for, not to watch you moon into the goddamn mirror! When are you going to teach me the runway tricks I need to know?"

He sighed in irritation as he put away his thoughts and turned to the business at hand.

"You've made your runway walk into an imaginary barrier," he told Tinker. "That doesn't mean that you don't truly believe in it, simply that it does not exist. You have two feet, two legs, you've walked all your life. All you lack is attitude, and attitude isn't *how* you walk but how you're *feeling about yourself* while you walk. I realize that you believe, in your negative way, that it has to be instinctive, that you haven't got the knack. You're wrong and I'll prove it. Can you dance?"

"Dance?"

"Yes, dance."

"I even stink at disco because I can't let myself go enough to do it right."

"Have you ever had dance lessons?"

"No."

"I thought as much. I'm going to have you taught to tango."

"What goddamn good will that do?" Tinker shouted in vivid disappointment, glaring at him, arms akimbo. "I've got two left feet. It's the most useless idea I've ever heard."

"Now listen to me. I've used the tango before with girls who had your problem, and it worked for them. You're too young to know, but the tango is the ultimate dance of passion. A dance of arrogance and authority, but above all, *passion*. Anybody, even you Tinker, can learn enough in a course of intensive tango training to absorb some of that passion. Then when you walk on the runway you'll *gather yourself into yourself* in such a passionate way that you'll move with the power of the tango, the seduction of the tango."

"Bullshit!"

Marco ignored her, putting a tape in a tape deck that lay on the accessory table.

"Tomorrow we work all day with my assistants, with everyone in the house I need to execute my sketches," he informed her. "After that, we'll work every afternoon, right up to the show if we have to. Each morning you'll have tango lessons with Señora Varga, a magnificent woman, the best tango teacher in Paris, who'll teach you the man's part since you'll be walking forward, not backward, as the woman normally does. You're going to tango three solid hours every single morning and tango in your dreams every night, and when I work with you, I'll play tango tapes. When you get the tango in your blood you'll be different in ways you can't begin to imagine now, so listen now, listen to the music while I unpin you."

Shaking her head in bitter dismay, Tinker listened as the taped music filled the room. It had a strong beat, sure, but how the hell was that going to give her an "attitude"? She damn well wasn't going to dance her way down the runway! Was Marco merely trying to use her as selfishly as possible, reducing her to a high-class fitting model who spent her mornings learning the tango and her afternoons being his "inspiration," for all the good that would ever do her? Would she ever learn enough to be competitive with Jordan and April, or was this just another cruel trick of a cruel man?

Marco finally released her from her lace cage.

"Put your clothes back on and sit down for a few minutes, while I talk to you. The tango isn't hard but it's a precise dance without a single sloppy move. It has clear, simple rules, and that's why you're going to be able to learn it—you will never have to 'let yourself go'—that thing that bothers you so much. You never have to improvise. *The movements of the dance itself will give you attitude.* A fat old woman becomes seductive when she does the tango. You'll learn exactly how to hold your whole body from the position of your head to the way you point your fingertips and toes. If you follow the rules it's impossible to fail."

"What kind of rules?" Tinker asked, interested in spite of herself. If she was anything at all, it was someone who had always been good at strict obedience to rules.

"In the tango you are attached to the earth. It's a level dance, no bouncing. Your whole foot is on the floor except when you have to lift your heel to move your foot. Your knees are *always slightly flexed.* That's the first rule, flexed knees. There is only one beat, no matter what the step. Slow, slow, quick, quick, slow. You never have to learn more than that. Flexed knees, slow, slow, quick, quick, slow—how difficult does that sound?"

"Too easy to be true."

"On your feet, you've rested long enough." Marco turned off the tape. "I'm going to teach you the basic step right now, so you'll understand how simple it is. Every other step follows the same exact beat."

"The man's part?"

"No. I'll lead, but you'll get the idea. Feet together, pull yourself up from your waist, shoulders level, but normal, not like a soldier, neck long . . . no, you can make it longer than that . . . head proud, eyes wide open, absolutely no smile. I'll walk you through the basic step very slowly without music."

Marco stood facing Tinker from a distance of some eight inches and put her left hand on his right shoulder. "Look over my shoulder, not at me." He grasped her other hand in dance position. "Now, flex your knees. *More!"*

Feeling utterly foolish, Tinker gazed into the corner of the room.

"When I say 'slow' walk back on your right foot and when I say 'slow' again, walk back on your left foot."

They took two deliberate, backward steps in slow motion. "Keep your knees flexed! Now when I say 'quick,' another step back on your right foot. On the second 'quick,' a step sideways, to the left on your left foot. Then when I say 'slow' drag your right foot across to your left foot and stop."

He led her powerfully through the last three steps, preventing her from wavering.

"That's it," Marco said. "You've just done the basic step."

"You were holding me up."

"Because we were doing it so slowly that you could have lost your balance. With music it goes so quickly that there's no problem. Now, we'll walk through it again without music. I want you to say the slows and the quicks with me out loud."

"Oh, for goodness sake!"

"Stop being such a self-conscious child! *Slow! Slow! Quick, quick, slow, damn it!* That's better. And again. And again." He led her twenty times around the room until Tinker found herself matching the steps and the words automatically.

"Now, with music," Marco said.

"Can't I wait till the first real lesson?" Tinker pleaded, panicked again.

"No, you cannot." Marco put the tape on and walked back to Tinker. "Doesn't that music make you want to dance?"

"No!"

"You're a liar. From now on, no more walking, no more talking. *Now!*"

They circled the big room, the only sound their feet and the music. After a shaky start, Tinker found the beat, and soon, sooner than she would ever have believed, she found herself dancing in a sense of heightened consciousness. She became a big, resplendent, masterful cat, a great, prowling, sure-footed, arrogant cat, full of indisputable pride, a cat whose territory no one would dare invade. The beat of the insistent music became her cavalier, the music infused her with its strength and grace, the music made her forget that she couldn't dance, because while it lasted, she could. She could!

"*Basta!* Enough." Marco danced her over to the sofa and released her so that they both fell backward, side by side. "You may rest a minute. So, now, what do you think? Unwilling to admit it, aren't you? But you were doing the tango, no mistake about that."

"I know." Tinker blushed with deep pleasure. She was dripping wet, her sweater clung to her in patches, and sweat ran down her forehead into her eyes.

"Here," Marco said, offering her a handkerchief. As she dabbed at her face he inhaled the pungency of her natural aroma with brutal pleasure, savoring the throb of his instant arousal. There would never be a better opportunity, he thought through a haze of lust. While she continued to dry her face he opened his trousers in a quick, stealthy gesture. With a deft, strong move and the advantage of surprise Marco grabbed Tinker's wrists and flung her to the floor, locking his knees around her body.

"Take it in your mouth," he ordered.

"*No!*" She screamed as loudly as she could, rearing backward.

"There's no one left in the building. Do it!"

"The hell I will!"

Her resistance inflamed him. It was exactly what he wanted.

"Have you ever had a hard cock in your mouth?" he asked, savoring the words. "Have you ever sucked a man until he came? No, of course not. This will be your first time."

"*Let me go!*" Tinker struggled as violently as possible but she was immobilized.

"Not until you've taken it between your lips. Not until you've tasted it. I won't permit you to stop. Look at it. *Look!*" He pulled her by her wrists until she was forced to bend forward at the waist. "How can I let you go when it's so hard? Don't you know that when I'm in your mouth you'll *own* me, you innocent child? Don't you want that power?"

"Power?" Tinker asked in a muffled voice, ceasing to struggle.

"I'll teach you something that will give you power over every man alive."

"That?" Tinker said wonderingly. "Only *that?*"

"Yes. That."

"You're hurting my wrists," she whimpered.

"Bend your head and take it in your mouth," he said, his voice thick.

"My wrists . . . I can't bend. . . ." She was on the verge of tears.

He let go of one of her wrists and put his free hand behind her head, pushing it toward his cock. Tinker stiffened her neck until his attention was focused on pushing her head down. Then, with a lightning movement, she grabbed his balls with her free hand and squeezed them as tightly as she could.

"Aah!" he screeched, gasping in pain.

"*You sick, evil bastard!* If you ever touch me again I'll kill you." With both hands free now she squeezed even harder. "I'll never be in a room alone with you again. Do you want to work without me? —I'll go or stay—your choice."

"Stay," he grunted.

"I thought you'd say that. I believe we understand each other now, innocent though I am."

"Let go!"

Tinker held his balls in one final wrenching squeeze. "Know what I was famous for in high school, Marco?"

"Damn you!"

"The best blow job in town. See you tomorrow."

Tinker was out of the door, shaking but still grinning at her lie, a long time before Marco was even able to move.

16

If I had to bet on it, I'd say that Tinker had unquestionably won the jackpot.

There had been a couple of free days during which Lombardi sent word that he didn't need any of the girls and didn't have time for Tinker. I was deeply concerned that he didn't mean to keep his promise to her, but at least the time was used by Mike, who had the three girls at his disposal by now he must have exposed enough film to fill ten issues of *Zing*. Then yesterday, Tinker had been selected for special treatment by Lombardi.

I didn't know about it until he called me a half hour ago, while I was eating breakfast, to inform me of her new schedule: tango lessons in the mornings, afternoons working for him in his atelier. I asked him what I could do to help and he said that since he had arranged for one of the limos to be permanently assigned to Tinker there was nothing else she needed. No, the photographer was most definitely not welcome to pollute the concentration of the tango lessons nor, most particularly, was Mike to interrupt his work with Tinker. We were to leave her to him and his staff and to Señora Varga, and not bother him with questions: his time was at a premium.

Naturally I immediately checked this all out with Tinker, the anointed, who, for a change, I managed to find in her suite taking a bath. She promised me that she could handle the pressure.

"It's an overly heavy schedule," I warned her. "You're spending almost every night on the Left Bank with some guy. Now you'll be dancing all morning and standing on your feet being fitted all afternoon—that's just crazy pressure, Tinker. You'd be giving yourself much better odds if you moved back to the hotel . . . at least you'd have your evenings free to soak your feet, get a good night's sleep alone in your own bed . . . I don't have to remind you how much there's at stake. I have a responsibility to you, Tinker, and you have a responsibility to yourself. You know what Justine would say."

"Oh, Frankie, I don't give a damn! I don't care what you say, I can't not be with Tom. He's what keeps me going. Oh, if you only knew him you'd understand!"

"So introduce me."

"I will, I promise, but not yet. It's too soon . . . I want him all to myself."

"Tinker, I hope to God that you're as strong as you think you are," I said with real worry. Tinker was so aflame with a combination of love and ambition that she was beyond reasoning with. If she insisted on burning the candle in the middle as well as at both ends, there literally wasn't anything I could do, short of physical restraint, to stop her. Justine and I both knew that she had magic and now Lombardi did too. Maybe, after all, it was this Tom who had given her the special visibility, the new glow of self-assurance that Lombardi responded to?

While I was mulling over how delicately I could break this significant, unwelcome, and sure-to-be-upsetting development to April and Jordan, Mike Aaron called on the house phone.

"Frankie, it's another magnificent day."

"Oh, be my guest, just take the girls again," I sputtered. "I don't care if it's good weather or bad, they're yours, all except Tinker, she has to work." Did it matter how many unnecessary pictures he took?

"No, that's not why I called. I've been feeling terrible about that lie I told the other night."

"Huh?"

"Telling everybody that we'd been at the Louvre. It eats away at me. And then you rubbed it in that none of them had gone. Don't you see that we've put ourselves into a position of cultural superiority that we don't deserve, and I feel that's distinctly immoral."

"I'm sure nobody remembers or gives a damn." What was wrong with him?

"No, they remember—I can see them thinking that Mike and

Frankie went to the Louvre and we didn't, we missed out on it—it's something you'd have to be a photographer to notice, but it's there in their eyes all right. A sort of sadness, a kind of *deprivation*."

"That could become a real problem," I said seriously, feeling my heart beginning to wake up and take notice.

"So what I thought is, you and I could sneak off to the Louvre today but we won't tell anybody, never mention it. That way we'll make reparations, even if we're the only ones who know it."

"Hmmm."

"Don't you agree that it's the only right thing to do?"

"I'm really not sure, morally speaking," I said thoughtfully. "You still told a lie, and this could be considered just another lie, coming on top of the first, a cover-up, compounding the first one. Maybe you should check with your rabbi." No way you get away with this so easily, Aaron, I thought.

"Jesus!"

"Why not? If you can reach Him."

"Frankie, will you please go to the Louvre with me today?"

"I'd enjoy that," I made myself say sedately. "But why didn't you just ask in the first place?"

"It made it seem like a date thing."

"Well, is it or isn't it?" I wanted to get this absolutely straight before I let myself get too excited.

"Well . . . yeah, it is. But date things—I haven't done them in years. That's kid stuff."

"Not where I come from. Your problem is you moved to the city. You're too far from your roots. Manhattan has crazy rules . . . in Brooklyn we still do date things, all the time."

"Could we possibly discuss this in person? I like hearing you tell me what's wrong with me, but it's more fun to watch you while you do it. This conversation is degenerating into what my mother calls 'hanging on the phone.' "

"I'll meet you in the lobby in an hour."

"Can't you make it sooner? Your phone's been busy or I'd have asked earlier."

"Date things never take less than an hour prep time," I said severely, dancing wildly around the phone cord.

"I guess, if you say so."

"See you later."

I hung up and rushed into the dressing room. I'd already had my bath and I'd been brushing out and admiring my new hair when Lombardi called. After several cautious attempts I'd finally dared to use enough henna to turn into a dark redhead. It was, I had to admit, rather becoming. Hell, it was magnificent.

Donna, I implored silently, help me out here, I've never been a redhead before. I need your great brain, Donna, my own has turned to electrified marshmallow. I made my way through the row of hangers, trying to think redhead thoughts.

Green . . . obviously there were a variety of greens, the natural choice, but was I going to make my debut as a redhead wearing green like the majority of other redheads on earth? No, for my coming out I intended to make a major redhead statement, and not in any of the subtle browns, blacks or ivories, some of which I'd already worn. Justine had been wildly generous but when I'd eliminated all the obvious colors, all that was left was a tunic with matching trousers. The tunic had a generously cut turtleneck and a wide belt, and both pieces were made in a stretch wool in a fascinating color that wasn't quite plum or precisely grape—more like an eggplant, a rich, luscious eggplant, a moody purple with a lot of black in it.

I held the tunic up to my face and even on the hanger I could tell that I'd found my answer. The eggplant made my hair come more burningly alive, in some way only an artist could understand. I was fast approaching a potential Paul Mitchell approval rating, I thought as I did my makeup with hands that stayed blessedly steady even though my mind was zigzagging with a thousand considerations. A *date!* And he'd figured out an absurd excuse to set it up, which made it so much more meaningful than if he'd just said, "Come on, we might as well go to the Louvre, I've got nothing better to do," which would have been perfectly natural and in his style.

Fact. Mike Aaron, after almost a week of seeing me daily, wanted to get me off alone, without the others knowing. Was there any other way to view this development except as a sign of some degree, however small, of . . . interest, no matter how mild?

As I zipped up my wonderful eggplant pieces, I thought that if there was ever a day to begin to lead a redhead's life, it was today. Big silver hoops for my ears, to match my belt buckle, and wide silver bracelets. The black coat over my arm, my black boots—I looked at myself in the mirror and shook my head in amazement. Why had I spent so many years dressing for a dance student role that was no longer mine, when I could have looked like a woman out to do damage of a very mature nature?

"Frankie, this is just a date," I said to the mirror, sternly. "Only a date. Nothing to get in a tizzy about. People have dates all the time. They don't mean anything special. Just a way to get through the day." The sound of my voice only made me feel more nervous. I don't normally talk to myself out loud.

I walked into the lobby feeling so self-conscious that I had to fight the need to put on my sunglasses, but I felt dramatic enough without going over the top. Mike was standing there with his back to the elevators, looking massively impatient. I stopped for a minute before he saw me, just taking him in from head to toe. It wasn't just his height or the field of energy he walked around in that made him stand out in that lobby. It was also the details; the fine, unkempt shape of his head, the arrogance of his big, handsome nose, the confident line of his lips, the muscles in his strong neck. And there was not one single camera hung around his neck! Oh, help me, Lord!

"Am I late?" I asked, slipping around into his field of vision.

"No, half an hour early."

"Then why are you looking like that?"

"Like what?"

"Impatient."

"I didn't know I was. Oh, shit! Hi, Jordan. Hi, April."

"Frankie! What did you do to your hair?" April asked, gasping.

"My God, it's—too beautiful! And where'd you find that marvelous thing you have on?" Jordan demanded.

"Sorry, girls, Frankie doesn't have time to gab. Hurry up, Frankie, the guys in the darkroom won't wait forever."

"What darkroom?" April demanded curiously.

"The *Zing* darkroom. Maxi Amberville sent me a fax—she

wants Frankie to look at the contacts and let her know what she thinks." He grabbed me by the arm.

"Can we come too?" Jordan suggested with lively interest.

"Maxi'd eat me alive if I let models see contacts. You ought to know that. See you later, girls."

"Why don't we all meet for lunch somewhere fun?" April said. "I'll let Maude know, she can join us."

"Impossible," Mike said firmly. "Frankie and I have to go scout locations in the Paris sewers. No lunch for us today. Go shopping, you two, take the day off. I've worked you hard enough."

"*Sewers?*" I heard April wondering, as we escaped toward the lobby door and into a taxi.

"What lies you'll tell not to tell a lie about a lie you've told," I marveled.

"I can't believe my imaginative capacities. Do you think they guessed?"

"They'll never find out," I said, comfortingly. "I almost believed you myself."

"But there is a famous sewer system and people really visit it."

"We should swing by the sewers after the Louvre," I suggested, "if that's going to trouble you."

"Maybe another time. It's dark down there, alligators all over the place most likely, like in New York. And sewers don't count, they don't give you the aesthetic stature of going to the Louvre."

"But they do show that you have a genuine interest in history, Mike. And archaeology. *And* sanitation. What is civilization without sanitation? That makes three more areas of superiority we'll appear to have. The girls will develop heavy-duty inferiority complexes—you should never have mentioned sewers. Did you see the look on Jordan's face? She was really impressed."

"I'm going to have to teach you not to laugh at me."

"You and who else?"

I guess I must have given him a smile loaded with redhead power because the next thing I knew Mike was kissing me in a way that shut me up as effectively as if I'd fainted. I may have actually fainted, because the next thing I clearly remember was the cab stopping. Could we have been kissing all the way to the Louvre? Considering my condition, the fact that I was more or less paralyzed, gasping for breath, yet more alive than I'd ever been in my life, there was every reason to believe that was what might have happened. One thing was certain, I hadn't played hard to get.

"Frankie. Open your eyes. I have to pay the driver."

"Bribe him to go away and leave us here," I whispered, keeping my eyes closed tightly, "make him rent us the taxi."

"I would but he's already stopped his meter and there's a policeman looking inquisitive and a couple of people who're waiting to get into this taxi. We have to get out. Let go of me, just for a second, you beautiful, silly baby."

"I can't. I would if I could but I can't." I really couldn't. I'd been waiting at least half my life to feel like this, but I'd never dreamed it would be so—there were no words for it. Whatever I was feeling, language couldn't express it.

"Sweetheart, we're at the Louvre."

"What about the Louvre?"

"We're going to go in, remember? We have a date."

"Really?" I tried to remember. Mike Aaron had kissed me, God knows how often. He'd called me beautiful, he'd called me baby, he'd called me sweetheart, and he expected me to remember something about a date?

"Yes, really. A Brooklyn-style date."

"I guess maybe you're right," I sighed languidly, opening my eyes. I unclasped my hands from around Mike's neck, finger by finger, and released him, or semi-released him, kissing his jaw with tiny kisses from his earlobe to his chin, and then down his neck, while he fumbled for his wallet. His neck alone was a place a person could kiss all day without getting bored, I thought as I pried myself reluctantly away. I felt that if I broke the contact between his skin and my skin some rending, terrible thing would happen.

Mike seemed to feel the same way because he managed to get his wallet open and pay the cabdriver with only one hand, while holding me very tightly with the other. All the way from the cab to the entrance to the Louvre, he hugged me hard with both his arms clasped around my shoulders, while he kissed the top of my head, which is not an easy way to walk, but in Paris who notices? We had to separate at the escalator, but we still managed to hold hands, and at the bottom we peeled off to one side and stood up against the first wall we came to and kissed a lot more, until it became a clear choice of stopping or making an outrageous spectacle of ourselves in full sight of everyone visiting the major tourist attraction in all of Europe.

"Just a whirl, darling," Mike muttered in my ear, "we'll just give it a quick whirl since we're here."

We managed to stagger over to a brilliantly lit display that showed us what was exhibited in the 198 galleries of the Louvre, and exactly how to get to each one of them.

"We could try the Crypt of the Sphinx," he suggested. "There shouldn't be anybody there. Or what about the Mastaba of Aakhtihotep, a Fifth-Dynasty sepulchre? Place probably only gets ten visitors a year."

"Neither of them *sound* like the Louvre. They might just as well be in the antiquities department of the Met," I pointed out with what small wits I retained. "We'll have made this whole trip without getting any authentic Louvre lore to prove we really came, in case anybody asks, and you know they eventually might."

"But think how cozy it sounds. A crypt, a sepulchre—we'll have them to ourselves."

"Mike," I said warningly, seeing exactly what he had in mind.

"There's no law against it, darling, darling, darling. I've simply got to kiss you some more."

"Me too, but not rolling around on the floor of a public building," I said regretfully. "Look, why don't we head straight for the Venus de Milo and the Winged Victory of Samothrace and get them over with quickly. That's what people expect you to see in the Louvre."

"We'd better do the Mona Lisa too. That's the biggie."

Nothing in the Louvre is quick, believe me, unless you've brought a skateboard. Those illuminated maps that make it all look so simple are diabolically deceptive. By the time we'd negotiated the trek from the Venus de Milo up the two staircases that led to the Winged Victory and then another staircase up and through a large gallery to the Mona Lisa, we'd had more than a major museum experience. We took one look at the large, jostling crowd blotting out what must be the Mona Lisa and turned away, down a long, wide, picture-hung, windowed corridor overlooking the Seine. It was called the Grande Galerie and it led, according to a sign, to an exit.

"Now I know why I never came here before," Mike said. "Call me a Philistine but this place is just too big. If you spend more than an hour in a museum your brain stops taking in and appreciating the things you see, and we're already overdue." We both walked quickly in the direction of the arrow.

"Why, oh why, didn't I listen to your suggestion about the Crypt of the Sphinx," I cried regretfully.

"Because you're a lady with ladylike delicacy and I respect you for it."

"I am? You do?"

"Yes, but I wouldn't want you to keep it up for too long."

"When do you want me to stop?"

"I'll tell you, in fact I won't have to tell you, you'll know."

"Stop talking to me like that. It makes me dizzy and we're not out of here yet."

"Dizzy? Head-whirling, fall-down dizzy? Want me to carry you?"

"No, crazy dizzy. Like this." I took the palm of his hand and pressed my mouth to it and then quickly tasted it with my tongue. He jumped two feet straight up.

"Don't *do* that!"

"I was just showing you exactly what I meant."

"That wasn't fair . . . unless you're ready for serious trouble, in front of all these guards. Oh, Frankie, darling, do you believe this hall? It's fucking *endless*," he said as we walked as quickly as possible, reading the names on the walls.

"Giotto, Fra Angelico, Botticelli, Bellini, Van Dyck, don't look, don't stop whatever you do or we're finished . . . have they no pity? Don't they know that some people have better things to do than look at pictures? Damn the French, once they've got you where they want you, they never let you go."

"Cranach, Holbein, Guardi, Tiepolo, Goya . . ." I panted, as we went so fast we were almost running.

"You don't suppose we've missed the exit?" I asked, after a long while, as the absence of other people suddenly registered and made me pull up suddenly.

We looked at each other in horror and disbelief. We found ourselves alone, without even a museum guard in sight, at the end of the gallery that now stretched back, way, way back into the dim rich areas we'd already covered, a distance you almost needed a telescope to see to the end of. Ahead of us was only a room full of El Grecos and, unbelievably, the end of the building itself, where windows looked out on the Tuileries gardens. There were two staircases, marked "vers Sculptures" and "vers Galerie d'Etude."

"We must have passed it somehow. Or else it's all part of a plot, I bet there never was an exit," Mike said grimly.

"Which staircase do you want to take?"

"Neither one of them is safe. We could be wandering around here all day. The only thing to do is to retrace the way we came. I learned that in Boy Scout camp."

I burst into tears.

"Baby, my poor baby, I'll carry you, I promise," he said, holding me against him and rocking me comfortingly.

"No . . . no . . . it's not that, my feet are fine. . . . It's the idea of you in a Boy Scout uniform . . . you must have been so adorable . . ." I sobbed.

"You're overtired, that's what it is."

"Admit you were adorable," I demanded through my tears.

"I guess so, yeah. I'll give you some old photos of me in my uniform if you'll stop crying."

"Do we really have to go all the way back?" I asked piteously.

"That or spend the night. Look, I have an idea, if you really won't let me carry you, it'll be easier if you look straight down at the floor and let me guide you. You're suffering from seeing all those pictures out of the corner of your eye. It's a case of sensory overload. But the floor has a repetitive pattern and it won't seem so far if that's all you see, without other distractions."

"All right. I'll put my hand over my eyes—it'll look as if I've been struck by a headache from absorbing too much beauty. The Stendhal Syndrome I think they call it."

Mike was absolutely right, the safari was much easier with visual monotony and just his big, warm hands to concentrate on. I *had* managed to get a look at the miraculous Botticellis and the glorious wall of Tiepolos . . . and a lot more—it seemed a crime not to peek. Since we were here.

"There's the exit sign!" Mike exploded after we'd covered about half a mile.

"Can I look at it, at least?"

"No, it'll break your heart. We could have taken a right after Fragonard and gone down those stairs next to the buffet and tea room. Damn sign's facing sideways, that's where we went wrong."

"BUFFET?" I stopped dead, incredulous. "Were you going to pass up a buffet?"

"Now you know why I never made Eagle Scout," he said sheepishly.

We devoured two huge ham and cheese sandwiches each, the kind the French make that are mostly divine bread and butter, drank two cups of milky coffee apiece and bounded down the stairs, which were a short distance from a door to the outside world I'd almost given up hope of seeing again.

As we stood there, revitalized, breathing in the fresh air, I realized that I felt deeply shy. I looked up at Mike and I could tell he'd been seized by the same emotion. "What next?" was what we were both asking ourselves, now that we didn't have the Louvre to go to or escape from.

"Is this still a date?" I asked finally, sounding as challenging as possible, "because if it is, it's up to the guy to decide what to do next. That's the way it works in Brooklyn and we're on Brooklyn regulations here."

He brightened and pushed me in the direction of a taxi stand where there were actually a couple of cabs waiting, probably because it was the lunch hour.

"Du Louvre" I thought I heard him say.

"Haven't you had enough for one day?" I objected incredulously.

"This is a different Louvre, on the Left Bank. It's our Louvre day, all day long. I thought Brooklyn girls let the man decide."

"They have a right of consultation."

"If you don't like it, Red, we won't go in."

" 'Red'?"

"Did you think I hadn't noticed?"

"I totally forgot!"

"Your mind has been otherwise occupied."

"I can't *believe* I forgot. What do you think? Do you like it?"

"I love every last hair on your head, I love your forehead, your eyebrows, your eyes, your nose, your lips, particularly your lips, and I love everything else all the way down to the soles of your feet. Brown hair or red, it makes no never mind. You're gorgeous."

"That's a lot of things to love," I mumbled cautiously. Was he putting me on?

"Barely enough. Less would be too little, more, lots more, would be much better."

The taxi pulled up at a modest-looking hotel on the busy Quai Voltaire.

"What's this?" I asked.

"The Hôtel du Louvre, so named because of the view."

"And why are we here?"

"As I said, more to love would be better. But that's up to you."

"Mike Aaron, it's the middle of the afternoon!" I said, surprised into being scandalized.

"Does the time of day bother you?"

"You want to go in and rent a room and . . . ?"

"I'm dying to. It's the only thing in the world I want to do. Don't you?"

"But . . ."

"What?"

"Is this still a date?"

"No, Frankie, this is not a date anymore, not if we go into that hotel room. I don't know what you'd call it, but I'd call it damn close to a matter of life or death, emotionally speaking."

"Oh," I said, blank as a piece of glass with pure dumb happiness.

"Does that mean yes or no?"

"Kiss me first," I temporized.

"No, I want you to decide without kissing . . . kissing makes you more impulsive than usual. And every time I kiss you I fall more in love, and if you don't want to go into that hotel with me, I don't want to be one bit more in love with you than I am right now."

"You never said anything about love," I gasped.

"Can't you tell?"

"Of course not!" I couldn't believe how indignant I sounded. "You're always around the most beautiful girls in the world," I cried in disbelief, "how could you possibly not be in and out of love with them all the time?"

"It just didn't happen. Lust, yes, love no. I must have been waiting for a bumptious, opinionated, obstinate, impossible girl from the old neighborhood like you. No, not 'like you' . . . you, *only* you."

He stopped and seemed to be thinking. I sat there, too astonished to breathe.

"It's the *personhood* of you that I love, the human *beingness* . . . the way your nutty little mind works, what passes for your sense of humor, your strong sense of values even when you're wrong, your wacky attitude . . . you know who you are and you *are* who you are. I love the way you make me feel that I'm a completed person. I love the way I want to take care of you. When I'm with you I feel that I've come home—home in the way everyone imagines home should be."

"But . . . ?" This was happening so fast I still couldn't believe it.

"But what?"

"When we met, you were so rude, and we had lunch at the Bistroquet only because you couldn't get hold of the girls that day. . . ."

"Don't you know that love is one big, fucking, scary number, Frankie? I was hoping I didn't feel how I felt. Even way back at the airport, I began to suspect that you were it for me. Aren't you scared too?"

"Not even one little bit," I said, looking in his eyes in a way that would tell him that every word I said was true. "I've been in love with you since your senior year in high school. I've never stopped. I decided it was hopeless but I still carried on."

"Really? Is that true?"

"Of course. Half the other girls in school had the nerve to think they were too, but I *knew* I was, the real thing. You're the love of my life."

"I'd better be," he said, gathering me up as much as you can in the backseat of a Paris cab. "Forever and ever, now that I've found you. Oh, Frankie, my overlooked, rudely treated baby. I don't want to rush you into anything, but I graduated from high school many years ago. Don't you think that we should do something to celebrate?"

So we did. With intermissions and catnaps, of course, all afternoon and well into the evening, together in a big bed overlooking the Seine, with street noise that made a rapturous bumble outside the double-glazed windows of our room. We didn't talk a lot. We were making our first trip together through a landscape too intensely interesting to be interrupted by words. I can't tell you the details, because I'm modest about things like that, but . . . never mind. Let's just say that when Mike and I made love I realized that I'd never truly been with a man before.

Finally, I had to rouse myself and convince Mike that our absence would be noticed by one and all, sewer trip or no sewer trip. We took a shower together and got dressed, congratulating ourselves on our striking resemblance to the people we'd been in the morning, even though we weren't them and never would be again. In the taxi going back we sat collapsed against each other in silent delight. If only, I thought vaguely, if only the fourteen-year-old me had known for certain that this day would come, I could have been looking forward to it all these years. But could I have endured the slow passage of time?

As usual, the gang, except for Tinker, was gathered in the Relais Bar, near the window.

"Better not stand too near me," Mike warned as we got out of the taxi. "We don't want to advertise."

"Then you'd better let go of my hand."

"And just how were the famous sewers?" Jordan asked as we sat down. She laughed in a way I didn't care for.

"As a matter of fact we went to the Louvre," Mike told her.

"The Louvre?" Maude Callender inquired snarkily. "You don't say? The Louvre *again?* Indeed? I suppose you saw the Mona Lisa?"

"No, there were too many tourists around it to get close," I replied.

"There usually are," she agreed. "What a clever thing to say."

"Of course you went to the Louvre," April snickered. "It's written all over you. Both of you."

"Doesn't the Louvre close much earlier than this?" Jordan asked.

"That's okay, Jordan," Maude assured her, "I'll fill you in later."

"You can see the effects of looking at great art in their glazed eyes, can't you, Maude?" April drawled.

"We walked the whole length of the Grande Galerie," Mike said indignantly. "It's the Stendhal Syndrome."

"You walked the entire Grande Galerie and lived to tell the tale? That's not just rare, it's unheard of in the annals of art appreciation," Maude laughed. "Now that was not a clever thing to say, Mike, I expected better of you."

"We damn well did! Both ways," Mike insisted.

"Have it your own way," Maude smirked. "You must have found a fountain of youth in there somewhere. You both look quite . . . peppy. Refreshed, ten years younger, if such a thing is possible at your ages."

"Oh, Maude, I don't agree with you," Jordan protested. "To me Frankie and Mike both look . . . wiped out, bushed . . . almost . . . *depleted* . . . congratulations, Frankie, you lucky thing, you."

"I'm not having a drink with you cynical, filthy-minded people," I snapped. "You're all just jealous!"

"Ah ha! Gotcha!" Jordan crowed.

"Jesus!" Mike asked, throwing up his arms. "Is nothing sacred?"

He grabbed me and we left through the side door into the lobby. They were all laughing so hard that they were crying. I didn't give a damn, I realized. I wanted to tell everybody, starting with the concierges, the cashiers, the waiters, the people in the lobby, the bellboys, and then I wanted the word to spread out in ever-widening circles of knowledge all over Paris—out, out, until the whole world knew about Frankie Severino and Mike Aaron and how much in love they were.

17

The last few days had been such an utter and complete shit storm that she might just as well have lunch with Dart Benedict, Justine thought. She was tired of making excuses to put him off and in the state she was in, she welcomed any diversion. She was mildly curious to find out why this man, who ran such an important and long-established agency, had kept after her to make a lunch date. Obviously he wanted something or he wouldn't be bothering with her, but at least there was no particular agenda of *presumption* involved. Even if there had been, Justine thought grimly, Necker and Aiden had already made her feel so intensely presumed upon that any further presumption would merely fade into the general murk.

How could Necker have dared to send her that outrageously lavish piece of unwanted furniture? It was such an obvious bribe, masquerading as a gift. Everything about the little desk reeked of the kind of largesse she could expect, if she had fallen in with his wishes. It was an utterly unwelcome responsibility. Justine wasn't at home during the day, so she hadn't been able to get it picked up and sent back. What's more, sending it back meant, infuriatingly enough, having it properly repacked and suitably insured since, as Aiden had pointed out, it must be exceedingly valuable.

She didn't want to owe Necker anything! Justine picked up the light desk and carried the damnably exquisite thing into a little dark room that she never used and tried to tell herself that it didn't exist except as a nuisance she'd have to deal with eventually.

But the desk refused to disappear from her mind. It was as if Necker had reached out into her house with a giant hand and placed it there himself. It seemed to exist—to be alive!—in its unlit room, as inescapably radiant in her mind as if there had been a spotlight trained on it night and day. She could clearly see the porcelain plaques on the drawers with their tender, gay bunches of brilliantly painted flowers, framed by a particular shade of apple green with a turquoise tint to it. The central plaque with its coat of arms, three towers with a coronet surmounting them, was unforgettable. If it hadn't come from Necker, she would at least have found someone to identify its first owner. Natural curiosity would have carried her that far.

If she'd come across the desk in an antiques shop—but only at a bargain price—even though it was so many light years more elegant than the objects she was normally attracted to, she might have been tempted by its supremely harmonious form. Then, Justine thought, she would have kept it in her bedroom to enjoy looking at, to wonder over. She might even have amused herself by writing a note on it, wondering about the generations of women who had sat there before her, writing to lovers, sending invitations to balls, confirming orders to their dressmakers. It must have been first made for a woman of taste, a woman who demanded luxury and quality. There was no question that the desk was a work of great craftsmanship, Justine had to admit that to herself. She didn't blame the desk, she blamed the giver.

She didn't want it! The mysterious object was a part of another civilization, an artifact of a way of life utterly foreign to her, and it belonged in a museum, not in her own, very personal, non-museum-quality home. It didn't matter what charm it had, the desk had invaded her privacy, as Necker had intended it to. Justine felt as if he had presented her with a magnificent tiara, held her down with one hand, forced the tiara on her head with the other, and informed her that she had to wear it every day whether she chose to or not.

Necker had *presumed,* unbearably presumed, for he had sent the desk before the blizzard, probably as soon as Gabrielle d'Angelle had called to spring the trap with the news that her three models had been chosen for the Lombardi prize. That haste showed how sure he'd been of her acquiescence, how easily he thought he could buy his admission into her life.

As for Aiden, there was only a difference of degree between his presumption and Necker's. Aiden—Justine brooded, feeling sick at heart—Aiden had become another kind of presuming invader in her life. She'd opened her door to an unknown contractor and the next thing she knew he was wrecking her furnace, kidnapping her and enticing her into a sexual enslavement. No man, ever, had reached her inner core as Aiden had. Passion, uncontrollable and overwhelming, had been irresistible for a few days, but how quickly it had led to demands on her privacy. He'd said he didn't "want any explanations" about the desk, when that was exactly what he wanted, what he *expected*.

Why the hell did the fact that a man could almost make you come by looking at you sideways, mean that you had to tell him things you wanted to keep to yourself? Wasn't it as basic as that? Wasn't that an example of classic male sexual control, the sort of control she'd always feared her girls would be exposed to by the model-collectors who pursued them, the kind of control that caused models to do things no sane girl would do*!*

She hadn't trusted herself to see Aiden again. She couldn't resolve his suspicions without revealing Necker's existence in her life. It would be equally impossible to spend time together pretending that the desk didn't exist. Worst of all, if she saw him for dinner, as he'd been phoning and asking her to do, she wouldn't be able to think of anything but whether it would be only decent to wait until after dinner to make love. Decent or indecent, it didn't matter, Justine admitted to herself. A quick fuck on her doormat, the second he put a foot inside her house, would do just fine. And then another. Her brain told her body that it was dangerously enraptured and that knowledge scared the hell out of her.

Yes, this was a good time to see what Dart Benedict was after. He was neither father nor lover nor friend. He was powerful and much gossiped about, but there was no emotional element involved in breaking bread with him. He was the kind of man who brought out all the cool, strong independence she had so recently, so foolishly, congratulated herself on possessing.

Dart Benedict was a long-range planner, blessed with a cold, accurate objectivity, so clear and powerful that he could use it on himself as well as on others. In the late-1970s, when he was a splendid twenty-five, he'd married, picking Mary Beth Bonner, a large, placid, utterly plain but immaculately groomed post-debutante who had the advantage of being an heiress in her own right as well as the only child of rich parents. Mary Beth, accustomed only to mild attention from the most hopelessly boring of society boys, was astonished at her luck in attracting Dart. He could have had any one of her friends he wanted, in spite of his being in the model agency business, an occupation that was regarded with the deepest suspicion in her conservative world.

In addition to Mary Beth's fortune, her other desirable attributes included old-fashioned good manners, a lack of imagination, a low sex drive, a passion for country living and a firm sense of self-discipline that ensured, insofar as such things could be predicted, that she would never embarrass Dart by running to fat or to drink. Most important of all—after her money—Mary Beth was a deeply religious Catholic. Dart converted from Methodism in order to marry her, knowing that Mary Beth guaranteed the background he'd decided he must have: a home life built on a rock and free from financial worry.

Dart had grown up in Philadelphia, where his family's justifiable pretensions to antiquity and status were being slowly and sordidly destroyed by divorce, drink and a chronic mishandling of funds. During his undergraduate years at the University of Pennsylvania, Dart distanced himself from his parents, looking for the quickest path to future security. He evaluated his own abilities with his unsparing clarity.

There was no question that he functioned best outside of any classroom. He had enormous success in dealing with the most ambitious and alluring of his female classmates. They flocked around him, treating him not as a possible boyfriend, but as someone whose advice they sought, whose judgment they valued and acted on. No question about it, Dart told himself, he had a God-given knack for dealing with women. What's more, he had the ability to judge degrees of female beauty. He had an inborn accuracy of eye for the often blurred line that separated the large number of girls who were pretty, even exceptionally pretty, from those few who had true, bone-deep beauty. His sexual needs were inexhaustible and he was careful to satisfy them with the pretty girls, not the beauties. When he graduated, Dart was able to get his first job in a modeling agency by persuading the two most beautiful girls in his class to follow him into the business that he had decided was made to order for him.

Soon after Dart married Mary Beth, he borrowed some of her money to open a small agency he called Benedict. Mary Beth busied herself creating a life of calm and elegance in the Fairfield County horse country just outside of North Stamford, to which Dart commuted every day. He had imagined that perhaps six months after the honeymoon he would resume his wallowing in the luscious variety of sexual pleasures the world of models offered him so freely. This was the only place in which his self-knowledge failed. Dart managed to hold off less than three weeks before he resumed his clandestine lunch-hour affairs in his old bachelor apartment in New York, but otherwise his plans were perfectly executed. Mary Beth was soon happily pregnant; she shopped in Greenwich, rarely ventured into New York and showed little curiosity about his work.

Now, not quite twenty years later, Dart and Mary Beth Benedict had long been pillars of Connecticut society. They had six children, ranging from nineteen to three, and Mary Beth, who adored her husband more than ever, was hoping for another baby. Dart's apartment remained a well-kept secret inside the modeling community and none of the hundreds of girls he'd brought there had ever expected more from this firmly married father of six than he was willing to give.

He had one hell of a good life, Dart thought as he waited for Justine Loring. On the one hand, it was beautifully centered, well rounded and full of calm contentment and dignity, the sort of life his parents had thrown away so selfishly. He and Mary Beth had founded a handsome, well-bred dynasty. On the other hand, he had married so intelligently that he was able to preserve an area of freedom other men could only dream of. Drugs—of course he sometimes enjoyed drugs, but as a connoisseur, a civilized gourmet, happy to share the best stuff available with those clients who expected it. And what real man should be denied women in all their variety? He'd organized his life around his most necessary pleasure, and when he'd finished with a girl, there was always good business use to be made of her. Both of them gained in the transaction.

But there was an area of his existence left to be satisfied, Dart told himself. As his success in the business had grown, so had his ambition. His agency, aside from three women's divisions, had a men's division, a children's division and a thriving branch in Hollywood, as well as profitable affiliations with major agencies in Paris and Milan. But Ford, Elite and Lunel were larger than Benedict in total billings. It infuriated him to own the fourth largest modeling agency in the world. There was something that fundamentally smacked of failure about being fourth in anything, he saw that all too plainly. It had an unpleasantly humorous flavor, like winning the gold medal for the luge at the Olympics. Although no one in his weekend world ever saw him as anything but a glamorous success in a field that had gained a certain respectability and enormous fascination, Dart could not escape the fact that after more than twenty years in the agency business he might never be the leader of the pack.

Unacceptable, he decided, as he rose to greet Justine. Simply unacceptable.

"Justine, you're more beautiful than ever," he said truthfully. He'd give damn near anything to have her working with him. There was no one in town to equal her reassuring way with young models, and young and younger were the key words today. Recently he'd lost several most promising kids to Loring Model Management because their mothers were more willing to entrust their daughters to Justine than to him, in spite of the relative smallness of her agency. And Justine had a tremendous eye for potential. Sometimes it was better than his, Dart had to acknowledge. She'd signed girls he hadn't wanted, and turned them into useful moneymakers, even potential stars. He'd turned down April Nyquist, for example, because she had impressed him as too classic a blond to be salable. He'd thought that one Daryl Hannah was all the market could absorb and he was still kicking himself for that mistake.

"You don't age, Dart," Justine said, equally truthfully. Dart's thick, sandy hair had been showing a little grey for a dozen years, but it was still all on his head where it belonged. He was handsome in a bluff outdoors sort of way, a tanned, tall, rugged man who looked as if he sat a horse beautifully, fly-fished the best streams and climbed dangerous mountains on his vacations. Amazing, Justine thought, as they sat down, to look at him you'd say he had to be a nice guy.

"I was surprised, and delighted of course, when your secretary called to say you could make lunch after all. I was sure that by now you'd be off to Paris to be with your girls. Congratulations, Justine! What a coup! When I heard that you'd swept the field I couldn't believe it, nobody could. You put everybody's nose out of joint, a small agency like yours getting all three of the picks. But when credit is due, I'm the first to admit it."

"I was just as surprised as you were—maybe more." Dart Benedict hadn't asked her to lunch to congratulate her, Justine thought. That much she was sure of.

"I'm curious, how come you didn't go to Paris? I'd be over there hovering over those girls if it had happened to me."

"Good Lord, Dart, I can't just pick up and leave Loring Management to run itself for two weeks. Frankie's more than capable."

"Frankie Severino of song and story. You're lucky to have her."

"How true," Justine said shortly, addressing herself to the menu. "Song and story?" What was that supposed to mean? He'd never met Frankie as far as she knew. She only knew Dart and his wife from parties they'd both been invited to. People in the agency business normally stayed out of each other's way.

"How many of your other girls are going to do the shows?" Dart asked after they'd ordered.

"Four or five . . . you know how it is, they won't make up their minds until the last minute."

"I've got a dozen getting ready to leave for Milan day after tomorrow. Or at least that's the plan . . . when did the inmates take over the asylums, Justine? Five years ago—no, *two* years ago, if I said I had a dozen girls going, a dozen girls damn well were on that plane. Now the best of them are bloody conglomerates, too busy deal-making to face the jet lag. And if they're not doing hostess gigs on television, they're bound by their cosmetic contracts not to do runway. The money is so big it doesn't seem to matter to them anymore."

"Don't forget the girls who are flying off to the coast, testing for movie parts." If Dart insisted on making small talk before getting to his point, whatever it was, she was willing to go along with it, Justine shrugged to herself.

"Tell me about it—that's what's happened to Elsie, and she's done Chanel faithfully for three years. Karl always gave her the bridal gown, so you can imagine how thrilled he is about losing her at the last minute . . . he'll never book her again even if she comes back."

"Elsie? What's the part?"

"Something Julia Roberts just fell out of, so it could be one of ten scripts. All I know is she left a message with her booker, didn't dare tell me herself."

"You're probably too strong a father figure," Justine said wryly.

"That's possible," Dart said thoughtfully. "But isn't a father figure exactly what young girls need? Look at you, Justine. You're what exactly? In your mid-thirties? But you give off a powerful mother figure aura—you make people think of someone baking great bread and making fabulous soups from scratch—all those things no one has time to do anymore. I think, with all due respect to your business acumen, it's that aura of safety, of home and hearth, that's made your boutique work so well."

"Thanks, Dart. If so, I don't know I'm doing it, but so much the better. There are things you just can't fake," Justine made herself smile graciously. Homemade soup her ass!

"You know, Justine, I'm a little worried about you. Here you are, stuck in New York, when by all rights you really *should* be in Paris making absolutely sure that each of your girls is okay. But you can't leave by your own admission because, of all your employees, Frankie is the only one who's totally trustworthy. None of your bookers can take over the agency for you, can they? What does that tell me? That your shop is paper thin in management. How can you grow quickly in that situation?"

"You're kind to be concerned about me, Dart," Justine said

coolly. "However, I've managed to keep growing at a rate that personally I feel comfortable with. Comfort and total control are important to me. I like being the boss, and I wouldn't want to share that position with anyone else. To each his own."

"I understand what you're saying, Justine, I used to feel the same way, but I didn't really start getting anywhere until I hired the right people, even before I could afford them, and made myself learn to delegate. When I think that even though Necker himself personally picked all three of your models, you actually didn't *go* to Paris . . . the man owns two other fashion houses, for God's sake— you could *pack* them with your girls if you chose to use your charms on him. I'd never have wasted such a clear shot."

"Dart, what makes you think that Lombardi didn't choose the girls himself?" Justine asked, going pale.

"Marco Lombardi and I have been the greatest of pals for years. Old, old buddies, veterans of the model wars you might say. He was so furious when Necker crammed your girls down his throat that he picked up a phone to complain to me for half an hour. How can you be sure that our charming mutual friend, that well-known scamp of a Marco, is being halfway decent to them? How do you know they're behaving themselves? Hmmm? We all know something about the temptations of Paris, don't we?"

"Frankie reports to me and there haven't been any problems." Justine managed to keep her voice level and light and semi-amused. Why was this insulting piece of vermin pushing his horror of a country-life nose into her business?

"Well, good for Frankie, but in your place, I'd be in Paris no matter what I missed in New York. I'm leaving in a few days as a matter of fact. Which brings me to my pitch, Justine."

"I've been wondering when you'd get around to it," Justine said, not bothering to suppress a chilly smile.

"You accepted my invitation, so you must be curious to know why I invited you to lunch."

"Perhaps a touch curious, Dart, but mostly polite. How many times could I turn down your flattering invitation?"

"I'm never ashamed to be persistent. Justine, you know how big Benedict is. I run a magnificent, well-oiled machine. We cover every branch of the business, and we make a fortune in commissions, yet I don't feel we've gone nearly as far as we can go. There's room to expand and this is the perfect moment to do it."

"Go for it, Dart," Justine said encouragingly. "Rah, team!"

"Be serious, Justine. I'd like to buy Loring Model Management at a price you'd be more than satisfied with and sign you to a long-term management contract on your own terms. It would be a win-win proposition. You'd come out of it with a significant fortune, you'd still be working in the field you've chosen, but you wouldn't have any financial responsibilities. No more Friday paydays, no more worry about your line of credit, no more concerns that a key booker might leave and take some of your best girls with her—all that would become Benedict's problem and Benedict is big enough to absorb them easily. You'd be free to do what you do so brilliantly: find promising girls and develop them into stars."

"Win-win? Who would I report to, Dart?"

"You'd run your own division, absolutely. And of course you could bring Frankie with you."

"But who would I report to?"

"Well, in the final analysis, you and I would have a pow-wow every now and then, but your contract would spell out the terms of the issues on which you'd defer to my judgment."

"So I'd report to you, and there'd be an area in which you'd have the last word. Have I got that right?"

"Correct. I can't pay a lot of money for your business and then give you an absolutely free rein . . . that wouldn't make sense. But there's no reason we can't hammer out an agreement that's satisfactory to both of us."

"It wouldn't work. I'm not interested, Dart."

"Look Justine, you haven't had time to give this any real consideration. Don't answer now, just think about it. But let me ask you this, do you realize that you're a slave to your agency? It's run in an old-fashioned way, as if you lived over a candy store. On the other hand, in spite of all my responsibilities, I have enough strong second management working in my shop so that whenever I feel like it, I can run off with Mary Beth and relax at our place in Hobe Sound. And when the kids are out of school we manage to get away for a real family vacation, a month, even six weeks."

"Relaxation's not my cup of tea, unless it's just a weekend."

"You're being deliberately frivolous, Justine. You know perfectly well what I mean. You're more than young enough to pick and choose from a hundred eligible guys—you should get married, have children, entertain, buy a place in the country, garden, travel —I don't have to spell out all the possibilities but they're as real as that salad you're eating. It's all out there for you but you've chosen to marry your business. That's not healthy."

"I could also sew my own clothes, Dart. I'll think about getting a life," Justine said sharply. Necker, Aiden, now Martha Stewart advice from a turd! Just what she'd needed.

"Look, we both know I'm not saying this because I'm disinterested. I really and truly *need* your talent at my shop," Dart said, undeterred. If you don't want to sell Loring Management outright we could still work out a different kind of agreement, some form of partnership, that would free you of business problems, afford me the benefit of your brains and give you a fair percentage of all the profits I'm positive we'd make together."

"Sorry, Dart, but I don't want to work with anyone as a partner. I like my independence."

"With all due respect, Justine, you must realize how vulnerable you are running what's essentially a two-woman shop. For example, what if somebody took it into his head to offer Frankie twice the salary you pay her? She gets seventy-five thousand a year—a hundred-and-fifty wouldn't be out of line, if you ask me, considering how good she is."

"How the hell do you know what she makes?" Justine asked, startled and angry.

"I asked her. I'm the guy who offered her double. And don't bother to say I'm a bastard, it was strictly business. I figured that if I didn't, someone else would."

"She never told me."

"Probably because she didn't want to seem to be pressing for a raise you couldn't afford. But the day might come, Justine, when she changes her mind. As I said, persistence pays off."

"Look, do you really want to know why I won't join forces with you, Dart, in spite of the very favorable conditions you've spelled out?"

"Of course I do, because it doesn't add up, and you're a sensible woman."

"The business of renting out beautiful young females should only be done by someone who's deeply concerned with what happens to the girls, someone who sees them as individual human beings, each one precious in her own way. As it is now, there are too many girls who don't get a contract without sleeping with an important man at a given agency or who can't get a booking without sleeping with the client. There's too much pimping the new girls to photographers and their reps. Young women who go into modeling are exposed to enough inevitable shit about their weight, their looks and their stamina without being pressured into sex."

"How can you stay in the business if you think it's so terrible?"

"Because someone, as you said about trying to hire Frankie, has to do it, and at least with me there's no abuse."

"So, you consider yourself a version of a mother superior?" he asked with a nasty edge to his voice.

"Dart, let me give you an example of the kind of thing I'm talking about here. There's an agency in this town in which girls are divided, unofficially, into three groups. There's a group known as the 'Untouchables'—the girls who are great enough to get contracts anywhere. They're left strictly alone, spoiled like princesses, sexual favors are never required of them. Then there's a second group, known as the 'Maybes.' They're watched carefully and brought along to see which of them has genuine potential. If they have what it takes they become 'Untouchables.' The others, unofficially again, are demoted into a third group, known as the 'Troops.' "

"Where do you pick up this stuff?"

"The Troops," Justine continued, "no matter how pretty they are, will never have a chance to get to the top. They're not told that fact in so many words, of course, but they're destined to have ordinary careers: catalog work, small print jobs, all the non-glamorous mid-level kind of thing every agency needs. They'll never do high fashion or television or runway, but they make good money for themselves and accumulate steady commissions for the agency—"

"Justine, every shop in town including yours has more girls

like that than any other kind. Only civilians don't know how tiny the percentage is of the so-called supermodels . . . we're talking about less than two dozen out of hundreds and hundreds of girls. Thousands if you count the girls outside of New York."

"The owner of this agency I'm talking about," Justine said, disregarding his interruption, "regards all the Troops as his private harem. When he wants to . . . use . . . them, all he does is tell them where and when to show up. They either comply or they're asked to leave the agency. There's no shortage of would-be models, is there, Dart, especially at the mid-level? Now, until the girl gets to this man's place, she never knows if she'll be alone with him, or if there'll be other girls working on him, or strange men she'll be required to service, or even other girls she'll be expected to perform with. And there's a lot of drugs around—a strong possibility exists that she may try them, possibly for the first time. Oh, I forgot, this scene only takes place at lunch. The amazing thing is that the agency owner who stages these . . . lunches . . . is happily married, with great kids, a real pillar of the community. What's more, his wife has never suspected a thing. No one would be cruel enough to tell her."

"And you actually believe that rumor? Where'd you hear all this nonsense?"

"Everywhere, Dart, *everywhere*. That's why I'm never planning to go into business with anybody else. You never know what's under the rock in someone's backyard until you move into his house."

"Suit yourself," he said with a shrug. "Stay out there on your own, if that's what makes you happy. But you'd better invest in some long johns made out of cashmere, you're going to need them during that long, cold, risky winter when the wind blows and other agencies start raiding your bookers and your girls."

"I've survived so far—in my pure silk scanties. Do you mind if I skip coffee? I have to get back to my candy store."

"Good-bye, Justine. I won't forget to tell Marco about our lunch when I call him, he'll be interested in news of an old friend."

Justine walked quickly out of the restaurant, without shaking hands. She'd known from the inflection in his voice when he was talking about "that scamp, Marco" that he was letting her know that he was in full possession of the details of her shameful, humiliating affair with Lombardi. Men like the two of them would never fail to report such conquests to each other, boasting about them in full detail. But for Dart to use it as ammunition so many years later, ammunition to soften her up, ammunition to put her in her place, before he made his buyout proposition! Wouldn't a really smart man have realized that it was the last thing he should have mentioned? And wouldn't a really smart man have avoided threatening her with raids on her agency when she'd made it plain that she knew what went on in his private lunches?

No, Justine told herself, it was simpler than that. Dart Benedict saw no difference between her and the girls he preyed on. He'd worked on her with the same combination of bullying and the promise of rewards that made them do his bidding. He wanted to fuck her brains, not her body—that was the only difference. And this was to have been the lunch in which her professionalism would be engaged, a lunch without emotions, without pressure, without an agenda of presumption.

As Justine hurried back to her office she tried to put any further thought of Dart Benedict out of her mind. He'd made an enemy and she'd made an enemy. So much for the business lunch. From now on it was a tuna sandwich, alone at her desk.

Later that afternoon her secretary put a letter from Frankie on Justine's desk. It had just arrived by overnight Federal Express from Paris.

> *Dearest Justine,*
> *I have to tell you and I couldn't fax it because someone might read the fax even if it's marked confidential and I didn't want to try and get you by phone because I couldn't interrupt you in the office to talk about this, but I'm so happy I don't know what to do with myself. I'm roaming around this huge suite like a madwoman, trying to believe it's really happened. . . . Mike Aaron and I are in love. Oh, Justine, I can't sleep, I can't make myself sit still, I can't do anything but write to you—the only person in the world I can confide in—and hope it calms me down. In love, can you*

believe it? I didn't know till this afternoon, but he's in love with me! You know how I've always said such awful things about him? Did you guess I was just covering up the way I'd loved him since high school? Oh, Justine, he's so magnificent! I wish I could write poetry—or even prose that could come anywhere close to how I feel. Mike's my dream come true ten thousand times over. I didn't know a person could be so happy. And you were absolutely right about my hair and my clothes—I don't know how much of that helped him to notice me, but it certainly didn't hurt. We spent all day alone together, at the Louvre in the morning and at the Hôtel du Louvre in the afternoon. Yes, Justine, yes! Now the whole mob here knows, they couldn't miss seeing it when we met them for drinks. Do you realize it wouldn't have happened if you hadn't sent me here? I still can't believe it! Everything's under control, I'm keeping my head, I'm not letting down on the job, don't worry about a thing. I faxed you all the details about Tinker this morning and there's been no new news since then. Except Mike and me. We. Me and Mike. Us. I don't know what it's going to mean—even if you don't believe in a personal God, pray for me, Justine darling. Pray that this isn't just a Paris version of a shipboard romance. I don't think I could recover from that—not after this afternoon. I hope someday you'll be as happy as I am right now. I miss you so much! With love and kisses,
  Frankie.

Justine reread the letter four times before she put it down and went over to the window and leaned her head on the glass. She nodded her forehead gently from side to side, as one would over the crib of a sleeping baby, a nod of wonder and apprehension and helplessness and love and hope. Let it go well, she thought, please God, let it go well.

18

I'm trying so hard to rationalize this," April said to Maude, her words rushing out passionately. "I'm trying to accept it, to tell myself that it isn't the end of the world, that I never expected to win anyway and all the exposure in *Zing* will be wonderful for my career, but I'm so disappointed I don't know what to do—" April dropped down on the edge of Maude's bed, and burst into tears.

Frankie had visited both Jordan and April in their rooms soon after they were awake that morning and told each of them separately that from now on they'd be seeing little of Tinker since she'd be busy with her tango lessons and working with Lombardi. In spite of her efforts to downplay any premature assumption that Tinker had won the Lombardi prize, Frankie hadn't convinced either girl that there was still an open competition. Jordan had received the news with composure, but April, still in her bathrobe, had brushed Frankie aside and rushed to take her emotions to Maude, who was sitting on her bed, her draperies still drawn, reading the *International Herald Tribune* by the light of her bedside table, before getting dressed for the day.

"Marco Lombardi should be drawn and quartered," Maude cried vehemently. "April, poor baby, don't sob so terribly. Oh, I know how you feel, I really do. I know how important this is to you. Remember how I told you that my story is based on your winning? It still is, this changes nothing. If the ending turns out differently, I'll make it perfectly clear that it was rigged against you, that no honest choice was ever made. Here, put this quilt around you, you're shivering. There, that's better, now blow your nose. Have you even had breakfast?"

"I'd just finished when Frankie came in."

"Want some of my coffee to warm you up? It's still hot, and it's chilly in this room. No place in France understands central heating, American style."

"No thanks," April answered, her tears reduced to a few sniffs by Maude's sympathy.

"Lombardi hasn't given you even a fighting chance at the contract. Or Jordan, for that matter. Of course you realize what has to have happened?" Maude said, soothingly. "Tinker must have let him make love to her when she went for that runway lesson, there's no other explanation. Maybe she even put the idea in his head, who knows what tricks she could get up to? But you'd think Lombardi would pretend that he hasn't made his choice so early in the game, you'd think he'd let it play out as a competition and declare a winner afterward. He's utterly shameless . . . what I don't understand is how he can *not* realize that after the show no one will believe he could have chosen her instead of you?"

"He doesn't give a damn, that's the only answer I can think of," April said thoughtfully. "Jordan won't be particularly upset, she hasn't believed she had a real shot because she's black, she told me that on the plane coming over and she's never changed her mind. To think I was worried because Necker took her to Versailles. I should have been worried about Tinker instead. But damn it, I don't see why any one of us, including Jordan, couldn't have ended up as the Lombardi girl if people played fair."

"April, darling, it was never going to be Jordan, she was right about that. But it should have been you."

Maude looked with compassion and adoration at April's face. Her beauty gave no quarter, there was no mercy in it, as there was in less perfect faces. It seemed indecent to her that there would not be a consensus about April's perfection for it rang so true.

"Do you think . . . ?" Maude began and then stopped.

"What? What were you going to say?"

"That maybe what Lombardi said *is* true, that Tinker's simply given him new ideas for design, who knows why, and that's the only reason he's working with her every day? That would explain why he didn't bother to pretend—nothing *is* settled in his mind, and we're jumping to conclusions, April! After all, Tinker only has a few hours a day for those stupid tango lessons, and from tango to runway is by no means a clear path. I think this story is very far from over—you've still got every chance to win, I'm sure of it!"

"Do you really believe that or are you only saying it to make me feel better?"

"I'd never give you false hope, April. I truly believe that nothing's been decided and once you're on that runway, you'll carry the day."

"Oh, Maude, I love you! You're the only person around here with a working brain." April flung herself at Maude and wrapped her arms around her, kissing her on the cheek in an exuberance of relief and renewed hope.

"April, you have no idea how good that feels."

"Good?" April looked at Maude inquisitively. "Does it feel good to be told you're a genius?"

"It feels good to have you kiss me. Even on the cheek. It's the first time I've felt your lips."

"Oh."

"Don't draw away like that, April. You've had to know that this was bound to be said sooner or later, haven't you?"

"I haven't thought about it," April quavered, still sitting on the bed and clutching the quilt around her shoulders.

"Not once, not even one little time? It never happened to even cross your mind?" Maude asked softly.

"Well . . . I guess maybe I did wonder . . . a little, I'm not stupid . . . okay, after I'd told you how I felt about men I started thinking about how you led your own life, and I realized that you . . . well I wasn't sure, but . . . you know what I mean. I guess it's because of the way you dress, otherwise I wouldn't have dreamed. . . ."

"Yet you've still spent every day with me exploring Paris. Do you understand what that means?"

"It means that I'm not afraid of you and I don't think any the less of you for anything you do. Whatever it is," April added with a nervous giggle.

"I know that and I'm glad, but there's something more, April, something you haven't even allowed yourself to understand. April, listen to me, don't turn your head away like a little girl, you're not a little girl, not at all. You're very much a woman and you wonder what it would be like with another woman . . . you wonder about it all the time, don't you, darling? Oh, April, it's the most natural thing in the world for you to think about. You told me that you don't like men, you tried with them but you couldn't go through with it because it disgusted you. You may be a virgin April, but that doesn't mean that you're not a normal human being with a normal body, so there's only one alternative."

"You make it sound so logical," April murmured protestingly.

"It *is* logical, April. What isn't logical is that a normal woman like you has no sex life at all. That's cruel, that's true punishment. I know you feel like an outcast and that doesn't make the slightest sense. It must be a torment to you. How long do you imagine it can go on?"

"I can't even bear to think about the whole thing, it's such a mess, I'm completely confused. . . ." April took refuge in muteness, bending her head to hide her blushing face, looking down at her shaking hands. Still she didn't move away from her perch on the side of Maude's bed.

"April, April," Maude said, her voice trembling, reaching out and caressing April's downcast head, "of course you're confused, you always will be until you at least bring yourself to make love with a woman, just once, and find out if that's what you like. Ideally, it should be someone experienced, someone who knows you're a virgin and doesn't expect fireworks—who doesn't expect anything   now how many people could that description apply to?"

April laughed and Maude felt her relax a little. She continued to touch April's hair lightly as she spoke quietly, evenly.

"I could be accused, rightfully, of being opportunistic, but you know you owe it to yourself to find out, or you wouldn't still be here with me, would you? You've almost made your decision, darling. It's going to happen sooner or later, that you know for sure. Don't let it be on a crazy impulse with a stranger, just to get it over with, the way you tried to with those boys. The first time should be with someone you can trust, someone you know as well as you know me, someone you've confided in, someone who understands you. Oh, April, sweet, confused April, I promise to be so tender, so gentle, I won't rush you into anything and if you want to stop, I'll stop, no questions or recriminations, the way there are with men. I promise you, a solemn promise, that I'll respect your wishes. It won't make any difference in the way I feel about you. You can't possibly go the entire rest of your life not knowing, so let me love you, my darling. All it takes is the courage to say yes."

April turned her head and looked shyly, indirectly, at Maude. Then she leaned forward from the edge of the bed and brushed Maude's cheek with a quick kiss, too embarrassed to say a word, not even the "yes" that she was bursting to say. How many nights had she lain awake thinking about Maude Callender? How long had she spent wondering about the sophisticated, dashing, fascinating woman whom she felt closer and closer to every day. She hadn't dared to imagine this happening . . . no, to be honest, she had imagined it, but not beyond the vague, frightening, quickly thrust away idea that something like this might be possible. At least . . . not impossible. Yet she didn't feel frightened now, she felt taken care of, she felt adored, she felt a curiosity so wild and powerful that her mouth was dry and her limbs trembled and her nipples tingled.

"Come to bed, April," Maude whispered, sliding the quilt away, putting her arms around April's shoulders and kissing her hair lightly. "Lean back on this pillow and close your eyes, just think about how you feel, that's the only important thing. You're so tense . . . don't be, I'm just going to kiss your face."

Maude kissed April softly, taking the girl's head in her hands and placing her lips gently on April's forehead, just at her hairline. Back and forth her lips traced a path that widened almost imperceptibly, until Maude was kissing April's small, lovely earlobes and her sublime jawline as well as her hairline, outlining the exquisite shape of her face. She felt April's body go limp with relaxation and she heard her sigh with relief that the die was cast, yet still Maude continued to press her lips only to the outer edges of April's face. Her iron self-control gave her far more pleasure than she would have gained if she had kissed April with the full violence of her excitement.

As Maude kissed April she drew back often to gaze at the girl's willfully expressionless features with amazed joy, almost unable to believe that the face she worshiped was abandoned to her touch. When April's closed lips finally parted slightly of their own accord,

Maude brushed them with one finger, floating that finger repeatedly over April's warm lips with the most delicate of contacts, until she saw that April's mouth was pouting, as if it had a life of its own and was reaching out for something April herself had no knowledge of. Only then did Maude kiss April on her lips, giving her dry, feathery, closed-mouth kisses on the sides and tops and bottoms of the proffered, expectant lips, never fully covering April's mouth with her own.

She felt April timidly pushing her lips forward, but she wouldn't allow her mouth to be captured, not yet, not until she'd driven April to demand it. Soon, sooner than she'd expected, Maude felt April's hands reach out and meet behind her head so that she could pull Maude forward toward her, until their lips met fully, the girl giving her kiss for kiss, whimpering with wordless pleasure as she tasted the woman's full mouth. Maude was determined that April would be the first to use her tongue and, as she kissed April lingeringly, but almost chastely, she felt a tiny flicker of the girl's tongue, almost imperceptible at first, but quickly growing more bold. She let April dart her tongue forward until she grew more and more demanding, until she was openly trying to get Maude to respond. Only then did Maude, unable to stop herself, finally suck April's tongue softly and steadily. Soon she quickly wet the fingers of one hand with her tongue and slid them under the girl's dressing gown and nightgown until she found the small, stiff, pointed nipple of one breast.

For a long dreamy time Maude continued to suck April's tongue and tantalize the tip, only the tip, of her nipple, knowing that the combination of sensations, isolated from any other touch, was intensely powerful. She was entirely focused on April's breathing, listening voluptuously as she heard it quicken, as the girl drew her head back and murmured "Don't stop" and tried, without success, to push more of her swelling, sensitized nipple into Maude's fingers. No, Maude thought, no, she wouldn't be rushed, she wouldn't let April do anything to get it over with, as she had with men, she'd rather go mad with her own piercing desire before she'd allow that.

Finally Maude felt the touch she'd been waiting for, the downward pressure on the top of her head that indicated, wordlessly, that April wanted her to suck her nipples, but she pretended not to understand, playing with the tip of April's nipple even more lightly than before. "Oh, please, *please* . . ." April sighed.

"What do you want, my darling?" Maude murmured. "Tell me exactly what you want, say the words."

"Suck me, suck my breasts!" April begged, and Maude, glancing at her face, saw that she was far beyond blushing. But before Maude could lower her head, April changed her mind as she felt herself invaded by sensations she'd never known before. The girl sat up in the bed where she had been lying so passively, and threw both of her strong arms over Maude, one on each side, immobilizing her.

"Unbutton your pajamas," April ordered. "I want your breasts, I want them now." And as soon as Maude's big, beautifully shaped breasts were revealed, April threw herself on them ravenously, handling them with firm, ardent, awkward fingers, sucking each nipple with her whole mouth, clumsy yet masterful in her suddenly understood greed, licking and biting in an attack so unleashed that she was astonished by herself. "I want you hanging over me," April commanded harshly, and slid down on the bed so that Maude could reverse her position.

When she saw Maude's breasts dangling over her face April felt herself grow wild and strong with a desire she'd never known, she pressed the breasts together so that she could suckle one nipple after another with lightning rapidity, abandoning herself utterly to the realization of a fantasy that had always, she now admitted to herself, lurked at the back of her mind. The abundance of Maude's breasts intoxicated her, she looked with wonder at their hanging ripeness, the full rosy firmness of their skin, the darkness and largeness of their mature nipples. She fed on them, shuddering with luxurious invention, pulling on the nipples, teasingly, imperatively, with a swollen mouth and careful teeth and a plundering tongue, imagining hazily that she was a baby, imagining that she was a man, until suddenly, she realized that she was a woman and she wanted to be fucked.

"Maude, Maude, what do we do now?" April cried.

"Do you want more? Say the words, just say the words."

"Please, Maude, I don't know the words."

"Yes you do."

"I beg you. I can't stand it anymore."

"What do you want me to do?" Maude was implacable. It was the only way to make April know herself.

"Between my legs . . . your hand, your mouth, everything! Quickly!"

"No, not quickly, never quickly, not the first time," Maude murmured. "Take off your nightgown, get under the covers." While April hastened to do her bidding, Maude slid out of the bottoms of her pajamas. "You've had my breasts, but I haven't had yours," she told April with mock sternness. "That's not right, not when I've been dying for them for so long, dreaming of them, watching you flaunt them without a bra under those tight sweaters, driving me mad . . . lie still, let me look . . . oh, your nipples are as hard as mine, and I've barely played with one of them . . . you were born for this, darling, born for it."

By the time Maude attacked April's lovely small breasts with her kisses, she had positioned herself in the bed so that April's nipples were on a level with her mouth and her hands were free to descend the length of the girl's body. Between kisses, with a reverent, hesitant caress she laid one hand on the girl's flat belly, waiting for the slightest hint of rejection. Instead, April arched her pelvis and threw the covers off the bed, so that the entire length of her naked, magnificent body was revealed. Her mound was covered with straight, silky hair, the same gold as the hair on her head.

"Yes, yes, there, *lower*, now, I can't wait!" April moaned. She heaved herself upwards in the bed, pushing Maude downward, away from her breasts, crying out, "your mouth, Maude, I have to have your mouth!" April opened her legs wide and spread her wet, congested lower lips apart with her hands. "There, put your mouth on me there," she demanded in a tone of domination that Maude had rarely heard, a tone for which she abandoned her own, unselfish plans to obey.

She swiveled on the mattress and crouched above April, enveloping the pink, enlarged bulb of the girl's clitoris with the pulsating, firm suction of her hot mouth. At the same time, she inserted two fingers gently into the entrance to April's vagina, remembering that she was a virgin. April cried out in ecstasy and pushed down on Maude's fingers as hard as she could. Then she pulled back until the fingers almost lost contact with her and immediately pushed down again, contracting her vagina and panting, "Push, push harder! Give me another finger! Don't stop sucking!"

Maude gave herself to her task with an intensity that blocked out anything but an awareness of April's sensations. It was as if she were being fucked for the first time herself, as she gave the girl what she'd wanted so desperately, for so long, without knowing it. April's vulva was open and distended, madly greedy, demanding, more engorged every second. Whenever she tried to slow the rhythm of her fingers and her mouth, to make the first time last longer, April spurred her on, as if she were riding a horse, and soon, from the tenseness in her thighs and the way she raised her pelvis, Maude knew that April's orgasm was approaching. She heightened the sucking rhythm she had established, making her lips and tongue as hard and tight as possible, letting April go faster and faster as she rode her three hard fingers until she felt the girl pause for a long, silent second and then come, shrieking and bucking, into her waiting mouth. Her fingers, deep inside April, were clutched and unclutched by the powerful spasms that lasted a long time until they eventually came farther apart and finally stopped entirely.

When the girl lay quiet at last, Maude lifted her head and looked at her face, not knowing what to expect; shame, a return of shyness, bewilderment, anything was possible. April's eyes were shining through her half-parted lids and she licked her dry, smiling lips.

"Just give me a minute to bask, Maude, my beloved, just give me a minute and then . . . then I'm going to fuck you, fuck you good. I'll be grateful to you every day for the rest of my life. I'll never be able to thank you enough."

"Listen, darling, you don't have to, honestly . . . I have ways."

"You don't understand. I want to, I'm dying to taste you, I can't wait for it . . . I'm just getting my strength back, is all. I'm going to fuck you and then you're going to fuck me again or we'll do it to each other at the same time. I'm just getting started, Maude. Think of how much I have to make up for. Oh, come on up here right away and kiss me, I'm going crazy just thinking about how good it's going to be."

Not only can she keep up with me, Maude thought, she's going to go far beyond what I can give her, and not that far from now. She's unstoppable. I'd better take what I can get before the word gets out, before she gets curious about other women. Or is she already? She's going to be the most wanted girl in town when we get back to New York. She doesn't need me, but she doesn't know that yet.

Maude moved up on the bed so that she could meet April's lips, her body so aroused that a touch would bring her to orgasm, her heart breaking.

19

Jacques Necker woke up each morning to the conviction that he would feel more rested if he could somehow make himself stay up all night and go without sleep entirely. He was plagued by brutally punishing nightmares that vanished before he opened his eyes, leaving him with a sensation of having been physically pounded into the ground. He was depressed to his very core, but without a memory to pin to the nightmares. Nevertheless, in the last week, they seemed to have become a part of the historic reality of his own life, as real as any of his achievements and as solid as any of his possessions.

The hideous miasma of the night was only slightly dispelled as he forced himself through his brisk morning routine and his rapid walk to his office. As spring collection week rapidly approached, he found some relief in thrusting himself into overdrive, not only making the usual important decisions that determined the overall course of his business empire, but also overseeing feverishly the small details that he normally left to the people who were well paid to do these jobs. He deviled the party arrangers about the work in progress for the showing at the Ritz, demanding to know if they had enough tens of dozens of flowering trees, wanting an explanation about the progress of their painted decors, insisting on changing the menu, even tasting the wines, as if the success of the Lombardi collection were the only thing on his mind. He worked later and later, driving his associates mad with his second-guessing of already-made plans, postponing the moment when he would have to leave the place where his word was law, and return home.

If his wife, poor Nicole, were still alive, he would have had an obligatory distraction every evening, Necker thought, with a grimace, since Nicole had expended most of her energies on entertaining with enormous style at least once a week and on being entertained in return. He remembered the shadow of distress that would cross her face if they dined alone together more than once in any given week. Unless her appointment diary was filled six weeks in advance, she quickly felt friendless, abandoned and, worst of all, unimportant. Knowing this, in spite of the pressure of his work, Necker had never protested at having to leave home, showered and freshly dressed, in time to be driven to yet another dinner party or gala. It was the least he could do for her, he had long ago decided, since he no longer loved her with anything but a reflex of mild affection, and hadn't given her children to occupy her life.

Even if Nicole were still alive he wouldn't have mentioned his nightmares to her, Necker realized. They had fallen out of the habit of personal revelations a very long time ago, less than two years after their marriage, when it became clear that her world consisted of fittings and lunches and consultations with florists and caterers, and his world consisted of business.

Not many weeks passed, after Nicole's death, before Necker began to receive twice as many invitations to dinner than he and Nicole had ever received as a couple. He refused them all, occasionally asking several old friends to dine at his house, merely to let people know that he hadn't become a morbid hermit. He had no interest in remarriage, but he realized that he had been targeted by every important hostess in Paris, each of whom had her own candidate, one of the many, still lovely divorcees or widows of suitable background and interests, to become the second Madame Necker.

It was unthinkable, Parisian hostesses agreed among themselves, that a fabulously rich man, a particularly handsome, alluring, vigorous man who was younger in so many ways than his actual age, should be allowed to draw another breath without a new attachment.

However, Jacques Necker managed to show himself so unresponsive, even rudely uninterested, when it came to that, that all but a very few of his oldest and most optimistic friends had given up arranging his future. Sometimes, in a rare moment in which he admitted his loneliness to himself, he asked himself why he didn't give in to the matchmakers and pick some perfectly agreeable woman to busy the corners of his life with the bustle of redecoration and the myriad irritations of domesticity known only to the enormously wealthy—someone energetic, he thought, who would consider it minimal to own the banalities of a yacht, a château and a villa at Saint-Jean-Cap-Ferrat, someone who planned safaris and skied and would bully him into taking time off and "enjoying life."

But he didn't intend to be condemned to repeat the pattern of his life with Nicole, the dining out and entertaining, chatting about nothing with the same three hundred people year after year. Until he learned about Justine, he had been, if not content, at least resigned to spending his small amount of leisure in collecting, reading art history and flying off frequently to Zurich, Amsterdam, Milan or London to see the newest museum and gallery exhibitions or to attend the latest of the annual antiques fairs to which dealers from all over brought their finest wares.

The only way he knew he hadn't turned into an antique himself, Necker thought, was that his sexual appetite was far from dead. He couldn't bring himself to keep a mistress, preferring the efficient, if joyless, relief afforded by the most exclusive call girls in Paris. He expended his supercharge of energy almost every evening in violent squash games at his club, often dining there as well, with one of his many squash partners.

The blow Justine had dealt him in not coming to Paris immobilized him for several days. One morning, while walking to the office, he suddenly asked himself why, now that a suitable amount of time had passed, he had not done the natural thing and inquired after her health. As soon as he arrived in his office he called Frankie and asked if Miss Loring's ear infection had responded to treatment.

"I'm not certain," Frankie answered, too surprised by the suddenness of his question to make up a lie.

"How is that possible? Don't you keep in touch on a daily basis?"

"No, actually we don't," Frankie said, recovering. "Justine has almost seventy other models to worry about. She knows where we are and that the girls are keeping busy—she counts on me to alert her to any problems, so I don't need to check in with her every day."

"Miss Severino, I consider you entirely capable, but it seems to me that with the Lombardi spring collection less than a week away, Miss Loring would find it more important to be here than in New York, where nothing this important can possibly be going on."

"I don't know what she could do here that I can't," Frankie said hardily. "Tinker doesn't have a minute to herself all day long, as you know, and Lombardi said he doesn't want to even lay eyes on April or Jordan until he's ready to fit them along with all the other models. He's expressly asked me not to disturb him for any reason. From what Tinker tells me, he's making new designs like mad and all his associates are working to keep up with him. Marco has his ateliers open and filled with workers night and day. I don't see what possible good Justine could do over here, except add to the confusion."

"It's a question of dignity," Necker heard himself say pompously. "Miss Loring's absence fails to reflect her consideration of the importance of the Lombardi contract. I assume she'd manage to come for the collection itself."

"Oh, certainly! Of course she will, if not before," Frankie said calmly.

"Are you all keeping busy?" Necker asked, forcing a friendlier tone.

"Now that the girls have finished working with the photographer from *Zing*, they're basically killing time . . . the club scene palled quickly for all of us. Maude Callender, the writer from *Zing*, and April have been sightseeing all over Paris and Jordan's usually off doing her thing at museums. Yesterday she spent almost all day again at that museum of decorative arts. That's become her favorite Parisian spot."

"Your little group seems amazingly dedicated to culture."

"Well, what's left, Monsieur Necker? The girls don't dare indulge in French lunches or dinners, the cooking's too fattening, there's nothing much to buy in the stores except leftover winter stuff on sale. They can't even shop! All the new movies are in French, even the TV's in French. It's too cold to stroll around for long or sit in the parks, Paris doesn't even have any decent workout clubs . . . how do women stay in shape here? If it weren't for the arts, what would we do with ourselves? Everyone in the couture is working in a frenzy of last-minute arrangements this last week but, except for Tinker, my girls aren't needed yet."

"Quite true. I hadn't thought of that. Are you part of the culture brigade?"

"I make it a point to spend as much time as I possibly can at the Louvre."

"An excellent focus for your energies."

"Thank you," Frankie said demurely. "It's the experience of a lifetime."

After he'd hung up, Necker drummed on his desk in a wave of pain, unable to collect his thoughts. Frankie Severino, that impossible creature, dared to lie to him, even to complain, and there was nothing he could do about it. It was beyond humiliation, beyond shame, almost beyond frustration. Pure pain, he thought, a pain that he felt as a vast punch in the stomach. It was so real he tried to find it with his fingers so that he could massage it away, so real that he was surprised that it didn't make him bend over when he walked.

Many tens of thousands of people were busy at this very minute, all working for him, busily turning out goods from textiles to perfumes, people to whom his word was all powerful, yet this impossible twit of a girl, who unquestionably knew the truth, could not be made to reveal a breath of it. He no longer could even try to believe that Justine intended to come for the collection any more than he had believed, from the first minute, that she had ever been sick. It was just as unlikely that Frankie was haunting the Louvre. It was, of course, possible that April and the journalist might be sightseeing but the only thing Frankie said that rang with truth was the brief picture she'd painted of Jordan at the Musée des Arts Décoratifs.

The museum was crammed with great furniture and objects, entire rooms preserved and arranged exactly as they had been during the life of the past, and for anyone like Jordan, there would be long hours in which other visitors would be almost absent and she could gaze at her leisure and dream herself back into another world.

Suddenly the thought of Jordan wandering around, peering

with fascination into those romantic, evocative rooms, but unable to enter them because of the velvet rope that protected them from the public, touched something in Necker that enabled him to put Frankie's lies behind him for a while, to allow the pain to retreat.

He could, at least, make Jordan happy for an afternoon, he thought. Jordan's pragmatic assessment of her position as a black woman had given him a perspective on her maturity and her self-reliance. He understood, after what she had explained to him about the cautious way in which she navigated the world, that she would almost certainly not go into a fine antiques shop by herself to look at things she couldn't afford to buy. It was only an unusually self-confident white tourist who dared to brave the imposing doors of the fine French antiques dealer, only those who were rich enough to feel at home anywhere and wise enough in the ways of such commerce to realize that one was free to "just look" at the best without the intention to buy. And even they usually came with a sponsor, a client of the house. The flea market dealers of Paris grew rich on the awe inspired by merchants of quality antiques.

Necker had his secretary reach Jordan on the phone and soon made his suggestion.

"I understand from Miss Severino that you've enjoyed the Musée des Arts Décoratifs. I know it well but it's frustrating having guards hovering over me as if I were going to steal something the minute their backs are turned. Would it be fun for you to go to some shops with truly fine things where you can open every drawer, turn over every piece of porcelain, inspect every hinge? Someplace where they don't expect you to buy?"

"Oh, yes, I'd love that!"

"I can pick you up at three this afternoon. How does that sound?"

"Perfect!"

After he'd made his arrangement with Jordan, Necker, after a moment's thought, called the House of Kraemer to make an appointment. All three of the Messieurs Kraemer would, most unfortunately, most unusually, be away that afternoon, a secretary told him. They were at auctions in three different cities, but Monsieur Jean, their chief assistant, would be delighted to assist him, to do the honors of the house for Monsieur Necker and his guest, Mademoiselle Dancer.

Normally he never bothered to announce his visits to the Kraemers but this time he phoned in advance because he realized that if he suddenly appeared on their doorstep with the most magnificently beautiful black woman anyone had ever seen, even the great poise of the Kraemers might not be able to prevent the momentary showing of the smallest hint of surprise or curiosity. He couldn't allow that to happen to Jordan while she was with him. Intelligent and wise in the ways of the world as she was, he found himself feeling strongly protective toward her . . . a protectiveness mixed with tenderness. He wanted only good things to happen to Jordan, Jacques Necker realized, and fleetingly wondered if she'd become a daughter-substitute to him.

Strange, Jordan thought, that Jacques Necker should have phoned just when she was feeling particularly abandoned. Tinker had been whisked away on her cloud of glory; April and Maude never seemed to be around or available; it was obvious that Frankie and Mike had their own, intense private life together, lucky, lucky them—there was nobody left to hang out with except, Lord have mercy, that old Peaches Wilcox, who was good fun in a crowd, but who gave Jordan a quick dismissive smile when they met by chance in the lobby. It was, Jordan thought, the sort of forgiving facial grimace a famous woman makes when someone doesn't recognize who she is. Jordan didn't hold it against Peaches. That was just the way it was.

Jordan had planned to go antiquing this afternoon in any case. She'd walked the streets of the Left Bank and found many of them lined with small, unpretentious shops whose windows displayed wares to tempt the devil. She felt so at home in Paris, she'd received so many glances that frankly admired her for herself without any racial overtones, that Jordan had allowed herself to investigate several of the smaller boutiques and discovered that antiques dealers liked nothing more than conversation.

Like the best of hosts, they gave the impression that they

opened their doors to her for no other reason than to meet her and chat. They were so low-key that Jordan had relaxed into a state in which she felt no obligation to buy anything at all. Somehow she acquired a set of charming old dessert plates and four irresistible chocolate cups with matching saucers and a chocolate pot, two vases and a dozen small botanical engravings, but the dealers seemed neither pleased nor displeased when their conversations terminated in a purchase, after the necessary minor bargaining that was part of the transaction.

The whole process was so delightful that Jordan had toyed with the fantasy of living the rest of her life in Paris, of working there until she was too old to model, saving her money like a frugal Frenchwoman and eventually opening a little antiques shop of her own. But even as she invented the dream, she read the newspapers and learned of the strong and ever rising tide of hate against black immigrants from North Africa, of the growing percentage of French who blamed blacks for all the complicated ills of the country.

She definitely had more options at home, Jordan realized, even as she relished walking the streets feeling all around her that special kind of homage that all Europeans accord to beautiful women of any race.

"No shop window?" Jordan asked as Necker's car drew to a stop in front of the Kraemer *hôtel particulier*.

"They're too famous to advertise with even a window. It's the sort of place you'd never go to unless you knew about it already, yet if you just showed up and rang the bell they'd be perfectly charming to you."

"So, in that way, they're no different from other antiques dealers?"

"You've been shopping?" He concealed his surprise smoothly.

"In a small way, a tiny way really, on the Left Bank. There's only so much room in my suitcases and I've already used it up. I wonder if they really want my business . . . is it my imagination or are they faintly let down when I actually buy something?"

"Oh, no, you're right about that. Imagine spending your life hunting for certain special things, finally discovering these things in the most unusual, unexpected places, persuading someone to sell them to you and then, after all that fun and trouble, having to resell those trophies to make a living. I think it's a particularly refined sort of torture, but dealers chose it, and the Kraemers have continued to do it for three generations. Of course they've kept many of the treasures for themselves, they must or die of broken hearts. Once I told Philippe Kraemer he was as self-punishing as a ballet dancer who chooses to dance in pain all her life, but he merely laughed at me. When you get down to it, he sees everything first. I'm sure he has better things than I do."

"How about models who starve themselves and spend their life in high heels, walking in agony and making it look like fun? It's always something, isn't it? What are the disadvantages of your business?"

"I've never thought about it. Perhaps there aren't any," Necker said in a startled burst of amusement.

"Lucky man. One yard of fabric is like another, one bottle of perfume like another, you don't deal in unique objects, except for your couture houses, and if one of your designers doesn't make the cut, he can always be replaced, right? It's the name that has to be established, basically to sell the perfume down the road."

"Precisely. That's why I'm launching Lombardi. But don't you want to go in?"

"I'm rambling on like a dealer," Jordan said with her habitual smiling composure as the chauffeur opened the door of the car. She was dressed in uncompromisingly well-cut jacket and trousers, and a turtleneck sweater, all of them the rich, deep dark brown of bittersweet chocolate. They made a background against which the splendid, unnameable tint of her skin created as vivid a contrast as if she were a very fair skinned woman dressed in black satin.

"Monsieur Necker, Mademoiselle, welcome, both of you, and please come in out of the cold," said Monsieur Jean, the slim blond assistant who knew so much about antiques that the Kraemers could, when necessary, leave their affairs in his hands.

"Jordan, this is Monsieur Jean," Necker said in English. "Monsieur Jean, this is Mademoiselle Dancer, who is an amateur of antiques."

"I'm delighted to meet you, Mademoiselle. May I offer you some tea? A drink?"

"No, thank you. Perhaps later. Jordan, is there anything special you'd like to see?"

"Oh no . . . I just want to look around," Jordan answered, in awed astonishment. Never in the world had she imagined that so much priceless furniture and so many exquisite jewels of smaller objects could be concentrated in one house, in just the entrance to one house—yet not priceless, she reminded herself, since they were all for sale. She had been antiquing on the far fringes of nowhere, she realized, talking to dealers who would themselves be stunned by a single pair of sconces at the Kraemers'.

For an hour, Jordan and Necker wandered at random through the nine salons of Kraemer et Cie. Gradually Jordan felt more and more at home. These armchairs, made for Versailles, were displayed to be sat on by prospective buyers—what woman would buy a chair without trying it out for comfort? This Louis XVI white marble and gilt clock with its three dials and three mounts for candles was meant for daily use, to be consulted for the time, to be lit as she'd light a lamp; the Boulle marquetry inkstand with its palpable sense of statecraft at its most powerful, was an object with a specific purpose, just as was the ballpoint pen in her handbag.

Was this glimpse into the possibilities of possession available to the richest people in the world going to spoil her pleasure in her small finds, Jordan wondered? Was she going to compare her dear little chocolate cups to the black and gold Boulle inkstand and find them wanting? No, she decided, no more than she found her own favorite clothes wanting in comparison to the ten-thousand-dollar evening dresses she'd worn at the last Bill Blass collection. For some reason or another, one thing had no connection to the other.

Jordan sat back, almost reclining, on a deep love seat and half-closed her eyes, savoring with all her senses the special aroma of perfection of upkeep, composed of wood and wax and something indefinable—perhaps the roses that stood in small glass vases here and there—that filled the crowded rooms. Necker was inspecting the edges of the carving on a table behind the love seat. In his still concentration, Jordan thought, he seemed so intense that she had the impression of motion restrained by force. At that moment, a door concealed in the molding of the wall opened, and a man dressed in a dark uniform crossed the room. He saw Necker and stopped suddenly.

"Ah, Monsieur Necker," he said in French. "Did Monsieur Jean report to you the safe delivery of the *bonheur-du-jour* of Madame de Pompadour to Mademoiselle Loring? I had the pleasure of accompanying the piece to New York myself—four days waiting for that blizzard to clear up, what a history!—but I promise you, I never let that precious crate out of my sight, except during the flight, naturally, until Mademoiselle Loring herself personally signed for it. Oh, yes, I insisted on that. I hoped she liked it, Monsieur, such a superb work of art."

"Yes, of course, thank you very much," Necker said, hastily, on a dismissive note. The courier disappeared as suddenly as he'd arrived, leaving a silence in the room that was very different from the silence that had filled it before his entrance.

Justine and Necker! So that was it, Jordan thought, holding her breath in shock. So that was the reason all three of them had been picked to come to Paris. A writing table that had belonged to the mistress of Louis XV—millions of dollars! He must be insanely in love with her . . . it explained all his questions about Justine at the Petit Trianon. She made herself take shallow breaths as a wave of pain replaced her first amazement. But why pain, she asked herself, why this terrible pain in her heart? What real difference did it make to her that Justine and Necker . . . oh no, oh shit *no!* This could *not* be! She was jealous, Jordan realized, as she'd never been jealous in her life. Jealous of Necker? But Necker was merely a man she'd been able to talk openly to, a good man, a decent man, a kind man who'd listened to her with honest interest. His power, his wealth, his possessions—was it that? Oh, if only it were, if only it were, Jordan lamented. It was the feeling of his big, warm hand on her elbow, it was the way his grey hair curled at his temples and vanished into the blond, it was the very sound of his voice, a sound so different, so much more pleasing than any other voice she'd ever heard, it was his rare, quick boyish smile, his look of melancholy when he thought she wasn't watching, it was—oh fuck—*everything* about him, from head to toe, and she was the worst fool on the planet Earth. Girl, you've fallen into it big-time, she thought, but you can't sit here forever. At least, thank the good Lord, she'd resisted the temptation to show off her French. Now all she had to do was pretend that she hadn't understood a word of what that delivery man had said. Nothing more complicated than acting out total ignorance while she was in a state of shock, and jealousy and other more impossible and impermissible emotions she mustn't begin to think about until she was safely back in her hotel room.

"I think it's time to go," Jordan said, rising in a liquid movement. Necker stood riveted to the parquet. "So many wonderful things . . . it's been a great afternoon."

"Of course, if you're ready . . ." Necker said, recovering himself. He trailed her out to the entrance where they said farewell to Monsieur Jean and returned to the car.

"Henri," Necker ordered the chauffeur, "take us to the Ritz, please, the Vendôme entrance."

"The Ritz?" Jordan asked in surprise. Hadn't he taken her where he'd promised to take her? Wasn't this horrifying afternoon over?

"We can both use a drink," he said grimly.

"I suppose so . . . I need something to counteract all that fine French furniture. Perfection makes me thirsty."

Babble on, Jordan told herself, babble on, because Jacques Necker can't say anything I'm ever going to believe again, and a few minutes more with him won't kill me.

Once inside the small lobby of the Ritz, they turned left into the main bar, all amber velvet banquettes, with a view of a wintry garden with high walls covered with a white wooden trellis on which realistic, but imitation, green leaves and flowers had been cleverly intertwined.

"Let's sit in the corner," Necker said, taking Jordan by the elbow. "What do you take at the twilight hour? Champagne? Please don't say tea."

"Champagne sounds fine." Flight sounds fine, Jordan thought, good-bye sounds fine, let me out of here sounds fine, I'm no Meryl Streep sounds fine.

The waiter quickly brought two flutes of champagne and Necker raised his glass. "To your health," he said formally, his face grave.

"It's quiet in here," she remarked nervously after a half minute of silence. "Where are all the people?"

"Dressing for dinner. They'll be down in the next half hour. The hotel's still fairly empty. All the fashion journalists are in Milan. Nevertheless in an hour from now you won't be able to hear yourself talk. Jordan, I've been thinking—"

"Now, that's always a bad idea," Jordan rushed in to interrupt him. "Never think when you can drink. Could I please have another glass of champagne?"

"Of course. I'll join you. Waiter, two more glasses and some of those nuts. Jordan, I know you speak French."

"How . . . I mean, what makes you think—?"

"Jordan, don't say anything. Just listen to me. I saw the way you reacted to what the courier said. You understood every word, I could see the surprise on your face, but your first instinct was to be tactful and play dumb and your second instinct was to get out of there as quickly as possible. You know I sent Justine a desk, don't you?"

"It's none of my business," Jordan insisted hastily. "There's nothing you have to explain to me, nothing I need to know or want to know. There's nothing I intend to repeat, ever. I give you my word on that."

"*Jordan, please be my friend.* I have to have someone to talk to about her."

"Look , Monsieur Necker—"

"How many times have I asked you to call me Jacques?"

"I don't intend to talk about Justine, if that's why you brought me here. I'm sorry, truly sorry, and I am your friend, Jacques, but there's no way I want to hear about it. You'll resent me for it eventually, I've never known it to fail. No matter what happens between the two of you, you'll be sorry for anything you tell me now. I was in the wrong place at the wrong time and learned something that's none of my business. Let's leave it at that."

"I don't blame you for jumping to conclusions."

Jordan sipped some champagne, looked into the garden and

prevented herself from raising even one eyebrow. She'd said her piece. Jacques Necker took the glass out of her hand and set it down on the round table. He leaned toward her and turned her chin toward him so that she had to look him in the eye.

"Justine Loring is not my mistress, Jordan. She's my daughter."

"That's impossible!" Jordan exploded. Necker sat perfectly still and continued to look at her, merely offering his face to her disbelieving gaze until she clearly recognized the resemblance that Frankie had noticed immediately. The spikes of ice in her heart vanished but there was no relief, only an emptiness that hadn't been there before.

"Yes," Jordan said at last, after she'd processed the undeniable information. "Yes, I see. Of course. If I'd been using my eyes. . . ."

"Will you let me talk to you now? Please Jordan, I implore you. No one in the world knows except Justine herself and possibly, I believe almost certainly, Frankie Severino. But she has steadily played ignorant and I can't force her to be disloyal to Justine. I've been going mad, Jordan. I don't recognize myself. I can't sleep without the most unspeakable nightmares, I'm not functioning rationally, I'm in absolute despair, at the breaking point. I need you, I need to talk to you. Remember when you asked me if I had children and I said my wife and I hadn't had any? That was only half the truth . . . please, Jordan, may I tell you about it?"

Jordan looked clearly at Jacques Necker and saw another human being in trouble, a man whose eyes begged her for the basic, necessary mercy of a listening ear. He might indeed hate her in the future because of what he wanted so desperately to tell her now, but she'd have to take that chance. She could not turn away from someone in so much pain, it was as simple as that.

"So what is the other half, Jacques," she asked softly, "what happened?"

"I didn't know Justine existed until a few months ago," Necker said with a great sigh. "I had no idea I had a daughter, none! I thought I was childless, I'd resigned myself to it. Helena, Justine's mother, had kept me in ignorance. I abandoned Helena when she got pregnant. Left her alone, on her own. I was a totally worthless young shit, a disgrace, a sickening rotten little coward—we were both nineteen but that's no excuse. Helena didn't want me to have anything to do with her child and who can blame her? When she knew she was dying, she finally decided to send me photographs of the only child I've ever had. Oh, such photographs, Jordan! Scrapbooks of pictures dating from Justine's birth, all the way until she stopped modeling. Helena had a rich revenge."

"Revenge? How do you know she wasn't giving you a second chance, a very late second chance?"

"Because Helena had turned Justine against me. Completely, thoroughly, over a lifetime, I imagine. Of course the first thing I tried to do was to contact Justine but she wouldn't have anything to do with me. She sent back all my letters, unopened. I understood that too. So I organized the Lombardi contest and sent Gabrielle d'Angelle to New York. I knew that as a businesswoman, Justine's agency would have to become involved in it, there was no way to hold out. In the contracts she signed she was supposed to come with you . . . my God! *Damn me for a total fool!* Why didn't I realize that the contest was the worst possible way to deal with her? What the hell put that idea into my head?"

"Only the devil himself," Jordan smiled. "To say that Justine does not respond well to pressure is an understatement. I imagine you're the same way."

"I am, I certainly am. So, at the last minute she pretended to be sick and sent Miss Severino instead."

"So that famous ear infection—"

"She's not going to come, Jordan," Necker cried. "Not ever. She doesn't want to have anything to do with me, nothing, no contact at all."

"Nothing?"

"Nothing."

"I couldn't stick to a decision like that myself," Jordan said, thoughtfully, "but Justine? She's one of the most strong-minded people I've ever known, and if her mother worked on her since childhood, I can understand her holding out, at least so far. I know how stubborn she can be. We all take her seriously, believe me. But this whole thing's crazy! Mad! You can't possibly let it go on, for God's sake. You're her father! Why aren't you in New York, confronting her?"

"How do you think she'd react to that? It was my first impulse, and my second and my third, but would it have worked? Justine hates the thought of me, the fact of me, the idea of me. I can't *make* her accept me as her father, it's much too late for that."

"Oh, I'm not so sure . . . maybe, just maybe a confrontation would have been a good thing to do. There's something entirely different about knowing you have a father, even one you believe is an unworthy, low-life son of a bitch, and meeting the reality in flesh and blood. There's a limit to how long she could have resisted you. You're pretty persuasive, Jacques. I think kicking in her door would have worked eventually, when you first found out, but you blew it, lost the momentum."

To soften her words, Jordan allowed herself to touch his hand. She drew back quickly . . . one more major mistake like that, she told herself angrily, and I'm out of here. She spent a reflective minute before she could continue. "I don't think it's too late . . . it's only been a few months. You shouldn't let yourself get in such a state. This isn't a situation that can possibly last. It's much too unnatural."

"I'd leave her alone," Necker rushed on, barely listening to Jordan's last words, "if only I could meet her once and talk to her, if she wanted me to I'd leave her alone after that."

"You just want to meet her? Is that all? I don't quite understand."

"See her and talk to her. I know so little about her life. I've had her investigated, of course, but all I could really find out are the facts; why is a beautiful woman of thirty-four unmarried, living alone, without a husband or children? How much of that is my fault, Jordan? It could *all* be my fault!"

"Whoa! Wait up, take ten, Jacques. You have one hell of an imagination! Think of it another way. Listen to me. I *envy* Justine. She's terrifically successful on her own, she's built a highly re-spected agency from a modeling career, she has a tremendous per-sonality, plenty of friends and an interesting life. I've never thought of her as unhappy or unfulfilled. And she's young and beautiful. A whole heap of women would trade places with her. I'll bet she could be married tomorrow if she wanted to be, and pregnant the day after that, if not before. Justine gets what she wants. Now, did you ever stop to consider those possibilities while you were so busy feeling guilty for the imaginary sorrows of someone whose life you don't know anything about, even if she is your daughter?"

"No, I didn't." Necker smiled at her, almost reluctantly, yet unable to hide his lightening of spirit. "There's nothing like an intelligent woman's point of view to make a man feel a bit of a fool. A lot of a fool."

"Ain't that the truth," Jordan agreed, relieved to see the smile change his tragic look, the desolation of his eyes. She tried to imagine him as a kid in a panic, deserting a pregnant girl, and failed. There was so much strength in him, even when he appealed to her, even when he found himself forced to turn to her to unburden himself because of an accident of timing. How alone did a man have to be to tell his deepest secrets to a girl he hardly knew and didn't care about? Very alone, she realized. More alone than any man should ever be. As alone as she felt right now, sitting at his side . . . or did being with him in this context of confidante make her feel worse than she would if she were truly alone?

"Jacques, I have an idea," she said impulsively. "Don't do anything more at a distance, it'll just get screwed up in the transmission or translation. Don't talk to anyone else. Wait till the Lombardi collection is over and there's no more pressure. Then get yourself to New York. You'll manage to see Justine, one way or another. It'll work out, I know it in my bones."

"That's good advice," he said, after a minute's thought. "I'll take it, on one condition—"

"Listen, you don't *have* to take my advice! I'm just offering it for what it's worth," Jordan flashed at him. "I don't have to give you any conditions to get you to do the right thing, at least what I think is the right thing. I'm not your reader and advisor, just a friend."

"Damn, I didn't mean it the way it sounded. I just want to be able to talk to you again, talk to you when I get discouraged . . . that's the condition, only I don't mean condition, I mean . . . please? *Can I see you when I need you?*"

"Well . . ." She couldn't bring herself to say no and she knew she shouldn't say yes. It was going to be hard enough to forget him without another word between them. Hard? It was going to be fucking impossible . . . who was she kidding? Deal with it, Jordan, deal with it!

"Thank you," he declared, taking her hesitation for agreement. "End of discussion. All right. How does Chinese food sound? Frankie told me you were all afraid to eat French cooking. I can promise low-fat Chinese food."

"You don't have to feed me again," Jordan said. God damn it to hell, didn't she even have the gumption to clearly resist a dinner invitation? She was like some crazed rodent storing up poison nuts for the winter.

"But can I, if I want to?"

"You can," she sighed, giving up, "and you *may*. An important distinction, Jacques. I'll explain at dinner."

20

Peaches Wilcox had made polite noises about giving a party for us when we first arrived in Paris, but I hadn't put any confidence in it. She didn't strike me as a female who would willingly entertain three glorious creatures less than half her age, much less like someone who'd actually plan a party in their honor. But Peaches surprised me; her cocktail party is set for tonight.

Maybe when you have as much money as she does, you're beyond feeling threatened by youth and beauty; maybe it's like being Elizabeth II and knowing, deep beneath any level of consciousness, that no matter who else is in the room, you're the Queen of England and they're not. Something as profound as that would approach the feeling of unutterable specialness I'm walking around with, which could be roughly translated as Mike and I are in love and every other human being in the world is living only half a life, but, fortunately for them, they don't know it.

There's Tinker of course, who's in love too, or at least so she tells me. But how can her born-yesterday infatuation with this Tom Strauss compare to the unrequited love I've nourished for Mike since I was fourteen? Of course I'm gloating, but can you find it in your heart to blame me? Justine phoned me the morning after she got my letter and raved on in a most deliciously satisfactory way. She knows Mike slightly, and she's always liked him and admired his work.

I promise you that even as she uncharacteristically burbled at me about the happiness and joy she felt, I could hear her mentally planning the wedding, deciding on what particularly becoming shade of off-white I should wear and beginning to worry about my leaving work as soon as I gave birth to our first child.

I didn't tell Justine not to worry about something that hasn't even been mentioned yet. I've had the same thoughts myself, I have to admit. Then I catch myself up short and change to the take-each-day-as-it-comes plan that Mike and I seem to have mutually adopted. This tacit agreement must have been made at some moment when I wasn't quite myself, because it doesn't *sound* like me, it doesn't ring even the faintest inner bell. However, I've learned that I can't trust myself to *be* myself lately. Thinking straight is getting harder and harder, and my job of keeping the girls under close surveillance, if not house arrest, has become as impossible as herding cats.

Of course I had to tell Justine about my conversation with Necker and his expectation that she'd be in Paris for the collection. Her abrupt silence at receiving this news made me decide not to add that I'd assured him that she'd be here. Okay, I'm a coward, but I knew that Necker didn't believe me anyway, so doesn't one lie cancel out an omission?

As the spring collection draws nearer I've made it a point to see Tinker daily and check on her. The only time to catch her is during a break in her tango lesson because I certainly can't interrupt her in the sacred, strictly-off-limits mystery of Lombardi's atelier, nor can I count on being around when she drops into the hotel at the most unexpected hours for a change of clothes and a long hot bath. Apparently Tom's studio isn't big on luxury sanitation but after Tinker's finally free to leave Lombardi's, and it's always far too late at night, she rushes off to be with her painter. I can imagine how she'd feel if I barged in on them.

I'm still not happy about this Tom Strauss although he doesn't fit the profile of your typical degenerate model chaser. He's not a playboy or a spoiled rich man's son or an older millionaire; he's not a photographer, a photographer's assistant, a model agent, a designer or involved with the production of any kind of film; he doesn't have a Porsche, a title or a rich business associate who's dying to invite her to dinner in his apartment. In other words he's not the typical horror your bumpkin model always manages to dig up from under a paving stone in Paris, but it's almost impossible to believe that he's not interested in exploiting her in some way or another. Exploitation is what happens to models. All the time.

Would he be so crazy about her if she weren't a model? Would all those wildly sexy women have thrown themselves at Picasso's feet if he'd painted houses?

Señora Varga's dance studio is on an almost inaccessible little street off another little street somewhere between the Place de la Madeleine and the Gare St.-Lazare—thank heaven for the one car and driver still left to us. La Señora, a small, stick-thin woman, must be at least fifty-five and looks as if she had never left Buenos Aires. She wears a tight, black, mid-calf skirt slit amazingly high up on her lean, muscular thigh, and a glittering black blouse. Her sleek dark hair is parted in the middle and drawn back into the classic chignon, ornamented with antique jeweled pins.

Although the Señora has the best posture I've ever seen, she barely comes up to Tinker's shoulder, and as they dance, with Tinker leading, I can tell that Tinker is dancing far, *far* above her innate ability, or, rather, lack of ability. She was born without a trace of the dancer's gene. To my trained eye, even as the Señora takes her backward steps, the knowledge in her muscles of where she should be next, is *leading* Tinker, without Tinker realizing it. No matter how hard she might try, Señora Varga is too powerful a dancer to merely follow anyone with as little control or training as Tinker, and I doubt that she's ever taught a woman to lead before.

Of course they're doing the American tango. Even a good dancer would need six months of steady work to get anywhere with the Argentine tango. I can't help but wonder just how, or even *if*, this one dance is going to change Tinker's walk. Yes, it's dramatic, arrogant, and mannered, but how will it translate onto the runway?

Every day Tinker's usual pallor becomes more pronounced. Her miraculous way of becoming what the eye is searching for is switched on while she dances, but it disappears as soon as we have the three minutes of time together that I'm allowed each day. I see a fragile, agitated, blindly determined girl who isn't getting nearly enough sleep, a girl who's overexcited, overchallenged and over-courageous. Oddly enough, she's never been more beautiful. Those gleaming Moonriver eyes are brighter than they've ever been— almost feverish—and she's thrilled about the clothes Lombardi is making. We haven't had time to discuss them in detail—the stern Señora doesn't allow her pupil enough breathing time for that—

but Tinker's convinced that he's working with great inspiration. I hope she's right and it's not just a case of being in love with herself as well as Tom Strauss.

I'll meet Tom tonight at Peaches' party. Apparently la Wilcox, an old friend of Necker's, has invited lots of people to meet everyone who has anything to do with the Lombardi collection, from Necker on down to models' boyfriends. It'll be the first time that Mike and I will be going anywhere in public as a couple. I can't wait.

She would never have believed this disgusting madness could endure, Peaches Wilcox thought. She'd been raped in her own bedroom by Marco Lombardi, he'd humiliated her and hurt her physically . . . and yet she wanted him, more ruinously than ever. She was obsessed by every second of the scene that had taken place a few weeks ago. Over and over again she found herself moaning, not at the rape itself, but at the fact that she'd been so angry afterward that she hadn't let him satisfy her. Each time she repeated to herself his last words, "I'll make you come now, with my mouth, the way you adore it," she felt like flaying herself for not having allowed it.

Perhaps that one final orgasm would have freed her from him, Peaches thought, perhaps it would have filled her with enough self-disgust at her weakness, her self-abasement, to put an end to her craving. But to have been left high and dry . . . bad choice, old thing, she said to herself. You saved what was left of your dignity and doomed yourself to whatever is the female equivalent of unfinished wet dreams. Peaches McCoy Wilcox of the sovereign state of Texas did not relish waking up in the middle of the night to the savage letdown of several crucial seconds before she was about to come in her sleep.

Peaches was trying to think of a face-saving way to revive her relationship with Marco when the memory of the party she'd idly promised Frankie and Mike sprang into her mind. It was the perfect answer to her problem. Marco automatically would have to be included in a party for the girls even if she had truly never wanted to see him again, especially since she was inviting Jacques Necker.

Peaches and the Neckers had run with the same set in Paris. She wasn't ashamed to admit that not too long after Nicole's body was cold, she'd cast her eye on Jacques—you'd have to be a fool not to. But it hadn't done her any more good than it had done two dozen other women she knew. Yes, that big, blond and, as far as she was concerned, extremely sexy Swiss would have made her the best possible second husband. She'd have cured him damn quick from being married to his business. Jacques would be passionate, if you could ever get him in bed, her infallible instinct told her, but it was not to be. Of course it was strictly his loss, Peaches philosophized, that he'd chosen to turn into a tycoon-monk, when life held so many other possibilities, but then the Swiss, unlike the French or the Italians, weren't a nationality anyone could generalize about. Perhaps he'd been really in love with Nicole?

Peaches wrenched herself away from the knowledge that in a few hours she'd see Marco again, and considered her guest list one last time. She'd invited some fifty people: all her closest French friends who weren't away skiing; those of her best American friends who had already gathered in Paris for the precollection week; Dart Benedict, that dear man, who'd just called to say he was in Paris, and of course, the three girls, Tinker's unknown Tom Strauss, Frankie, Mike, and Maude. She'd told Jordan and April to bring their own escorts, but they'd both said they'd rather come alone. She didn't see any need to invite men for them. It was hard enough to forgive them for their youth, without going to the trouble to fix them up.

She was really a remarkable woman, if she did say so herself, Peaches ruminated. She'd spent hours with these young girls, each of whom was far more beautiful than she'd ever been on her best day of her life, and she'd managed to endure it. She'd watched keenly the heedless way in which they inhabited their long, long slim limbs, the careless, carefree way—which amounted to arrogance in her opinion—in which they accepted their gifts of grace and beauty, and yet she almost genuinely liked them.

Yes, that was one of the things money *could* buy, the comforting realization that the girls wouldn't keep those looks for long, and they'd never have the money to properly maintain them. Chances were they'd run to fat, after depriving themselves of a decent meal for years, and start to sell real estate, like most of the ex-models she'd known. You could just about count on the fingers of two hands the girls who were still working at twenty-eight, and Tinker, the youngest of them, was already eighteen, whereas, ten years from now, she, Peaches, would still be going strong, God and Dr. H., willing. Once you'd faced up to forty-seven, fifty-seven, with increasingly vigilant upkeep, didn't look all that terrible. Youth was equally over in both cases.

Yes, Jordan, April and Tinker were doomed, if they were lucky, to a future of suburban life and child raising, with nothing but a lot of yellowing tear sheets to remind them of their glory days, not that they'd want to be reminded. Of course, lightning might strike and one of them might marry well, but that wasn't as easy as it sounded, Peaches thought with the relish of one who had succeeded.

If she had to say which of the Loring gals she envied the most it would be ol' Frankie, who didn't depend on how she looked to keep working. Frankie had charm and jazz and a blazing personality that would keep her alluring long after gravity took its toll.

Just what, when you came right down to it, would she give to be instantly reincarnated as young and beautiful as April or Tinker, Peaches asked herself? To be a girl who could have Marco with a lift of her eyebrow? Not a penny more than four hundred million dollars, she decided after long speculation. That would leave her with a hundred million, or a minimum of at least six million dollars to spend annually after taxes, enough income to live on very well if she didn't go crazy acquiring jewels or art. Lordy, she could even sell the ranch if she had to, it just ate money and she was so rarely there.

Of course the greatest beauty among the three girls was Jordan, but no matter how much youth and beauty Jordan possessed, Peaches wouldn't pay a dime to be reborn black. No, not even if talent were thrown in. There were just too many cards stacked against you, it was too tough a row to hoe. She wasn't being racist, just realistic, she ruminated, as she set about arranging for the caviar, the fresh foie gras, the crabmeat mousse, the white Norwegian smoked salmon—no, she wouldn't call room service, she decided, but the banquet manager himself. She intended tonight to be an occasion that would bring home to Marco a fresh understanding of just what he had almost lost.

There was a moment, like a distinct click, that happened in the course of every large party she'd ever given, after which Peaches could legitimately relax. It took place when enough people had been introduced to each other—she was very clever about introducing people flawlessly—so that they were well mingled and talking easily. That was usually the time when the majority of her other guests were crowding into her rooms too quickly to expect to be introduced, unless there was a special reason why she should lead someone from one group to another.

It was at that precise instant that she considered a party successfully launched: people could be counted on to introduce themselves to each other; like would discover like; anyone who was stuck in a conversation could easily drift away to another part of the room, and basically her job as a hostess was over. Her staffs were always drilled in every nuance of food and drink. From now on Peaches was as free as any other guest at her own party, and it amused her to drift from group to group, never letting anyone pin her down, picking up tidbits of gossip and information and flattery from a multitude of sources.

This party, however, didn't promise that moment of relaxation. Marco Lombardi, although he didn't know it, was the only guest of honor on her secret agenda and in her mind's eye the only important click would come when he realized that he must win her forgiveness.

All the rest was background, Peaches thought as she finished dressing. She had devoted the day to every beauty treatment in her considerable armory and she radiated natural health, her wide-screen, mature glamour enhanced by the most expensive professional attention. Almost all, if not all, of her French women friends would be wearing elegant black in one form or another, Peaches knew, as would her visiting Americans—it was still the one way never to set a foot wrong, especially in Paris, and nothing would ever replace it.

Peaches decided to stand out in Saint-Laurent's latest, timeless white dinner suit. It had been tailored for her compact, superbly toned body at a cost of twenty-five thousand dollars, yet its jacket and trousers, made from a thin wool and trimmed with white satin lapels and cuffs, were so strictly cut that she could wear all her diamonds with it . . . well not all of them, Peaches decided as she reluctantly removed a favorite lapel pin the size of a zinnia. Around her neck she wore five diamond necklaces in graduated lengths, designed, as she had collected them one by one, in a way that allowed them to fit into each other until they looked like one wide collar. There was a resplendence of diamonds at her ears, and three wide cuff bracelets on each wrist; hundreds and hundreds of carats of the most rare and valuable of all diamonds, those certified D flawless. Peaches knew that none of her guests would be inspecting her with a jeweler's loupe, but she had never settled for less. She wore only one ring, her forty-two carat, square, cushion-cut engagement ring.

Over the top? Of course she was over the top, Peaches thought in delight, smiling her famous good-time smile into the mirror and shaking her freshly blond head approvingly. It was her damn party, wasn't it? She rapidly replaced the lapel pin as she heard the first guests arrive.

Peaches had expected that the girls would probably all show up together, in a gaggle, for moral support; that the French, as was their way, would be on time and the Americans late. She was delighted and surprised when many of the French and Americans arrived almost simultaneously in one party-hungry, luxuriously black-clad, importantly jeweled group and her party started out in that explosively exciting confusion every hostess dreams of. For a half hour her large sitting room was filled with excited conversation as people who hadn't seen each other for a few months delighted in renewed acquaintance, kissing, laughing, catching up on the latest scandal, and drinking champagne as quickly as it was offered by the many busy waiters. Suddenly a hush descended on the crowded room. Peaches turned toward the door, expecting to see the three girls making their entrance together. But it was Jordan who stood there alone, Jordan who had reduced the room to this tribute with the fire of her unexpected presence.

Peaches collected herself and her smile and advanced toward

the girl, who, unpardonably, was also wearing white, a totally un-adorned, sleeveless white satin mini-dress with black satin pumps and a fresh white gardenia pinned in her hair. Jet button earrings were her only jewelry. As her compatriot, LBJ, was known to say, Peaches thought, looking at the murderously chic girl, she felt like shittin' a squealin' worm.

She guided Jordan around the room to meet the other guests, feeling that she must resemble a short, glittering tugboat leading a sleek yacht. A part of Peaches' brain noticed that Jordan greeted the natives in a French that caused them all to express the immedi-ate appreciation the French reserve for those who speak their lan-guage with the right melody.

The instant she spotted Jacques Necker enter the room, Peaches unceremoniously abandoned Jordan.

"Jacques, I didn't dare to believe you'd really show up! The most infamous hermit in Paris! I'm absolutely thrilled," she told him, kissing him on both cheeks and throwing back her head to look up at him in barely concealed covetousness.

He looked down at her with a tolerant smile. "Am I such a total recluse that you think I'd miss a party for my own models?"

"You've missed most of my others," she pouted.

"And everyone else's—to be fair. You're looking gorgeous, Peaches, it's a treat to see you."

"Come with me and I'll introduce you to some of the Ameri-cans who are here—all future Lombardi supporters," she said, taking him by the arm.

"Thank you for watching out for my interests," Necker re-plied, his eyes rapidly taking in the room, "but I think I'll go rescue Jordan first. Those men look as if they're about to eat her up alive."

Peaches found herself standing momentarily alone at the en-trance to her big sitting room, watching Jacques Necker's back as he cut through the crowd, waving at the people he knew, and headed directly for Jordan. "Rescue Jordan?" she muttered in of-fended surprise. "What the fuck from?"

"Since when have you started talking to yourself at your own party?" Dart Benedict asked, grabbing her and spinning her around.

"Dart, darling! Welcome!"

"My God, Peaches, you've never looked better! Mary Beth

told me to be sure to send her love. What's new in your life, beautiful girl?"

"This and that, and quite a bit of the other," Peaches said, giving him as subtly insinuating a smile as she could summon up. "Nothing" was not a possible answer, even when it was true.

"Hmmm, some lucky guy agrees with you, and don't think I won't find out who he is. Now tell me, where are the guests of honor? I'm panting with curiosity."

"Two of them haven't shown up yet, if you can believe such rudeness, but that's Jordan Dancer, over there, having her little triumph."

"Hmmm . . . the politically correct inclusion. Necker's instinct is good," Benedict admitted. "I'd say there's room for one, or at the most two, more top black girls in the business."

"Could Jordan be one of them?"

"I'd have to study her carefully to answer that. But as far as attracting a crowd goes, she'll win that prize any day. Has Marco arrived yet?"

"I haven't noticed," Peaches answered vaguely. "Come on, I'll introduce you around."

"Don't bother, love, I know lots of these people. I'll take care of myself."

Dart Benedict melted away in Jordan's direction as Peaches expected he would. Professional curiosity was something she could understand. Quickly Peaches found herself caught up in the next wave of guests. Maude Callender, in a formal frock coat of black cut velvet and a ruffled, white, lace-trimmed shirt, was the only one Peaches felt was enough of a stranger to be introduced to a few groups before she could be left on her own.

"Aren't the girls here?" Maude asked as they moved through the noisy room, from one group to another.

"Only Jordan."

"I can't imagine what's happened to April," Maude said, mystified. "She said she was going shopping but she should have been back hours ago."

"And what about Tinker—can't they tell time? Guests of honor should always be early, damn it, everybody knows that."

"Why didn't Frankie round them up?" Maude asked.

"Even Frankie isn't here," Peaches said, sharply annoyed. "What a joke of a chaperone she's turned out to be."

"But Peaches, her mind's on more important things, surely you've made allowances for that."

"What's more important?"

"Mike Aaron of course. Where have you been not to have heard?"

"Oh, Maude, don't be absurd, Mike can have anybody he—"

"Would you care to bet cash on the line against it?" Maude asked. "Oh, Kiki, here you are! I have a million things to tell you. . . . Peaches, I'll just stay here with Kiki, don't bother about me. . . ."

Peaches took a flute of champagne from a passing tray and drained it. She looked around the room with a feeling of unreality. Who were all these loud, gesticulating, gossiping, hand-kissing, cheek-kissing, eating, drinking, shriekingly elegant people; what were they all finding so amusing, why had she invited them in the first place?

"Mrs. Wilcox, I'm Tom Strauss. Tinker told me to meet her here. Thanks for inviting me."

"So you're the mystery man!" Peaches said, recovering quickly from her moment of self-doubt. "Well, it's about time! We've all been dying to lay eyes on you. Hmmm . . . I can certainly see why Tinker went missing so fast."

"You'll make me self-conscious," Tom said, grinning down at her easily. He liked a genuine, all-American, flirtatious broad as well as the next man.

"Somehow I doubt that," Peaches said wryly. "I suppose you want to know where your girl is?"

"She promised me that for once she'd get here on time. Lombardi's been working her so late that I barely see her, and when I do, she's whimpering with exhaustion. She falls asleep while she's soaking her feet. It's pathetic."

"Don't worry, they're probably on their way over this minute —you, of all people, must know how artists get carried away."

"Of course I do. I've worked into the next day myself, a hundred times, but I didn't have to get up every morning for tango lessons."

"If she wins, it'll all have been worth it."

"And if she doesn't, Mrs. Wilcox? Sorry, I shouldn't have asked you that, I shouldn't even think it."

"Call me Peaches. If she doesn't, at least she'll know that she gave it her all. Isn't that what you're doing?"

"Yeah, I'm giving it my best shot. Say, that must be Jordan Dancer. *Wow!* I can certainly see why Tinker's so nervous about her. Who's the older guy hovering over her?"

"Hovering?"

"Right, a big blond type, greying at the temples, hovering protectively, as they say."

"You can't mean Jacques Necker?"

"That's the guy. I should have recognized him from Tinker's description. Now *that* doesn't look too good for Tinker's chances, does it?"

"You're imagining things, Tom. It's out of the question." Peaches turned to look in the direction of his eyes.

"Why? I hope you're right, but who's going to make the decision anyway? As I understand it, nobody really knows, but it seems to me that the man who owns the business would make it his personal choice."

"Tom, use your head. Would a hardheaded businessman build a new couture house's image on a black girl, no matter how lovely?"

"You're probably right . . . but that isn't stopping him from hovering."

"Well, yes indeed, so he is," Peaches said slowly, as if to herself.

"Peaches, we're so sorry we're late!"

"Oh, Peaches, there just weren't any cabs!"

She turned to confront Frankie and Mike, their arms intertwined, both of them glowing with a visible aura of romantic excitement and satisfied sexuality that was as good as an engraved announcement.

"I'm glad I didn't make that bet with Maude," Peaches said slowly. "When did you two happen, Mike?"

"I thought everybody knew. You ought to hang out in the Relais more, that seems to be where all the rumors start," Mike said laughing.

"Only I assume this isn't a rumor?" Peaches asked him.

"It certainly doesn't feel like one to me. Does it to you, darling?" he asked, turning to Frankie.

"I can't answer that," she said, hesitating as she saw the look of fury in Peaches' eyes.

"Well, Frankie, that's wise of you," Peaches drawled. "I wish I had a ten-dollar bill for every poor deluded girl I know who's thought Mike Aaron was going to stick around. I usually give him two months before he loses interest, a few weeks more at the outside. I rated three full months, didn't I, Mike? I've always considered that a major compliment, considering your notorious hit-and-run habits."

"It was seven years ago, Peaches," Mike said quietly. "You weren't a bitch then. And I wasn't in love. I never claimed to be, if you remember. Come on, sweetheart, let's get a drink." He turned away, taking Frankie with him.

Peaches bit her lip. This was turning out to be the worst fucking party she'd ever given. Everybody was having a superb time and she was hating each minute of it more and more.

As she looked at the retreating figures of Mike and Frankie, Peaches spotted a girl paused in the doorway, posing for effect. Obviously she had to be a model, for she stood at least six-feet-four in her exaggeratedly high platform-soled shoes, but a model such as Peaches had never seen. Her face was dead white, her lipstick was a dried-blood red that looked black, her eyes were rimmed thickly with sooty black charcoal, her platinum-white hair was no more than four inches long and teased out every which way as if it had been electrified instead of cut. The ribs on her amazingly elongated torso could be counted through a dress that looked like a whore's tattered nightgown. It was made of black satin and mousseline, sheer and deeply cut, revealing her breasts to the top of her nipples, torn here and there, its hem vanishing in jagged shreds high on her thighs. Her astonishing long and exquisite legs were visible almost to the crotch and the white skin between the top of her black stockings and her black lace panties was framed in the ribbons of a bright red garter belt. She looked utterly dissolute, depraved and totally divine.

Silence descended on the party as every head turned.

"Oh, Peaches, I feel awful about being so late, but that genius hairdresser took forever," the girl said, her voice issuing with incongruous sweetness through her carnivorous lips. She strutted through the room with every eye on her until she reached her hostess. She was like an alien form of life, utterly fascinating in her vampirelike, decadent allure, a New Age Shanghai Lil.

"*April!*"

"Makeover city, darling. I couldn't stand being a nice girl for another minute. You like?" April struck a pose, with one lean hip jutted forward, her exposed legs scissored wide apart, her neck and head thrown back as if in the moment of orgasm. "I think it's heaven! You'd never believe how much this dress cost, almost as much as these blissful shoes."

The silence of the room turned into a hubbub as dozens of voices rose at once, each one with an opinion. The only people who weren't talking were Maude, who was paralyzed by shock; Frankie and Mike, who'd stopped in their tracks and returned to Peaches' side; and Dart Benedict, who had instantly made his way to April and turned her toward him.

"April," he said hastily, "I'm Dart Benedict. *You're the New Thing.* Brilliant! Sheer genius! Congratulations! But you've gone a tad over the top, love, just a tad. I'll help you perfect that great look. My Paris affiliate can get you the next cover of French *Vogue*, *Elle*, Italian *Vogue*, maybe even American *Vogue* next month, and just about everything else you want, but we have to work quickly. I can pick you up first thing in the morning."

"But . . . but what about Justine? . . . I mean, that's impossible, isn't it?"

"Of course not. You work for yourself, April. Justine only has you for Lombardi. You've got to strike out now, and I mean immediately. She doesn't have the expertise to handle you the way I—"

"Don't talk to this man, April," Frankie said, elbowing him aside. "He has no right to be soliciting you. You're under contract to Loring Model Management. What's more, when the Lombardi show is over you may be tied up for the next four years—"

"In the next few *days* I'm going to make April famous," Dart interrupted, pushing past Frankie and standing between her and

April. "Loring can't. April, you're not a slave. Justine isn't even here. And you, Frankie, good as you are, you can't possibly have my contacts. April, tomorrow at nine?"

"Well . . . sure, why not?" April said excitedly, "I don't see the harm in testing the waters. Does anybody know where Maude is?"

"Right here," Maude said, as she joined the group.

"Darling!" April reached out, put her arms around Maude's shoulders and, bending down, looked her in the eyes for a long minute before she kissed her full on the lips. "I hope you realize this is all your doing, if it weren't for you I'd never have had the courage."

"I never said anything about changing your looks," Maude cried out, still unable to believe how April had transformed her priceless classic purity.

"You'll get used to it, darling, it's still me, and I'll prove it," April laughed, and kissed her again, slowly, aggressively, defiantly. "Doesn't that feel familiar? Listen, you guys can keep fighting over me to your heart's content," she said airily to Dart and Frankie. "Maude and I are going to have some champagne. Come on, darling, let's find a waiter."

"Sweet Jesus!" Frankie breathed under her breath.

"I hadn't heard April was gay," Dart Benedict said reflectively. "Interesting. And how brilliantly clever of dear old Maude to have figured it out."

"It must be something in the water," Peaches laughed delightedly, knowing that April's startling arrival and that erotic second kiss, which had been observed by everybody in the room close enough to gawk, had made her party a mad success that would be a choice topic of conversation everywhere in Paris. Tomorrow her phone wouldn't stop ringing.

"Peaches, sweet, of course she was, she just hadn't found out," Dart protested. "And it's perfect timing, perfect! She's kinky and exquisitely glamorous at the same time, trisexual, at the very least, more than a little threatening and deeply erotic, beyond grown-up, beyond funk, light years beyond waif, perfect for today . . . we're all desperate for a new direction, something that isn't recycled Cindy or that shiksa shepherdess, Claudia. April's going to be *so fucking big* even *I* don't believe it."

"I'd like to hear what Marco will say when he sees her, that is if he ever bothers to honor us with his presence," Peaches wondered, unable to hide her impatient longing.

"He just walked in," Dart answered, looking over her head and beckoning to Marco, who brushed through the crowd toward him, with Tinker at his elbow.

The two men clasped each other in a bear hug surrounded watchfully by Peaches, Mike and Frankie. Unnoticed by anyone, Tom Strauss stood behind Mike.

"Remember the girl I phoned you about?" Marco said to Dart. "Voilà! I present Tinker Osborn, my muse, my lovely inspiration. How does she please you, old friend?"

"Your taste is improving, just when I thought it couldn't get any better," Dart answered, taking Tinker's hand and brushing it briefly with his lips.

"Now I understand what Marco's been raving about," he added, still clasping her hand, and talking to the girl as intimately as if they were alone. "We were all wondering if he'd actually stop working long enough to bring you to the party. I can certainly see why he wasn't in a rush to share anyone as beautiful as you with a crowd full of people. Marco, you've simply got to stop being so possessive."

"When a man finds a woman who can make him dream, Dart, he wants to keep her close to him. But when that same woman can cause him to create—ah, then you don't let her go if you can avoid it. Hands off, my friend," Marco said, putting his arm firmly around Tinker's waist. "I only told you about her, I didn't *give* her to you."

"Then you should never have introduced us. Tinker, I've just asked April to meet me tomorrow about doing some major magazine covers, and she's agreed. I think I can do as much for you as I can do for her. Will you join us at nine? I want everyone who works in my Paris office to see you and brainstorm on the best ways to position you."

"I have my tango lesson at ten but yes I—"

Tom Strauss moved quickly around Mike and jerked Marco's

arm away from Tinker's waist. He grabbed Marco by the shoulders and shook him fiercely. "You touch her again, you little shit, and I'm going to take you apart!"

Without warning, Marco punched Tom viciously in the midsection. Quickly Tom landed a brutal right to Marco's jaw. Marco staggered, his lip bleeding, as Mike and Dart jumped in to separate the two men. Their combined efforts managed to stop the fight, while Frankie flew across the room to Necker's side, speaking urgently into his ear.

"Tinker," Tom said grimly, as he and Marco were finally quieted. "I'll get your coat, we're going home."

"Tom! How *dare* you act like that? How could you? Are you completely crazy?"

"We're leaving," he insisted.

"But, but . . . I just got here!" Tinker sputtered furiously.

"Every time you come home you damn near fall down because you've been on your feet all day. Have they suddenly stopped hurting?"

"No," Tinker answered, wearily, tears starting in her eyes at the roughness in his voice. "I'm in pain, all right. I'm always in pain. That doesn't mean I don't want to have a little fun. Oh, Tom, you *ruined* it! And I promised everybody that they'd meet you."

"They'll survive. We're going home."

"Tom, you can't steal one of my guests of honor," Peaches said sharply.

"The lady doesn't want to leave," Dart Benedict told Tom. "Haven't you made enough trouble for now?"

"He's the little boyfriend, Dart," Marco spat out in contempt. "You ought to know they're always jealous."

"*Oh, stop it everybody!*" Tinker's voice rose above the sound of the party, a shrill sharp scream of rising hysteria. "Just stop it, *stop it!*"

"It's all right, Tinker." Jacques Necker loomed up behind her, tucking Tinker's arm protectively under his, as Frankie stood beside him. Tom, Marco and Dart all fell silent at the authority of his tone.

"Now, all of you, *everybody*, I suggest that you leave Tinker to me for a few minutes. I'd like to find out how she's bearing up under her schedule." He looked directly at Dart.

"Mr. Benedict, April, Tinker and Jordan are all under contract to me until the Lombardi show is over. I don't want them distracted by your attempts at poaching. Is that understood?"

"Monsieur Necker, I assure you—"

"You heard me, Mr. Benedict. No poaching. Not if you want to do business with any of my companies again. Now Tinker, you and I are going into the other room and have a nice, quiet talk."

Peaches glanced around the circle of antagonists left by Tinker's departure. Marco, his lips pressed together in rage, blood on his collar, refused to even look in her direction.

"I'd better go play hostess," she faltered, and turned on her heel, plunging back into the fascinated, still-watching crowd.

"The cavalry to the rescue?" Dart sneered, raising an eyebrow at Frankie. "Nice work but it'll only work once. Even Necker can't be everywhere."

"Maude will kill herself for missing all this, Benedict," Mike said. "I'll fill her in. *Zing's* readers will be fascinated by your hustle."

"Just spell my name right. Marco, let's get a drink."

"And then there were three," Frankie said. "Tom, I'm Frankie Severino and this is Mike Aaron."

"Hi. I'm sorry about that but I couldn't stand there and watch those two bastards treating Tinker as if she were a piece of meat. She didn't even realize it . . . shit, is it always going to be like this, flattery mixed with slime, everyone trying to use her?"

"They happen to be particularly repulsive, but pretty typical I'm afraid," Mike answered, with solid concern. "It isn't always that bad, is it, Frankie? Frankie? Now where the hell did she disappear to? Oh, right, Frankie's mad at me too. Peaches is some piece of work, you've got to say that for her. Hey, Tom, great punch, guy. No, waiter, no champagne, thanks, bring us two double Scotches, no ice."

I'd had it! Enough already! I beat it the hell out of that party and got on the phone to Justine. Listen, I said, April's turned herself into some kind of intergalactic slut but it's nothing I could have prevented. She'll stop the show, one way or another. But Dart Benedict is here propositioning our girls and if you don't get your ass on the next Concorde he's going to move in big-time. The only thing that broke it up, at least for now, was your old man. April and Tinker were all set to meet with Dart tomorrow. How? I told Necker that Dart was trying to steal your girls, that's all. What more does a father need to know? He took over damage control. Plus Tinker's boyfriend tried to kill Lombardi, unfortunately without success. You've got a problem with Tinker too. Something's wrong there. Jordan's the only one I feel is solid. We can share this suite, I'll expect you tomorrow. I'll send the car. Start packing.

I was so mad I hung up on her, not waiting for Justine to agree or say good-bye. I knew she'd be here tomorrow and high time. How long could she continue to thrust her responsibility on me?

After I'd finished yelling at my boss, I realized that the party was still going on and it was my duty to get back to it. But I had to sit down for a few minutes, take deep breaths, and talk to myself sternly. So Peaches and Mike had had a fling seven years ago—I could live with that. But what about all the other girls she'd accused him of? He hadn't denied anything. He'd told me himself there'd been a lot of girls in his life but he hadn't loved any of them. I *couldn't* be destined to be one of the string of women he'd lost interest in. I had to believe that I was different for Mike—the final girl, the one he'd been looking for—or I'd spoil everything we had. What we had *was* everything, for me anyway. But my little bubble had definitely been pricked.

After I'd given myself this wise advice I had a really good, really loud, five-minute old-fashioned cry that traveled all the way from my toes to the ends of my hair. I repaired my makeup and went back to the festivities. Was it just this morning that I'd actually been looking forward to them?

21

Justine glared at the phone receiver in her hand as if by sheer mental force she could eliminate the flood of words that it had just brought her. Playing for time, she forced herself to concentrate on the fact that Frankie had hung up on her. Actually flat-out *banged* down the bloody phone. An unthinkable act of downright mutiny, an unleashed exhibition of flagrant rudeness. Ha! So that was the thanks she got from someone she'd done everything for! Give a girl a job, promote her, let her worm her way into your affections, allow her to become your second-in-command, wangle her a trip to Paris, buy her a wardrobe of new clothes, make it possible for her to attract a man who never would have looked at her otherwise, and of course she turns into a viperous ingrate, so high and mighty and full of herself that she starts giving duchessy orders . . . "Start packing" . . . "I'll send the car" indeed!

However, even Justine's formidable powers of denial were unable to focus exclusively on Frankie, no matter how satisfactory that felt. Soon she was forced to try to process the information she'd just received. The notion that April would become any kind of a slut was absurd. If anything was bothering Tinker, Frankie had only suspicion. Lombardi was still in one piece.

Which left nothing to really worry about except Dart Benedict.

"Phyllis," Justine said, buzzing her secretary, "get me a seat on the next Concorde, and if they don't have one, tell them I'll stand in the aisle or sit in a cage in the baggage compartment like a dog."

Dart Benedict. How could she not have expected this? What the fuck else would that criminal be doing in Paris days before the collections started but trying to steal her girls? How many of her

New York—based girls had he already reached, girls who hadn't yet found the courage to tell her that they were jumping ship? And what about her bookers? Which of them were busy making copies of all her computerized files, filled with invaluable information, quietly getting ready to flit in the night? Did she still have an agency or was it about to fall apart? And wasn't it all her fault?

If she hadn't let Dart know that she was wise to his sickening little lunchtime orgies, if, instead, she had strung him along, pretending to be flattered by his desire to go into business with her, if she had told him that she'd be talking to her financial advisors about it and getting back to him, none of this would have happened.

Dart would be on his best behavior with her for months . . . she could have strung it out almost indefinitely if she'd been even semi-smart. But no, she'd had to show that she was as tough as he was, that she was too independent to be co-opted into his agency, she'd had to challenge him. She must have had a turd for a brain that day. It had never been about Dart, it had been about Aiden. But basically the fight with Aiden was really all about Necker. And now Necker had stepped into her world again, and, if Frankie, that pretentious, cocky bitch, was to be believed, and of course she was, Necker had done her a major favor.

Okay, Justine thought, this was the moment to look at her options. Coldly, dispassionately, unblinkingly. Option time, she thought, writing the words on top of a fresh yellow pad.

Option One, she wrote, and underlined the words. For a long while she sat, gnawed by confusion. No, maybe it would be easier to write down the options she *didn't* have, so as to make Option One stand out inevitably from the rest.

"You've got the last seat on the Concorde tomorrow," Phyllis' voice came through the intercom. "And five girls want to see you about problems with their bookings that the bookers can't handle."

"Tell them to wait a half hour. I'm clearing my decks," she said, bent over the pad.

Nonoptions:
1. Stay in New York until the collection is over, with head in sand.

2. Prevent the girls from listening to Benedict. Chain them in dungeon.
3. Do not have any contact with Necker while in Paris. Become invisible.
4. Do not share suite with Frankie so don't have to listen to drivel about Mike Aaron.
5. Pray.

It wasn't a long list, Justine thought, considering it. Praying and not sharing a suite with Frankie were the only items she could cross off. Unfortunately she had to admit that love-struck drivel about Mike was exactly what she was looking forward to hearing. And prayer was always a good idea, just in case.

Where was the option that was going to present itself, clear, shining, obvious? She ripped the sheet of yellow paper in four pieces and threw them in her wastepaper basket. On the next sheet she wrote two words.

CALL AIDEN.

Well, Justine said to herself, mentally flinging her hands in the air, what else was there left to do? If she couldn't run her agency, at least she could make a stab at running her life, particularly when she knew she couldn't endure one more day without speaking to him. No reason, as the world fell apart around her, to deny herself the sound of his voice.

She dialed his beeper number and told Phyllis to send in the waiting girls, one by one. She was in the middle of working out a booking conflict with the second girl when Phyllis announced Aiden Henderson returning her call.

"Oh, Josie, would you please excuse me for a minute, it's my impossible contractor," Justine said. "I'm going to have to be rather unpleasant to him."

When Josie had taken herself out of the office, Justine picked up the phone.

"Hi, there," she said, in a breezy voice.

"If you hadn't called me today," Aiden said, not bothering to hide his happy relief, "I was coming over there to get you and drag you out by the hair and how would that have looked?"

"I was worried about something like that happening, and I

have a reputation to protect," Justine replied casually as her tense shoulders relaxed.

"I'm still planning on doing it, unless you meet me after work."

"Are you trying to intimidate me?"

"Absolutely."

"Then I give up. In Zen that means that I win. That's why I called you first, it's part of telephone Zen."

"I'm a good loser. Where would you like to eat?"

"Well . . . now that the furnace is working, we could eat at my place, in the kitchen."

"It's more convenient," he agreed. "What should I bring?"

"I don't have any food in the fridge. That's the first rule of eating Zen. Bring whatever you're in the mood for . . . there's a saying, 'When the student is hungry the food will arrive.' Why don't you pick up some lobster Cantonese and sweet-and-sour pork and vegetable fried rice, and maybe some egg rolls and those little spare ribs, hot mustard and tons of duck sauce, of course."

"How did you know that authentic Americanized Chinese food is the latest foodie thing? You're on. How about seven?"

"How about six-thirty?"

"I could make it at six."

"Swell. See ya."

"Bye."

Justine sat at her desk, joyful tears, unnoticed, running down her cheek. She buzzed for Josie to come back in.

"Justine!" the girl said, astonished. "Did he give you that bad of a time?"

"No, I straightened him out," she sniffed. "But you know contractors, living hell, every last one of them."

"Yeah, I know. That's what my mom says. You can't live with them and you can't live without them."

"Exactly."

"You even remembered fortune cookies! It was when Chinese restaurants stopped serving fortune cookies that things went off the track. Aiden, you're seriously gifted at take-out."

"Hey, a guy's gotta do what a guy's gotta do."

"So what do you *think*—I've been talking all through dinner and all you've done is nod from time to time. You're worse than a shrink, at least they don't chew."

"Are you asking my opinion about the situation you're in, or my advice, or what?"

"Naturally I expect some sort of minimal comment," Justine said in an aggravated tone. She'd told him everything, every last one of her secrets, and except for a raised eyebrow and a noncommittal motion of his head she hadn't received any feedback at all. "I mean obviously I have to go to Paris, but what happens with Necker when I'm there? What would you do?"

"You really want to know what I'd do, the unvarnished, you-won't-like-this version? Remembering that I haven't lived your life and I didn't know your mother?"

"Absolutely."

"I wouldn't have gotten into this mess in the first place. I would have put my mother's and father's mistakes where they deserve to be, *in the past,* and I would have responded to my father's letters, met him and made up my mind about him without fighting my dead mother's battles for her."

"Twenty-twenty hindsight! Typical of a man!" Justine burst out with indignation.

"You asked," he said mildly.

"What do you mean, 'my mother's mistakes'—are you blaming her for getting pregnant?"

"Don't be dumb. And I don't blame her for not letting him know about you at first. He'd abandoned her, what else could she do? But later on, when she knew his whereabouts, I think she should have tried to bring the two of you together."

"For the money?" Justine asked, incredulously.

"For the *relationship,* sweetheart. You would have had a father in your life while you were growing up. She should have swallowed her pride as soon as she could, and not hugged you all to herself, her own private treasure, keeping you out of Necker's life as her revenge."

"But my mother *needed* to have some kind of revenge, Aiden. You're not making any allowance for human nature. She'd given up so much, she did a brave and difficult thing, bringing me up on her own."

"Her revenge wasn't fair to you, not to my way of thinking. If your mother hadn't died, you *still* wouldn't know you have a father."

"Unfair! Oh, that's such a perversion of the way she was! You never knew her, she *devoted* herself to me, don't you see?" Justine cried, growing more and more irritated at the way he didn't give her mother credit for anything.

"Who says a mother should devote her life to her kids? A lot of it, sure, but never all of it. Justine, look, I have a feeling that your mother did too well at her job not to have enjoyed it. I know how much you love your work. I bet she was a lot like you that way. She had an entire working life that didn't revolve around you. I think your mother was stubborn, too stubborn for your own good."

"But look how she sacrificed herself to give me everything!"

"Justine, I understand why she acted the way she did," Aiden responded, clinging to his point. "But just think, if she'd been able to bring herself to try to share you with your father, she'd have freed herself too. Who knows, maybe she'd have married again, even had more kids? But she made a decision to avoid any chance for a normal, healthy situation. One thing I know for sure, it would have been better for you to have had a father, and in this series of unhappy events the only person whose happiness I care about is you."

"You're making a big assumption here—that Necker would have wanted me all those years ago, while his wife was alive. I could have been a real embarrassment to him."

"And you're assuming that he wouldn't have wanted you, this man who doesn't have a single child? But one way or the other, your mother should have given him the chance to know you were alive. Then, if he hadn't responded, she would never have had to tell you about him."

"Oh, you make me so mad!" Justine shouted.

"I'm just telling you what I think, the way you asked me to."

"I hate the way you're so logical and sensible and plod along putting things together, looking at both sides as if they're *even.*

That's such a typically male reaction. You don't have a touch for the human factor, you don't have any imagination, any passion!" Justine raged at him. "If the world were left to people like you there wouldn't be any drama, any tragedy, any conflict, you'd solve everything so sensibly, with one and one always making two."

"But they do. Always. It's just one of those crazy things."

"Oh, I give up talking to you about this. You never knew my mother and there's no way you can realize what a wonderful woman she was. You only see the downside. And not only that, you still haven't given me any advice about what to do in Paris, and I specifically asked for advice."

"But you're not getting it. You're on your own there. Anybody who can return Madame de Pompadour's writing desk can make up her own mind about a little thing like a long-lost father."

"How do you know who it belonged to?" Justine's startled eyes flew open.

"I researched the coat of arms. Couldn't resist. The woman with the greatest taste in the history of France commissioned that particular piece of furniture."

"I wonder . . . do you suppose she used it?"

"She possessed a number of châteaux, the Marquise de Pompadour had a passion for acquisition, she owned as many objects as three queens put together, but I have a strong feeling that she kept that particular desk in her bedroom."

"Do you?"

"It gave off a definite bedroom vibration when I touched it. Uncanny."

"Did it?"

"Yeah. And something even more weird. While I was working on the pipes in your bathroom, I walked through your bedroom and there was a space exactly the right size for that particular desk, a space that cried out for a little place where you could sit and write me love letters in the middle of the night."

"And why on earth would I want to do that?" Justine demanded.

"Because you're so considerate. See, this is the thing, you'd wake up in the middle of the night and see me lying there sleeping happily beside you and you'd get this terrible urge to tell me how much you love me, but you'd realize that I needed my sleep because I have to get up so early in the morning. So the only way you could do it would be to write it down and leave it for me next to my shaving stuff."

"What a touching fantasy."

"It's not a fantasy, Justine," Aiden said, shaking his head solemnly. "I can show you the exact place in your bedroom and if you can swear to me that it isn't crying out for a little desk, I'll . . . I'll . . ."

"You'll what?"

"I'll make you another Tequila Sunrise. Right now."

"That's pretty tempting," Justine said, relenting as she looked at him sitting there so earnest and hopeful. So, for some reason . . . absolutely swell. Yes, swell, that was the exact word. And beautiful. Heart-meltingly beautiful, it was the broken nose that did it. And his eyes, how could they be bluer than her own? And masculine, flesh and bone-meltingly masculine, and edible . . . no! She wasn't going to go that route again, not tonight. She'd picked up the phone first, she reminded herself, sternly. A woman has to have pride. Pride was important, essential, men respected a woman with pride.

"I'm not packed," Justine said firmly, "and I leave for Paris tomorrow. I can't drink and pack at the same time."

"How long does it take you to pack?"

"Golly, who knows? Paris, with all the fashion people there— I can't just throw things in a suitcase the way they do in movies. I have to be coordinated, organized, mostly black naturally," Justine babbled, "and then I have to pack my shoes, my cosmetics . . . hairspray . . . vitamins . . . antihistamines. . . ."

"Tell you what I'll do, I'll come up and help you. I'll focus your mind. I'll make a list while you decide what to take. I'll quiz you on coordination. I'll fold things so they don't wrinkle. As you put each item in your suitcase, I'll check it off the list. You'll be done in half an hour."

"Never, ever in my whole life have I packed in half an hour, even for a weekend."

"Never, ever, have you had such a good reason to get it over with. Because as soon as that suitcase is closed, I'm going to make love to you."

"Oh." Justine's whirling mind came to full stop. Pride, she thought, pride was some sort of a *sin*, wasn't it?

"Don't you want to?"

"Could we do that *first?*" she asked, giving him a laughing, unpremeditated kiss. Pride wasn't what it used to be, whatever it had been. "And pack later?" Justine got up quickly from the kitchen table and started in the direction of the staircase, reaching out for Aiden's hand.

"That makes sense," he said as they took the stairs two at a time. "You're right about me, I do tend to plod along. Maybe one and one doesn't necessarily make two. Hey, it's nice and warm in your bedroom. I think I'll get undressed."

"I really feel much better about everything now that we've talked, even if you won't tell me what to do," Justine told him from the bathroom where she was taking off all her clothes with hands that shook with eagerness. As gracefully as a mermaid she slipped into her bed and beckoned to him.

"Nope, I won't give you advice," Aiden agreed, joining her without ceremony, and looking into her eyes with such flaming, uncomplex, uncompromising tenderness that she shivered, and lowered her lids. "But, on another subject, do you think you might possibly consider marrying me?"

"I think . . . perhaps . . . maybe . . . I could," Justine allowed, burying her nose in his neck so that he couldn't read her astonished face. "Consider it, that is."

"How long will it take to decide?"

"Oh, I've decided already." She managed to keep her voice light and wonderfully careless, as decades of fearing to trust any man crumbled in seconds, and a conviction of absolute rightness took the place of all her well-cultivated defenses.

"Justine!"

"I'll tell you later." She smiled infuriatingly, savoring a last moment of maidenly hesitation. Aiden had built his fortress right in the middle of her unwilling heart.

"When?"

"There's sure to be a right time eventually . . . maybe when we've gotten to know each other better, maybe when Rufus is ready to share you."

"Justine!" He grabbed her threateningly. "Yes or no?"

"Okay, okay! *Yes.* Satisfied now?"

" 'Satisfied'?" he cried, incredulously. "Would it be too banal to say I'm the happiest man in the world? Would that begin to explain how I feel? Do you want me to try and find new words, because if you do, I'll start thinking and—"

"Actually, I wouldn't mind if you said it again. That first thing, about being happy, it sounded just right, just enough . . . would it be too banal to say 'same here'? Or how about this—I love you as much as life itself?" Justine asked, suddenly intensely serious. "That's pretty banal too."

"I don't need fancy," Aiden told her, with sudden tears in his eyes, taken off guard by perfect joy.

22

I thought you'd want to know," Frankie said as soon as she'd been connected to Jacques Necker at his office. "Miss Loring is on her way to Paris."

"Are you sure?"

"She called me to confirm it right before the Concorde took off. She'll be here tonight, our time, which means she'll be at the dress rehearsal tomorrow."

"I'm glad to hear she's well enough to fly," he said flatly.

"So am I," Frankie said, wondering why her news wasn't being greeted with more warmth. She'd been so delighted that she was finally able to give him news of Justine's arrival that she'd called him the minute she was certain Justine was in the air. Now, instead of sounding joyous and relieved and anxious and excited—all or any of the reactions she'd imagined him having—Necker seemed merely businesslike.

"Thank you for talking to Tinker last night," Frankie ventured.

"Frankly I was amazed at the way she's let Lombardi take advantage of her. To use her for inspiration is entirely justified, but he has no right to keep her working such long hours, with daily tango lessons on top of it. Couldn't you have done something to put a stop to this, Miss Severino?"

"I've been trying, Mr. Necker, believe me. But Tinker is more fiercely determined than you imagine and I can't physically restrain her from working as hard as she wants to. Not a day has passed without my asking her if she's okay, and she always says she's fine."

"Nevertheless, you should have called me."

"I didn't realize you'd want to be bothered—" And he doesn't even know about Tom, Frankie thought. Or does he?

"Let me be the judge of that."

"Yes, Mr. Necker. I'll keep that in mind from now on," Frankie said meekly.

After he'd hung up, Jacques Necker sat motionless, staring into space. Of course Justine was only coming to Paris now, at the last moment, because of the threat posed by Dart Benedict, he had no illusions on that subject. But she would be right here, in his city, within his grasp, and between the dress rehearsal and the collection itself, there would be dozens of natural opportunities for him to see her. She had to be as aware of that as he was.

How should he handle this chance? His daughter had no idea of the extent of his remorse for the past. All she knew about him was whatever damning things her mother had told her. But he'd been too pigheaded to let that fact deter him, warn him, even, at the very least advise him of how set Justine must be against him.

No, he'd gone right ahead and done the most unwise, ill-considered thing he could have done; he'd overreached. From the day he'd conceived of the Lombardi contest, he'd overreached every time he'd tried to take a step toward his daughter. Mistake, mistake, mistake! That damn desk, he must have been insane! He knew so much about Justine now, he mused, so much he would never have known without Jordan.

From everything Jordan had told him, he could conjure up Justine's prickly sense of self, her need to achieve on her own, her fierce attachment to her independence. She clung to her ideas and her ideals, she was unyielding, she was loyal, she had a sense of fairness that made her stubborn to a fault. He understood her because he was like her. Or was Justine like him? Could character, flaws as well as strengths, be inherited without contact between father and daughter? No matter—now, when he stopped to put himself in her place, he could see how his tyrannical pursuit, his entrapment, if you called it by its right name, had only served to make any future approach more difficult.

He couldn't make another mistake, Jacques Necker resolved. He would leave Justine alone. He wouldn't lift a finger toward a rapprochement. Unless they were actually brought face-to-face by some unforeseen event, he wouldn't make the slightest gesture toward her, not so much as sending flowers to the hotel.

Justine had had months to take his measure, she knew how far he'd go to get to her, yet she'd never found it in her heart to give him a chance. Not even curiosity had made her read his letters. If that was the way she felt about him, realistically there was nothing he could do to change her. The next move was up to her. If there was to be a next move.

Justine moved into action as soon as she reached the Plaza. She had her bags put into the bedroom, tracked down April and asked her to come to the suite immediately. April obeyed, too astonished by the sound of Justine's voice to mention that she and Maude were on their way out to a late dinner.

"My, my," Justine said as she kissed her, "I'm not sure I would have recognized you on the street, but I like what I see."

"You do! I thought you were going to be horrified," April breathed in relief, her new swagger only skin deep in Justine's magisterial presence.

"Not at all. Sometimes there's a look like yours that's so strong in one modality that we're blinded by it. I thought of you as the next great classic blond, but in a way that everyone understands. Now there's nothing classic left. You've achieved a look nobody else has, and that's the one thing a top girl has to have. I just wish I'd thought of it myself."

"Maude thinks I look freakish," April blurted.

"Ah, but then Maude's not in the business," Justine said crisply. "The thing is that you're not just a divine vanilla blond, you're a red-hot, musky blond, and nothing can beat that. All you need to modify is your hair, otherwise you're magnificent. But your hair's on the verge of punk, and we've been there before and we don't want to go back, do we? Let me find out exactly what that hairdresser did." Justine ran her fingers through the wild remains of April's once-glorious hair, pushing it this way and that without managing to make any change in its comic-book frizz.

"Was this permed, after the bleach job and the cut? No? Just set? That's a piece of luck. You've got enough split ends as it is. Frankie, look in my cosmetic case. There's some gel there and a comb."

When Frankie returned, the three women went into one of the bathrooms, and April sat on the toilet lid while Justine dampened her hair and carefully rubbed gel into her platinum disaster.

"See, April, you can't have too many things going on or people won't know where to focus. Now your mouth and your eyes are both dynamite so I'm going to take the hair way down. A gent's look, I think, from the Arrow Collar days . . . always loved that handsome guy."

She parted April's hair sharply on one side and combed it back from her face. There was enough of it to form a low, smooth pompadour that fell just behind April's lovely ears, in small points, emphasizing the beauty of her skull. Suddenly the heavy makeup April wore, combined with the severely modern, shingled hair, fell together to make one strong, single statement of outrageous sophistication.

"Take a look in the mirror," Justine told her. "No, the full-length mirror, or you won't get the full effect."

"Oh, my God! It's divine . . . but you don't think it's too . . . too . . . boyish?"

"You've never looked more feminine," Justine said honestly. "A man's hairstyle on a girl with that great big emphasized mouth of yours, and those enormous Dietrich eyes, creates an elegant sexual tension you'd never get with curls or long hair. It's a bit Berlin in the thirties, I admit, but not boyish. Ambiguous, that's what it is . . . ambiguous and tantalizing. Now, what's this I heard about Dart Benedict?"

"He came after me at the party. He said if I worked quickly he could get me *Vogue* covers."

"And so he could. Two days from now, after the collection, the doorman at this hotel will be able to get you *Vogue* covers, because *Vogue* will be coming after you. But I don't think you'd be happy at his agency."

"That's what Maude said. She's heard some strange things about him."

"All of them true, and more. If you want details, I have them. However, after this collection's over, I only represent you at your request. Until then, I'd appreciate it if you stayed away from Dart."

"Oh, Justine, I don't intend to leave you! Not ever! I wouldn't be in Paris if I hadn't been at Loring Model Management. I'd still be the same know-nothing, mixed-up child I used to be, with my old mistake of a life."

"But it's just makeup, April, don't go overboard." Justine looked puzzled at April's outburst of words.

"Ah . . . yeah . . . well . . . I'll let Frankie fill you in. Bye Justine. Thanks for my hair. Gotta go. Maude's waiting."

April fled the room as Frankie hugged herself, rocking with silent laughter.

"Will you stop that! What the hell's so funny?"

"Oh Lord," Frankie panted between howls, "oh, Lord have mercy, she came out before fifty people but she's afraid to tell you!"

"Came out? As in 'to come out'? *April?* April's gay?"

"For the moment anyway."

"With—Maude?"

"Who else?"

"Damn! I missed all the fun. You might have said something in your phone call."

"I thought I'd let you find out for yourself. No sense in spoiling all the surprises around here."

"Hmm . . . I must have got a subliminal message, that's undoubtedly why I thought of the gent's cut."

"Back in charge, already, I see," Frankie said, as sarcastically as she could manage.

"Isn't that what you wanted?"

"Oh, Justine, I'm just so damn glad to see you, I don't know whether to shit or go blind."

"Neither, please, my darling mouse. Now, shall I tackle Jordan?"

"About what? She's the only one who hasn't given me a minute's trouble."

"It's too late to get on Tinker's case, I suppose?"

"Even if it weren't, she isn't here. She's at Tom's."

"At Tom's? Is Tom a man or a woman, Frankie?"

"A very adorable guy. They're, and I quote, 'madly in love.' "

"And when did that start?"

"The second night we got here."

"Frankie, I'm beginning to question your performance as a chaperone."

"I warned you it wasn't my gig, not that I didn't give it my best efforts."

"We'll go see Tinker in the morning. Meanwhile, let's order dinner in the room."

"So you can ask me all about Mike?" Frankie said eagerly.

"Eventually. First I'll tell you all about Aiden."

"Aiden?"

"My husband to be," Justine said with dignity. "Aiden Henderson."

"You don't even know a man named Aiden."

"I've known him for almost two weeks."

"Any other girl on any other planet might, just possibly, get engaged to a guy she's known for less than two weeks, but not you, Justine. You're simply not the type. I'm the one with the guy, not you. Stop teasing me."

"Do I look as if I'm teasing you?"

Frankie took a good close look at Justine for the first time since she'd arrived. The changes she had missed, the luminous expression on Justine's face, the way she said the name "Aiden," a new lightness of being, almost like a halo, that seemed to emanate from her friend, all rushed at Frankie in one affirmation of an unlikely but unquestionable truth.

"Caramba!" she shouted.

"I know. I can't believe it either."

"But . . . but . . . *how?"*

"He broke my furnace, and then . . . it's complicated, but one thing led to another. There was an absolute inevitability."

"Ah ha, the old broken furnace ploy! Why didn't you say so in the first place? That's a mating call on the molecular level if there ever was one. Or you could blame it on the Bossa Nova. Okay, okay! I'm listening!"

"I wonder how long that elevator's been broken," Justine said as she and Frankie climbed the four flights of stairs to Señora Varga's studio.

"Since I've been coming here and probably for the last decade. No wonder the Señora is made of steel. Here we are. Don't ring, she keeps the door open so I can just creep in and wait until she allows Tinker her break."

The two women entered quietly and sat down without being noticed. They watched the two dancers for five minutes before the Señora noticed them and reluctantly released Tinker with a few words of praise.

"Justine! You made it!" Tinker cried. "Oh, I'm so happy to see you, you can't imagine, it's so exciting, I've never been so excited in my life, did you see me dance, today's my last lesson, what did you think, I'm getting really good, I never knew I could do this, and wait till you see the clothes, Marco's finished most of the last-minute changes, and we did a final accessory rehearsal just for me, oh, Justine, there's so much going on I couldn't close my eyes last night, Tom tried to make me eat a steak but I couldn't get it down, not a bite, just soup and bread, that's all my stomach wants, it's probably the endorphins, they cut the appetite, all I could think about was the other girls, working with them tonight at the dress rehearsal, Karen, Carla, Helena, did you know Necker finally got them all, even Claudia and Kate and Linda, almost all the top girls, Justine, the real ones, he paid them three times as much as anyone else does because otherwise they don't do un-knowns, not even for GN, it's going to be so exciting, being out there with them, being the first girl out, opening the show, of course it's a lot of responsibility but Marco's sure I can do it, and I have to, Justine, I have to, because that's the way the show is planned, my first dress, wait till you see it, he's starting with eve-ning clothes instead of the usual way, with day clothes, it's a divine coral chiffon, five ruffled skirts, different lengths, very flamenco, they whirl and whirl, it's cut down to *here* in the back and *here* in the front, you can see everything, lucky I'm thinner than I've ever been, tiny straps, with a full-length cape made of nothing but hundreds of organza roses in the most beautiful shade of pale, pale, *pale* yellow, as if there's a spotlight on me, I take it off at the end of the runway . . . no . . . no, what am I saying? . . . not then, not until just *before* the end of the runway, facing the photographers, and I don't drag it in the old way, I lift it and throw it as far as I can backward, to show how light it is, I've practiced and practiced—"

"Sit down, Tinker," Justine said quietly.

"Oh, I can't sit down, it's easier if I stay on my feet, if I sit down I might never get up and Señora Varga wants one last half hour before she lets me go to Marco, she's a perfectionist, I wanted to learn another dance, not just the tango, but she wouldn't let me, said I wasn't ready, the silly thing is I'll never be able to dance it with a man because I only know how to lead, isn't that ridiculous, silly, so silly, it won't even do me any good on the dance floor, and the silliest thing of all is nobody dances the tango anyway, do they, Justine?"

Justine stood up and pressed her hands firmly on Tinker's shoulders. "Sit down, Tinker, you're overtired."

Tinker burst into a passion of tears. "No, no, I'm not," she kept talking, weeping all the while through her words. "I told Tom I wasn't, he tried not to let me out of the house this morning, and now you're telling me the same thing, you *want* me to be tired, you don't understand, I can't be tired, it's impossible, it's only another day away, the spring collection, it's tomorrow, I can't let the house down, that's what Marco says, I can't let them down, you understand, Justine, you know how it is, you understand, don't you? Frankie, don't you understand?"

"Take her other arm, Frankie," Justine said, locking one of Tinker's arms in hers. "We're going to get you some rest, Tinker, so that you'll be perfect for tomorrow. You're overrehearsed, that's the only thing that's wrong with you. One good day's rest, and one good night, just till tomorrow and you'll be perfect, on top of your form, but you need to rest, you can understand that, can't you, Tinker?"

"But the Señora . . ."

"I'll say good-bye for you, you can come and see her after the collection if you want to, now we'll go back to the hotel and put you to bed."

"*But Tom!*"

"We'll get Tom and bring him to the hotel. He'll stay with you there and help take care of you. Frankie will get him as soon as you're in bed. If you don't go to bed, Tinker, Frankie can't go get Tom. I'll talk to Marco, he'll understand perfectly, this happens lots of times, they can do the dress rehearsal with somebody standing in for you, you've already had your final accessory check, so they don't need you, doesn't that make sense, Tinker? There, that's better now, isn't it, here, blow, good, don't let go, Frankie, we've still got those fucking stairs, grab her coat, okay, let's go, back to the hotel, some nice hot soup, you'll be perfect for tomorrow, Tinker, you just need to get off your feet."

"But you'll talk to Marco, you promise? You'll explain?"

"Oh, I'll talk to Marco, Tinker, you can count on that."

23

I realized that I was holding my breath as Justine, Mike and I shepherded April and Jordan to the elevator that would take us to the underground space at the Ritz where the Lombardi spring collection was going to be presented tomorrow night. Tonight was the dress rehearsal and the first time Jordan and April would find themselves in the company of the top girls in the world.

It had been a long day and the hard part was just starting now, after eight at night. We were late, on top of everything else, because of an unexpected traffic accident that had tied up the Place de la Concorde.

It seemed years ago, rather than just this morning, that Justine and I had settled Tinker in her room and made sure that she ate every last bite of a light lunch. When we'd last looked in on her, before leaving the Plaza for the Ritz, she'd had another meal and was sound asleep. Tom, reading in a chair, was riding shotgun.

"Just what kind of favor is Necker doing our girls by making them hold their own with all the superstars?" I'd asked Justine in the afternoon, hours ago, after she'd returned from her confrontation with Marco, filled with the glowing, righteous satisfaction of someone who has finally performed a major public service in a woodshed. "That sadistic, sick little creep won't give us any more problems," she told me. Her victory-blue eyes had never been so vibrant a color, every individual one of her blond hairs seemed to have an energetic life of its own, and I had felt a lift of my spirit every time she flashed her familiar smile that combined mirth, courage and pride in the same moment.

"Face it," Justine replied, suddenly serious. "GN hired the

stars to give the first Lombardi collection borrowed status. The fashion press always expects to see the most important girls doing the most important shows. But it could be exactly the sort of gesture that backfires and makes our three girls look even more inexperienced than they are."

"Look at the bright side," I had urged her. "The photographers and editors must be getting damn sick of all the familiar, predictable models, they'll take a really good look at our girls, three fresh, unknown faces who've had a huge PR buildup. Each one of them is as beautiful as the big girls, they're simply not famous. You know that the hotter a girl is, the closer she is to being history."

"Maybe you're right," she had replied dubiously.

"And maybe you are," I had said gloomily. "But, on the other hand, even if our girls don't grab the limelight, what difference does it make? The real competition is only among them. The others are just there to show the clothes, so what are we getting in such a twist about? It's a win-win situation."

"I don't believe in 'win-win,' " she had said, shaking her head competitively, her stubborn streak taking over. "It's a myth, one of those expressions that's easy to say and too good to be true."

The reception desk had called, interrupting the seesaw of our discussion, and announced that Gabrielle d'Angelle was in the lobby and would like to come up. When she arrived, looking far-beyond-sleek in black, she announced that she had been delegated by Necker to be our guardian angel from GN until the spring collection was over. Believe it or not, I was so nervous at this point that I actually welcomed the distraction of her sharp-edged, beady-eyed, bred-in-the-Parisian-bone hardness, although how she could help to protect my beauties from disappearing beneath the shadow of the great perfect pumpkinhood of Claudia-Linda-Yasmeen-ness, I couldn't imagine.

"Well," Gabrielle said, as she shook hands with Justine, "I'm glad that you've finally recovered. Your illness seems to have left you looking extremely well."

"Antibiotics often have that effect," Justine answered smoothly.

"How is poor Tinker?"

"Sleeping peacefully."

"She'll definitely be all right by tomorrow?"

"She will, in spite of Lombardi. Who did you get to take her place tonight?"

"Fortunately Janine, Marco's former house model, is helping out. She's still loyal to Monsieur Necker."

"What I don't understand is why is the dress rehearsal starting so late?" Justine protested. "Eight in the evening is a ridiculous hour—it might run all night."

"At no price would the Ritz allow us to rent the space earlier in the day. As it is, they exacted an incredible amount for the use of the swimming pool for twenty-four hours, as if anybody has time to swim during collection week. We'll be using the beauty salon, next to the swimming pool, for dressing, hair and makeup. Their last hair client is scheduled to be finished just before seven to-night."

"But what about the hotel guests who want to get their hair done tomorrow?"

"Tomorrow the Ritz has made arrangements to send them to Alexandre by car and driver, all at GN's expense. Months ago I suggested that it would be more practical to set up the runways and hold the rehearsal elsewhere than in the hotel, but Marco fought for the actual location of the show so that the girls and their dressers will know exactly where they are to be tomor-row night."

"He makes sense about one thing, anyway," Justine grumbled.

"Do you two have any idea how different this is going to be from the ordinary show?" Gabrielle asked. "The normal show lasts forty minutes, costs about two hundred thousand dollars and the editors leave unfed. This show will last less than a half hour, and cost well over half a million dollars."

"We haven't been given any of the details," Justine replied, interested in spite of herself.

"It's a black-tie dinner of the most lavish kind. Champagne and caviar will be served before the show, dinner afterward. Only the crème de la crème of the press and customers have been in-vited. Normally there are two thousand people, tomorrow night only three hundred, plus the most important photographers of course. Remember, GN is one of the world's biggest advertisers. No editor of importance can ignore Lombardi. We kept this deliberately small and exclusive but nevertheless the media coverage will be huge since Monsieur Necker has spent money with an open hand."

"What about the runways?" Justine asked, unwilling to be drawn into a discussion of Necker's financial excesses.

"The crew from Belloir et Jallot will get started tonight at seven sharp. Their first job is to cover the pool and set up the runways. They'll be arranged in concentric circles with the banquet tables between them, so that everyone will have a front-row seat."

"Belloir et Jallot?"

"The great experts on location backgrounds: sets, lights, seating, the musicians' bandstand, everything that you need for transformation of any space into a great party."

"Musicians." I asked. "Aren't you using a DJ?"

"My dear Frankie, this is not going to be like all the other Paris collections, so many of which have turned into vulgarity contests. Lagerfeld actually played something called 'Don't Want No Short Dick Man' last season, and he began the show with a soundtrack screaming 'Turn This Fucking Music Up!' "

"Good God!" I couldn't believe those words had issued from Gabrielle's elegantly made-up mouth.

"Marco," she continued, not turning a single glossy hair, "decided he wouldn't be like everyone else, in competition with those ridiculous people who call themselves 'soundtrack stylists.' So he persuaded Monsieur Necker to import a band called Chicago."

"But they're an American rock and roll group from the late seventies," Justine said surprised. "Why them?"

"They're favorites of Marco's," Gabrielle said, shrugging in a way that clearly showed her lack of enthusiasm. "He arranged for them to supplement their group with other musicians, singers and a backup group. He commissioned them to reinvent music from the nineteen thirties in a new idiom. There'll be twenty musicians in all not counting the vocalists."

"Are his clothes also a reinvention of the nineteen thirties?" Justine asked. "I didn't expect him to steal—borrow—from that far back."

"I haven't seen them," Gabrielle replied snippily. "He may be fabricating a new kind of neutron bomb, for all I know, or even bringing back the high-button shoe. However, the key words he gave the PR department were 'gaiety, freshness and charm.' "

"*You* haven't seen them?" Justine and I asked together, equally amazed.

"Marco has been 'too busy' creating to show me anything. He refused to show clothes that were in the 'formative state,' except to the other people concerned in the design process."

"But if you haven't seen them, what about the PR people? They must be working in a vacuum?" I asked, feeling sympathetic to Gabrielle for the first time since I'd met her.

She gave us an I've-been-there-and-done-it-all shrug. "Worldwide, only a dozen or so designers are important. PR will not decide if Marco is to become one of them. But I do know quite enough to tell you that he is playing all his strongest cards, even though I haven't seen the clothes."

"So," Justine said slowly, "you mean seduction."

"Exactly." Gabrielle looked at her with a new appreciation. "Seduction. What else can it be with sets that have been executed at vast expense to turn that enormous space under the Ritz into the terrace of an outdoor café surrounded with one thousand flowering cherry and apple trees? Marco is invoking the spring of some vague, entirely idealized year between nineteen thirty-four and nineteen thirty-six."

"But nobody remembers that far back," I objected.

"And that is exactly the point. The present is not particularly alluring, is it? Marco wants it to be an imaginary year during which nobody had any reason to worry about the future or brood on the past. The seduction of the senses will begin as the press enters the hotel from the cold night and finds the lobby banked in springtime."

"Have you any idea what music Chicago is going to play? New stuff in the thirties idiom?" I asked.

"You didn't think they were doing original music, did you?"

she asked, horrified at the idea. "No, only the interpretation, the orchestration, is original. Marco wouldn't leave something that important to these musicians," Gabrielle said, taking a notebook out of her purse. "Here are some of the titles from the medley that will set the mood before the show and you tell me how original it is. 'Lovely to Look At,' 'Isn't This a Lovely Day—to Be Caught in the Rain?,' 'I'm in the Mood for Love,' 'Blue Moon,' 'All I Do Is Dream of You,' 'My Romance' . . ."

"Stop!" Justine cried, laughing as hard as I was. Even Gabrielle was smiling. "We get the idea. Cornball as all hell but if it doesn't put people in a receptive mood, nothing will. So you've got a dazzling replica of Paris in a never-never spring, music from the highest period of Hollywood musicals, a banquet provided by the Ritz, all the top models available—Marco won't be able to say that they didn't like his clothes because they weren't presented with a maximum of schmaltz."

" 'Schmaltz'?" Gabrielle asked.

"Chicken fat," I explained, but she still looked puzzled.

"It's another way of saying charm," Justine explained.

"And I thought I spoke perfect English," Gabrielle murmured. "Chicken fat? Highly idiomatic, I imagine."

"Highly," I reassured her. "You had to be there." It's at a moment like this that I find it easy to understand that French custom-designed clothes actually *lose* four million dollars a year.

"But," Gabrielle reminded me, "with luck, tonight is the first step to the Lombardi perfume. And the perfume market is seven and a half billion dollars a year. Monsieur Necker plans for many years in the future."

This conversation was cut short by Jordan and April, who beat on our door, closely followed by Mike and Maude. The girls were showing clear evidence of opening-night shakes.

"What are we supposed to do with ourselves until it's time for the rehearsal?" Jordan asked plaintively. "We've taken bubble baths until our fingertips shriveled, done our toenails twice, shaved our legs, washed our hair and we're afraid that we might start tweezing our eyebrows and not be able to stop until there isn't a hair left."

"There are still two more hours till we have to leave for the

Ritz," April said, looking faint. "I haven't eaten all day. I'm weak from hunger but I'm afraid I'll throw up if I put anything in my stomach."

"I have an idea," Mike said. "Do you all play poker? No? Only me and Maude and Frankie? Well, we'll teach the rest of you until you catch on. Then we'll play for money till it's time to leave."

Justine gave me an approving nudge that unmistakably meant, "you done good." I didn't deign to reply to such an obvious truth, but called room service for some playing cards and platters of food. The next two hours passed quickly as some very fast, loose and highly unorthodox poker took over. Soon everyone relaxed enough to consume the food, and Jordan, a beginner, or so she'd claimed, ended the session by raking in over three hundred dollars. Mike sat next to me, occasionally shooting a few pictures when he wasn't trying to look at my cards.

"Stop cheating!" I finally objected.

"But your cards are my cards, darling. Share and share alike. Wanna see mine?"

"Is that the way it works?"

"Sure." I was about to take a peek at his cards, under the influence of his grin, and the way his eyes lapsed with pleasure when he looked at me. But Maude caught us and put a stop to it.

Now even the memory of that fun was almost forgotten. Maude and Gabrielle had gone ahead of us in the small Ritz elevator, and on the second descent Mike, Justine and I stood in the back, while Jordan and April stood in front of us, backs straight, shoulders squared, exquisite heads held high on their exquisite necks, looking totally confident and self-possessed. Only their hair distinguished them, Jordan's dark cherubim ringlets and April's platinum nape. Suddenly Mike's flash went off and I saw what he had noticed: the two girls were holding hands so tightly that it must hurt.

"Heartless cannibal!" I hissed at him. "Possible cover shot," he hissed back at me and took another shot as the elevator door opened. "Go, girl, go!" Jordan encouraged April with a sudden smile, and the girls advanced, still holding hands, into the cigarette smoke–laced air of the white and pink marble reception room. In the background you could see stacks of little gilded chairs

being carried by, three models so famous that they could be identified by one feature alone and dozens of black-clad proles who were
either the Belloir et Jallot crew or people connected with the
business of inserting girls into clothes.

"What do we do first?" I asked Gabrielle.

"The girls should report to Marco so he knows they're here.
I'll take charge of them."

"No, I will, Gabrielle," Justine said quickly.

"No one who isn't necessary is to be allowed backstage, and
you're not directly involved with showing the spring collection. It's
going to be a madhouse tonight. I'm sorry but you'll have to wait
here, Justine. I thought you understood that."

"Balls, Gabrielle. I'm going with the girls. And so is Frankie.
They need us. And of course Mike and Maude have to be everywhere."

"Mike and Maude, yes. But as for you and Frankie, it's absolutely impossible."

"Why don't you go ask Marco?"

A minute later Gabrielle returned, looking as astonished as
her features would allow. "He's says you're both welcome anywhere, so long as you keep out of his way. I'm sorry, Justine, I
didn't know an exception was being made for the two of you."

"That's okay. You couldn't know. Come on everybody. Mike,
remember, no photos of Ms. Schiffer naked, or even in her undies.
She may be trapped in a look that she can't change, but she's not
giving it away when she's not being paid. It's a rule."

"Ah, shucks!" my beloved whined.

It was at that moment that Chicago struck up the first strains
of their version of "Goody Goody" and I felt immediately corrupted
with pleasure. It was strongly syncopated, extra fast, and with a
beat so empathic that no one could miss it. Something about the
music contained the very essence of expectation and dapper, light,
uncomplicated fun. All around me people started to smile and with
a gesture as natural as a child scratching a mosquito bite, Jordan
swept April into a little dance step.

"Not so bad, this Chicago," Gabrielle said in what was, for
her, a deeply approving voice.

We threaded our way into the large beauty salon, which

served very well as an improvised dressing room, since the enormous amount of beige marble counter space gave all the makeup artists and hairstylists room to place their tools, the lighting was brilliant, and by taking away all the leather chairs and replacing them with banquet chairs, an adequate space had been created for the dressers and the girls to make their changes.

As our little group paused in the doorway I realized that I'd never guessed just how smack-in-the-stomach the collective presence of the top girls in the girl business would be. Now they weren't clacking, one by one, in and out of Loring Model Management, each an individual, as I had come to know them. Now they were banded together in a cloud of heightened awareness of themselves that raised their power to the nth degree. As a group they were plunged into a dense atmosphere of dedicated self-absorption that was deeply knowing and totally privileged, in equal proportions. They were wrapped in the knowledge of their meritocracy, which consisted of the dead-simple fact that at this particular moment in time they were the chosen of the chosen, the anointed. Rules that bound other women had been suspended for them. Their faces, in spite of their youth, carried the weight of so much fantasy that walking into a room filled with top models was ten times more impressive than finding yourself backstage in the presenters' makeup room on Oscar Night.

"April! Jordan! Stop gaping!" Justine hissed at them. "In six months you'll both be as bored by this as they are. Can't you hear them thinking 'another day, another dollar'?"

"Nice try, boss," Jordan muttered, unable to take her eyes away from the girls who were harem-esque as they sat, half in and half out of their Ritz peignoirs: chatting animatedly or intimately on cellular phones with their bare legs flung up on the counters as if they were alone; sipping out of bottles of Coke and Evian as they compared Filofax entries; scrutinizing their toenail polish, curling their eyelashes or inspecting the all-but-invisible veins in the whites of their eyes; a minority reading paperback books, one or two humanly imperfect enough to wear glasses; groups of them locked together in whispered gossip; clearly none of them interested in the clothes, since getting paid triple to show the work of an unknown designer must mean the stuff was a disaster. There were girls lighting cigarettes, girls putting out cigarettes and girls lost in a cloud of smoke. I blessed, for the thousandth time, the luck of the draw that had given me three nonsmokers to chaperone. A scattering of girls turned to wave at Mike, several at Justine, but their eyes became blank as they passed over Jordan and April. We're the original Broadway cast, their lack of interest seemed to say, we're in and you're out, make no mistake, the two of you are a couple of understudies, hired for a single day's stunt.

"Where's Lombardi?" Justine demanded.

"Probably behind those girls," Mike said, pointing to a lineup of six models who stood in a row with their backs toward us, their legs hidden by a table. From our vantage point they were wearing identical suit jackets in a marvelous hyacinth-blue wool; snugly fitted, small shouldered, narrowly belted.

Justine herded the girls in Marco's direction, her hands on their shoulders. "Jordan and April are here," she said to him as he sat behind a table covered with accessories like a giant mosaic.

"They're late," he said, not looking at her.

"Paris traffic," she informed him without apology.

"Take them to their dresser," Lombardi said to Justine. "Put on the hats," he ordered, turning away. I watched his assistants adjust close-fitting, hair-covering, pistachio-green felt cloches over six of the highest-paid heads in the world. Each cloche sported a single white rose and the skirt of each of the lightweight, elegantly pared-down suits was in a different length, from a slightly-less-than-fingertip mini to a skirt that ended at the ankle bone. The skirts had the same modified A-line shape, widening as they grew longer. Each of the girls wore sheer beige hose and identical medium-heeled black patent leather pumps. It was impossible to say that one length was more becoming or more fashionable than another. Marco stood up, giving Kate Moss' knee-covering skirt a tug at the waistline.

"Divinity," he cooed at her.

"He never even looked at us," April wailed as we pushed backward through the crowd. "Didn't say so much as hello."

"It has nothing to do with you, he'll come around." Justine reassured her. "Not a dumb idea, those different lengths," she commented to me, annoyed but honest.

"Fence sitting," I grumbled, but I had to admit that if fashion editors still thought skirt lengths were any kind of an issue—and didn't they all?—Marco had just made a dramatic statement, too convincing for the media to overlook.

We finally reached the two racks of clothes with April's and Jordan's names marked in crayon on a cardboard sign. The girls, their patience at an end, lunged for the clothes, paying no attention to the flustered, protesting dresser. They flipped through the racks like dogs chasing a rabbit, exclaiming with excitement, their yelps of approval growing louder and louder, while Mike photographed them looking like crazed shoppers on some game show.

"Girls, for God's sake!" Justine protested. "Control yourselves!"

"Look at this," April screeched. "A mohair cape in fire engine red, lined in pale pink satin and a dress that matches the lining . . . I crave it!"

"I've got the reverse, cape in pink, dress in red!" Jordan exclaimed.

"Hey, hey!" April exclaimed, holding up a wide-skirted, strapless lilac satin ball gown with an intricate pleated chocolate sash and a tiny, snug bolero covered with chocolate glitter, a dress worthy of a young Sophia Loren.

"I have it too," Jordan breathed, brandishing a hanger with the same gown in biting brown, the sash in lilac and the bolero flashing lavender sequins. "Are we twins?"

"Don't know. Wow, princess coat, princess coat!" April squealed, showing us a flared, tucked and buttoned coat in a featherweight, dove-grey flannel with a deceptively demure sliver of a white silk dress. "A person could get married in this . . . Jordan, you?"

"Same coat, in apple-green tweed, one-shouldered dress in pale turquoise organza . . . look at this yellow velvet jacket over a lipstick-pink chiffon cocktail dress . . . yummy! But velvet for spring?—still, isn't it exactly the *right* yellow? Justine, is this the most perfect yellow or what?"

"Let me try it on," Justine begged, stripping off her own jacket.

"No way. You'll get it dirty . . . here's one in sky blue, it's almost the same cut. . . ." Jordan threw the velvet jacket deftly at Justine and flipped fast forward through the masses of juicy, joyous, jubilant color on her rack, as if she had exactly one minute to shop for the rest of her life. "Look, just look, each dress has a coat or jacket, every cocktail dress or ball gown has a long cape or a coat or a bolero . . . somebody finally realizes that women spend most of their time in air-conditioning. Oh my God! Look at this!"

Jordan grabbed a ball gown in plaid taffeta woven in a half-dozen exquisitely melting pastels. "Hoop skirts! As I live and breathe! And the cape, did you ever see a more marvelous pink, oh, oh, here's a hood lined in plaid!" She flung the cape around her shoulders, snuggled into the ravishing frame of the hood and preened beatifically in the mirror. "I'm never taking this off, not for anybody!"

April gave a hair-raising Confederate yell. By this time the noise and excitement generated by our two girls had aroused enough attention to set the superstar models to investigating the contents of their own racks, the same clothes they had been ignoring while making themselves comfortable and staking out their territory. Soon the entire dressing room was full of girls exclaiming and comparing, pouting in disappointment at the rare sight of grey or navy or black and, their superiority swept away by enthusiasm, posturing in delight behind a garden of pure, intense spring colors.

"Girls!" Marco yelled, standing up. "Don't exchange clothes! Don't even try on another girl's clothes! Stop it immediately! If you behave I promise that as soon as they're finished being photographed I'll give them to you and you can trade to your heart's content. There's enough of my perfect pinks for everybody, enough daffodil yellows, enough new grass greens, enough apple blossom whites—put the hangers back where you found them, this minute! Pay attention to your dressers. Now, I want Karen, Kate and Shalom dressed in their first numbers, and make it quick."

"That maggot is in pig heaven right now," Justine whispered in my ear as she wriggled into the intricate column of Jordan's bias-cut, lilac chiffon ball gown. "The girls have told him all he needs to know about his success. Nobody cares less about clothes than they do." She wrapped herself in a sweeping Parma-violet cape with a deeply ruffled taffeta collar and hem. "How do I look? Is this me, mouse, or is this me?"

I was too busy trying to get into April's slinky navy satin cocktail suit with Mae West white marabou collar and cuffs to answer.

24

I heard the bell to my room ring at a delicious moment in a dream that vanished forever as, blinking and swearing, and falling out of my nightgown, I automatically staggered out of bed.

"Who the hell is it?" I barked through the door, in a way that made it plain that my much·needed and ·deserved sleep had been outrageously disturbed.

"Tom. I didn't want to wake you, Frankie, but Tinker insisted."

"What time is it, for crying out loud?"

"Three in the afternoon."

"Oh good God! Tom, wait a minute, I've got to put on a robe."

As I splashed water on my face and quickly brushed my teeth, I found it damn near incredible that I'd slept so late. We'd all returned to the hotel at seven in the morning, granted, and then wound down over a gigantic breakfast in my sitting room, but still to sleep to mid-afternoon . . . I'd never done it in my life. I can imagine what my mother would have thought.

"Poor Tom," I said remorsefully, as soon as I joined him in the sitting room. "Tinker must be going crazy with curiosity. I was sure I'd be up earlier so I didn't set my alarm. No sign of anybody else, not even Mike?"

"Nope. I've been sitting in her doorway, halfway into the corridor so I couldn't miss any of you. The only person I saw to speak to was Peaches and she couldn't tell me anything."

"How much sleep did you get?" I asked.

"I don't think I got any. I lay on top of the covers with Tinker's arm tied to mine by the belt of her bathrobe so she couldn't get out of bed without my knowing it, but I kept myself awake so I wouldn't roll over on her."

"Enjoying the fashion business?"

"It wasn't the worst ordeal in the world."

"How's she feeling?" I asked, afraid of the answer.

"She insists that she's totally recovered. She's raging because I won't let her out of bed except to go to the bathroom."

"No more crazy talking?"

"Not crazy . . . well maybe a little crazy but more like compulsive impatience," he sighed.

"Tom, listen, you're the only one who's seen anything of her. Tell me if you think Tinker's on any sort of drug—she's in really weird shape."

"It can't be speed, that's for sure. I knew lots of people on speed in the ad business and they didn't totally fall apart after work the way Tinker does, like a rag doll. She doesn't unwind, she drops in her tracks. And if she's getting any other drug from that shit-faced little creep she's working for, I haven't noticed it. Señora Varga? No, why would she be giving Tinker anything? It might disturb her concentration on the sacred fucking tango. If you ask me the drug she's on is pure raging ambition, that crazy feeling she has that getting a runway walk and winning this contest will give her an identity. What she keeps saying is, 'I just want to get up there, that's all, just get up and do my stuff'—over and over again."

"That's natural talk, Tom. The best runway girls are like race-horses, they can't wait for the show to begin. If someone didn't control them they'd all come swarming out at the same time, tripping each other up on purpose."

"If that's the case, she's got it made. Please, Frankie, take pity on me and go tell her every last detail about last night. I'm falling asleep talking to you."

"Take the couch. I'll go see Tinker and have something to eat with her."

I wrapped a coat around my bathrobe and rushed down the corridor of the hotel. Tinker was lying back on the pillows, one leg lashed firmly to the bedpost, the phone too far away for her to reach it, looking like the heroine in a comic book who's been tied down on the train tracks and is about to be run over.

"You've got to admit that he's thorough, that Tom," I said as I untied her, trying not to laugh at her expression of fury.

"I'm going to *kill* that motherfucker." Tinker's voice sounded like an out-of-tune harpsichord with shredded velvet strings. "You have no *idea* what he subjected me to all night. He's criminally insane."

"Now be fair. He was only doing what we asked him to do. Don't have a hissy fit, Tinker, Tom was good, loyal and true."

"Every last one of you is overreacting," Tinker moaned, rubbing her leg and then jumping up and pacing around the room. "There's nothing wrong with me, you can see that, can't you? Nothing! Nothing! *What cunt wore my dresses?*"

"Gee, Tinker, I remember when you wouldn't even say 'damn' —in fact I think you spelled out 'darn.' " Cunt! No wonder Tom said she was talking a little crazy. "As it happens, the lady who wore your dresses was Janine, a former house model Marco had fired. She's chic but dull-looking, but she still managed to look fabulous because your clothes are far and away the best in the show."

I was trying to reassure her, of course, but everything I said was a fact. "Marco's really done you proud, Tink. And your dresser has everything lined up, totally accessorized, just waiting for you. Of course your skirts were way too long on Janine, but it didn't matter. Even without them the show would have been a total sensation. An absolutely genuine smash, the kind of turning-point show fashion people talk about for years. Everybody's sky high about it. Everything you said is true—Marco's a genius, much as I hate to admit it."

"I told you!"

"There was a real breeze of fresh air—no, make that a tornado —and it didn't stop all night."

"I knew it! Tell me more!"

"The clothes had that thing editors always pray for . . . I guess it's a quiver of something genuinely new. Nothing was reminiscent of any other designer, and his color sense—my God, Justine and I were fighting to try on April's and Jordan's clothes. They made me feel that no matter how expensive they were, they were worth it —transfiguring, flattering, luscious, *edible*—yet everything was so basically wearable that it's hard to believe that not a single piece was dull. It was *awful*—I *had* to have them and I knew I couldn't possibly afford even one. I've never felt that way about clothes before. It was like sex! No, *better!*"

"What about April and Jordan?" Tinker asked sharply. "How did they look?"

"Well . . ."

"Tell me, Frankie! Damn it! *I have to hear the truth*," Tinker demanded roughly.

"Extraordinary. Each in her own way—of course, in those clothes they couldn't miss."

"I'll look better."

"Damn right." It wouldn't be a good idea to disagree with her, I thought, looking closely at Tinker's essential magic. If she *was* on drugs I knew she couldn't have had access to any since early yesterday and she hadn't changed all that much even after a good rest.

Tinker's normal expression was a tender, somewhat brooding joy, attentive to the world around her, rather than to herself. Today, as she quizzed me, she blazed with attention and impatience, all turned inward toward a vision of how she would look tonight. Her pale skin had more color in it than I'd ever seen, her eyes glittered harshly, almost dangerously, even the flags of her hair seemed a brighter shade of red than usual, as if she were on fire. Overrehearsed, I thought, trying to calm my fears, overrehearsal followed by frustration, followed by first-night nerves. But she'll settle down once we get to the Ritz, once she's back on the job. She had to.

"I'm ordering from room service, Tinker. What can I get you?"

"Nothing, damn it . . . what the fuck makes everybody think I'm hungry? Tom's been force-feeding me ever since I got here. I *know* I've gained two pounds," Tinker said angrily.

"Nobody can gain two pounds in twenty-six hours," I said in my most reasonable voice. "Two pounds of fat equals eight thousand extra calories."

"But how can I burn calories normally when I'm imprisoned in this fucking bed with my muscles atrophying? Listen, Frankie, there's still time for another tango lesson before tonight! Call Señora Varga and tell her I'm practically on my way."

"Tinker! If there's one thing you don't need it's another tango lesson. You could tango in your sleep."

"It'd warm up my muscles," Tinker pleaded, rapidly stripping naked and hunting for her clothes.

"We have to be at the Ritz in a little more than two hours, for hair and makeup," I said, sternly. "What you need is to take a long shower, have something to eat and calm down, you're not as rested as you think you are and it's going to be a long night. You're not leaving this hotel until we all go together. I'll sit here until you've finished in the bathroom. Then we'll go to the suite and play poker, like last night."

"I'll meet you there."

"No, I'll wait for you."

Tinker glared at me and slammed the bathroom door behind her. I called my suite and got Tom to wake Justine.

"Tinker's in a rage . . . wanted to take another tango lesson . . . asked 'what cunt' had worn her dresses."

"Is she tripping out like yesterday?"

"Not quite as bad, she's not raving, but she's not like herself either. But Tom doesn't think she's on anything—I just can't tell."

"Damn this timing! It's driving everyone around the bend. She'll calm down once the show starts."

"You honestly think so?"

"Frankie, what's the choice? As long as Tinker's upright, she has to have her chance."

"Wake everybody, will you, Justine? And get out the cards. We'll be along as soon as she gets out of the shower."

"Frankie . . . how nervous are you about tonight?"

"Not more than you are, kiddo."

"And we're not even *doing* the show. Come back soon. It's worse when you're not here."

25

The two chauffeured cars drew up to the employees' entrance of the Ritz. A group of burly young men, clad in sober dark blue suits, each sporting a dark red tie, guarded the door.

"Where'd they come from?" Frankie asked.

"They're called Les Cravates Rouges," Justine answered. "Up-scale bouncers who keep out the unwanted and uninvited. Everybody uses them. They weren't here last night. There's undoubtedly another, bigger mob of them in front of the main entrance. Gate crashers are a nightmare at every collection."

Justine led the way to the door. One of the Cravates Rouges approached her, his arms filled with magnificent bouquets of spring flowers.

"Madame Loring?"

"Yes?"

"There is a bouquet for each of the mannequins, and these envelopes are for you, Madame Severino, Madame Callender, Monsieur Strauss and Monsieur Aaron." He handed her five square white envelopes. She opened one and discovered an engraved dinner invitation and a card indicating a table number.

"We won't be needing these," Justine told the stolid young man. "We're going with the girls."

"I regret, Madame, but Monsieur Lombardi has insisted that no one but the mannequins be allowed backstage tonight."

"When did you get this order?"

"This morning, Madame."

"Who sent the flowers?"

"I don't know, Madame, they were waiting with the concierge when we arrived."

"April, is there a card with your bouquet?" Justine asked sharply.

"Wait . . . yes . . . it's from Mr. Necker. It says, 'Good luck tonight.' Oh, what heavenly flowers! This is so sweet of him . . . I feel like a ballerina."

"I demand to speak to Monsieur Lombardi," Justine told the Cravate Rouge.

"I can do nothing, Madame. I regret, but it is impossible. My orders are formal. Monsieur Lombardi cannot possibly be disturbed at this time."

"Where's your boss?"

"I'm the senior man here, Madame Loring. The office is closed until tomorrow. All complaints will come to me. I regret Madame, I wish I could accommodate you, but it is impossible."

"Girls, go on down," Justine ordered. "I'm going to find Gabrielle. We'll be there as soon as possible. Tinker, your rack is right next to April's, just follow the others."

Justine hurried off, followed by Frankie, Maude, Tom and Mike. Within an hour of frantic searching and futile telephoning it became evident to all of them that Marco Lombardi had effectively shut them out of the spring collection except as spectators. Gabrielle d'Angelle, even if she had agreed to take up their case with Marco, was already downstairs, out of range of any message. The only concession Justine had been able to ring out of the chief Cravate Rouge was a promise to inform the girls of what had happened. He came back from his mission to tell them that Mademoiselle Osborn had sent a message that they were perfectly capable of taking care of themselves.

"Christ!" Tom exploded. "That's aimed at me."

"No, at me," Justine soothed him. "She'll be her usual sweet self tomorrow, Tom. This isn't an unusual reaction. It's like a feisty kid on the first day of school who doesn't want to be kissed good-bye in front of the others."

"Why don't we all wait in the bar?" Mike suggested. "I'm the one who's been treated worse than anybody, unable to shoot backstage. Doesn't anybody realize that?"

"Poor darling," Frankie jeered at him. "Trust a photographer to feel sorry for himself first."

"Children, children," Maude said soothingly, "we're all in the same boat. Let's not shove each other overboard quite yet. There'll be plenty of time to do that later. I'm with Mike, we need a drink. And it's at least an hour before we can go down as guests."

"Assuming the Cravates Rouges let us into the bar," Justine snapped.

The group from Loring Management and *Zing* sat gloomily in the Ritz bar, at the table with the best view of the entrance, drinking Evian and herb tea, except for Maude Callender who ordered her usual Scotch. They barely spoke to each other, watching the invited guests arriving, each one of their invitations carefully checked by the swarming corps of Cravates Rouges, who were wearing dinner jackets with dark red bow ties in honor of the occasion.

As far as Maude was concerned, this contretemps was all wonderful grist for her mill, infinitely better than it would have been to be downstairs taking notes on the oddly well-ordered hysteria associated with any fashion show. She'd picked up more than enough backstage stuff last night, and most of it was unusable anyway. How many ways can you describe a superbly functioning, yet incredible sloppy, madhouse of careening girls, aided by their nerveless dressers, changing with ripping speed from one outfit to another, throwing the most delicate garments on the floor once they were finished with them, any normal concepts of modesty, assuming they'd started with such an outmoded idea, checked at the door? How many times can you describe the self-important ministrations of hairdressers, bending over the girls with their rollers and combs like so many Pygmalions, or makeup artists wearing clear-plastic tool belts to hold their favorite brushes and tubes of color? After a few minutes the only thing that made it interesting was the beauty of the girls, and that had already been captured in Mike's pictures of last night.

"Listen," Frankie said, suddenly, "do we want to be the last people to arrive at this party? Are we just going to sit here—hey! Hold up there. Do you all think you're sticking me with this check?"

" 'Night and Day'? What the hell are they playing that old stuff for?" Tinker asked Jordan.

"It's the mood, lovey," Jordan said over her shoulder. "You'll get what they're doing in a minute, just keep listening."

"I don't like it," Tinker said in a flat voice.

"It'll grow on you. Give it a chance."

"I can't dance to this shit. It's a fucking foxtrot."

Jordan turned abruptly. Tinker was standing up, bare breasted, fists clenching and unclenching, a look of violent rage on her face.

"It's just the party music, Tink, don't let it bother you."

"Party music? Is that all this is, a party? God damn it to hell, don't they realize this is a matter of life and death? How can they subject us to this crap while we're waiting to go on? Don't any of you have the slightest sensitivity? It's a fucking insult! I'm going out to tell those bastards to shut the fuck up."

"No Tinker, no, I'll do it. You stay here, you haven't got any clothes on. *April!* Come over here, talk to Tinker, while I go tell Chicago to stop playing."

"Huh?"

"Just do it! Come over here. Listen," Jordan bent forward and whispered in April's ear, "there's something wrong. Don't let her get away from you, for God's sake. Sit on her if you have to."

"Right."

Jordan sped away, threading her way through the crowded beauty salon until she found Lombardi laughing with Claudia and Linda, both of them dressed in their first ball gowns, and, except for shoes, completely ready to go on the runway.

"Marco, there's a problem with Tinker."

"Dio, not again," he groaned. "What is it this time?"

"I'm not sure but she's not acting normally. She hates Chicago, it's freaking her out. You've got to talk to her, she won't pay any attention to me."

"Do you think I have nothing better to do right now than worry about her taste in music? Is this the time to bother me?"

"Yes, if you want the show to go on."

"Excuse me, my beauties. I'll be right back." Marco followed Jordan leisurely.

"So, Tinker, what's the problem now?" he asked as he arrived to find her slouched down in her chair, with April rubbing the back of her neck. "More complaints? Even at the last minute?"

" 'The problem'?" Tinker echoed. "There's no problem, who said there was? I'm not going on to the sound of that incredible crap, but that's not a problem, is it Marco? You've got someone else who can wear my clothes, don't you? Let that short French cunt wear them, because I won't submit to this foul excuse for music, and there's no one who can force me to. Whatever they think they're playing, it's not a tango."

"Tinker, you couldn't possibly have expected them to play tangos," Marco said, turning white. "I told you a hundred times, the tango lessons were only meant to give you an *attitude*, a feeling for your body, a way to hold yourself, a way to *think* about yourself —my God, how often did we talk about it?"

"I don't remember," Tinker replied stubbornly. "I *intend* to tango, Marco, surely you understand?"

"Tinker, we need to talk seriously," Marco said, forcing his most charming smile, his most persuasive voice. "Come with me, *cara*, we'll go to one of the treatment rooms and find someplace quiet for a little chat."

"I'll come with you," Jordan said. "I'm all dressed."

"No. She'll be more reasonable with fewer people around. It's too crowded in here, too much smoke, that's all. Believe me, I've coped with nervous models for years."

"Justine's upstairs . . . do you want to send for her? Or Frankie?"

"It's not necessary, Jordan, I assure you. Remember I've been working with Tinker every day for two weeks, I know her moods better than anyone."

"But this is more than a mood!" Jordan insisted fiercely.

Ignoring her, Marco took Tinker by one hand, flung a big towel over her naked shoulders and led her away, out of the beauty salon, across the reception room and into the calm of the locker room that led to a series of luxurious, quiet marble rooms designed for various beauty treatments. Finally, inside the door of a massage room he stopped and sat down on the toweling-covered table.

"Here, isn't this better?" he asked, patting the toweling invitingly. "There's a big Jacuzzi next door, eight people can use it, but this is more relaxing, don't you think, Tinker? Sit down, *bella*."

"Just for a minute," she said sullenly, hugging the towel around her.

"Ah, poor Tinker, I deeply apologize for the band. If only you'd been here last night and I'd discovered our misunderstanding, I'd have ordered them to change their sound, to play only tangos."

"It's too late now. I won't go on."

"But, Tinker, this is your big chance. And you walk beautifully now, I've seen you do it over and over. Tinker, remember, you and I know that you have the best dresses, that you'll be the star of the show."

"I'm going to tango," she repeated. Marco looked at her carefully. She hadn't listened to a word he'd said, this mule of a girl. If he could strangle her, he'd do so happily, but he needed her, she was essential.

"Of course Tinker," Marco said gently. "No problem. So—I don't know about you, my little darling, but as for me, this is the moment that I have a sip of Goddess to quiet my nerves."

"Goddess? What's Goddess?" Tinker asked sullenly.

"A cocktail, something quite marvelous. Actually it was invented especially for runway models. No matter how high strung they are, Goddess makes them feel wonderful, calm and collected, at their very best. I find that in this business, even a designer needs a nip of Goddess before the collection. All the top girls take it, you know, they never go on without something to soothe their nerves."

"I've seen those pictures," Tinker mused, distracted from her anger. "A last puff of a cigarette and a glass of champagne—the supermodel special. Do they drink Goddess too?"

"Of course they do. But not when the photographers are looking at them. It's a secret of the inner circle. Here, smell it." Marco took a small flacon out of his pocket, uncapped it and offered it to Tinker. She sniffed cautiously.

"It doesn't smell like alcohol."

"There's very little in it . . . it's mostly herbs." He lifted the flacon to his lips and then stopped. "Forgive me, Tinker darling, what bad manners I have. I should have offered you some first. Here, while we still have a peaceful moment to unwind, try it."

"Oh, I don't know . . . I think that maybe a glass of champagne is a better idea."

"Nonsense . . . Goddess is better and it lasts longer. Champagne is only enough to give you the courage to step out on the runway, then you burn it up quickly. Goddess lasts through the whole collection, with no hangover, because of the herbs. Here, let me give you a sip."

"Oh well, I guess so, if you really think I should." Tinker wet her tongue with the liquid. "It doesn't have a taste, Marco. No taste and no smell. How bad can it be?"

"I told you, *bellissima*, it's good, very, very good, and calming. Now, allow me my little nip, if you please."

"You don't have to walk down a runway in front of hundreds of people, Marco," Tinker said with a sudden, mischievous smile. "You don't really need it. Anything called Goddess is obviously meant for women anyway." She lifted the flacon again and took several big gulps. "There's not much left," she giggled. "Here, you can have it now."

Marco took the almost empty flacon and slipped it in an inside pocket. "How do you feel? Better?"

"*Much* better! Oh, ever so much more relaxed. It works so fast, it's amazing. Why did you never tell me about Goddess before, Marco? Were you saving it for someone else?"

"Actually, I'll tell you the truth, sweet Tinker, I was saving it for myself—you know how much this collection means to me— but I could see that you needed it more."

"You're an angel, Marco! I'll never forget what you've done for me!"

"But Tinker, if you tell anyone about it, they'll all want some Goddess, and there isn't enough left to make a difference. Promise me you won't tell. *Not anyone.* You must promise me. Especially April and Jordan or they'll accuse me of favoring you . . . they think that already, and this will make it worse, you understand that, don't you?"

"Of course I do. I won't say a word. I'm the one who gets Goddess, not them. I'm the one who did all the work, aren't I?

Standing up all day, the tango lessons, never complaining about anything, inspiring you? I deserve Goddess because I'm the best, aren't I?"

"You are, my darling, you are." He glanced at his watch. Goddess worked quickly. Tinker had responded beautifully. Her eyes were brilliant, and the consuming need for affection and attention that motivated some runway models to perform had expanded beyond what he had hoped. And, as he'd hoped, she'd forgotten her obsession with the tango.

"We still have a little time, Tinker, my beloved little girl. We don't have to go back to that crowded dressing room for a while," Marco said caressingly. This was his last chance to be alone with her, his last opportunity to make her pay for the way she'd treated him, the way she'd kept him at a distance and played her filthy games with him.

"Ah, good . . . I feel so happy—I'm floating—I feel as if I can do anything now. I'm not afraid of the runway."

"Tinker, do you know the reason why some girls glow so much that they seem to explode in beauty out there on the runway, and others, equally beautiful, pass unnoticed, as if they didn't count?"

"Goddess?"

"Not Goddess alone, my love. Goddess helps, of course, but there's something else too."

"Then I want it, Marco!" Tinker sat bolt upright, her eyes gleaming with insistence, her freckles showing clearly in her excitement.

"It takes two to create that glow, *bellissima*, it requires a man's help."

"A makeup man?"

"No, darling, not a makeup man, but a man who loves the model, a man who allows her, who *permits* her to take him in her mouth and satisfy him completely, before she goes on the runway. Nothing else can give a girl that special glow, *nothing*. It's exactly like being in love."

"I've never heard that," Tinker said without any sign of surprise. "But then I'd never heard of Goddess either . . . there's so much to learn, isn't there, Marco?"

"Shall I do that for you, Tinker? Shall I allow, shall I *permit* you to satisfy me so that you'll have that extra winning glow on top of Goddess?"

"I don't know . . . is it the right thing to do, Marco?"

"Of course it is, my darling. You're the one I owe the most to. You deserve it. Here, put your hand here, feel me, yes, it's big already, from being close to you, but you must keep both hands on me so you'll feel it grow bigger. It's all for you, *mi amore*, all for you, but you must take it only in your mouth, and only when I tell you, you understand."

"Only in my mouth," Tinker whispered, "I understand."

"Kneel between my legs," he ordered, suddenly harsh and avid with his own excitement. Too bad that she was willing, he thought, yet with that much Goddess in her he could hardly expect the thrill of resistance. But she was his abject slave at last and that had a flavor of its own. If he only had more time, the things he would make her submit to. . . . "Kneel there, at my feet. And now, lean over." Marco guided her bright head quickly down toward his heavy, straining penis. "Suck me and then drink me. Don't stop, not for a second, I'm almost ready now. Yes, that's the way, but harder, you must suck harder, you must open your mouth wider, you must take it all, you must drink every drop, you must earn it, earn the glow."

26

There she is!" April exclaimed. Tinker glided rapidly toward them, the big towel wrapped around her head and falling to cover her breasts, her cheeks rosy, her smile blissful.

"Feel better, baby?" Jordan asked anxiously.

"Piece of cake," Tinker answered, with a radiant look, taking her seat at the makeup counter. "What's one more fashion show anyway? You just get yourself together and do it. It's another gig, that's all. It's a mental place you put yourself into."

"Is that what Marco explained?" April asked, stunned by the change in Tinker.

"He made it all so simple."

"Will you let me do your face now, for God's sake," a makeup artist asked nervously. "You realize you're on first and I haven't had a minute with you, damn it. Do you want to hold up the show?"

"I'm sorry, I'm really sorry," Tinker said sweetly. "I must have been a bit nervous. I'm okay now. Do whatever you want to do, I'm all yours." She closed her eyes and relaxed, the smile never leaving her face until he asked her to open her lips so that he could fill in her lip liner with color. He leaned closely toward her mouth and worked on it with sure, delicate strokes. "Somebody just got real lucky with this one," he muttered to himself as he smelled the sperm on her breath.

Soon Tinker was ready, her hair brushed out loosely and naturally over her shoulders, dressed in the all-but-naked, coral chiffon ball gown. "I don't know why I'm so cold, does everybody feel as cold as I do?" she inquired mildly.

"It must be the yards and yards of fabric in that four-inch bodice," April answered. "Here, put your cape around you. Oh, Tinker, it's like a feather! Who would believe how light it is?"

"I know," Tinker laughed, "isn't it wonderful? Give me that towel again, will you please, Jordan? I don't want to get the cape messed up. Oh! Have you seen yourselves? The two of you look so beautiful that I could cry. I wish I'd been here last night . . . are you doing the runway together?"

"No, first Jordan in the brown and lilac and then me in the lilac gown and brown bolero. Marco wants the audience to immediately realize the importance of color in this collection. He says because Jordan's black and I'm white, they'll think we're showing two entirely different dresses for just long enough to get the point. He's a game player."

"Marco's wonderful," Tinker breathed. "He made me feel so much calmer, yet I'm ready for anything . . . anything at all."

"How'd he get you to listen to reason?" Jordan asked curiously.

"It's so strange, Jordan, I don't seem to really remember . . . he just made sense." Tinker knit her brows for a second and then, still smiling, gave up trying to catch the fleeting memory.

"Girls! Girls!" came Marco's voice. "Everyone get in position. We start in three minutes. Up here, right at the entrance, behind the curtain, quick, quick, watch your feet, don't step on any hems, shoes *on* everybody, cigarettes *out*, not another drop of champagne, in line, you know your order, come on girls!"

"I have a feeling he means us," Jordan said nervously. "Give me a kiss, Tinker. And you too, April, baby. Oh, good luck to all of us! What are they playing? It sounds so familiar, it's on the tip of my tongue. . . ."

" 'Goody Goody,' again," April answered. "I guess it's suitable."

With an indifferent toss of her head, Tinker thrust her arms into the all-but-luminous flood of organza roses and led the way to the beginning of the line. She stood straight and light and beautiful beyond beautiful, looking at Marco as blankly as if she'd never seen him before.

Lined up immediately behind Tinker, Jordan couldn't stop herself from leaning slightly forward and peering through a tiny gap in the curtain. She gasped at the sight of the immense room packed with glittering, expectant people, all of their eyes, eyes that had seen it all too many times, trained on the beginning of the runway, as ready for defeat or victory as any crowd at a bullfight.

Last night Jordan had become familiar with the circular runways, but she'd denied the potential presence of an audience, even to herself. She forced her eyes away from the curtain with a quick prayer. Deep breathing, she thought. Deep breathing. Tinker still stood calmly, barely tapping her foot, smiling with a vague eagerness.

As the exciting syncopated sound of Chicago blended into the soulful ballad, "Sophisticated Lady," Marco gave Tinker a slight push. "Go!" he ordered. She turned to him with a bewildered look. "But it's not a tango," she murmured.

"This isn't the moment to joke! Remember what I told you. Now go! You're on!"

Tinker shrugged her shoulders with a hint of resignation, adjusted the cape to its best advantage, pulled herself up high from her waist and moved smoothly and gracefully onto the wide runway.

Slow, slow, quick, quick, slow, Tinker thought, blocking out the rhythm of the orchestra. To the pounding, inescapable beat of the tango in her head she stalked forward, haughty, territorial, magnificent, her proudly angled head held high on elongated neck, her hands positioned to clasp a nonexistent partner.

The room fell quiet, people fascinated by this original concept of presentation. Yes, it was excellent, the clever, sweet nostalgia of the unusual musical arrangements combined with the majesty of the classic dance pose, unexpected, original, above all, original. A girl dancing a tango like a giant cat, ignoring the familiar foxtrot, yes, amusing, different, not seen before. *Génial, quoi!*

A barrage of motor-driven flashbulbs went off from the photographers' vantage point, illuminating the scene with continuous bolts of white light. Down the concentric circles of the runway Tinker continued in her swooping tango, never losing her poise, never faltering.

Tinker had been instructed to stop as close to the photographers as possible before she opened the cape and revealed her dress. As she reached the perfect spot she executed a *corte*, lifting her left arm high, her right arm pointing toward the runway, bending her left knee and sinking down on it, in the formal bow to signal the end of the dance. Then she straightened up, turned toward the photographers and let the cape slip off her shoulders, revealing the dress beneath, turning slowly so that everyone could see it. Applause filled the room as she whirled faster and faster, her pale coral-red hair flying above the many flamenco fluted skirts of barely darker coral chiffon, in as dramatic a moment as even the jaded fashion media could ask for.

Tinker lifted the cape from the runway and with a practiced gesture threw it into the air, where it seemed to hang for seconds. She tangoed back up the runway to more applause and retrieved the cape, even as Chicago swung into the fast beat of "Take the A Train." Tinker raised her arms and flung the cape back toward the photographers. She continued to dance toward the mass of pale yellow flowers, picked up the cape and launched it up the runway with the same sweeping movement as before. She swiveled, and retrieved it once again. She reversed, utterly unable to break loose from the tyranny of the rhythm that had been imprinted in her brain. Just as she was about to raise her laden arms for the fourth time she slipped suddenly, in the middle of a step, swayed danger-ously, fell heavily to both knees and knelt on all fours during interminable seconds on the runway before she managed to rise, awkwardly and unsteadily to face the orchestra.

"God damn it!" Tinker stood stock-still and screamed at the top of her voice. "Can't you asshole motherfuckers play a tango, for Christ's sake? What the hell is wrong with you?"

Chicago played on while an entire roomful of people froze in their seats. Only Jacques Necker had the wit to move instantly. He jumped up from his table in the center of the room near the end of the runway, and leapt up three steps, moving swiftly toward Tinker where she still stood motionless, her hands on her hips, glaring at the musicians.

"Allow me, Tinker, my dear," he said with a smile, taking the cape away from her. He clasped one arm tightly around her waist, and, with a cheerful salute to the photographers, he led her firmly back down the steps, across half the room, guiding her smoothly between the tables until he'd reached the exit that led to the reception room.

April and Jordan immediately appeared on the runway, smiling brilliantly, arms linked in defiance of Marco's orders, the attention of the crowd quickly diverted toward the startling pair swaying toward each other in their huge skirts and sparkling boleros.

"Stay here, Frankie!" Justine commanded. "I'm going after Tinker. We can't make a group exit. That Cravate Rouge must have seen enough to realize he doesn't dare let her get away from him."

Slipping deftly around the edge of the room, behind the round tables, Justine managed to leave without attracting attention. The large reception room was empty. On one side lay the beauty salon, jammed with models and dressers, on the other the locker room. Justine poked her head into the beauty salon. There was nothing in the disciplined hush, the unbroken backstage silence that lay over the assembled company, to indicate that Tinker was in there. She turned away and walked quietly, unseen, toward the doorway to the locker room.

"Why did you stop me, Mr. Necker?" Justine heard Tinker's voice ask plaintively.

Justine froze, unable to make the slightest move forward. *Necker?*

"I was doing so well, I just lost my balance for a second, that's all," Tinker continued, "why did you make me leave the runway? People liked me, didn't they? The Goddess was working fine, wasn't it? I was doing so well, it's not fair—"

"Goddess?"

"The cocktail that Marco . . . oh, I forgot, it's a secret. But, why, *why* did you stop me?"

"You were wearing yourself out showing the cape—I was worried about you, that's all. But you were marvelous, Tinker, you were delightful, every minute, the press loved you, everybody loved you, you're warmer now, with the cape around you, aren't you? It's all right, Tinker, yes, cry, cry as much as you like, my poor girl, I understand, you're disappointed, it's been a long day but now everything's going to be all right."

"I want Justine," Tinker's voice said on a rising sob. "Oh, I want Justine!"

"So do I, God help me, Tinker, so do I," Jacques Necker said, his voice stiff with pain.

"But I *need* Justine, Mr. Necker, I want to see her."

"I'll send for her as soon as I can, Tinker. But first you have to go back to the dressing room."

"Why can't she come in here where it's quiet?" Tinker demanded childishly, still weeping.

"Please, Tinker, let me help you up."

"*No!* I don't want to, they'll all laugh at me, I need Justine."

"I know Tinker, *I know*. Please, stand up, Tinker, let me take you back—"

"I'm here, Tinker," Justine called, making herself walk forward on trembling legs. "I'm here."

"Oh, Justine!" Tinker sobbed. "Justine, hold me tight!"

Justine sank down on the long bench on which Tinker and Necker were sitting and took the girl in her arms. Tinker gave herself over to a full-blown flood of uncontrolled weeping, burying her face in Justine's shoulder.

Over the top of Tinker's head Justine's eyes met those of Jacques Necker. Before he could turn his face away, she saw how they burned with naked longing, eyes that were so much like those she had faced in every mirror for as long as she could remember.

For a long moment the three of them sat motionless on the bench in the locker room of the Ritz health club, the crying girl and the silent, stiff figures of the father and daughter. When Justine spoke, her voice was unsteady. The same eyes, she thought, the same expression, the same hairline, the same coloring, even the geometry of his features . . . anyone who saw them together would know. . . .

"I didn't realize—I thought you were a Cravate Rouge," she said. "Thank you for acting so quickly."

"No. *No!* Don't thank me, I had no idea that she was so—as you see her," he said, looking down at Tinker. "Everything, even this poor girl, everything is my fault—the prize, the contest, everything! I should never have tried to . . . to force you to come to Paris, with the lure of the contest. It was unfair, utterly unfair and unforgivable, but when you returned all my letters unopened I lost my sense of what was wrong, I was ready to do anything, I *had* to see you, face-to-face, or it seemed that my life wouldn't be worth living."

"Why? Why did you need to see me now, after all these years?" Justine kept her eyes unreadable, her voice uninflected. She tried, and failed, to forget the words she'd overheard him say to Tinker only moments before, words of such raw yearning and hurt that they'd made her heart break in spite of herself.

"You're my child. I didn't know you existed . . . but once I knew . . ."

"Where were you when I was born?" She had to ask him, she owed this much, at least, to her mother, no matter what Aiden had said.

"As far away from your mother as I could get. I was a foul coward. Faithless, gutless. I have no excuses for myself, for the young man I was. None are possible. None are admissible. That history can't be changed."

"Yet you wanted to see me. Why? To tell me what I knew already?"

"I hoped. . . ."

"You hoped?"

"I know, I have no right to hope for anything. Yet—I admit I hoped, stupid as it was, as little as I deserved it, I was human enough to hope—I hoped that there might somehow exist a chance to know you, to find out if you were happy, to make some kind of contact—"

Necker shook his head helplessly at his inability to find the right words. "I wanted to give you . . . what could I give you? To give you *anything,* to make you happy if you weren't happy, to *know* . . . just to know you, one human being to another, to learn the story of your life, to ask if you distrusted men because of me, to tell you that most men aren't as rotten as I was, to say that you shouldn't judge them by me, to—"

"To play the father," Justine said slowly.

"Yes! Exactly! To play the father. It was a foolish idea but I have it. I admit it, to play the father, to *have* a daughter, to *be* a father to my daughter—you can't imagine how I want it, how I cling to it, how I dream of it . . . even now. Yet I've understood at last. I've come to my senses. If you don't want to have anything to do with me, Justine, it's your decision entirely, and I'll accept it. I won't bother you again."

"Is it still up to me?"

"Do you doubt it?"

"No, I don't doubt it . . . but . . . it's too late."

"I don't understand."

"I want . . . I want to play the daughter," Justine said in an almost inaudible voice. "Don't ask why. I just do."

"Justine—"

"I said not to ask why," Justine said, scowling fiercely to keep her tears from falling.

"I won't," Necker said, keeping himself in check with all his forces. "Not a word. But the collection will be over in a few minutes, and I've got to make the announcement about who will be the Lombardi girl."

"You? Not Marco?"

"Never Marco," Necker said, scornfully.

"Well?"

"Jordan and April. Both of them. Okay with you?"

"Same fees for each?" Justine laughed.

"Obviously."

"You'll make history."

"No, they're the ones who will make history."

"Poor Tinker." Justine looked down at the now sleeping girl. "I heard what she said about Goddess—that criminal gave her some drug, it's the only explanation. But she was never meant to do runway. I blame myself for letting her come to Paris . . . I know I couldn't have stopped her, but I should have been here to watch over her—I was afraid of you—"

"Stop that, Justine, stop it right away," Necker ordered firmly. "You can't rewrite that script. Now, you sit here with Tinker, I'll send Frankie to help you, make the announcement and come back as soon as I can. Understood?"

"Bossy, aren't you?" Justine challenged him.

"Can you figure out a better way to do it?"

"Well, actually . . . no."

"So?"

"I didn't say bossy was bad, I merely said you were bossy. Honestly, Jacques, or whatever you want me to call you, haven't you got something else to do than stand here arguing? Listen, they're applauding, the bride must have come down the runway, now they're cheering, it's an ovation—for goodness sakes—*hurry!*"

Jacques Necker stood up, sweeping Justine into his arms in a huge hug, tears streaming down his face. "So you think I'm bossy, do you, my daughter? Well then, call me Papa. For once in our lives I want to have the last word with you. It may never happen again."

27

Good morning, Monsieur Lombardi! What a triumph!" Necker's secretary gushed in excitement at speaking to the hero of the hour. "Monsieur Necker will see you right away, as soon as he gets off the phone. May I offer my congratulations on your great achievement! This morning all Paris is talking about nothing but your collection—it's sublime!"

"Thank you, Madame, but the week of the spring collections is just starting," Marco said modestly. "Who knows how the editors will rave about other designers? I'm just happy that they liked what I showed them."

"Liked? They adored it! The front page of every newspaper in Paris! And how wise of you to choose both girls . . . I thought it was impossible to pick which one was the most beautiful."

"So did I. Although there is much that is more important in a woman than mere beauty, wouldn't you say?" Marco asked her, automatically turning on his charm for any woman who might someday prove useful.

What the devil was taking Necker so long, he wondered. He'd been requested to come to Necker's office before lunch, in spite of the fact that yesterday seemed to have lasted forty-eight hours, and now he was being kept waiting for a mere phone call.

Probably Necker was having a last-minute consultation with his lawyers before beginning the renegotiation of his contract, Marco told himself. Obviously Necker understood that to keep him happy after last night's triumph, a triumph that rivaled Saint-Laurent's first collection, he must be given a piece of the business. An unhappy designer was the last thing Necker would want. And he would be a most unhappy, most unproductive designer unless a highly satisfactory piece of the house of Lombardi belonged to him. A percentage of the ready-to-wear line, the accessories, the licensing, the perfume . . . he was a rich man at last. Everything he'd been working toward lay within his grasp. But he'd been wrong not to have brought a lawyer with him. Even Coco Chanel had never made more than a ten percent royalty on her "No. 5" although she'd fought the Wertheimer family for it all her life. He'd sign nothing today, he'd hold out until he was certain he was getting the most lucrative deal possible.

"Please go in, Monsieur Lombardi. I'm so sorry you had to wait."

Jacques Necker was standing up, behind his desk, as Marco, repressing his grin of anticipation, advanced toward him, his hand outstretched for the usual handshake.

"No, Lombardi. I will not touch your hand."

"What?"

"I will not touch the hand of a man who drugs a model he has already overworked into a state of frenzy."

"What are you talking about?"

"*Goddess*, Lombardi." His words came across the desk with the force of an expertly thrown knife. "I know what you gave Tinker, I know why she acted the way she did. This morning, Miss Loring and I investigated the entire episode. We questioned the other models, we questioned the makeup man who was the last person close to her after you took her into a private room. We know what you made her do, how you took sickening advantage of that helpless, drugged girl who trusted you. You deserve to go to prison for that."

"The girl's quite out of her mind," Marco replied, springing into indignation without a quiver of hesitation. "You must be equally mad to listen to a raving neurotic with no talent. She'd make up anything, anything at all, to excuse herself. Her first day in Paris that little tramp had already picked up a boyfriend, some American, ask anyone, Necker, they all know about him, but her real fantasy has always been about me. I had nothing to do with her except professionally, no one in my entourage ever saw anything wrong—a makeup man, no, please, don't make me laugh. I see what you're trying to do, Necker. This is only an excuse not to give me a fair piece of the profits. It won't work. I know that I'm worth a fortune to you, I know my bottom line, and I know it's all that matters."

"Your bottom line, profitable though it will be, is no longer my concern, Lombardi. We're not in business together anymore, so don't waste your time lying to me. You have a new employer now, try to convince her."

"A new—?"

"I've sold your services. I found a buyer for your contract with one phone call to my old friend, Mrs. Peaches Wilcox. I warned her about you, of course, in complete detail, but she said she's perfectly aware of the kind of man you are. She's often told me that she wanted to own a couture house and she has more than enough money to finance one. She also acquired the contracts of Jordan Dancer and April Nyquist, so you can do nothing to change their positions. From now on, Lombardi, Mrs. Wilcox is your only boss. Your future is entirely up to her. You'd better do your best to please her in all things, even in her smallest whims. Mrs. Wilcox has always enjoyed the exercise of power. She'll be a most exacting employer."

"No! I refuse!"

"As you choose. It makes absolutely no difference to me. Mrs. Wilcox now has a lock on your services as a designer. She alone can decide how much she'll spend to produce your next collection. Down to the price of a yard of fabric, down to the last button on the last dress, your working freedom will be up to her. I believe you'll find she has a vast, untapped talent for domination. In effect, she *owns* you, Lombardi, at least as a designer. If you refuse to work for her, you're prohibited by law from working for another couture house for five years. Still, slavery no longer exists. If you prefer, you can always go into any other line of work. Pimping would suit your talents. Mrs. Wilcox expects you for lunch in her suite in half an hour. You'd better hurry, she doesn't like to be kept waiting."

"Frankie, where were our brains?" Justine asked, as they ate lunch together in their suite. "Shouldn't we have expected that there'd be this much publicity? I have a stack of requests for interviews with the girls from damn near every place on earth but the former Yugoslavia, and that's probably on its way. CNN, Barbara Walters, Diane Sawyer, the BBC, Canal Plus, Tele Luxembourg—you name it, and they all want it today or tomorrow. All the big magazines want cover stories, the major newspapers want Sunday magazine stories, and as for the fashion press . . . !" She threw up her hands. "Don't even ask."

"And Maude and Mike have scooped them all! I bet Maxi'll rush out a special issue of *Zing*." Frankie gloated, gleeful and proud. "It's become a bigger story than if they'd won Oscars—maybe because there are two of them, twin Cinderellas, black and white, unknown until yesterday, both making all that money and both guaranteed to be public faces for years. The public's panting to know all about them. Your old dad certainly made the right decision."

"Don't you *adore* him! And, all else aside, is he or is he not the best-looking thing you've ever seen?"

"Worship. Revere. Venerate—adore's too small a word. But, for his age, Mike's the best-looking thing I've ever seen."

"Thanks for not telling me what an idiot I was."

"I can't find words strong enough. But I'm working on it."

"Oh, Frankie, what are we going to do? We need the best PR experts, we need advice and we've got to get back to Loring Management, the business will be going to hell with both of us away. I'm totally confused."

"I suppose I could go back," Frankie volunteered with a visible lack of sincerity or even a trace of integrity.

"Oh, sure, you're prepared to miss all the fun, leaving Mike still here, taking a whole new set of pictures of April and Jordan together . . . tell me another."

"You could go back," Frankie suggested sweetly.

"And leave my father? No way!"

"Let's all go back together," Frankie said, in a sudden rush of inspiration. "I'm sure your father would come with us. We'd wait and do the PR in New York, do it carefully. Remember that just because the media's making all these demands doesn't mean we have to give in to them. Let's play hard to get, pick and choose. We don't want to wear out April and Jordan and doing PR's an absolute bitch no matter how important it is. Remember, Mike's pictures take priority and he can do them in New York. Your father said he wanted to meet Aiden as soon as possible, anyway."

"You're a genius!" Justine jumped up excitedly. "Okay, let's get organized. Start making phone calls."

"Justine, grab hold of yourself," Frankie said patiently. "There's nobody we have to tell except your father. The concierge can worry about the tickets."

"You've been living in a luxury hotel for too long, Miss Severino."

"I can't wait to get out of here. Enough is enough."

"Pining for Brooklyn, are you?"

"Pining for real life."

"But what about Tinker?" Justine asked anxiously.

"My God, I'd forgotten . . . what's she going to do? Stay here with Tom or come back to New York and make a fortune doing ads?—the latest fax from the office said every ad agency and fashion magazine in New York wanted her."

"Tinker's going to have to make that decision herself. I can't begin to advise her on her love life . . . it's definitely not my field of expertise."

That evening, at dusk, Jordan sat alone at a quiet table in the Ritz Bar, too preoccupied to notice that almost everyone in the amber-lit room had recognized her and was glancing in her direction with curiosity and admiration—politely concealed, but still inescapable.

She was early for her appointment. Jordan barely touched her lips to a glass of white wine, thinking fiercely that the only true humiliation would lie in *not* speaking, in not having the courage to bring to light the discoveries she had made about herself. Probably she'd regret this decision for years, she told herself, tilting her chin resolutely, but if she didn't speak out, lifelong regret was not a probability but a certainty. Humiliation couldn't kill her, could it?

"I'm not late, am I?" Jacques Necker asked, sitting down beside her.

"No, I was early." She turned to look at him and the sight

of her profile lightened the hearts of the people privileged to see it.

"Jordan, I know the reason why you wanted to see me alone."

"Do you really?" Her eyebrows raised in wonder and the bridge of her nose twitched delightfully as they lifted, although her lips remained pressed together seriously.

"Yes, and I refuse, absolutely refuse, to listen to it. Not one word. There's nothing to thank me for. Whatever you think, I didn't choose you because you're black or—"

"I know you didn't, Jacques. I won fair and square, the same as April. We're much better together than apart . . . more interesting by light years, but each of us could have done the job by herself."

"I know that, everyone knows that, but then . . . ?"

"Then why did I want to see you alone?"

"It can't be to say good-bye, since we're all going to New York together tomorrow, so what—"

"Jacques, I need your advice," Jordan said gravely. "I would never have asked for it if you and Justine hadn't gotten together at last. You weren't in a fit condition to listen to me or advise me until you'd found your daughter and she'd found you, but now. . . ." her determination faltered and her words dried up.

"Jordan, there isn't anything you can't ask me, don't you know that by now?"

Necker bent toward her, thinking that no matter how beautiful she'd seemed to him before, the look on her face, a look of blinding courage blended with intense timidity, touched his heart more deeply than any smile of hers ever had.

"*Jordan!* We've had so many long talks together, in just two weeks we've discussed so many things I've never spoken of to anyone, don't you realize that you've become my friend? My only friend, as a matter of fact, I've never had time for friends, male or female. Come on, think how I always feed you," Necker said, trying to ease the terrible emotional tension he felt in her, "isn't that enough to make you confide in me? Have you been hiding some sort of trouble because I was so upset about Justine? You should have told me, you shouldn't keep things from me, not for any reason."

"It's not . . . a trouble exactly, but a problem."

"A problem with a man?" he asked, his face hardening.

"Yes, with a man. A man old enough to be my father."

"What's he done to you? If he's done anything, he won't get away with it!"

"Jacques, lower your voice, people can hear you," Jordan protested.

"I don't give a damn, not if some old bastard has hurt you."

"He's not old, he's not a bastard, he hasn't hurt me, not yet, anyway, but possibly, quite possibly he will. . . ." She grew mute again, her courage faltering.

"For heaven's sake, Jordan, you're driving me crazy with all this mystery. Just say it!"

Her eyes looked intently into the glass of wine, and her hands gripped the stem of the glass. "I've fallen in love with you."

Jordan spoke in a level, emotionless tone she'd been practicing for days, trying to say the words every way but backward, so that she wouldn't shame herself or alarm him.

"That's not possible," Necker said after an empty, echoing minute, in a voice squeezed dry of expression.

"Would I say such a thing if I weren't sure?" Jordan asked, determined to continue to sound reasonable. "Believe me, it wasn't my intention, but there wasn't much I could do about it. I had to tell you before we left for New York. Once the PR starts, I won't have a minute to be alone with you."

"You can *not* be in love with me," he said, sounding as sure of his right to pronounce the words as if he were a judge handing down a sentence.

"Jesus, Jacques Necker, you are a stupid, *stupid* man!" Jordan cried, her composure lost to a boiling whisper, tossing her short curls in reaction from her hard-won calm. "Do you want me to have my love notarized, you damned cautious Swiss? Even a saint wouldn't have spent hour after hour listening to you talk about how rotten you'd been, unless she were falling in love with you, you idiot! You know *nothing* about women. Less than nothing!"

"That seems unfortunately obvious," Necker said dryly.

At least he's still sitting here and listening, Jordan thought, as she continued. "You asked me about my life, as no one ever has before, and you were truly interested, I could tell. You listened, because you cared about me, or at least I was dumb enough to think so. You managed to find reasons to take me out, and we both knew it wasn't merely to expand my French culture, didn't we? And this last week, having dinner almost every night, can you still pretend that it was only to talk about Justine?"

"No. I admit . . . it wasn't only . . . I suppose . . . I guess . . . I must have wanted to be with you," he muttered, woodenly.

"All that while I was falling more and more in love with you, and you speak as if you noticed *nothing*. Nothing! No wonder you don't have any friends. You never even tried to kiss me. I'll never forgive you for that, never!"

"Damn it, Jordan! I didn't *dare to kiss you*, you're so *young*," Necker exclaimed, his composure deserting him entirely. "You take my breath away! You entrance me! You're a gala, every minute with you is a celebration, for God's sake! You're the most ravishing, fascinating, original woman I've ever met, but you're so terribly damn *young*. Ask yourself how it would have seemed if I'd tried to kiss you in the context of the contest, when I was the one to decide the winner?"

"So you *were* thinking about it, at least?"

"*All the time*. Even when I was talking about what a shit I was, I was thinking, in the back of my mind, about kissing you, which makes it worse! Don't you see that? Yes, I wanted to talk about Justine, but I wanted to talk about myself too, and about you, and, oh about everything. . . ."

"How shameless of you," Jordan said, smiling for the first time. "How imprudent. But now the contest's over. Now you're not even a shit, except retroactively."

"No, Jordan, it's impossible, just as impossible now as it was before."

"How can it be impossible—if I entrance you?" she asked with a proud lift of her superb little head.

"Because, oh, Christ, Jordan, don't you realize I'm fifty-three, and you're what? Twenty-two. That's thirty-one years younger than I am—thirty-one reasons why we can't be in love."

"Is there some law that says so?"

"There should be!" Necker answered fiercely, pounding the

polished wood of the table. "It wouldn't work out, Jordan, no matter how delicious it could be in the beginning, don't think I haven't had these same fantasies too . . . you and me together . . . but I keep coming back to reality. Too much separates us, I've lived too long. You've lived too little. That gulf of experience between us would grow more and more important once the initial thrill was gone."

"It must be wonderful to have the gift of seeing into the future," she said, shaking her head in wonder that she could love someone with such an unromantic turn of mind. "And to have such a pessimistic view of it. What if the initial thrill grew better in time? What if the gulf narrowed? That's been known to happen."

"I'm merely trying to be *realistic*. One of us has to be! We have such different expectations of life. I've lived the most important years of mine, I'm set in my ways, I'm known as a confirmed hermit, for God's sake! I've grown used to being essentially *alone* with my business, my routines and my interests. It's not a wide existence but I've been satisfied with it. But you! My God, Jordan, you're just beginning a wonderful adventure, the whole world is opening up for you, there isn't any way to know how high you'll fly. Why would you want to settle for a man like me?"

"Damned if I know, now that you've told me what a miserable old creep you are, but unfortunately I still do. Tell me something," Jordan asked, curling the corners of her lips provokingly, "this little hermit's life of yours, is that going to seem so safe and cozy when you dream about what you might have had with me?"

"Would being with me be exciting and fulfilling enough for you, when you'd realize what you'd missed, what you'd thrown away?"

"You didn't answer my question."

"Jordan, I simply don't have the right to you. I can't make love to you unless I marry you."

"Have I said anything about *marriage?*" she pounced, furiously. "Did I propose to you without realizing it, did they just declare a new leap year?"

"Do you think I'd let you be involved with me *without* marriage? Do you think I'd ever allow myself to look like one of those rich old men who buys himself a beautiful young mistress? And how could I dream of putting you in the position of looking like a girl who plotted successfully to marry money?"

"Now you're thinking like Peaches Wilcox! You make me sick! This is you, Jacques, and me, Jordan, not two people your society friends gossip about at lunch."

"But they would, ferociously. You'd never, never be free of the gossip, the envy, the peeking around corners to see if we were still happy. You'd always be suspect, you'd be considered a successful gold digger, there isn't a hostess in this city who'd trust you."

"Don't you really mean that there isn't a hostess who'd invite me?"

"On the contrary. You'd be a wild social success, for all the wrong reasons—curiosity, malice, a constant barrage of inspection as to whether you were doing it right or doing it wrong."

"I've been dealing with that all my life, or have you forgotten? I can handle it. Only the surroundings would be different, and the manners. And somehow, I think I'd manage to find a real friend here and there. I didn't grow up an Army brat for nothing."

"You have an answer for everything," Necker said. "But what about children?"

"What about them?"

"You'd want children, wouldn't you?"

"Eventually, yes. Not as many as Charlie Chaplin and Oona O'Neill, but a few."

"And what kind of life would they have?"

"The best we could give them, nothing's guaranteed. Unless . . . of course . . . unless you'd hate to have kids."

"How do I know? My only child happens to be a thirty-four-year-old woman I'd never seen in the flesh until yesterday."

"Let's forget the kid problem, then. Why worry about something that can't happen unless we get married first?" she asked, with a glint of victory in her voice. How many more objections would he raise, she wondered, before he realized that love was too rare to turn his back on it?

"Jordan, you have a way of brushing aside reality that amazes me."

"You mean because I haven't brought up the racial problem?"

"What?"

"The racial problem," she repeated, implacably.

"Jesus . . . your parents . . . as if I weren't too old, I'm also the wrong race."

"That's the racial problem?"

"What else could it be?" he asked, puzzled.

"You can be as oblivious to reality as I can, when you want to be, Jacques. If you don't even recognize it, then there isn't any racial problem, as far as I'm concerned. My parents would come to appreciate you . . . eventually . . . so long as you didn't try to call my father 'Dad.' I'm leaving now. Just promise me one thing, think about everything we've talked about. That's all I ask. Think about it tonight. Sleep on it. And remember, you haven't managed to say you're not in love with me and that's the only thing that matters."

Jordan rose, in a liquid movement, and vanished rapidly from the Ritz Bar, taking all the magic in the room with her.

28

I found that I was slipping into my
usual airborne reverie of where-and-whither almost as soon as we
took off for New York in GN's 727 private jet.

Could it really be only a little more than two weeks since we'd
left New York for the Lombardi spring collection? I actually had to
count from one date to another on my fingers, just to make sure,
because that trip, so much of which had been interrupted by Maude
Callender's interrogation on the habits of models, seemed to have
taken place an eon ago. In another world. On another level of
existence.

Looked at from one point of view, the last two weeks had
been like an extended, real-life episode of the "Love Boat." I've
watched a few cable reruns of that show, when I needed to choose
between mindless entertainment or brooding myself to death. At
the beginning of the hour a whole bunch of strangers meet, and by
the end of the show, they've all paired off. I guess life no longer
imitates art, but TV, except that our version hasn't worked out as
neatly as I remember it.

Did people on the "Love Boat" ever get off at a port and never
get back on? That's what's happened to Tinker. She came to the
hotel yesterday afternoon and informed Justine and me that she
would be staying on in Paris. Maybe, just *maybe*, drug-induced
freak-outs are good for some people, the way electroshock therapy
has come back into use for clinical depression, but the experience
with Goddess had left Tinker feeling, in her own words, "born
yesterday."

Looking happier and more relaxed than we'd ever seen her,
Tinker told us that she wasn't sure if she'd ever model again, but

that if she did, it wouldn't be in any continuation of her search for identity, but solely for the bucks.

"I'm over the proving-who-I-am-by-winning thing," she said. "The beauty contests, the contest for my mother's affection, the runway walk contest, the contest for Marco's attention, the contest for the Lombardi contract and, God knows, *any* kind of dance contest. I know you two probably think I'm just saying that to put up a good front, because I didn't win, but you've got to believe me, something snapped—not just my mind—last night, and I felt a load of gigantic pressure just blow away, pressure I hadn't even realized I was under. Maybe falling on my face in public was exactly what it took."

"Then what are you going to do with yourself?" Justine asked her.

"I'm going to stay here, get myself a studio apartment, or even live in some little hotel if I can't find anything else. I'm in love with Tom but living with him . . . no, that's over for now. I fell into it much too quickly because I needed him. I adore Tom but I'm not ready to get into a whole domestic thing, and now that the spring collection's over, that's what it would turn into. I didn't come to Paris to play house and sit around watching him paint, and I don't believe he'd really want me to . . . he's into a different trip. Another thing, maybe you haven't noticed, but he can be awfully possessive. Possibly that's going to work out, possibly not, but right now I'm giving myself time to simply find out what *I* need, as opposed to what other people expect of me. Even Tom, or *especially* Tom."

Under Tinker's bright glance there was a resonance that had a density rare in an eighteen-year-old. "I have that hundred thousand dollars, minus your commission, from doing the show—or rather from not doing it—and the way I plan to live, it should last a long time . . . years and years if I want it to. I'm going to read and go to galleries and walk all over Paris and maybe learn French . . . oh, there's so much I don't know! Damn-near everything. I can't wait to find out who I am when my looks don't matter to anyone, even to me."

Justine and I exchanged glances, deciding in an instant, that it would be plain and simply wrong to tell Tinker about the enormous clamor there was for her back in New York.

"Remember, Tinker," Justine contented herself with saying, "if you get restless or bored or need money, you can always pick up a phone and call me collect and I'll get you a job right here. You don't have to make any final decision about working for a long time. You're still so young. Who knows, maybe you'll want to go to college, you've got a million options."

"That's exactly why I'm going to do nothing," Tinker said with the smile that had sent both of us reeling around the bend with excitement about her potential. At that moment it suddenly occurred to me that her face had lost its chameleon quality. It no longer was the perfect blank canvas, ready to be painted, with which she'd left New York.

Whoever Tinker Osborn was, she was definitely somebody with a mind of her own, a mind that would be interesting to watch as it developed.

So we'd lost Tinker, at least for now, but we'd kept April, I thought. She'd left New York an underappreciated Minnesota ice-princess and now she was returning in triumph, boasting the freshest, most original look in the world of modeling, a look that makes all the other blonds—even Elle and Claudia and Karen—who still cling to their long manes, look like dated versions of each other. Sure, men will always go for surrealistically big and prodigiously beautiful blonds, clonelike, glorious Amazons, with hair growing down to the crack of the ass, but April will intrigue and fascinate all the sexes with the element of wildness she'd tapped into.

I'm willing to bet that April has a lot more metamorphosing to do, that this is only the first new version of April Nyquist, that there'll be change after change in the face and attitude and version of sexuality she'll present to the world. Somehow she'll escape the frozen fetishism of the camera yet, because of the relentless classicism of her features, there's no way she can fuck up or be fucked up. How do I know? I don't *know*—as some great mind once summed up Hollywood, "nobody knows anything"—but looking at her, I get a strong feeling about her future, and I've learned to trust my feelings more than my more logical thought processes. Remember when I thought that I couldn't stand Mike?

I didn't have to lean on my judgment when it came to April's future with Maude. April was deeply engaged in a giggly, whispered exchange with a dark-haired French beauty, a startlingly sultry little piece named Kitten, whom April had managed to pick up somewhere, somehow, after the Lombardi show. She'd simply brought her along to hitch a ride to New York, where Kitten had an appointment to meet Katie Ford, and nobody'd asked any questions. Maude was sitting alone, as far away from them as possible, working steadily on her laptop. Personally I'd rather have flown commercial than punish myself that way. I felt truly sorry for her, but of course it was bound to happen. Still and all—so soon?

I looked around the interior of the jet with unjaded wonder. I'd never imagined that somewhere there had to be someone who understood how to design aircraft seating. Our various lush swivel chairs were a combination of love seat and Barcalounger that gave comfort a new meaning. I was having such a delicious time with my thoughts that I had to fight to keep myself from drifting off, as Jordan had done, falling instantly asleep as the jet left the airport. I wasn't surprised, not after last night.

Jordan had been quiet as we all packed after a final dinner at the Relais Plaza, where we'd amused ourselves by the sight of Peaches Wilcox, brilliant, beyond-bejeweled and looking as bloomingly rejuvenated as a vampire after a particularly tasty feast. Last night she'd reigned over three large tables of her guests, the cream of the small clan of American socialites who are rich enough to order from the couture. Marco, whose new affiliation had been fully explained to Justine by her father, glued himself to her side all through the meal, attentive, adoring, hanging on every word she said; the only thing missing were his leg irons and handcuffs, which, I assumed, had been left in her suite.

Peaches' taste in men goes way beyond kinky, if you ask me, but if it makes Marco's life a misery, why not? I haven't forgotten what a malicious snake she was to me about Mike, but now that her venom will be channeled toward Marco, I can afford to feel mellow about it. There's a couple I feel will be around for a bit, until Peaches tires of him. He'd better not lose any of that Renaissance hair, he'd better not get fat, he'd better not have an un-charming minute or an unsuccessful collection. Most of all, because of what I suspect about our Peaches, he'd better be ready to get it up—and keep it up—at a snap of her imperious, diamonded fingers. Alas, I've never heard of a man yet who could flex that particular muscle on command.

But back to Jordan. She failed to join in our conversation during dinner, she seemed to be sleepwalking and daydreaming simultaneously, polished by silence, and I had the feeling that she was immensely sad to be leaving Paris where her life had taken such a new direction. She and April would be back soon, of course, for the Lombardi ready-to-wear collection in March, but no show would ever equal the drama she'd just gone through.

Since Jordan was exactly Tinker's height, and their measurements were the same, she'd had to show all of Tinker's outfits as well as her own. I sensed such a deep weariness in her that I dropped in, uninvited, to help her pack since of all of us, she was the only one who'd bought so many antiques that she'd had to send a bellman to buy her an extra suitcase at the last minute.

"Promise me you'll go to bed early," I asked her. "You seem desperate for a decent night's sleep. Your eyes look feverish to me."

"Okay, Mom," she agreed, "but I'm really not tired, my mind's racing—I bet I'll be up all night." I made sure she was in her nightgown and ready for bed before I left her. I even tried to talk her into drinking a glass of warm milk, but Jordan balked at that, pushing me out of her room before I could tuck her into bed. Then Justine came back from dinner with her father and the two of us drifted off to our rooms and settled down for the night, worn out by too many decisions, too many emotions, too much excitement.

A few hours later, when I was deeply asleep, just at that moment when the mind and body are finally totally at rest, I was aroused by a combination of pounding on the door and ringing of the doorbell. I didn't remember where I was for a disoriented minute and then my first thought was that the hotel must be on fire. I flew into my bathrobe, and opened the door the smallest possible crack, expecting to see the corridor filled with smoke. Instead, at eye level, I saw Jordan's gorgeous bare legs kicking to get free, trapped by an arm covered in a man's jacket.

"What the fuck!" I gasped, opening the door wide and gaping at Jacques Necker, holding Jordan struggling in his arms. "Let me go, you oaf!" she cried, hitting him with her fists. "Put me down!"

"I needed witnesses," Necker said to me, carrying Jordan into the sitting room like a blond King Kong, sounding as if he were making a perfectly normal request. Justine staggered through the doorway.

"Papa? What are you doing here?" she asked groggily. Jordan fought harder and harder to get free of his unrelenting grasp, muttering curses.

"Two witnesses, excellent. That makes it official. Jordan and I are getting married."

"Monsieur Necker," I said soothingly, drawing on all my experience with dealing with wigged-out, complaining, fit-throwing, should-be-committed models, "that's very interesting, very, very interesting news. It's nice, really nice as it can be. But wouldn't you be more comfortable if you sat down and told us about it slowly, *very, very slowly*, with all the details? Maybe you'd be even more comfortable if you put Jordan down, so I could give her a sweater, look, she's freezing, she's shaking, now you wouldn't want her to catch cold, would you, Mr. Necker?"

"I'm laughing, you idiot," Jordan managed to croak out, "not freezing."

"You're a big help," I hissed at her. "It's not funny."

"I can't believe it! How could this have happened, what's been going on here, for heaven's sake?" Justine looked intently back and forth from Necker to Jordan, weighing up what she saw in their faces. "It's impossible! It's crazy it's . . . *I don't get it* . . . but . . . whatever . . . hell, I don't know, it just *feels* right!" Justine cried finally, flinging her arms around both of them, kissing them at random all over their faces like an overexcited dog. "Papa, you have incredible taste! Jordan, you'll make him so happy. Damn, I wish I'd been here to watch this whole thing developing between you two."

"If you'd been here," Jordan said, suddenly serious, "it would *never* have happened, not in a million years. Thank you for not coming sooner, Justine."

Were all three of them insane? Necker loosened his hold on

Jordan so he could include Justine in his hug. I stood, looking at the happy group, trying to make sense out of this loony scene. Necker and Jordan? For real? He glanced at me, and read my mind.

"Jordan incapacitated me for any normal life, Frankie," he explained with a great big, astonishingly sweet smile. Well! How about that? First time he'd called me anything but Miss Severino. First time he'd really smiled at me. Someone had loosened this guy up, and it wasn't Justine.

"Incapacitated"—there is more than one way to declare your love, I guess, and looking at the illumination that was Jordan, I realized that my ability to empathize hadn't been working with her. She hadn't been desperately tired, she'd been desperately and unhappily in love. And I hadn't seen it coming, not for a minute, even though all last week I'd watched them set off on those cultural excursions of theirs. Had they been to the Louvre too? Maybe, but something tells me it wasn't the same Louvre Mike and I had frequented every afternoon. Necker was too proper and so, in her own grown-up, sophisticated way, was Jordan.

So there's your "Love Boat" complement; Jacques, as he now insists I call him, and Jordan, holding his hand in her sleep; Maude lovelorn and loveless; April and Kitten and whoever takes Kitten's place, and so on and so forth, I'll bet, for years into the future; Tinker, who jumped ship; and Justine and Aiden, the contractor, who still remains to be inspected but can't possibly be half as . . . well, let's agree on it, no way can he be anything like half as *divine* as Mike, who's up in the cockpit showing the pilot how to fly the plane.

The only person Jacques asked to come along with us to the airport was Gabrielle d'Angelle. He told her about his forthcoming marriage; news that you would have thought should have provoked some reaction bigger than her startled congratulations. While he gave her a list of things to supervise for him during his trip to New York, Gabrielle seemed to be working out the answer to some kind of vexing long-standing question. Yet when Jacques, almost casually, told her that he was promoting her to executive vice-president of La Groupe Necker, she broke down, literally bursting into tears of joy, and didn't stop for ten minutes. She pulled a real weeper. I believe Gabrielle must be the most dedicated, least romantic career woman I've ever met in all my years of working with women. You can't generalize, not even about the French, can you?

Of all of these recent romances, please notice, I'm the only one who's engaged to her long-lost true love—no quickie romance for me—and, as it happens, the only one with an engagement ring.

While he was running around yesterday, taking more pictures of the girls, Mike found time to nip into Van Cleef and buy me a ring that's embarrassingly big, if you're the kind of person who's easily embarrassed by mere material possessions and I find, to my surprise, that I'm not. I guess that must have something to do with learning to wear Donna Karan.

Justine wants to give our wedding reception at her house and I want to have it at Big Ed, because she'll have enough to do getting married herself, to say nothing of whatever sort of ceremony Jordan and Jacques are planning after he meets her parents. Gracious! If it weren't for weddings, what would happen to the American economy?

The event I'm looking forward to almost more than getting married is the tenth reunion of my class at Abraham Lincoln High School this spring. Two weeks ago I'd been planning on skipping it. Almost every one of my nine hundred or so classmates could be counted on to drag a spouse or partner of some persuasion to this particular reunion, and I didn't know anyone I cared to bring.

But when I show up with Mike Aaron—the legendary star who's never been forgotten—and they find out that I'm Mrs. Mike Aaron—*Caramba!*

Okay, call me a show-off, call me ostentatious, call me pretentious, but how can I resist a chance to prove to all those fellow students who teased me about being too skinny to look good in a leotard and tights, that even a kid with a big nose, who wore her hair screwed up in a bun, whose finest feature was her big feet—that even Frankie Severino could grow up to accept, with grace and dignity and passion, the heart and hand of the once and forever prince of Brooklyn?